C000241412

Lilian Faschinger was born in Austria in 1950. She has received literary prizes both for her own writing, and for her achievements as a translator of such authors as Janet Frame, Gertrude Stein and Paul Bowles. Her debut UK novel, *Magdalena the Sinner*, achieved widespread critical acclaim.

Also by Lilian Faschinger

Magdalena the Sinner

Vienna Passion

Lilian Faschinger

review

First Published in Great Britain in 2000
by REVIEW

An imprint of Headline Book Publishing

First Published in paperback in 2001

10 9 8 7 6 5 4 3 2 1

ISBN 0 7472 5850 3

Printed and bound in Great Britain by
Clays Ltd, St Ives plc.

Headline Book Publishing
A division of Hodder Headline
338 Euston Road
LONDON NW1 3BH

www.reviewbooks.co.uk
www.hodderheadline.com

To my parents

'All men are liars'
(Psalm 116 v 11)

'In short, I began to think,
and to think is one real Advance
from Hell to Heaven'
(Daniel Defoe, *Moll Flanders*)

1

On the day I saw Magnolia Brown for the first time, my mother woke me at three thirty-three in the morning. And for the first time I held it against her.

I'd been suffering from a very nasty attack of bronchial catarrh for the last four days, going out only to buy medicines from the St Mary Magdalene Pharmacy on the corner of Kettenbrückengasse and Rechte Wienzeile and to visit the produce stalls in the Naschmarkt for a piece of beef fillet, a large marrowbone, some pot-herbs and a couple of onions, the ingredients for good nourishing beef broth. Good nourishing beef broth is the only food I can take when I have one of these dangerous infections, which have been plaguing me as long as I can remember. All my life I've had inadequate immunity to viruses, and in winter I'm a martyr to assorted colds and chills practically the whole time. If I go to my regular coffee house, the Café Anzengruber in Schleifmühlgasse, and there's only a seat near the door free, it's almost a cast-iron certainty that the draught entering with every new customer will give me acute bronchitis within a couple of days, keeping me bedridden for days on end. If I have to stand in a crowded tram in cold, wet weather I can expect a nasty attack of catarrhal tonsillitis. If I come home late at night in early December, making my way, lost in thought, past the empty stalls of the Naschmarkt, the gusts of autumnal wind typical of Vienna, reinforced by the architectural bottleneck there, are bound to trigger a bout of flu with a high temperature and a muzzy feeling that may have been brewing for quite some time, and was just waiting for its chance to develop.

Of course Vienna, with its dreaded Viennese wind and alarmingly low temperatures in winter, isn't the place where someone of my delicate constitution ought to be living at all. The pharmacist in the St Mary Magdalene Pharmacy, a sensitive woman who genuinely understands vulnerable natures like mine, says I ought to go south like the swallows around the feast of the Birth of Our Lady in early September, and come back at Lady Day in late March. Did I never think, she asked that day, of going to Madeira like our Empress Elisabeth back in the past, the island climate there did wonders for Empress Sisi's infected lungs, in her opinion the secret lies in Madeira's volcanic origins, quite recently she read a scientific article in her trade paper, *The Lady Pharmacist's Companion*, supporting the theory that the felicitous combination of volcanic phenomena with a maritime climate will cure people who are chronically susceptible to colds. Or if Madeira is too far to go, she suggested, I could try the Lipari Islands, Stromboli is probably another very healthy place, likely to stabilize easily inflamed respiratory passages. There is obviously great healing power in the mysterious combination of volcanic and maritime features, she said, fire and water, two opposing elements existing side by side. I refrained from contradicting the pharmacist, who seems to be well informed and always listens patiently to accounts of my lamentable state of health, I merely pointed out that my meagre income didn't allow me to take such long trips, Empress Sisi had had entirely different opportunities at her command, why, Queen Victoria herself placed a ship at Sisi's disposal for the voyage to Madeira, a measure upon which the Vienna Regional Health Insurance scheme is hardly likely to decide even if a person's membership premiums have been paid on the dot for decades. At this point the pharmacist's young assistant joined in the conversation, saying that when her uncle contracted a nasty case of pneumonia all of a sudden, just like that, the Vienna

Regional Health Insurance paid up without a murmur for a Mediterranean cruise, second class, so cruises for the sake of your health aren't anything unusual, and her uncle landed in Trieste three weeks later with his lungs perfectly well again. Here the old lady from the building at 14 Kettenbrückengasse, who had just come into the pharmacy with her toy spaniel, raised her failing voice and said Empress Sisi was nothing but a malingerer, there was evidence to prove it, and who, pray, paid for the Empress's expensive trips when she imagined herself unwell but the ordinary people of the Austro-Hungarian monarchy, victims bled dry by those vampires of the imperial house, victims including her late father, a man who had held the reputable position of retired stipendiary councillor in the civil service at the time of his death, and where would we be if we went running to the health insurance scheme for every little ailment, her late father had suffered his painful rheumatism without a word of complaint, and for years she herself had tried to alleviate her far from imaginary rheumatoid arthritis with medicinal herbs laboriously gathered in the Vienna woods, she did think one might show a little solidarity towards people who really were severely ill.

I asked the three ladies to let me finish what I was saying, and explained that quite apart from the fact that it was financially impossible for me to take long trips abroad, my pupils kept me in the city, and anyway I loved Vienna.

But of course you love Vienna, cried the pharmacist, the old lady and the pharmacist's assistant, of course you do, it isn't only the Viennese who love Vienna, the whole world loves Vienna, you have only to look at the statistics for overnight stays published by the Viennese hotel trade to see that. They themselves, although they hadn't been born in Vienna, loved the place dearly, you didn't have to be a native of Vienna like me to love it with all your heart and feel the deepest affection for the city.

Yes, naturally you love Vienna. You love it as dearly as your own mother, even if the harsh climatic conditions in Vienna in autumn

3

and winter don't make such a depth of affection easy for a person susceptible to bronchial asthma.

After I'd bought a small bag each of violet-leaf tea, lime-flower tea and dead-nettle tea in the St Mary Magdalene Pharmacy, as well as two little bottles of *atropinum sulfuricum* D3 and *arsenicum* D6, I went back to the Death House. I walked slowly, stopping as usual for a short rest in the tobacconist's on the corner of Kettenbrückengasse and Schönbrunnerstrasse, because in the long term chronic colds have a dreadfully debilitating effect on the organism. Usually I sit down on the folding chair near the little iron stove and have a chat with the lady in the tobacconist's about preventative health measures in general, since she isn't by any means blessed with a robust physical constitution either. That day, however, I saw with some annoyance that the lady in the tobacconist's was already sitting on the folding chair herself, and before I got any chance to describe my own symptoms she began complaining about the unbearable back pain which was making it quite impossible for her to stand behind the counter. I leaned against a pile of copies of the weekly magazine *Profile*, because I was fighting off a nasty stitch in my side as a result of the effort of walking, and advised the lady in the tobacconist's to seek medical advice at once, to which she replied that she couldn't leave the tobacconist's just like that, her tobacconist's shop was a place where people liked to meet, and moreover the locals had a right to their daily newspapers and their tobacco, she'd been running the tobacconist's shop for twenty-two years now to the satisfaction of the inhabitants of the administrative districts of Vienna 4 and Vienna 5, you couldn't unexpectedly confront those people with such a drastic change as the closure of their tobacconist's shop, even temporarily, to which I said that in principle, if it was really urgent, I'd be happy to stand in for her in the shop, although only if my own state of health allowed, and my health, as she knew, was almost always poor. Then, looking around, I asked where her husband was, because normally, as I said, her husband helped out behind the counter. Oh, but surely I knew, cried the lady in the tobacconist's, looking at me in surprise, surely I knew her husband was disabled, a tragedy in one way, of course, but lucky in another because if he hadn't been disabled he'd have had considerably less chance of getting the tobacconist's, since the disabled, particularly if disabled in the war, were given strong preference over healthy folk in the allocation of franchises for tobacconist's shops, which after all were a monopoly of the Austrian state. Cold, wet late-autumn weather like this was the worst possible thing for her husband, the weather around All Saints' Day always gave her husband phantom pain in his lower leg, so unfortunately missing, and forced him to take to his bed.

By now I had recovered slightly, and since in the circumstances I saw no chance of describing my bronchial catarrh at greater length and the lady in the tobacconist's made no move to offer me the little folding chair to sit on, I said goodbye and left the place in some haste, a haste I regretted after struggling on another ten metres or so against the wind, when I noted, to my dismay, that I'd left my pure hand-spun wool scarf behind in the tobacconist's, a slip of the mind that could have serious consequences in this kind of weather. I immediately turned my coat collar right up to my chin and retraced my steps, to find the lady in the tobacconist's shop already waiting for me with the snow-white scarf I'd knitted myself in moss stitch, and I wrapped this item of clothing, which I treasured, round my neck three times and closed the door of the tobacconist's behind me again. I could expect a deterioration in my condition, since through my own stupid carelessness my windpipe had been exposed entirely unprotected to the wind and weather, and I could already feel a distinct constriction in that area, so I made haste to get back to the Death House before I was totally exhausted by my difficulty in breathing.

As I was climbing upstairs, clinging to the banisters, I met my neighbour, a nice woman who used to be a church pastoral assistant and has family living in the attractive Bucklige Welt

5

countryside area of Lower Austria. She very kindly sometimes brings me back a jar of lime-flower honey from her brother-in-law's apiary and queen-bee breeding farm, organic lime-flower honey undamaged by pasteurization is one of the best of medicines for sensitive bronchial tubes, very soothing to people who get attacks of coughing. Fräulein Haslinger looked at me in alarm, asked if I was all right, and helpfully offered me her arm, which I took with relief, and then she led me to my apartment next door to the room where Schubert had died and helped me to open the front door. I thanked her, closed the door, and lay down on my bed without removing my coat and scarf.

Sometimes I wonder what I did to deserve being brought into this world so ill-equipped for the battle of life. I was always sickly. While other children flew high in the air on the swings in the playground, rushed squealing down the slide, clambered rung by rung up the climbing frame and ran tirelessly after shuttlecocks, I would sit listlessly on a bench at the side of the playground, wrapped up in a woolly rug by my mother and not yet entirely recovered from a painful attack of inflammation of the middle ear. And while I listened to the carefree cries of neighbouring children playing volleyball on the grass outside the building, all they could hear from me was convulsive coughing from my room on the ground floor when I was in the throes of a violent attack of whooping cough. I can imagine how difficult it must have been for my mother, herself rather fragile, to bring up a child as delicate as I was, in the absence of a father. Although she was naturally melancholy and subject to frequent mood swings, no doubt because of her outstanding artistic talent, she did what she could to cheer me during my periods of sickness, which often went on for weeks. As a trained pianist, she tried to hasten my recovery through the art that meant so much to her. If I was in bed with swollen tonsils and a high fever because of a sudden drop in the temperature, she would sit at the piano and play me songs by her favourite composer Gustav Mahler, particularly the

Kindertotenlieder, which she loved. Those songs, she used to say, were the tenderest things Mahler ever wrote, so very tender, lyrical and full of tragic premonition. As she played the introduction to the last song, she murmured *sempre molto espressivo*, then looked sorrowfully at me and began intoning, in her dark mezzo-soprano, 'With stormy weather and wind about, / I would never have let the children go out, / But oh, they were carried, were carried away.' And bringing me a hot lemon drink in bed, she would sing softly, 'Ah, too quickly, too soon extinguished light of joy, extinguished light of joy.'

My mother was firmly convinced of the healing powers of music, in fact so firmly convinced that she thought traditional medicine unnecessary. If lovely songs don't cure you then antibiotics won't make you better either, she said; codeine and penicillin are not going to succeed where Schönberg and Berg have failed. When the lady who lived above us and felt bothered by both my mother's piano playing and my own persistent coughing, which could easily be heard through all the walls, came to our door with some Ems Salts, my mother said no thank you, not without politely suggesting that hard as it might be for lay people to imagine such a thing, it could still be annoying for a sensitive pianist kept out of the concert hall only by bad luck of the most fateful kind to have her concentration on the dense thematic structure of the piano accompaniment of a Hugo Wolf song disturbed by her neighbour's ringing of the doorbell. And when the neighbour said she wasn't interested in Hugo Wolf, she was just afraid the poor child might choke to death in one of his coughing fits, my mother said sharply that the methods used to treat me could be left to her, my mother, whose right it was to bring me up. And when, at this, the neighbour turned away, sighing, my mother called after her that the usual medicaments you could buy killed far more people than they cured, it was a well-known fact, and she for one would rather not subject her child's growing and therefore very vulnerable organism to the influence of strong doses of Ems

Salts and other medicinal drugs, preferring gentler methods in line with her little boy's gentle nature. And what could be gentler than music therapy? She could well believe that a woman like her, our neighbour, born and bred the daughter of a working man who lived in Ottakring, a woman who hadn't gone beyond the eight years of compulsory state schooling, had never heard of music therapy, the art of healing through the influence of music on the mind, but it was well known that David, a character in the Old Testament, had cured people by playing the harp, and Orpheus, a name with which she, our neighbour, was unlikely to be familiar, had even snatched his dead wife back from the god of the underworld by the power of his singing. The beneficial power of music had been successfully tested on countless schizophrenics, stammerers, insomniacs and people suffering from war trauma, so did she really think her Ems Salts were on a par with the greatest of all the arts? Our neighbour, who by now had reached the half-landing between our two floors, said a few more things, which I didn't understand apart from a few disquieting words such as custody, irresponsibility and child abuse, whereupon my mother closed the door and sat down at the baby grand again, shaking her head.

I dwelt on such thoughts of my childhood, a sad one clouded by illness, yet also happy because it was irradiated by the unique personality of my dear mother, as I lay in my coat and scarf on the bedspread I had crocheted out of remnants of wool during the forced inactivity of a long period of convalescence. I would have liked to indulge my memories longer, but I had decided to hang some damp sheets up in the room to humidify the air by evaporation and thus relieve my inflamed bronchial tubes, so I got up and took off my scarf and coat, and although I was a little dizzy I found my Swiss-made stepladder, stretched a washing line right across the living room, hung three white linen sheets on it, and after that I really did soon feel some relief. Encouraged by this improvement in my condition, I went into the kitchen and began making the beef broth. I quickly browned all the ingredients except the beef in a large pan, added water and salt, and once the liquid began to boil I added the meat and let it all simmer over very slow heat, so that there was soon a pleasing aroma in the flat, reviving me sufficiently to sit at the piano and venture on playing the song 'The Hurdy-Gurdy Man' from Schubert's *Winterreise*. I'd loved this song, with its heart-rending text, ever since my mother played it to me while I was suffering from diphtheria. At the time, the doctor claimed my childish larynx was already affected, and he strongly advised several weeks in a clinic, to which my mother quite rightly objected that the invisible notes of Schubert, that most spiritual of all the Viennese composers, would certainly do more to cure my pharyngeal and tracheal area than time spent with a set of invalids who were strangers to me, among overworked nursing staff and in a non-musical environment. It is from this decision of my mother's that I date my love of Schubert, a love that has never diminished but has grown ever stronger in intensity year by year, and in view of its warmth and tenderness can be compared only with my feelings for my mother herself. I picked up the battered Volume One of the Schubert album for voice and pianoforte accompaniment published by Anton Rückauf, newly revised and printed with additional expression marks, opened it, and abandoned myself entirely to the song: 'There beyond the village the hurdy-gurdy man / With his frozen fingers plays as best he can. / Barefoot on the ice he totters to and fro, / Not a single coin in his dish will go. / No one wants to hear him, no one's eyes will scan / Him, and all the dogs growl at the poor old man.' As usual, I felt a spiritual affinity with this pitiful figure, as susceptible as I am to cold winter weather, still turning his hurdy-gurdy to give other people pleasure despite the danger of contracting a severe cold, in fact even catching his death of it. The second half of the song always reduced me to tears while I had diphtheria, which my mother took as a certain sign of the efficacy of Schubert's music and my imminent cure: 'So he lets the world go by, go by as it will / And his hurdy-gurdy never once is still. / Strange old music-maker, shall I go with you? / Will you play your music for my own songs too?' In my feverish delirium I followed the shadowy figure of the old man further and further out on the ice. I would have liked to sing the words as I played, but that was naturally impossible, since my bronchial catarrh had a devastating effect on the state of my larynx, my glottis and my vocal cords. To enjoy the song properly, however, I rose from the piano stool and put on the LP of Hans Hotter singing the *Winterreise*, an old recording made in 1942, but of remarkably good quality.

Schubert. He and my mother made life bearable for me, and once I begin to love a human being I am very faithful and seek that person's company as often and as much as I can. The fact that Schubert died on 19 November 1828, one hundred and forty years before my own birth, didn't really make much difference to my efforts. As soon as I realized how strongly I felt about him, I began visiting those places in Vienna which he had frequented during his short life, in the firm belief that his spirit must linger there. First I did some research into the location of the inns and cafés where Schubert used to go with his friends, the Café Bogner in Singer-strasse, the Café Hugelmann on the bank of the Danube, the Oak and Starr inns, the Hungarian Crown, the Green Huntsman and the Red Rooster, the Wolf Preaching to the Geese in Wallnergasse, the Green Anchor in Grünangergasse and the Red Cross on Himmelpfortgrund. Only the Green Anchor Restaurant was still in existence, and the proprietor, a very pleasant man, claimed credibly enough that Schubert had frequently eaten and drunk there over a period of two years, so I ate lunch at the Green Anchor for months on end out of fellow feeling, a habit that finally led to an attack of gastritis. Even more interesting than the inns and cafés were the buildings in which he had lived, particularly the house where he was born at 54 Nussdorferstrasse, known as the Red Crayfish, which today contains a museum, but I also sought out the building at 9 Spiegelgasse in the centre of the city, to which

Franz von Schober often welcomed his friend, and inquired about the apartments in Tuchlauben and Wipplingerstrasse where the composer had also spent a considerable amount of time, and as the years passed by I redoubled my efforts to move into one of those apartments, or at least into one of the buildings. The folder in which I filed my correspondence with the owners and tenants of these apartments and buildings and with the Vienna City Council still bears witness to the difficulties with which I had to contend. My dearest wish would have been to live in the building where Schubert was born, but owing to the City Council's lack of understanding I soon realized this was an impossible aim, and my persistent attempts to rent a place in 9 Spiegelgasse, where Schubert had composed the Symphony in B Minor, the Unfinished, weren't as successful as I had hoped. Renting a place in 6 Kettenbrückengasse, known as the Death House, did not at first seem to me particularly desirable, for the simple reason that the place was linked to an irreplaceable loss for mankind, and consequently I feared that living long-term in that fateful spot might further reinforce my tendency to melancholy, probably inherited from my mother and manifesting itself more particularly in the cold months of the year in the form of depression, a fear which I'm happy to say has turned out to be only partly justified.

When all my attempts to live where Schubert had lived had come to nothing, I decided to find out about the Death House after all, and on the occasion of a visit to the room on the second floor where Schubert had died I asked the lady who sat there, knitting with great concentration and selling tickets, who owned the building, to which she replied that these were all council apartments, and then immediately put her tongue firmly between her lips again, for she was obviously engaged in the rather tricky business of turning the heel of a pale blue woolly sock. Nonetheless, I ventured another question – did she know if one of these apartments might fall vacant in the near future? – and she looked at me suspiciously, returned her tongue to the inside of her mouth

11

and said that as far as she knew the Turkish family of seven living in the three-roomed apartment right next to this room, Schubert's death chamber, was to be evicted in the course of the next six months because the head of the household, who sold fruit and vegetables in the Naschmarkt, was so far behind with his rent, and what's more the tenants' association had unanimously spoken out against the affront of having members of a foreign ethnic group constantly present in Schubert's Death House, in view of the fact that Schubert wrote music that was so very German, so profoundly German. I thanked her for the information and asked her to sell me an entrance ticket, a request with which, after casting me another suspicious glance, the lady complied. I stood in the death chamber for a long time, gazing at a lock of Schubert's hair in a locket and a silver toothpick the composer himself had used, and then listened through headphones to the Sanctus and Benedictus from the E Flat Major Mass, and tried to hide my inner emotion when I went out again past the knitting lady, who now seemed to have mastered the difficulties of the heel, since she was sitting there looking very relaxed.

Soon afterwards I visited the Vienna 5 Accommodation Advice Bureau on the second floor of 54 Schönbrunnerstrasse, door 18, and told the clerk on duty that I'd heard, from a reliable source, that a council apartment might soon fall vacant on the second floor of Schubert's Death House at 6 Kettenbrückengasse, as a result of an eviction, and as I had the deepest veneration for Schubert as both a composer and a human being I would very much like to move into the building where he died. The clerk, a remarkably stout young man with sparse fair hair and a thin, reddish moustache, looked me up and down and then asked if my circumstances justified my applying for a council apartment, not everyone in Vienna had the prospect of getting a council apartment, it was a privilege reserved for only a few, and the selection criteria were rigorous. I apologized for my ignorance and said, well then, what *were* the selection criteria, whereupon the clerk inspected me thoughtfully again, twirling the left-hand side of his moustache, and said that I'd have to prove that the state of the place where I was living at present had already impaired my health. When I made haste to say that I'd been unusually susceptible to illness since early childhood, the clerk became rather impatient and said my only chance was to show I lived in a damp basement apartment without its own toilet and had to use one out in the corridor, and that I suffered from severe arthritis as a direct result of living in such conditions, to which I replied, rather discouraged, that unfortunately I was living in my mother's large, comfortably furnished four-roomed apartment near the Church of Maria am Gestade in Vienna 1 and couldn't fulfil either of those stipulations. In that case, said the clerk, leaning back, in that case he could only advise me to rent a place for a while of the kind he had described, and then reapply, showing unmistakable symptoms of arthritis, and if my veneration for Schubert was really as great as I said, he was sure I could make that small sacrifice.

On the way back to my mother's apartment in the little street called Stoss-im-Himmel near the Church of Maria am Gestade, the advice of the clerk in the Accommodation Advice Bureau kept running through my head. His were terrible demands. Delicate from early childhood as I already was, must I deliberately move into a place injurious to my health in order to get the council apartment I longed for in Schubert's Death House? That was not, as he claimed, a small sacrifice but a superhuman one. Such a step could lead to my early death, and I didn't want to emulate the composer in that respect, since I had pupils who needed me. On the other hand, the prospect of living in Schubert's own aura was tempting. As I climbed the stairs to my mother's apartment I decided to discuss the problem with her – a woman with so much experience of life, such perspicacity, such a sense of realism. She did not disappoint me.

My dear child, she said, I've always been anxious to pass on to you the love of music that, as you know, fills every fibre of my being, and I have every reason to suppose that I have achieved that aim in your upbringing. Of course health is a very precious thing, undeniably we must do all we can to preserve it, and for you in particular even greater caution than usual is advisable, since yours is a delicate constitution. However, sometimes an extraordinary chain of circumstances can lead to a situation where considerations of physical well-being must take second place to some higher endeavour. If ideals are involved, and in the case you describe they undoubtedly are, the consistent pursuit of those ideals demands the commitment of one's entire person, even one's life. You mustn't think I shall find it easy to go on living here without your familiar presence, but calling on my maternal authority, which, as you know, is something I seldom do, I advise you – no, I require you – to make the sacrifice of living under insalubrious conditions for a while, for the sake of Franz Peter Schubert. You will be amply recompensed for this sacrifice by the good fortune of knowing yourself, later, to be always in his spiritual presence.

I looked at my mother standing there before me, very upright, one hand laid on the black lacquer lid of the baby grand. What a woman!

So it was that I spent the next few months in a one-roomed basement apartment on the Lerchenfelder Gürtel, with mould creeping up its walls. The desired symptoms set in within a gratifyingly short space of time: first fatigue and loss of appetite, then swelling of my joints and lymph glands, slight distortion and stiffness of my hands and feet, and the appearance of several rheumatic nodes, and when I had also contracted synovial bursal inflammation of the right shoulder because of the damp in the basement flat, I thought the time had come for another application to the Accommodation Advice Bureau. I got my mother's doctor to make out a certificate and went off to Room 18 in search of the stout clerk, who seemed to be impressed by both my sickly appearance and the medical certificate, and promised to support my application.

14

In this way the knitting lady, the stout clerk and my mother helped me to realize the dream of my life. I have lived in the building where Schubert died for over three years now, and I've never regretted taking the step I did. The quarter is a pleasant one, I can easily get all the provisions I need in the Naschmarkt, the St Mary Magdalene Pharmacy is reassuringly close, the proprietor and proprietress of the Café Anzengruber and the Golden Bell Restaurant like a chat with me, and the other tenants in the building are quiet, friendly people who, I am glad to say, don't seem to mind the sound of singing and the piano that go with my profession.

By now the beef broth was ready, and I drank two good bowls of it, then swallowed the requisite amount of *atropinum* and *arsenicum* pills and made myself a large cup of violet-leaf tea, and before I went to bed I took a bath with the water at body heat, adding a few drops of oil of thyme. Just before lying down I decided to make a hot compress for my chest, to be on the safe side, since my temperature had dropped slightly but was still above normal, and to help me get to sleep I played part of Brahms's *German Requiem*, a choral work said to have been written by the composer in memory of his dead mother. I fell asleep in a mood of cheerful relaxation, not without including my mother and Schubert affectionately in my thoughts first.

But once again my mother wasn't going to let me have a good night's sleep. The terrible nightmare that had plagued me so often recently came back. I was standing in a dark cemetery beside her last resting place, and I heard a hollow voice call: Dig me up, dig me up! I began digging in the hard, black earth with my bare hands until my fingernails broke. Faster, called the menacing voice, faster, my child! I dug and dug until two hands came into view, two dreadful hands, their yellowish bone structure exposed but still partly covered by blackish-brown scraps of skin and flesh. These hands reached out for my snow-white pure wool scarf, which was wound three times round my neck, and began pulling the ends of it

15

tighter and tighter, until I thought I would choke. Come, my child, called the voice, it is quiet here, it is good here! Normally I would wake up at this point, bathed in sweat, and it would take me some time to recover from the nightmare. I never tried defending myself against my mother's hands. But tonight the dream took a new turn; before the hands could seize my scarf I tore it from my neck and threw it in the hole I had just dug. Leave me alone, I cried, find someone else to share your eternal rest! At this my mother rose entirely from her grave, half decomposed, a terrible sight, and grew taller and taller until she was towering high above me. She picked me up with her huge hand of worm-eaten flesh and porous bones, raised me to the level of the black holes that were once her eyes, and then opened her skeletal yellow jaws to swallow me. But before her teeth crushed me I woke with a shriek. It was three thirty-three in the morning. I was trembling all over.

I couldn't understand my dear mother's ghastly behaviour. She was dead, of course she was, she'd died on 28 December three years ago, Holy Innocents' Day. Her mortal remains were buried in a grave in Vienna Central Cemetery, and I took the 71 tram there at least twice a week to talk to her. How could she repay such devotion, enduring even beyond death, in such a disgraceful way? I'd put up with my nightmares for a long time, feeling defenceless and incapable of protest, like a small child. I was surprised by my own untypical conduct in the dream from which I had just woken, by my conspicuous lack of respect for my late beloved mother, but on the other hand I was gradually beginning to lose patience with the selfish, unloving conduct of the dear departed, and I decided to ask her to explain herself when I next visited the Central Cemetery. And my next visit would be on the very day that had begun three hours thirty-three minutes ago, All Souls' Day, a very suitable date for such a confrontation. After these reflections, I managed to fall asleep again remarkably quickly.

2

The day I met Josef Horvath was 2 November, All Souls' Day, John's birthday. I had been in Vienna for three days, and by now the flight from Kennedy Airport to Vienna-Schwechat felt as if it had been a kind of journey in time, taking me back a hundred years into the past.

Only a few days ago I'd still been hurrying around Manhattan in sunny weather, making my last purchases for my journey to Europe, forcing my way past vehicles jammed solid in the streets amid the hooting of horns, the sound of alarms, police cars and ambulances. I'd raced down the steps to the subway and watched the rats scurrying along the lines as I waited for the train, water from a faulty pipe dripping on my head before I got into one of the graffiti-sprayed carriages, where the handsome young man sitting opposite me in jeans, T-shirt and trainers changed all his clothes during the journey. He took his fresh clothing, including a snow-white shirt and a pair of expensive-looking shiny brown shoes, out of a yellow plastic bag.

And that evening there'd been the view from the plane of the violet sky, a gleaming Atlantis, Brooklyn Bridge hanging like Christmas lights over the Hudson River, the bright oval of the Shea Stadium, the diadem on the roof of the Chrysler Building, the gold and silver streets, the red lights blinking on the skyscrapers.

My neighbour on the plane was a grey-bearded antique dealer from Vienna. He'd come to New York primarily, he said, to see an exhibition of netsuke, those little figures of ivory, jade, pottery or wood that you fix to the belts of Japanese kimonos. Collectors from all over the world paid very high prices for these little sculptures, he said. Life was a funny thing, he added, after a longish pause, he had come across a woman, a young woman who needed his help. He brought his mouth close to my ear. Crack, he whispered, I'd know what he meant, cocaine mixed with water and baking powder and boiled up. Her name was Maria Mercedes and she was only sixteen, it had been love at first sight, he'd already spoken to her mother, the family had emigrated from the Dominican Republic a few years ago and were very happy about his feelings for its youngest member. When he left he had given Maria Mercedes his most valuable netsuke, as a kind of pledge, and she'd be following him in a few weeks' time. Her problem would very soon be solved entirely of its own accord in Vienna, the city of waltzes, he was sure of that, Vienna, the city of waltzes, had a very beneficial effect on all kinds of dispositions. And then they'd get married in the Nine Choirs of Angels Church. I said he was quite right, you should do as your impulses dictate, it's the only sensible course of conduct, and I wished him the best of luck. He could do with that, he said, nodding, he could really do with that. Then I turned my head aside, thinking I'd sleep for a while, but the thin brunette sitting on my left addressed me. New York was impressive, she said, it was certainly very impressive, but personally she preferred Paris. During the entire two weeks of her visit to New York nothing out of the ordinary had happened to her, whereas it was absolutely impossible to stay two weeks in Paris and not have some kind of unusual experience. The first time she visited Paris her mother had asked her to go to the Musée de Cluny on the Left Bank of the Seine, because her mother, who had been a widow for over thirty years, spent her time embroidering copies of famous tapestries. In their original size, said the brunette, raising her right forefinger, mark that, in their original size, well, there weren't many ways for a widow to amuse herself in Salzburg. So when she went to Paris, she continued, her mother had just finished a copy of one of the six famous tapestries now in the Musée de Cluny, the set known as the Lady and the Unicorn tapestries. It had taken her mother five years to copy the tapestry with the sad-looking lady, the blue tent, the lion and the unicorn. Anyway, her mother had asked her to go to the Musée de Cluny and see exactly how the border was worked, because she, the brunette's mother, was having difficulty with the border. The thin brunette leaned back and paused for a moment. So she went off to the museum, she added, and being rather short-sighted she had to bend down and get quite close to the tapestries hanging on the wall, to take a good look. That had set off the alarm system, and an attendant came along and turned her out of the building. However, she said, smiling, she'd already memorized the style of the border, so there wasn't any way the attendant could bother her. Well, now I could see what she meant about something unusual always happening in Paris.

Europeans do seem to have odd experiences, I thought, and then I fell asleep and I didn't wake up until the plane had landed, and there was waltz music coming over the loudspeakers, Johann Strauss's *Vienna Blood*, as the brunette from Salzburg readily told me when I asked her. The stewardesses were standing at the exit from the aircraft dressed in bright red, nodding and saying *Grüss Gott!* over and over again. I almost slipped on the marble tiles of the arrivals hall in Vienna-Schwechat Airport, they were polished to such a shine.

When I stepped out into the open air, a cold wind was blowing in my face. It wasn't difficult to find the building where my relation lived on the corner of Blutgasse and Domgasse, since she'd given me reasonably clear instructions in a letter and said she was sorry she couldn't come to the airport to welcome me in person, but for a number of good reasons she hardly ever went out.

I took a taxi the last part of the way, and I was impressed by the generous scale on which the city was planned, with magnificent palatial buildings lining the broad streets around the city centre. This was my first visit to Vienna, and I had no real idea of the city at all, although I knew my maternal grandmother had been born there. My mother seldom talked about her family, so seldom that I'd wondered whether she was still in contact with her relations in Europe. Was there a gulf of some kind that couldn't be bridged, had there been bitter hostility, terrible quarrels, had my grandmother emigrated to the United States because of irreconcilable differences? Could there be dark secrets that my mother had never told me, painful conflicts upon which she didn't want to touch? When I told her I was planning to spend several weeks in Vienna taking an intensive course of singing lessons, she looked at me in surprise and said that as far as she knew Aunt Pia, not really her aunt but a cousin once removed of her mother's from the Pilsen line of the family, though she'd called her Aunt as far back as she could remember, still lived in that spacious owner-occupied apartment on the corner of Blutgasse and Domgasse, and she'd give me Aunt Pia's address. It would be only right and proper for that selfish creature Aunt Pia, who'd never paid a penny for her two-hundred-square-metres apartment, to put me up while I was in Vienna, eccentric egomaniac that she was, Aunt Pia had never done the slightest thing for the rest of the family, and it was high time she made up for it. After making these remarks my mother began rummaging about in a shoebox full of photographs and brought out an old, hand-coloured wedding picture of a woman with a happy expression and yellowish-green hair, and a serious-looking, rather older man with cherry-red lips, wearing uniform. Poor Major von Hötzendorf, she said, indicating the uniformed man, whom Aunt Pia had married not without ulterior motives, was dead and buried long ago; she remembered receiving an ostentatious death announcement. The Major had survived two battles of Isonzo safe and sound and then, a quarter of a century later, came home from the Ardennes offensive without a scratch, but Aunt Pia was more than he could survive, said my mother, Aunt

20

Pia had managed to infect that sober and deliberate man with her own crazy ideas and crack-brained delusions. But she wouldn't succeed with her daughter, my mother added after a brief pause, with a triumphant smile as if to herself, oh no, Aunt Pia would fail with her daughter. I must write to her, said my mother, I must write to Aunt Pia at once, she could hardly refuse my request.

When I protested, on the grounds of these dark hints, that it might be more sensible to stay in a hotel, my mother cried what, a hotel, what could I be thinking of, a good hotel in Vienna cost the earth, who was going to pay for that, not she for one, and she was really surprised to find that after going for months without any engagements and consequently without any money I was even contemplating such an eventuality. She had bled herself dry to finance my drama studies, absolutely bled herself dry, my training at Herbert Bergdorf's studio, for which she'd paid out of sheer sentimentality, sheer sentimentality because Bergdorf was an Austrian and the blood in my own veins was twenty-five per cent Austrian anyway, had brought her to the brink of economic ruin. And now I was a qualified actress I was always out of work because I was so pig-headed and demanding. I thought I could walk straight into Lady Macbeth or Desdemona instead of being content with smaller parts, like other beginners. And to put the lid on it I wanted to stay in some luxury hotel in Vienna, my self-absorption amazed her, and she didn't know whether this egotism was an unfortunate legacy from Aunt Pia or something to do with my Austrian genes, but anyway it was high time I met Aunt Pia, whom I obviously resembled so much and who'd always been an actress herself, a truly first-class actress, for otherwise the Major, a man out of the very top drawer, would never have fallen for her. Go and write her a letter this minute, my mother repeated by way of conclusion, and she put the photo back in the shoebox.

My mother's account of Aunt Pia, which wasn't entirely free of contradictions, made me curious to meet this relation of mine. The taxi driver was going along the side of a park, and some way off a

21

gilded statue of a man in tails, playing a violin with verve and standing on a tall plinth, gleamed briefly in front of a pale stone arch. Then the driver turned into a narrow street and stopped. I'd have to go the last few steps on foot, he said, Blutgasse and Domgasse were both traffic-free areas. So this was where I lived, he added, right by the Figaro House, he could never hear Mozart without shedding tears, the late works were particularly moving.

I paid him, took my case and stepped out on the cobblestones of the narrow little alley. As I looked for the building where Aunt Pia lived, my heels stuck twice in gaps between the cobbles. The second time around the narrow high heel came off my right shoe. Aunt Pia looked rather surprised when I finally reached her front door carrying my indigo-blue Samsonite case in one hand and my burgundy-red heel in the other. The old lady stood at her brown double door wearing a quilted pale blue dressing-gown, half open, with a long, high-necked pink flannel nightie under it. She had dirty white plush slippers on her feet. Oh, so it was me, she said out loud, and chuckled, Flora's little mistake, a remark that stopped me in my tracks on the doorstep, rendered speechless by this greeting. Well, I'd better come along in, she added, crooking the index finger of her right hand, come along in and put my case down. Whatever was that I was holding, but I must let her have a look at me.

I put the case down on the wooden floor, and she removed the heel of my shoe from my hand and turned me right round in a circle a couple of times, with a strength and agility remarkable for a fragile old woman.

Pretty child, pretty child, she chuckled, but blacker than she'd expected. She'd thought I would be pale brown, pale brown like milky coffee, even medium brown like a hazelnut, but as dark as this – oh dear, as dark as this, poor Flora.

A little later I was sitting opposite her in a living room full of shining dark brown furniture and equally dark but threadbare rugs. The heavy wine-red curtains were pulled over the tall windows, and the only illumination in the big, square room with its moulded stucco ceiling came from the weak light of a pale green porcelain globe above the round table in the middle of the room where we were sitting. As soon as I had become more used to the dim light, I saw that the whole room was full of dolls. There were dolls standing, sitting and lying on the chest of drawers, the bookshelves, the occasional tables, the sofa, the upholstered arm-chairs, even lined up in rows on the tall cupboard and on the floor.

My relation noticed me looking at them, and said ah, her dolls, I'd noticed her dolls, it was the dolls that kept her confined to her home, the dolls and her poor hearing. I'd have to shout at her or she wouldn't catch a word, her middle ear had suffered irreversible damage and it was much too dangerous for her out in the street, her eardrum was perforated, and it was no use a pedestrian going about the Inner City of Vienna with a perforated eardrum. But come along, I must have something to eat, a nice hot plate of tripe soup was just the thing for this time of year, around All Saints' Day.

I found myself confronting a thick white plate filled to the brim with an opaque, greyish-brown liquid which had white strips of something floating in it. I said I wasn't hungry, I'd had something to eat on the plane, and when Aunt Pia stated again that tripe soup was the very thing for this cold, wet weather, I must eat up, I shouted that I really wasn't hungry, I'd already eaten.

Aunt Pia looked at me with clouded eyes. She must have been about eighty. Sparse hair lapped round her small head like little white flames. Wilma never would eat either, she said, oh, these children, they simply didn't eat. We'd look at the dolls, then, she added, reaching a withered, arthritic hand across the table and energetically grasping my forearm. Wilma never did like playing with them, she said as we stood looking at the dolls arranged in a row on the sofa, she'd bought Wilma the most enchanting dolls, but Wilma never played with them. This one, for instance, she said, pointing at a particularly handsome specimen in a long white dress with a tiny pearl tiara in her hair, this one, said Aunt Pia, had glass

23

eyes that opened and shut, the ribbons and flowers on her tulle gown were hand-embroidered, she had real hair and her head would turn on its neck. And look, she said, pointing to the doll's little ears, which had pearl earrings hanging from them, the tiny lobes of her ears were pierced. She'd bought that doll in the Vienna Dorotheum, a valuable item made by Simon & Halbig, and Wilma never deigned to give it a glance.

The doll beside it wore a red cloak with a white fur lining. Aunt Pia pointed to the little handbag hanging from its arm. Embroidered damask, she explained, and then she picked up the bag, opened it, and took out a little oval hand mirror and a deck of tiny cards. Fifty-two cards, she said, not one missing, a complete pack, and the mirror was made of horn. And this one, she added, pointing to a large doll with a straw hat adorned with flowers and a dress with polka dots, the flounces were edged with handmade lace, a porcelain doll from Thuringia, just look at her eyes and that expressive glance, the lower lashes were painted on with a very fine brush. She raised the skirt of the dress. And the shoes, real kid, a very expensive doll, but Wilma had thought nothing of her.

My mother had hinted at some tragedy in Aunt Pia's life, a misfortune for which, however, she herself wasn't entirely devoid of blame. I felt rather uncomfortable under the gaze of all those painted pupils and movable glass eyes, and shouted that I was a little tired and would like to rest for a bit.

Of course, said Aunt Pia, naturally, she'd show me my room at once, she was putting me in Wilma's old room, Wilma's room was perfect for a young girl like me.

She took my hand and drew me purposefully after her down a long corridor and into a room the sight of which made me jump, because it, too, contained dozens of dolls, looking at me with their big round eyes from the bed and the bedside table, the window sill, the writing desk and the top of an old chest. They were even peering through the leaves of a philodendron.

She'd lit the tiled stove so that I'd be nice and warm, said Aunt

Pia, Wilma did like to be warm, she never could get warm enough. And now I must have a nice rest, pretty little thing that I was, chuckled my aunt, I must recover from the strain of the journey.

With these words she closed the door behind her.

It was very hot in the room. I looked around me. The pattern of the wallpaper, small pink roses on a white background, was in curious contrast to the heavy, dark brown furniture. I sat down on the tall bed with its ornately carved headboard and the crochet bedspread of scarlet roses. The soft mattress sagged in the middle. There was a lamp on the marble top of the bedside table; it had a brass stand and a shade of pleated fabric with a pattern of white roses on a yellow background. I went over to the window, removed the dolls from the window sill, put them on the floor, pulled back the curtains of a pattern that matched the wallpaper, opened half of the double window, and looked down into the yard of the building, where there was a bare plane tree with a stout trunk listing to one side.

I asked myself what on earth could have induced my mother, a woman who in general had always given me the impression of having my welfare at heart, to send me off to this gloomy doll's house, to stay with an old witch who, furthermore, had immediately shown herself to be a racist. At least, my mother's relations in Europe seemed to have been told that she'd married an Afro-American, and to deplore the fact. I couldn't possibly spend several weeks in these bizarre surroundings, at close quarters with a more than peculiar relation, I'd take my indigo-blue Samsonite case, creep out of deaf Aunt Pia's weird home, and get a room at the König von Ungarn Hotel, which I'd passed on my way to the apartment on the corner of Blutgasse and Domgasse and which looked agreeable if expensive. John would understand about this unexpected change in my plans and foot the hotel bill. After all, it was he who'd persuaded me to come to Vienna, saying that anyone who was going to play Sigmund Freud's daughter Anna in a musical about Freud must get to know something of the city where that remarkable woman had spent an important part of her life. He didn't believe anything happened by chance, not the slightest, most insignificant incident, and he considered it no coincidence that my family on my mother's side, like the Freud family on its father's side, came from Vienna and one of the north-eastern provinces of the Austro-Hungarian monarchy, and my singing lessons were of course even more important than some knowledge of what, so John had heard, was still the imposing former centre of a huge empire. For a variety of reasons he saw me as the ideal casting for Anna Freud, but my register was just a fraction too low, a mezzo-soprano would never do as the leading lady in a Broadway musical, ever since the invention of that entertaining theatrical genre every leading lady in a musical had been a lyric soprano, just as the leading men, without exception, were never tenors or basses but baritones, and if I didn't want to lose the role, for which I'd been cast only through his, John's, initiative, I must work my way up to the register of a lyric soprano with the active assistance of a competent and able singing teacher. And what could be more obvious than to seek such a singing teacher, either male or female, in Vienna, the city of music, where Schubert and Mozart had once lived and worked? My family in Vienna would surely be happy to help me find some suitable person.

I'd asked my mother's advice, and she said Aunt Pia would certainly be able to recommend someone; as far as my mother knew Aunt Pia had forced her unfortunate daughter Wilma to learn the piano for years, and she was sure to be close to the musical circles of Vienna. So I wrote my unknown relative a letter making a request along those lines, to which she replied at once, saying it would be a pleasure to introduce Flora's daughter, who obviously hoped for a career in opera or operetta, to the son of the former piano teacher of her late daughter who died twenty-three years ago as the result of an unfortunate accident, she didn't know the piano teacher's son personally, but she had spoken to him on the telephone and she heard that he was a young and very talented singing teacher, and a former member of the Vienna Boys' Choir. John was full of enthusiasm when I told him about this letter.

It was his capacity for enthusiasm that had won me over in the first place, his exuberance and his unstoppable optimism. I'd met him about five months earlier when I was resting, waiting tables in the café of an off-Broadway theatre. I was standing behind the counter working the Italian espresso machine when he came in, saw me, and approached me with arms outspread, crying, Anna! I told the attractive man in the pale, loose-fitting linen suit, with his hair cut very short, that he must have mistaken me for someone else, my name was Magnolia, and as far as I knew I'd never met him before. He seemed not to have heard me correcting him, because he kept coming towards me, reached his right hand over the counter, took hold of my chin, pushed it up a little higher, put his head on one side, closed his right eye and murmured, after a brief pause, wonderful, wonderful, exactly what he was looking for. Then, ignoring my protests, he drew me away from the espresso machine and out from behind the counter, and looked me up and down. A couple of centimetres too tall, he said, but never mind that, never mind that, and he absently smoothed down my white apron. Feeling impatient, I said couldn't he see I was busy, he'd better explain his mysterious comments rather more clearly at once, because I had to get back behind the Gaggia and finish what I was doing, making a cappuccino. Here he untied the wide, well-starched and ironed bow of my apron, threw this item of clothing down on the counter, saying I'd never have to work a Gaggia again in my life, and then took my hand, led me out into the open air and a little way down the street, and finally through revolving doors and into the lounge of an elegant hotel, where he made me sit in a club chair. The clerk at the reception desk greeted this impetuous stranger in friendly tones, and scarcely raised an eyebrow when he saw my high-heeled white slingback waitress's shoes.

27

Anna, repeated the impetuous stranger, looking at me affectionately, can you sing?

Rather impatiently, I withdrew my hand, which the man was
still holding, and asked what he thought he was doing, I was an
actress, currently resting, so I depended on my job waiting tables,
his impulsive behaviour could cost me that job, which just about
enabled me to keep my head above water, in fact it very probably
had cost me my job already. An actress, the exuberant stranger
exulted, he knew it, every other waiter or waitress in Manhattan
was an actor or actress out of a job. Then he repeated his question:
can you sing, Anna?

Rather annoyed, I said my name was Magnolia, Magnolia
Brown, and perhaps he'd be kind enough to tell me what he was
getting at. He did not by any means comply with this request but
asked me to sing a song there and then, in the lounge of the elegant
hotel. Caught off balance by the man's determination, I involuntarily struck up the first verse of Schubert's song 'The Trout', which
my mother had taught me, a circumstance that caused the receptionist to raise his eyebrows a little higher, the uniformed porter to
step through the revolving door into the foyer with his mouth
open, and the elderly couple sitting a few metres away to stare at
us in surprise. The purposeful stranger seemed satisfied with my
performance, interrupted me after the second verse, and urged me
to give him another song so that he could get a more reliable idea
of my voice. Again, his sheer energy confused me so much that, as
if of my own accord, I launched into the tune of 'Swing Low, Sweet
Chariot', which my father had sung me when I was a child. The
reactions of the receptionist, the porter, the elderly couple and the
dynamic stranger left me in no doubt that my offering had moved
them. The receptionist sat down, rested his chin in his hand, closed
his eyes and moved his eyebrows up and down, the coloured
porter began smiling and nodded his head slowly back and forth,
the elderly couple held hands and hummed quietly along with me,
and the dynamic stranger leaned back in his club chair and sighed

28

several times. Wonderful timbre, wonderful, he murmured, just a tad too low, but something could be done about that.

At this moment the owner of the café where I worked, who was also director of the off-Broadway theatre, came racing in through the revolving door, looked inquiringly around the lounge, saw me and marched up to me. He planted himself in front of me, hands on his hips, and shouted that I was fired, what did I think I was doing leaving the café at its busiest time of day. His Gaggia, which he personally had brought from Florence to New York, was a highly sensitive machine, you couldn't just stop in the middle of operating a machine like that the way I had, the Gaggia was now out of order, it wouldn't froth the milk any more, he was going to deduct the cost of repairing the machine, assuming it could be repaired at all, from the wages still due to me, and if it couldn't I'd have to pay for a new Gaggia myself. Then he came a step closer, lowered his voice, and said that in the circumstances there was obviously no chance of my getting the role of Ophelia at the theatre next season, although it had been as good as mine, and he'd have to look around for someone else for the part. Then he turned on his heel and left. I sat there, looking at my high, strappy waitress's shoes, and said nothing.

I mustn't be upset, said the dynamic stranger, placing his left hand on my knee; who wanted to be Ophelia if she could play Anna Freud instead, and when I asked him to be kind enough to tell me just how I had deserved to make his acquaintance, and what his intentions were, because I found it difficult to explain them to myself, he said his intentions were of the very purest, as I would understand in just a few moments. With these words he offered me his right hand and said his name was John F. de Luca, John F. de Luca Junior, son of John F. de Luca Senior, he was a Broadway writer and producer, and right now he was busy preparing a sensational musical on the life of Sigmund Freud, founder of the science of psychoanalysis, the libretto of which he'd written, and all the parts were now cast except for the role of Anna Freud,

Sigmund Freud's daughter, a difficult one to fill. He'd noticed me at once in the café of the off-Broadway theatre, I was undoubtedly ideal for the role, and after the little musical recital I'd been so kind as to give he could congratulate me on getting the part. I said I was pleased and honoured by his confidence, but artistically I felt little interest in Broadway melodramas, comedies and musicals, ever since I took my final exams it had been my ambition to play nothing but Shakespearean roles, however small. I'd rather play a lady-in-waiting, a serving wench or some little shepherdess in a Shakespeare play than any big part in a musical, and furthermore as far as I was aware Sigmund Freud and his family had been white, which, as he could see if he had eyes in his head, was not the case with me.

Of course he had eyes in his head, cried John F. de Luca Junior, of course he could see my skin wasn't snow white, pale as milk and red as blood, but that was by no means a disadvantage in this case. And anyway he didn't see people unhesitatingly handing me the part of a Shakespearean shepherdess or lady-in-waiting, not in view of my skin colour, and he supposed he'd be right in assuming I wasn't exactly overwhelmed with offers. I said such reservations might be true of conventional theatrical people, but luckily there were others who modelled themselves on the English director Peter Brook, who as no doubt John F. de Luca knew cast members of all kinds of different ethnic groups in his productions of Shakespeare. Although I had to admit that, no, so far my skin colour hadn't been exactly helpful in my search for parts.

Peter Brook, cried John F. de Luca, he'd been just about to mention Peter Brook, a brilliant man of the theatre whom he'd been emulating for decades. Who said you couldn't stage a musical about Sigmund Freud with all the parts taken by black people, there was nothing against it at all, such an idea was perfectly plausible, weren't the Jews the blacks of Europe, the Afro-Americans of the Old World, couldn't their marginalization and social exclusion be very convincingly represented by such a device?

Some years ago he'd written a libretto based on *Uncle Tom's Cabin* in which the whole cast was Asian, and he'd produced this admittedly daring adaptation as a musical on Broadway. He'd been aware from the outset of the risks involved in such a radical experiment, but he never let risks deter him; on the contrary, risks always had an invigorating, stimulating effect on him. It was true that the musical had flopped, it was a fact that the expensive production had meant financial disaster for him, there was no denying that he had recovered from this financial disaster only with the active support of his father, the producer John F. de Luca Senior, but what were these drawbacks by comparison with the thrill, the daring represented by such an attempt?

John F. de Luca Junior took his hand off my knee, glanced at me, and said he knew how difficult it was to make your way as an actress in New York, looking at me anyone could see the privations I suffered, the disappointments I had to overcome as I attempted to win professional recognition. Well, the moment I accepted his offer there'd be an end to those privations and disappointments, he begged me to realize what a chance he was giving me, an opportunity like this turned up once in a lifetime, no more, he though it not out of the question that my performance as Anna Freud would win me a Tony, yes, a Tony was a distinct possibility. He'd be the last man to say a word against Shakespeare, I must believe him, but you had to keep your mind open to the more modern trends in the entertainment industry too, and no good would come of despising the musical, which after all was the contemporary version of a total art form and demanded a wide range of talents in its cast, who had to be able to sing and dance as well as act. Did I want to carry on chasing from agency to agency with the Ross Report in my hand, going from one unsuccessful audition to another, from one failed casting session to the next, did I really want to go on earning a living as a waitress now I had the prospect of such a quantum leap, a real quantum leap in my career?

I looked at John F. de Luca Junior. He had talked himself into a

state of high excitement, there were two small round red patches
on his cheekbones, his eyes were blazing like the eyes of a religious
fanatic. The man was probably crazy. On the other hand I'd had
more than enough of the life I was leading, with its constant
financial worries, the little room I rented in East Village, my
cheerless relationships with other actors who were just as poor and
unsuccessful as I was. I had nothing to lose.

A knock on the door brought me back from my thoughts.
Without waiting for me to ask her to come in, Aunt Pia entered
the room. There was a gentleman on the telephone, she said with a
giggle, a gentleman with a lovely voice, she couldn't understand a
word he said but he had such a lovely deep voice, and I rushed out
of the room, over to the old-fashioned black telephone with the
big receiver, the metal rest and a dial with holes for your fingers,
that stood on a little table in the corridor.

So how was his delicious little coffee bean, his divine little
hazelnut cake, his captivating fudge brownie, asked John, to which
I replied that contact with my Viennese family had turned out to be
a terrible mistake since it consisted of a monster, a witch who kept
me shut up in her dead daughter's overheated room and was trying
to poison me with suspicious-looking things to eat. John's soft
laughter at the other end of the line infuriated me. I wasn't staying
in this place a moment longer, I went on, no one could expect me
to, there was a proper hotel quite close, and considering all the
expenses of the musical to date, the hotel bill would hardly make
much difference. John stopped laughing. How could I say that, he
asked, he was trying to save wherever he could on production
costs, and now I wanted to spend weeks in a Viennese four-star
hotel, I must surely be reasonable and see how outrageous my
demands were. Look, he said, I'd only just arrived in Vienna, the
unfavourable impression I'd formed of my relation would surely
very soon turn out entirely unfounded, old ladies in general and
old Viennese ladies in particular might be a little eccentric but
ultimately they were very kind and affectionate, over the last few

32

months he'd already noticed my distrust, my scepticism, and I must try to shake off this negative way of thinking because it was counter-productive. After all, it was a wonderful opportunity, a privilege to stay in an old apartment in the district of Vienna 1, it meant my view of the city wouldn't be confined to the tourist angle, and even if my relation might be a little odd she'd give me a real insight into the old capital, an insight that was absolutely essential for my performance in my part, and what was more he was amazed by my lack of family feeling. I refrained from pointing out that maybe I was lacking, but as far as I could see he wasn't, and just said I was rather surprised by his lack of empathy for me in my situation. How could I say such a thing, cried John, he had empathy to an unusually high degree, if he hadn't then would he ever have picked me to play Anna Freud? He hoped I wasn't going to force him to put his foot down about this; after all, I was part of a whole, part of a huge piece of theatrical machinery, and I must put that before my personal comfort just as he and everyone else involved did. The production of a Broadway show was a tremendous venture, he was risking everything, costs had risen to dizzy heights in the last few years, costs had positively gone through the roof, the public demanded star casts, perfect technical standards and spectacular sets and costumes, he couldn't afford another flop, not even his father, the famous producer John F. de Luca Senior, whose second and favourite son he was, would be able to bail him out a second time. He didn't want to dwell yet again on the positively fantastic opportunity the chance of playing Anna Freud meant to my career, he wasn't asking for gratitude, but he did expect a certain amount of compliance with the group structures represented by the ensemble engaged exclusively for the production of our musical. This was not a matter of purely individual aims, hadn't I realized there was much more at stake here, the show meant unreserved commitment to the victims, the scapegoats, the oppressed and excluded of this unjust world, wasn't I capable of subduing my egotistic interests to a higher aim?

33

I gave up. As usual, John had talked me round. His idealism, his certainty that visionary endeavours could be successful, his belief in the realization of his utopias had won out over my scepticism, suspicion and selfishness.

Oh, very well, I said, I'd stay.

3

It was All Souls' Day, the day of the dead, a festival introduced to the calendar by Abbot Odilo of Cluny in the year 989, according to Fräulein Haslinger, who as a result of her decades working as a pastoral assistant is a reliable authority on all matters pertaining to the Catholic Church and its rites.

A nasty cough woke me early. Drowsily, I placed one hand on my forehead, and at once put the other hand out for the thermometer on my bedside table. My forehead felt hot. I shook the thermometer and put it in my mouth, and even this exertion, not excessive in itself, instantly exhausted me. I'd guessed as much: I was paying for my carelessness in walking part of the way home without my white scarf of pure hand-spun wool. The whole area behind my breastbone felt sore. In general I preferred to treat my bronchial catarrh without consulting a doctor, merely taking advantage of the wise advice of the pharmacist in the St Mary Magdalene Pharmacy, but this time I'd have to make the journey to the Vienna General Hospital, a journey I hated, because my mother had reached the end of her life as a pianist of melancholy disposition on Holy Innocents' Day three years ago in one of the many artificially lit wards of that ugly building. I would have to ring Dr Leupold-Löwenmaul, a medical authority and lecturer well known as a pneumologist far beyond Vienna and indeed the Austrian border, and make an appointment, and he would very probably do a bronchoscopy, an uncomfortable procedure to which I'd been obliged to submit myself once already. I wondered how, in the circumstances, I was going to manage to take the 71 tram to the Central Cemetery, because there could be no question of my denying my physical presence there to my dear mother and Franz Seraphicus Peter Schubert on this important day. I took the thermometer out of my mouth. Thirty-seven point seven degrees Celsius, nothing to panic about, but cause for concern all the same. The most sensible thing would be to inhale the vapour of a herbal decoction brewed from equal parts of coltsfoot, sundew and corn poppy; an inhalation had always brought me considerable relief. I let myself fall back on the pillow, closed my eyes, and tried to conjure up the image of my mother as she was in life, so as to get rid of the horrible apparition in my nightmare. She had been such a beautiful woman, tall, with expressive dark eyes and long, nut-brown hair, and had been compared, not entirely without justification, to the late Empress Elisabeth who perished in such unfortunate circumstances and about whom the old lady from 14 Kettenbrückengasse had made such unkind remarks. For a while I gave myself up to the pictures in my mind's eye, then I got out of bed, made my way past the sheets, which were now almost dry, and brewed my herbal decoction. Finally I put the pan on a chair, sat in front of it, draped the crochet bedspread over my head and breathed the vapours well in. The burning sensation did subside slightly. As I sat there in the dark, my back bent, I thought of a couple of lines from the *Kindertotenlieder*: 'Ah, my heart, you do not wish those wounds to heal / You have something still, while with pain they burn, / but when pain is stilled then all is dead and gone.'

Someone rang the doorbell. I rose, went to the door with the bedspread still over my head, and opened it. Through the crochet pattern of large star shapes, I saw the familiar figure of Fräulein Haslinger.

Oh, how I'd frightened her, she cried, taking a step back and putting a hand, so far as I could make out, to the collar of her white blouse. She was so sorry to bother me, she'd only wanted to quote me a biblical text that made a very suitable subject for meditation today, All Souls' Day. She opened what, if my limited vision did not deceive me, was a fat red paperback held in her left hand, probably the standard version of the Old Testament with the Apocrypha, and read:

Ecclesiasticus, Chapter 41, verses two and three: 'O death, acceptable is thy sentence unto the needy, and unto him whose strength faileth, that is now in the last age, and is vexed with all things, and to him that despaireth, and hath lost patience! Fear not the sentence of death, remember them that have been before thee, and that come after; for this is the sentence of the Lord over all flesh.'

I had an idea. I folded back the crochet bedspread and said I was sure she was going to the Central Cemetery today to put a bouquet of evergreen foliage and chrysanthemums on the grave of her late confessor and spiritual counsellor, Monsignor Gaspero, who died five years ago of the effects of an undiagnosed attack of gastroenteritis. Why didn't we go together, on the 71 tram? I was feeling very debilitated by the side effects of severe bronchial catarrh, and would be extremely glad of her company and support. I knew how her deep feeling for Monsignor Gaspero had survived his earthly existence, just as I still felt tender emotions for my dear mother, and I was sure she would appreciate the importance to me of visiting her grave on a day when everyone cherished the memory of the dear departed. To this Fräulein Haslinger replied that of course she understood my wish, she'd be delighted to render this small service to a fellow human being, and would also take the liberty of bringing me a bottle of cough syrup, a very efficacious medicament that she had made herself by a complicated process of distillation from fresh fir shoots taken from a wood belonging to her family in the Bucklige Welt countryside region.

So a few hours later we were standing in the crowded 71 tram with a great many other Viennese on their way, like us, to the

Central Cemetery in Simmeringer Hauptstrasse, which is open to members of all confessions, to pay tribute to the dead buried there. I had carefully turned up the collar of the thick, dark green loden coat made by the firm of Resi Hammerer, inherited from my mother, a garment of discreet elegance and indestructible quality, and I had wound the white pure-wool scarf several times round my neck. Fräulein Haslinger had also been kind enough to lend me her fur cap, made of valuable fine-haired sable and given her by a Russian soldier in the forces of occupation during the particularly severe post-war winter of 1947 to '48 in return for a small favour, so that my sensitive head area was protected. Did I know, asked Fräulein Haslinger, that five hundred and twenty-five trams made the journey to the Central Cemetery every year on All Saints' Day and All Souls' Day, including several cemetery specials that ran only on those two days, carrying a million passengers in all, and did I know that the bereaved mourners placed five million chrysanthemums and five hundred thousand cyclamens and pansies on the graves of their loved ones?

At the main entrance, Gate Two, where the office building and the two mortuaries are situated, we got out of the tram and mingled with the crowd mourning their dead, wandering around in the sleet among the many stalls selling flowers, hot dogs and roast chestnuts that had been set up in honour of the day. Fräulein Haslinger said that if I didn't mind she would leave me now, she must just pop into Grabsteinland, the biggest of the stonemasonry firms surrounding the cemetery, to find Kubicek the master stonemason and discuss a possible change to the wording of the inscription on Monsignor Gaspero's gravestone, a very fine slab of grey-blue conglomerate stone from a quarry in the Bucklige Welt. I said I thought I could perfectly well make my way to Schubert's tomb and then to my mother's grave on my own, the proximity of the mortal remains of those two beloved persons would give me strength, in fact I felt stronger already. Finally, Fräulein Haslinger cast a glance at the main entrance and said, shaking her head, three million dead people in over three hundred thousand tombs and graves, amazing, two hundred and fifty graves of honour, an Austrian pantheon! So saying, she turned and set off for Grabsteinland.

I walked on as best I could in the sleet. Fräulein Haslinger's mention of the two hundred and fifty graves of honour had revived unpleasant memories. After my mother's death I had sent a written application to the City Council, Department Seven, asking for her mortal remains to be granted a grave of honour, one of those graves held in perpetuity for which the city of Vienna pays all fees and which it undertakes to tend. I told the authorities that my mother had been a singularly gifted piano virtuoso who was prevented from offering her talents to a wide public only by circumstances of the most adverse and unfortunate nature. I therefore felt justified in petitioning for her body to be buried in the Garden of Remembrance for figures of cultural importance laid out a few years earlier among the graves of honour in Group 40. The letter I received from the official responsible was discouraging: it said the members of the committee had decided that while a bereaved son's assessment of his late mother's musical gifts was understandable and touching, it was by no means in itself a good enough reason to justify my late mother's burial in the Garden of Remembrance for graves of honour, or in either of the other two large departments of such graves, namely Groups 14A and 14C, and 32A and 32C. They did not wish to hurt my feelings, but with the best will in the world they could not class my late mother among the ranks of the famous names now resting there. I was not so easily discouraged, and made a further application to the department of the City Council concerned, asking them at least to grant my mother a grave *honoris causa*, as the slightly less prestigious are called, even if it meant that the erection of the gravestone and care of the grave would be my responsibility as her next of kin. When this application, too, had been turned down, I ventured to try one last petition for what is called a dedicated grave, which although it would not be in perpetuity like the graves of honour and the graves *honoris causa* would at least be granted for a period of ten years. Two months later I received an answer, written in tones of some annoyance, from the ultimate authority in such matters, the office of the Mayor of Vienna, asking me to desist from my efforts, my string of applications was merely causing an unnecessary amount of extra work for an administrative system already stretched to its limits.

By now I had reached the place where the tombs of composers stand, a beautiful and usually quiet spot where I always lingered for a short time before visiting my mother. Knowing that I was in the spiritual presence of Brahms, Beethoven, Wolf, Gluck, Schönberg and above all Schubert was a comfort. I sometimes regretted the fact that Mahler's last resting place was in Grinzing Cemetery, and Berg was buried in Hietzing Cemetery, but still, that gave me an opportunity for relaxing walks in these two well-tended grave-yards, the former a pretty place with many expressive funerary sculptures and well away from the noise of traffic, being laid out on terraced and slightly rising land, whereas the latter, with its hedges and handsomely designed rows of vaults, suggests the English landscape gardening style. I stopped in front of Schubert's tomb and gave myself up for a while to contemplation, in which I was sorry to be seriously disturbed by the conversation, conducted in unnecessarily loud tones, between an old lady and her compan-ion, a dark-skinned young woman, thin as a rake, with her hair curiously arranged in countless little plaits. In some annoyance, I placed the little bunch of red-berried holly sprigs bought from the pleasant woman in the florist's shop in Kettenbrückengasse on the tomb, and went off towards my mother's resting place in a rather remote part of the Central Cemetery, where old chestnut trees towered above it. For the gravestones I had chosen a plain but handsome piece of pink-flecked Untersberg marble, a mineral known here as trout stone, and the inscription engraved on it was two lines from the *Winterreise*, 'A stranger came I hither, / I leave a stranger still'. Above this inscription I had had a small, glazed oval photograph frame fitted, from which my mother's portrait looked at me as if out of a locket.

The walk to this rather inaccessible part of the cemetery, which was also covered by a thin, wet layer of snow, had tired me so much that despite the danger of further deterioration in my state of health I sat down on the low wall of mica slate surrounding the grave. My mother's dark eyes rested on me with gentle sympathy. When my glance happened to fall on the grave next to hers, a showy construction made of some synthetic-looking snow-white material and adorned with tasteless statues of angels, I realized that the two women conversing at such irritatingly high volume who had made such an unpleasant impression on me at Schubert's tomb were busy about it with a watering can and a rake. I tried to close my eyes and ears to them, and after a short salutation to my mother began talking to her, an exchange of ideas which her glance positively invited. It wasn't easy for me, I said by way of introduction, to broach the theme of those nightmares in which, unfortunately, she played such an unappealing part, but concern for my psychic welfare obliged me to do so. Since I remembered her as a loving, warm-hearted provider, it was very distressing for me to see her in the nightmares I'd mentioned as a monster making unreasonable demands, a horrific and life-threatening figure, a devouring spectre. Was it really necessary to undermine the positive impression she'd made on me during her lifetime? I'd be glad to help her in any way I could if she didn't like it in the next world as much as she had expected, but she really couldn't ask me, not yet past my thirtieth year, to follow her there just yet. She'd always had the good of her own pupils at heart, so surely she could understand that I, her son, had not yet fulfilled the purpose of my earthly existence, I had to pass on the musical abilities which I owed mainly to her, I must convey them to those who found music as great a need, as powerful a preoccupation, as it had been to her and as it was to me. I fell silent and waited for my mother to react.

One of the two women, who happened to be passing at that moment with a green watering can, stared fixedly in my direction. My mother said nothing, but the kindly and serious expression in her eyes showed that she had understood.

A dry cough shook me, and I stood up, took the little bottle of cough syrup so kindly provided by Fräulein Haslinger out of one of the pockets of the Resi Hammerer loden coat, and sipped the dark liquid. This measure brought me momentary relief, but soon the urge to cough became so irresistible again that I had to give way to it, causing the two ladies to put their right forefingers to their pursed lips in a request for silence which I thought outrageous, since they themselves continued to talk audibly and so clearly that I couldn't help hearing parts of a rather uninteresting conversation about the fate of some Major or other and a girl called Wilma who had obviously died young. To avoid giving the pair of them any further cause for complaint, I took out the two bottles of *atropinum sulfuricum* D3 and *arsenicum* D6, carefully slipped ten little white pills of each out on the palm of my hand, and swallowed them. As I did so a couple of pills fell to the ground. I bent down to pick them up, and in the process I noticed that the pretty wrought-iron lantern I'd put in front of the small yew I myself had planted on the grave was gone. Incredible as it might seem, there were obviously grave robbers at work in Vienna Central Cemetery, persons of the worst sort who didn't shrink from approaching items placed on graves out of love and affection for the dead. In the sleet that kept falling and the biting wind, I might conceivably have been able to light the red candle I'd bought from the candlemaker and ginger-bread baker in Margaretenstrasse, but without the protection of the glazed lantern the flame would go out again at once.

I straightened up, and I could hardly believe my eyes: the white-haired little old lady at the grave next to my mother's was in the very act of placing a white candle inside my lantern. I strode furiously towards her and addressed her, whereupon the old lady tilted her head to one side, cupped her right hand under her right ear, and asked me to speak up, because she was almost stone deaf on the right side, having a damaged eardrum as the result of a severe inflammation of the middle ear. I shouted at her to give me back the lantern she'd stolen from my mother's grave this minute, or I wouldn't hesitate to go to the cemetery staff and complain of her shameless theft. Here the old lady raised her voice to a volume that was astonishing in view of her frailty, and asked what on earth I was thinking of, this lantern was hers, she'd bought it for two hundred and ninety-nine schillings in the Baumarkt in Erdberg a week after the Major's death, she knew perfectly well she had, and I'd better refrain from using underhand methods to winkle decent folk's property out of them. The lie the old lady was trying on made me so indignant that I grabbed the little lantern without a word and attempted to wrench it away from her, a venture that turned out to be first difficult and finally futile, since the old lady clung to her ill-gotten gains with remarkable tenacity. To put the lid on it, the young black woman with the little plaits now intervened in the argument and began tugging at the lantern herself. In the middle of this argument I was overcome by a severe coughing fit, probably as an immediate consequence of the over-exertion and emotional agitation involved in the dispute. I gave up and fled from the scene, pursued by the screeching of both women.

4

After two days in Vienna I can't say I was particularly taken with the place. The sky above the city was grey and overcast, there was an icy wind blowing, and now there was wet, cold sleet falling all the time too, covering the streets with a thin layer of dirty snow on which you could easily slip. I had slept badly the last two nights, the room was too hot, and the big round eyes of the dolls followed me into my dreams. During one of our meals in the living room I plucked up all my courage and asked Aunt Pia's permission to remove at least some of the dolls from Wilma's room, a wish that I thought perfectly reasonable, although it set off a surprisingly violent reaction in Aunt Pia. Every single one of those dolls, she told me, had stood in a certain spot ever since it was bought, decades ago in many cases, it was out of the question to put even a single one of them anywhere else after all these years, her dolls had souls, she was sure of it, they had acquired habits of their own like everyone else, and being made to move would be as painful for the dolls as if she, Aunt Pia, were transferred to some completely unknown place, she was willing to oblige Flora's daughter in many ways, but she felt unable to comply with my wishes in this particular respect. Rather intimidated, I tried another question – would it be at all possible to keep the tiled stove a little less hot, I couldn't tolerate such heat, it prevented me from getting to sleep, and if necessary I was perfectly ready to look after the stove myself. Once again Aunt Pia's answer was surprisingly emphatic: I had no idea of the difficulty of heating a tiled stove of the Viennese Biedermeier period, Viennese Biedermeier stoves were particularly complicated to heat, she didn't want to offend me, but she couldn't think that being half black African I was in the least familiar with European tiled stoves of the kind first used in Switzerland and the Tyrol. It could hardly have escaped my attention that the tiled stove in Wilma's room was an especially fine example, ornamented with reliefs and tastefully painted, a stove like that had to be handled with great caution, inexpert handling might crack its tiles, leading to an acute risk of those near the stove being affected by escaping gases, and possibly, in the worst case, to tragedy. In addition, getting a professional stove fitter to repair cracked tiles cost a fortune, quite apart from the fact that professional stove fitters could hardly be found at all these days, not even in Vienna, which had been a positive El Dorado of stove fitters in the nineteenth century, and furthermore she was surprised that I didn't appreciate the comfortable warmth of the tiled stove in this nasty late-autumn weather we were having; no, she was sorry, but she must strictly forbid me to touch that tiled stove, she merely expected that as a young woman, and strong too, I'd be prepared to bring up beech logs for the stove from the cellar of the building, a task previously performed by the Bosnian caretaker's husband and for which he charged an outrageously high price, conduct not untypical of his ethnic group. Rather discouraged, I looked at the plate of tripe soup in front of me and replied that of course I was ready to lend her a hand in this small way, and I had another request as well, to do with the question of food: I was sure she wouldn't mind if I used her kitchen to prepare my own meals, because as she could imagine everyone has his or her own tastes and doesn't like departing from them, and in addition my preparation for the part of Anna Freud, who had been petite and delicate, meant I had to stick to a certain diet.

Diet, cried Aunt Pia, what on earth did I mean, diet, well, excuse her, but so far as she could see, with her poor eyesight, I was nothing but skin and bone, after all she was responsible to my mother for my physical and mental well-being, surely I could understand that. Tripe soup, a pan of which she always had on the stove, was a very healthy Bohemian dish, just the thing for adolescents from the over-civilized Western industrial states who suffered from that fashionable new sickness anorexia, and might she make so bold as to ask me, since not only African blood but also, thank goodness, a large amount of the old Austrian variety ran in my veins, what I had against a national Bohemian dish made exclusively from natural, nutritious foods, including besides the main ingredient – the finely sliced lining of the stomach of a cow, calf or pig, otherwise known as tripe, chitterlings or pluck – flour, butter, onions, a bunch of soup vegetables including celery and root parsley, salt, garlic, paprika and a little marjoram. She didn't mean to boast, but since we were on the subject of this recipe she would permit herself to say that its preparation was anything but simple, in fact it was very laborious, you had to wash the tripe thoroughly, rub it well with salt, scald it with boiling water, rinse it, then put it on the stove in a pan of cold water and simmer it for forty minutes, and that was only the first step in the method. After that you drained the tripe, covered it with fresh water and simmered it for about three hours more, and that was the second step. She hardly needed to point out that the tripe had to be of prime quality, which was difficult to obtain, what with the general decline in food standards these days. Every week, not without danger because of her deafness, she ventured out to the butcher in Schönlaterngasse, who sold what as far as she knew was the last tripe of absolutely reliable quality in Vienna. She wasn't going to tell me the third step in the method, because it was a matter of principle to hand on recipes of this nature only to your fellow countrywomen, with whom I could not, unfortunately, be classed without reservations, and anyway what she'd already told me was certainly enough to give me some idea of all the work that went into making traditional Bohemian tripe soup. I protested that I had no intention of criticizing an old Austrian dish, but I was used to rather lighter cooking, and anyway I didn't eat meat, or very little. Doesn't eat meat, muttered Aunt Pia, shaking her head, the child doesn't eat meat. Then she sat up very straight, raised her voice and said I could eat what I liked, in these extreme circumstances she wouldn't be responsible for my state of health, but she couldn't let me use her kitchen stove; like most kitchen stoves in Vienna it was fuelled by natural gas from the Schwechat oil refineries, and she could not allow me, the inhabitant of another continent and wholly unfamiliar with Viennese customs and habits, to have anything to do with that highly explosive Lower Austrian gas mixture. I said as calmly as possible that I was used to gas stoves, I cooked on gas myself in New York, but Aunt Pia wouldn't change her mind and said petrochemicals were a very dangerous area, and at my tender age I had better not venture into it. I refrained from telling her that I was going to be thirty-three on the twenty-eighth of February next year, and asked to be allowed to leave the table.

Such futile discussions were not the only trying aspect of those first few days in Vienna. On All Souls' Day, John's birthday, my relation asked me to accompany her on the arduous journey to Vienna Central Cemetery, where she wanted to tend the grave of Major von Hötzendorf and her daughter Wilma, placing on it a simple little wreath of pale purple heather, the Major's favourite flower, and a bouquet of pine branches and Christmas roses, of which Wilma had been particularly fond. There was a cheerful fairground atmosphere in the huge cemetery which seemed to me in odd contrast to a day set aside for remembering the dead, with the Viennese eating and drinking at the many stalls outside the main entrance, while their children ran around among the rows of graves with balloons, candyfloss and coloured paper hats.

We would make a little detour past the tombs of the composers, said Aunt Pia, perhaps I'd give her my arm, the Central Cemetery was a very handsome one, but unfortunately open to members of all confessions, you couldn't help wondering what business dead

Jews had here when the Christian part of the cemetery was so neat and tidy and the Jewish part dreadfully neglected, a terrible muddle, she'd spare me the sight of the Jewish part. It was a disgrace to German-speaking Austrians with patriotic and Catholic feelings, as the Major always used to say when they went for a walk in the cemetery. Thank goodness there was a corrective in the form of the composers' tombs, the composers' tombs were among the finest to be seen in the cemeteries of Vienna, just as the cemeteries of Vienna were among the finest sights of the whole city.

Aunt Pia stopped at a tomb with a stone statue of a woman seated in a graceful attitude on it. Only a cenotaph, unfortunately, she said. Mozart's mortal remains lay in the Cemetery of St Marx, what an inspired artist, such very German music. She sighed and folded her hands.

In front of Schubert's tomb, apparently lost in thought and muttering to himself, stood a man wearing a monstrous black cap made of the skin of some furry animal, who for reasons I couldn't fathom cast me an angry glance.

Later we passed an imposing work of sacred architecture. The Dr Karl Lueger Memorial Church, explained Aunt Pia, a remarkable building, named after a remarkable mayor, an upright and patriotic Viennese who laid the foundation stone but didn't live to see the church completed. Oh yes, *tempus fugit*, she added, *tempus fugit*.

My relation seemed very proud of the grave of the Major and her daughter. Imitation alabaster made in the foothills of the Alps, she said, deceptively genuine-looking, easy to look after and frost-proof, Grabsteinland had excellent connections with the manufacturers. The putti were copied from the Stiftskirche at Melk. She was going to weed it, weeds spread everywhere, and meanwhile, she said, pressing a large, dark green plastic watering can into my hand, would I get some water from the tap?

On the way to the tap I saw the man in the fur cap again. He was sitting on the grave next to Major von Hötzendorf's, talking out loud to a photograph on the gravestone. When I came back, he was still sitting there talking. I decided he must be one of those unfortunate lunatics more and more frequently found in big cities these days, unhappy souls who can't tolerate their loneliness and engage in conversations with themselves. He gave me another unfriendly glance, and then fished a small flask out of the pocket of his old-fashioned coat and took a long gulp from it. The poor man was probably an alcoholic too.

The Major had been a distinguished man, said Aunt Pia wistfully, removing a wet reddish-brown horse chestnut leaf from the curly head of a putto, a quiet man. Distinguished and quiet. He'd always hated domestic altercations, perhaps because of being involved in so many altercations of a warlike kind during his career as an army officer. A life devoted to the service of the fatherland. He and Wilma had been very close, probably because their natures were fundamentally similar. Two angels in human form. She tugged hard at a tall plant. Shepherd's purse, a pernicious weed, she said, difficult to root out, and now we'd light the candle, the pretty white candle with the golden dove from the shop selling devotional items in the Domplatz, please would I hand her the little lantern on the grave.

The harmless lunatic by the grave next door began coughing unbearably loudly, and we made discreet gestures indicating that he might show a little more respect for the dead. Aunt Pia was just in the act of placing the lighted candle in the grave lantern, not an easy task on account of the icy wind, when the mentally deranged man in the monstrous fur cap suddenly attacked her, accused her of grave robbery, and tried to tear the lantern away from her by physical force. In the course of a short hand-to-hand struggle, our united strength managed to wear this nasty customer down so much that he made off, coughing. When I breathlessly told my relation not to take the man's malicious insinuations to heart, it looked as if he was just some poor lunatic, Aunt Pia chuckled and said to tell me the truth, she really had appropriated the grave lantern; her ridiculous widow's pension, the pittance that was all the Austrian state allowed her, was too much to live on, too little to die on, as they say, and of course didn't run to the purchase of such luxury goods as wrought-iron grave lanterns.

That evening I called John from the telephone kiosk behind St Stephen's Cathedral to wish him a happy birthday, but unfortunately I couldn't because he wasn't at his office, and when I tried his home number, one of his three school-age children answered the phone. On the way back through the drizzling rain to my relation's apartment on the corner of Blutgasse and Domgasse, I remembered an Indian clairvoyant I'd visited three years ago in her little consulting room furnished with handmade Navajo rugs on the Lower East Side, and how she had gazed steadily into her glass ball and told me that a man with the sun in Scorpio would appear to me in a bright white garment and break my heart within a few months.

Next day I took my burgundy-red heel and the rest of the shoe to the cobbler in Postgasse recommended to me by Aunt Pia. His family, she said before I went out, came from Eger in north Bohemia and was distantly related to ours, ours being from the Pilsen area, which meant I could insist on a price well below his usual charge, and I was to give him her regards and tell him who I was. The cobbler, a friendly red-cheeked man with jug ears, was surprised first by my good Viennese German and then to hear of my northern Bohemian origins. A northern Bohemian woman of my skin colour and with a hairstyle like mine was something he'd never seen before, he said in surprise, nor one with a shoe like this either, whereupon I patiently explained that my mother, my father and I had all been born in the United States, my father's ancestors had been brought from their African home in Dahomey to the so-called New World by slave traders, which explained my appearance, that my family on my mother's side came from around Pilsen, and my grandmother, who was born in Vienna and had looked after me a great deal when I was little, had been very keen

51

to talk to me in her mother tongue, so that accounted for my perfect Viennese. As for the shoe, I'd bought it and its companion in a second-hand store in East Village. The cobbler hastened to assure me that it would be a pleasure for him to repair such an exquisite shoe, although a repair like that called for craftsmanship far beyond the normal standard and must be paid for accordingly, I could collect my shoe in a week's time. And my regards to your lady aunt, he called after me as I left the little shop.

On the afternoon of the same day I had my first singing lesson with the teacher Aunt Pia didn't know personally but felt she could recommend with a clear conscience because of her acquaintance over several decades with his late mother, who had been her own late daughter's piano teacher, and also on the grounds of the recommendation of several persons of high standing in the musical life of Vienna. As I went west from the Inner City through the pouring rain in the direction of Vienna 4, I tried to picture him. No doubt he would be a sensitive teacher and interpreter, an elegant young man with expressive hands living in tasteful surroundings, going from recital to recital when he wasn't giving lessons to a few privileged pupils, conversing fluently in several languages, and perfectly at home in all the capitals of Europe. His sophistication and European refinement would probably make me seem clumsy and wooden with my North American cum Afro-American lack of subtle aesthetic feeling. Such ideas went through my mind as I walked along under the large purple umbrella fringed by an optimistic sunshine-yellow edging that I'd borrowed from Aunt Pia, passing a temple crowned by a golden globe, making my way past two long rows of stalls in a produce market. Outside a subway station I unfolded my city map of Vienna to get my bearings again.

Then a little old woman not unlike Aunt Pia came towards me, accompanied by a yapping spaniel. Get her, she told the dog, go on, get that nigger! What were things coming to if such creatures were taking over our attractive district of Vienna 4 too, she added, populating it with their repulsive black brood, going to stay at Bad

Gastein, Bad Hall and Baden bei Wien one after another to take the waters, all paid for by Austrian taxes from the Vienna Regional Health Insurance scheme, whereas she was obliged to relieve her multiple arthritis with medicinal herbs laboriously gathered in the Lainzer Tiergarten. Her father, who had retired as a stipendiary councillor in the civil service, had always thanked God he wouldn't live to see our blessed country overrun square metre by square metre by African negroes. And as usual her father had been right. The little dog jumped up at me, and in sheer alarm I dropped my city map and fled. I marched straight on, feeling indignant and confused, until I had calmed down to some extent and decided, now I'd lost my map, to go into a florist's and ask about the singing teacher, who would surely be a well-known and highly esteemed character in this quarter.

The lady behind the counter, who was busy tying up a bunch of bright red anemones, asked in friendly tones what she could do for me, and when I said I was looking for a famous young singing teacher called Josef Horvath who lived somewhere in this area, and did she perhaps know him, she cried oh yes, poor Herr Horvath, of course she knew him, he lived in the Death House at 6 Kettenbrückengasse on the other side of the street, just a few steps further on, only the other day she'd sold him a very special bunch of holly. Poor Herr Horvath, whose mother had died three years ago, and to the best of her knowledge he still hadn't got over it, oh dear, poor Herr Horvath had a nasty attack of bronchial catarrh again. Feeling slightly disorientated, I thanked her for the information and left the shop, and the florist called after me that he was on the second floor, right next to the death chamber itself. Soon afterwards I was standing at the entrance to the building at 6 Kettenbrückengasse. A brass plate said Josef Horvath, Master of Arts, Singing Teacher, Second Floor Right. I went through the doorway, climbed the stairs to the second floor and turned right. A matronly lady sat knitting at a table just behind an open door, and when she heard my footsteps she raised her head and said she expected I wanted to see the death chamber. What was this death chamber they all kept on about, I asked, no, I didn't want to see any death chamber, I was on my way to Herr Horvath, the gifted singing teacher. Oh, so I was going to see poor Herr Horvath, said the matronly lady with the knitting, looking at me suspiciously, he was coughing again so badly you could hear it through the wall, which bothered visitors to the Death House, very unfortunate for the city of Vienna, because naturally visitors to the Death House didn't want to be disturbed as they devoted their thoughts to the genius who composed such profoundly German music. Here the matronly lady paused briefly and let her knitting sink to her lap. Such profoundly German music, she repeated, looking me up and down. I politely asked her if she would be kind enough to tell me what genius she was talking about, to which she said, well, Schubert of course, who did I think, Schubert had died here, the apartment had been too damp and that was what finally did for him. Herr Horvath lived right next door, and now please would I leave her alone, you had to concentrate hard to do a Norwegian cable pattern.

I had arrived at another of those tall double doors obviously typical of Vienna, with a little nameplate fixed to it. Josef Horvath. I rang the bell. Footsteps slowly approached, and the door opened.

I could hardly believe my eyes. The man standing in front of me was not the engaging young aesthete, the sophisticated virtuoso I'd been expecting, but the maniac from the Central Cemetery. He was dressed in a frayed salmon-pink towelling dressing-gown, the same dirty white scarf as he'd been wearing in the cemetery was wrapped round his neck, and there was a thermometer in his mouth. The fur cap was missing. He slowly removed the thermometer from his lips and looked at me blankly. I took a couple of steps back, unable to utter a word. He was the first to recover his powers of speech.

Oh, so it was me, he said, and cleared his throat. I'd better come in.

I hesitated for a moment, and then went through the doorway into a spacious entrance hall with piles of sheet music on the floor. He preceded me into a big room where several large, white linen sheets were hanging on a washing line, and having made our way around the sheets we fetched up beside a baby grand in the middle of the room. On its lid stood a portrait in a gilt frame measuring around thirty by twenty centimetres, and showing a thin woman with a long nose, low forehead and penetrating glance. Herr Horvath turned round.

If I was the actress from New York, the one my relation had phoned him about, then she, my relation, must have been that raving lunatic of an old lady in the cemetery, he said, and although I entertained no very deep affection for Aunt Pia I felt obliged, as a member of her sex, to speak up in her defence, so I replied that if anyone had acted like a raving lunatic in the course of that extremely unedifying scene, then he had.

He, a raving lunatic, cried Herr Horvath, clutching at his breastbone, he a raving lunatic? How, might he ask, could anyone with severe bronchial catarrh act like a raving lunatic, the quarrel in the cemetery had taken so much out of him that he was forced to spend quite some time sitting in one of the pews in the Dr Karl Lueger Memorial Church, struggling to get his breath back, before he could venture on the journey home.

Well, I replied, if a young man like him felt so exhausted after that unpleasant scene, then perhaps he could imagine what it was like for a poor lady of eighty, almost deaf and with a weak heart into the bargain.

A weak heart, cried Herr Horvath, I must be joking, that poor old lady of eighty was far superior to him in physical strength, and would easily have put him to flight even without my assistance, but be that as it may, he wouldn't hold me responsible for my relation's theft, and he'd forgive me for standing up for her. And what could be more suitable than music, than song, to resolve any differences of opinion? However, he didn't feel up to going through with the

55

planned lesson, his body temperature was hovering around thirty-seven and a half degrees Celsius, and a temperature like that was no laughing matter, so we'd better postpone the lesson until Thursday.

So saying, Josef Horvath collapsed on a tattered claret-coloured sofa, and reached out to an occasional table for a small bottle that I recognized as the hip flask from which he'd been drinking in the cemetery. Herr Horvath was certainly still behaving rather oddly, but not quite as absurdly as in the Central Cemetery, so deciding to put up with his company I said we all had our weak moments now and then, but that was no reason to knock yourself out with strong liquor, the only thing that did any good at such times was self-control, and I had no reason to doubt him when he said he didn't feel well, but all the same I insisted on having my lesson, since I wasn't going to stay in Europe long and had no time to waste, the premiere of the musical was early next year, and by then I had to push my voice up to the lyric soprano which was my natural register although unfortunately, for lack of practice, it had dropped to a mezzo.

Strong liquor? said Herr Horvath. What on earth did I mean, strong liquor? Then he asked me to do him the small favour of going into the kitchen and boiling a pan of water for his violet-leaf tea.

I spent the next half-hour in Herr Horvath's little kitchen, making first the tea and next, on his instructions, a cup of hot milk with honey, then taking down the sheets in the living room, folding them and putting them away in the cupboard, draping a hideous crochet bedspread over his head before he inhaled some disgusting herbal decoction, and heating up the pan of beef broth standing on the stove. He thanked me effusively for each of these little attentions, saying he couldn't imagine life without the assistance of such helpful ladies as Fräulein Haslinger, the pharmacist from the St Mary Magdalene Pharmacy, the kind florist and myself. I looked at Herr Horvath, who was lying on the sofa sipping his violet-leaf tea. He must be about forty, his unkempt curly hair had grey strands in it, there was a permanent expression of surprise in his blue eyes, he had a very pale complexion and a round, smooth face, and he was of medium height and rather stout. It wouldn't have been fair to call him ugly, but he was far from being an attractive man as he lay there, looking listless and neglected in his dirty scarf, his shabby dressing-gown of that ridiculous shade of salmon-pink, his ribbed woolly socks and his thick, dark-grey felt slippers. I was severely disappointed. An unwelcoming city, a grotesque great-aunt, and a useless singing teacher. For with the best will in the world I couldn't imagine this melancholy hypochondriac, who didn't seem fully responsible for his own actions, preparing me efficiently for the starring role of my life. I'd call first John and then the airport and catch the next flight back to New York. Any other course of action would be preposterous.

As soon as he had recovered slightly, said Herr Horvath in a weary voice, interrupting my meditations, we would begin with the voice exercises and then go straight on to Mahler's *Kindertotenlieder* and the *Winterreise*; we'd skip the rest, we could leave the rest out. His methods, by the way, were the training methods of the Vienna Boys' Choir, to which he had belonged for several years. Did I play an instrument?

Since the man could be extremely unpredictable, as his conduct in the cemetery had clearly revealed, I decided not to confront him immediately with my decision, just in case I set off another of his fits of rage. It would be more sensible to call him next day and present him with a *fait accompli*.

Well, yes, in a way, I truthfully answered his question. I'd taken drumming lessons from a shaman born in Senegal who now lived in the Bronx, and I could play assorted wooden, pottery and metal drums, including bongos, congas, tom-toms and timbales, as well as various kinds of African drums, and I could also get by on conventional percussion and tubular bells, rattles, celesta, vibraphone and gong. Herr Horvath thought for a moment and then said he wasn't sure whether these skills would be much use while my voice was being trained along Viennese Classical lines, proficiency on an instrument such as the piano or violin, or maybe the viola or cello, was a better basis for a good, thorough training of that nature, and anyway my relation hadn't told him when she phoned that, as he could now see for himself, my ethnic origins didn't necessarily suit me for voice training by the rules of Western music theory, although in his view that presented no insuperable difficulties, and after all, music knows no frontiers.

I decided to ignore these outrageous remarks, since my decision to leave the city made it superfluous to risk any further differences of opinion. As for the song cycles he'd mentioned, I didn't know either of them, but the rather elegiac connotations of titles about dead children and winter journeys didn't suggest to me that such compositions would be particularly useful in preparing my voice for the usual kind of entertaining Broadway musical. I also felt slightly wary of his training methods, since I connected the Vienna Boys' Choir with boys in sailor suits luring crowds of homesick, waltz-loving Austrian expatriates and other sentimentally minded people into concert halls on their tours.

As if he'd guessed my thoughts, Herr Horvath gestured feebly in the direction of the large quantity of photographs covering one wall of his living room. I went closer and looked at the pictures, which showed the Boys' Choir in the concert hall, against the background of the Eiffel Tower, the Statue of Liberty, the Acropolis, at receptions held by the Emperor of Japan, the King of Spain, the Queen Mother of the Netherlands, the Prince of Wales. I tried to find my singing teacher in the photographs, and wondered if he was the pretty, slender boy with black curls and a girlish face who looked so sad in all the pictures.

His years in the Vienna Boys' Choir had been the happiest of his life, said Herr Horvath quietly, even if it meant being separated from his beloved mother during that time. As soon as his state of health allowed he would get me a ticket for one of the Sunday services in the Court Chapel with musical accompaniment by one of the four Vienna Boys' Choirs. These Sunday services in the Court Chapel were among the top musical and social events of Vienna, tickets were as good as unobtainable by outsiders but he would pull strings, he was still in touch with his former Choir Tutor, and for the sake of their old friendship the Choir Tutor was unlikely to turn down his request for a ticket.

Herr Horvath fell silent, carefully took several small white pills out of two bottles standing on the occasional table beside the sofa, and swallowed them. As a matter of fact, he then said, smiling for the first time since I'd met him, as a matter of fact a severe attack of diphtheria was the reason why he became a member of the Boys' Choir. His mother, a remarkable woman and a notable pianist, who had unfortunately passed away on the twenty-eighth of November three years ago as the result of so-called malpractice on the part of a so-called Viennese medical authority, had cured him of his diphtheria by playing him Schubert lieder. Strangely enough, one particular song, rather sombre in both melody and text, had hastened his recovery in an unexpected manner, and this amazing cure both intensified his affection for his mother and was the beginning of his love for Schubert. He began studying the composer, discovered that he had been a member of the Vienna Boys' Choir from 1808 to 1813, and from then on he pestered his mother incessantly with his own desire to join the choir, until at last she gave way to his pleading and allowed him to audition at the Augarten Palace, the headquarters of the Vienna Boys' Choir. In spite of an incipient attack of tonsillitis which was already slightly affecting his vocal cords, he had passed the entrance exam, not least on account of the depth of feeling his heartfelt devotion to the composer had enabled him to express in his rendering of 'The Hurdy-Gurdy Man', which he had been allowed to sing, yet another proof of the theory backed by himself and other noted singing teachers both at home and abroad, to the effect that a larynx of perfect proportions in anatomical terms, and a body functioning faultlessly in physiological terms, are no more the guarantee of a convincing creative performance than a Stradivarius is all by itself, and ultimately the artist's personality is what matters.

Herr Horvath looked at me. No doubt I knew the song 'The Hurdy-Gurdy Man', he said, and perhaps I would sing it to him so that he could get some idea of my register, to which I replied that I was sorry, I wasn't very familiar with Schubert, and the only song by that Viennese composer I really knew well was 'The Trout', which my mother had taught me as a child.

Yes, well, 'The Trout', repeated Herr Horvath, clearly not much impressed, typical early work, very pleasing but of course not to be compared with the tragic depth and transcendence of the *Winterreise* songs. However, I'd better go ahead and sing, although unfortunately it would have to be *a cappella*, since I didn't play the piano and in his present state of health, as he was sure I would understand, he was in no condition to sit at the baby grand, so would I please go over to the piano and sing.

I complied with Herr Horvath's request, laid my forearm on the black lacquer lid of the piano, concentrated my gaze on the piercing eyes of the woman in the gilt frame, and sang all four verses of the song.

Serviceable raw material, said Herr Horvath, when I'd finished, but we'd have to do some intensive work on my breathing technique. Then he laid his head on the back of the sofa. He hoped I would excuse him, but listening had been a strain on him, we'd meet at three in the afternoon on Thursday if his general condition permitted.

When I left the building where Schubert had died, it was already dark. The wind had dropped, and it wasn't raining any more. I walked past the stalls in the food market, their shutters down now, their counters folded and leaning up against the walls. Pigeons were cooing as they strutted through the puddles where the moon was reflected. For the first time I felt I liked Vienna.

I went into the public telephone kiosk in the Domplatz and called John in his office on the corner of Fifth Avenue and Fifty-first Street. He wasn't there, so I left a message on his answering machine asking him to call back.

I had difficulty dropping off to sleep that evening, since I felt those dolls were watching me, and finally I got up and decided that in spite of my fear of Aunt Pia I'd put some of them away in the big chest standing in a corner of the room. I opened its heavy wooden lid. The chest was full of old odds and ends, clothes smelling of mothballs and mildewed books. Out of a vague sense of curiosity, I picked up a large, thick notebook with holes punched in the longer sides of its pages and string tying them together. The blue of the two covers, which looked as if someone had cut them to size rather clumsily, was faded. I opened the notebook. There was a single word on the first page.

Preamble

I closed the lid of the chest, sat down on it and began to read.

I, Beata Maria Postl, a member of the community of the Sisters of the Good Shepherd since the year eighteen ninety-seven, do hereby declare that I received the following writings from the hands of their author Rosa Havelka, née Tichy, a woman who had strayed far from the path of righteousness under the pernicious influence of the Prince of Hell and Lord of Darkness, Antichrist, the Devil himself, and that I did so on the twenty-ninth day of April nineteen hundred in the condemned cell, as it is called, of the Provincial Court in Alserstrasse in Vienna 9, where the condemned woman, then awaiting execution, handed me her closely written pages with the words, uttered in surly rather than amiable tones: do what you like with this! Furthermore, I declare that I have made no changes of any kind to the following authentic account of the woman's life with the intention of falsifying or distorting in any way either the character of Rosa Havelka, née Tichy, clearly displayed here in all its human frailty and its dubious nature, or the destiny assigned to her by the mysterious and unfathomable will of God, as revealed in all its ineluctable consistency in the present document. I have merely allowed myself to bring the now outmoded spelling up to date, refine the writer's style and adapt it to the requirements of educated, modern Christian readers, and to exercise careful censorship with regard to the unfortunate woman's vocabulary, which on occasion deviates into blasphemy. In making these changes, entirely in line with the dictates of a vigilant Catholic conscience, I never lost sight of the aim and purpose of my work: may the reminiscences of this sinner, deserving of our pity on the one hand but on the other hand extremely obdurate, may these reminiscences, which will arouse both pity and terror in every God-fearing soul, serve as a warning to those young women in the middle of the present century who do not always feel strong enough to offer vigorous resistance to the many and various temptations of these days, assisting them at such times as they are inclined to lend an ear to the deceitful blandishments of Beelzebub and the insidious suggestions of Lucifer. It would be my best reward if this account of one who was led astray were to move but a single reader to a life more pleasing in the sight of God.

Vienna, in the year of Our Lord nineteen hundred and fifty, on the twenty-second day of July, the name day of Saint Mary Magdalene, witness of the Death and Resurrection of Our Lord, the penitent fallen woman from whom seven devils were cast out, ennobled by her true love for Jesus Christ, liberator of prisoners and patroness of seafarers.

It took me quite a long time to decipher the first page and a half of the document I had discovered by chance, since it was handwritten in the old-fashioned German characters my grandmother called Sütterlin script. I remembered her using this script sometimes to write labels for preserving jars or make shopping lists, and she wrote her letters in it too. I thought the characters looked interesting and asked her to teach me how to write them, which she did by fitting a special metal nib into a pointed, brightly painted wooden pen holder, dipping the nib in a small, round glass jar of dark-blue ink, and guiding my hand as I copied the characters. The pages of the thick notebook on my lap were covered from top to bottom and from left to right in small, closely written script in black ink. I turned the page.

Foreword

So here I sit, my hair cropped short, in Cell Fifty-five of the grey building in Alserstrasse, looking at my signature, which like most of the prisoners who occupied this room before me I have added to the block of stone in front of the window, just below the signatures of the maidservant-murderer Hugo Schenk and his accomplice Karl Schlossarek. Rosa Havelka, accused and found guilty of the murder of the imperial-and-royal court coachman Karel Havelka, her husband before God and man. Although the day of my execution by strangulation, the method employed throughout the Austro-Hungarian monarchy ever since 1873, is not far off now, although it will be only a few more weeks before the former coffee-house proprietor Josef Lang, recently appointed imperial-and-royal executioner, whose method is said by well-informed inmates of Vienna Neudorf Women's Prison to be considered particularly humane, places the short, soft, well-soaped double cord made by the court ropemaker around my neck from behind me, I can only reiterate what I said during my trial: I regret nothing.

If I set out today to write down the extraordinary events that have befallen me in my thirty years of life, using the finely lined pale green prison paper readily allowed me by the prison authorities on the grounds of good conduct, it is only partly to relieve the indescribable monotony of everyday life in prison, the endless emptiness of these months. There is another reason as well, one that has nothing to do with either this dreadful tedium or a desire to justify myself or unburden my conscience: I wish the calamitous course of my existence recorded here to demonstrate clearly, to any who chance to come upon it, that for individuals like myself the way of life prescribed by religion and the law can lead to nothing but disaster, and must certainly be their downfall.

I am not afraid of death; indeed, I long for it. I take the consequences of my actions upon myself, and am prepared to enter the gallows yard in the early morning, my hands tied with a thin black silk cord, accompanied by the executioner's two assist-ants, the priest and the prison governor, and flanked on each side by four guards with bayonets at the ready. I do hope, however, that the executioner Josef Lang will carry out his task swiftly and with professional skill, that when the execution is over he will remove his top hat with relief and, satisfied, will place his black kid gloves beneath the stake according to the custom, and that it will be granted to me to be reunited soon, in a juster world than this, with my beloved mother and my dear friend Olga, women whose lives, like mine, were ruined by the malicious machinations of envious, power-hungry, avaricious and heartless people.

One

In the beginning there was paradise. A paradise where one of the four elements reigned supreme: water. I remember rivulets, springs, streams, fountains, pools, ponds, a murmuring and gurgling, a dripping and a rushing and a roaring, the taste of salt in my mouth, I remember being immersed in cold water, warm water, dense steam, I remember warm water and cold water running over my body. This was in Marienbad, the newest of the Bohemian spas, between the towns of Eger and Pilsen on the southern outskirts of the Kaiserwald.

And I remember a body that was round, round and soft and warm, a body smelling of fresh bread, cake, and eau de Cologne, I remember white skin with golden down growing on it, smooth blonde hair brushing my face, covering me, small hands with short fingers and a firm grip, a broad forehead above light brown eyebrows, pale blue eyes with thin yellowish lashes, tiny pink veins on white cheeks, reddened feet, and a navel lying deep in firm flesh. I hear a voice too, a gentle sound, its notes rising and falling, loud and soft, soothing, admonishing, cross words, amusing words. There's a taste in my mouth of sourish milk and cinnamon, salty skin and some kind of bitter liquid, and my fingers touch soft, warm skin, feel smooth nails and hard bones. This was the body of my beautiful young mother, who was called Libussa and was a cook in the house of the Marienbad Deputy Spa Director, a house set in extensive grounds designed by Wenzel Skalnik, court gardener to Prince Anton Lobkowitz, in the style of an English landscape garden.

My earliest memories also include the sight of a great many elegant, fat people who came to Marienbad by mail coach, had their baggage carried for them, and walked with some difficulty from one end to the other of the spa promenade, which was three hundred metres long, from the Kreuzbrunnen to the Ferdinands-quelle, from the Ambrosius and Karolinenbrunnen to the Rudolfs-quelle, and then back again. They strolled up and down among the colonnades, they talked to other fat, elegant people, and they drank enormous quantities of salty water scooped from the springs in tumblers. Most of the spa guests at Marienbad were not seriously ill, like those who visited Karlsbad, Franzensbad and Teplitz; they were fat people whose doctors had recommended a slimming cure, melancholy hypochondriacs who suffered from constipation and hoped the waters of Marienbad's thirty-nine cold springs would alleviate their complaints.

The family of the Deputy Spa Director was of bourgeois Viennese origin. When I was born my mother, the last but one of a Bohemian smallholder's nine children, had been in service with them for about three years. We might think ourselves lucky to be living in the Gerstner family's grand house, even if our own accommodation was just a servant's bedroom about two metres broad by four metres long, up in the attics of the house. You reached it by climbing a broad flight of stone steps with shallow treads, then a rather less comfortable wooden staircase, and finally a narrow spiral stairway. I remember the loud noise of rain falling on the roof, the scurrying of mice among the rafters, the cold of our little attic room in winter and the heat of it in summer, the top of the spruce tree swaying in the wind outside the attic window. At first I shared my mother's bed, and later I slept on a straw mattress at her feet.

I spent most of the day in the kitchen. I loved the big room with its stone-flagged floor, the walls covered partly in white tiles and partly in oil paint, with gleaming pots and pans of brass, copper and iron hanging on them, the enamel kitchen range with the coal box beside it, and the long wooden table. I helped my mother, eagerly wielding such implements as the cucumber slicer, apple divider, onion chopper, cherry stoner, butter pats, potato ricer, peppermill, egg slicer, yolk separator and coffee mill. While my mother worked she talked to me. People like us were chosen by God to serve, she said as she rubbed the flat iron with a mixture of salt and vinegar, chosen to work from early morning till late at night. It would be not just nonsensical but an offence against divine order to rebel against the life of a servant, she said, carefully pouring hot raspberry jam into jars which she then sealed with waxed paper. A servant's way of life was pleasing to God, she explained, raking up the glowing embers in the stove and adding a piece of wood, the well-being of our masters was our best reward. Jointing a chicken with a long knife, she confessed that she could imagine nothing more satisfying than to place her energies at the service of others, offering up her whole life as a gift. The wish to help other people, support them and make life easier for them was a natural desire of the feminine soul, she said, cleaning the globe of an oil lamp, and when she had polished a silver spoon with cigar ash and held it up in the air to check its shine she told me she was glad she didn't belong to the upper classes, who could never compete with servants in the richness of their inner lives. I nodded, and impressed on my memory every word spoken by my beautiful young mother as she sat there before me in her high-necked cook's dress and clean apron.

On Sundays my mother put on her flowered hat, took my hand, and went with me to the Church of the Assumption. The gist of what the priest said in the pulpit appeared to me to coincide largely with the ideas my mother was trying to instil in me. He stated that although a servant's rank was considered lowly, yet in reality it was noble, since a life of poverty, obedience and labour was closer than any other to the life of our Saviour himself; the

Son of God had been made man not to rule but to serve, and in the next world servants would be richly rewarded for their pains, since those who took adversity upon them for the love of the Almighty would be granted his grace. It was plainly written in Holy Scripture that servants must be obedient to their masters, the service of man was the service of God, and consequently domestic staff should do their work industriously, willingly, conscientiously, circumspectly and in purity of heart, so that they and all they did would be pleasing in the sight of the Lord. I tried to take good note of what that imposing man the priest said too, delivering himself so eloquently from his elevated position.

The Gerstners were a family of four: Deputy Spa Director Gerstner, his wife, and their daughters Helene and Marie, who were a little older than I was. My first language was the Czech I learned from my mother, but I soon joined Helene and Marie's lessons with their Viennese governess Fräulein von Roth-Rothenhorst, who taught me German, and later on German literature and history as well as Latin and French. My mother was always telling me what an extraordinary piece of good fortune it was for the child of a simple Bohemian cook from the lower classes of the peasantry to have such an education, saying that I owed the Deputy Director and his wife a deep debt of gratitude, and naturally it was my duty to show my appreciation to the Gerstners through blameless and discreet conduct, and include all the members of the family in my prayers every evening. My mother believed firmly in the grace and goodness of God and the effective intercession of all the saints, more particularly Our Lady and the Bohemian national saint and martyr St John of Nepomuk. She confided to me that it was her dearest wish, just once in her life, to go on pilgrimage with me to Lourdes, where the Virgin Mary had appeared in a grotto to the child Bernadette, a simple peasant girl like me who had seen the vision eighteen times in all, just imagine, eighteen times. There was a little statue of the Madonna of Lourdes on the enamel washstand in our attic. My mother had

saved up the money for it from her wages and ordered it from
Father Method Jelinek, vicar of the Capuchin Church in Vienna,
who had imported one thousand one hundred of these statues
from the firm of Raffel in Paris. The water from the springs of
Marienbad, mixed with Glauber's Salt, was undoubtedly good for
your health, said my mother, it gave you a good appetite, a
cheerful mind and refreshing sleep, but it was as nothing compared to the miracle-working water of the spring that had flowed
straight from the stone of the grotto on 25 February 1862 and
healed the halt and the blind, why, it could even raise the dead.
Every month she set aside a small sum in the tenacious hope of
making that pilgrimage with me some day, for if we called upon
the Virgin Mary often enough, said my mother, she would hear our
request at last. So in my evening prayers I politely asked God, the
Virgin Mary and the saints to grant the Gerstner family health and
wealth, enable us to go on pilgrimage to Lourdes, and save and
protect our Emperor Franz Josef and our beautiful Empress Sisi.
This last petition had been fervently recommended to Helene,
Marie and me by Fräulein von Roth-Rothenhorst, for the life of the
imperial couple and in particular the period of their courtship and
their first years of marriage was a subject on which she loved to
dwell. Helene and Marie were always begging our poor but
well-born governess to describe all the details of every item in the
trousseau which Sisi had brought to Vienna with her. There had
been twenty-five trunks, said Fräulein von Roth-Rothenhorst, her
eyes shining, twenty-five large trunks, dozens of Bavarian dress-
makers, embroiderers and milliners had worked on the trousseau
day and night for months. The fine dresses, cried Helene and
Marie, tell us about the fine dresses. So Fräulein von Roth-
Rothenhorst patiently described the pale lilac dress embroidered
with silver clover leaves and the silver lace cape that went with it,
an outfit Sisi had worn for her brother's wedding in Dresden,
carrying a bouquet of camellias and with a sparkling diadem in
her elaborately braided chestnut-brown hair, yet again she readily

71

told us about the gossamer-fine pink silk dress with its wide crinoline, the white lace mantilla and the little white hat in which the future Empress had gone by boat to meet her bridegroom, and described the expensive blue velvet cloak with sable trimmings and a sable muff that was a present from the Emperor, and then the beautiful wedding dress with its silver watered-silk cloak. And the diamond coronet, demanded the girls, clapping their hands. Oh yes, the diamond coronet with its matching diamond corsage, said Fräulein von Roth-Rothenhorst, and her gaze grew a little more sombre, an old example of the goldsmith's craft, set with emeralds, the most valuable wedding present of all. A few days before Sisi's arrival the coronet had fallen to the floor and had to be hastily repaired: a bad omen.

The Deputy Spa Director's daughters idolized Empress Sisi, just as my own ideal was the holy Madonna of Lourdes, whom I adored with a devotion for which Helene and Marie felt nothing but mockery and contempt. They didn't believe that the Madonna could raise the dead as I claimed, women couldn't raise dead people, it was beyond women to raise the dead, that was something reserved for men, namely God and Jesus Christ.

Long before I was given the German poems of which Fräulein von Roth-Rothenhorst thought so highly, to learn by heart out of little Reclam editions, my mother used to tell me stories in Czech before we went to sleep: tales of her namesake Libussa, who had founded Prague, of the lovely and patient Griselda, of the life and death of St John of Nepomuk, who was thrown off the Charles Bridge in Prague into the River Vltava in 1393 by order of King Wenceslas IV. She explained the significance of the illustrations in the religious broadsheet entitled *The Life of the Devout Maidservant Katharina*, which she had pinned to the inside of the wardrobe door, and she taught me prayers from her well-worn, dark-red prayer book. But her greatest treasures were four cookbooks by Magdalena Dobromila Rettigova, entitled *The Domestic Cook, Good Advice for Farmers' Wives and Country Girls, Sweets and Desserts* and *The Coffee Book,* published in 1843, and also the *Dream Book of the Pharaohs,* with the aid of which she tried to interpret her dreams, as well as the *Housewives' Golden Treasury* by Rosa Lindenmeyer, a fat blue linen-bound book with a cover bearing the title in gold letters and a picture of a golden keyring with eight keys. Its subtitle was: *Two Thousand Helpful Hints for the Practical Housewife, in Words and Pictures, for the Best and Cheapest Way to Keep House in Town and Country, for Every Household and Every Family, with Time-Saving Household Plans for Every Day and All Occasions.* I loved these books and their illustrations, and frequently leafed through them and read them, particularly the cookbooks, for I was often hungry, since Frau Gerstner, a tall, pale, thin woman who wore her greying brown hair in a knot at the nape of her neck, gradually withdrew her favour from me and my mother, and became more and more grudging in the amount of food she allowed her cook and her cook's daughter. I couldn't account to myself for this change in our circumstances. While the Deputy Director would stroke my hair, pat my cheek and give me sweetmeats if he met me alone, his wife pulled my plaits when no one was looking, kicked my shins and pinched my arms. Her two daughters imitated Frau Gerstner's behaviour if they found me when my mother, the Deputy Director and Fräulein von Roth-Rothenhorst were not around, and added verbal insults to their surreptitious physical attacks on me, calling me a vulgar Bohemian peasant and a servant's ugly bastard. Since my mother never tired of dwelling on the kindness of all members of the Gerstner family, and praising the favours they showered on us poor folk, especially me, since she was constantly urging obedience and gratitude on me, I dared not tell her about these incidents, which became increasingly frequent as time went by, and suffered in silence. When Fräulein von Roth-Rothenhorst praised me in lessons for the good progress I was making, her approval filled me with pride in one way but with fear in another, since I could be sure that her praise would make Helene and Marie

73

feel resentful, and provoke further spiteful acts on their part.

My gradual expulsion from Paradise continued. There was another circumstance that inspired me with fear and horror: the nocturnal visits my mother received from a shadowy figure, which meant I had to give up the place I loved in her bed and be content with the straw mattress. I was often woken in the middle of the night by the sound of footsteps on the narrow spiral staircase, and then the door would open, creaking, and the broad, indistinct outline of a human form moved towards my mother's bed. I was deeply frightened by the whispering, murmuring, sighing, groaning and the sounds of my mother's wailing that followed; I lay in the darkness and dared not move. One day, when I was sitting in the kitchen with my mother, a bowl of apples that I was peeling and coring in my lap, I ventured to ask her about the ghostly apparition that visited our room almost every night. My mother glanced sideways at me and said she didn't know what I was talking about, the apparition I spoke of was probably a dream-like vision, I'd had a lively imagination from my earliest childhood, a characteristic of children born on 29 February and a Saturday at that, and it would be this lively imagination, together with the darkness and silence of the night, that made me see such things. I said it was certainly dark but by no means silent, since on these occasions she, my mother, made all kinds of noises, filling me with great alarm. My mother gave me another odd look, and then said that just as you could have visual hallucinations, you could imagine hearing things too, illusions particularly common among people with a vivid imagination like mine, and I'd better pray to the Madonna of Lourdes, the Madonna would help me and free me from the nightmares and delusions tormenting me. Then she rose, took a dried bay leaf from a little bag and gave it to me, telling me to chew it well, because bay, like the Madonna, protected you from all kinds of illusions. I said nothing, I ate the bitter bay leaf and knelt before the enamel washstand and the Madonna every evening, but neither of these measures banished the phantom, and indeed it seemed to me that its outline was coming to bear an increasingly close resemblance to that of the Deputy Spa Director.

To divert my thoughts and feelings from the unsettling things that went on in our servant's bedroom by night, and from the even more disturbing idea that they were not real at all but mere figments of my childish imagination, I tried to concentrate entirely on acquiring the knowledge that Fräulein von Roth-Rothenhorst earnestly and conscientiously tried to instil in us. I was greedy for it, and I had a good memory. I was slightly disconcerted, therefore, when Fräulein von Roth-Rothenhorst kept indicating that some restraint on the acquisition of certain kinds of knowledge was necessary, and as members of the female sex we should take care not to show off our proficiency in the presence of any male persons, male persons could easily be made to feel insecure by directly revealed evidence of our historical, literary and linguistic knowledge. The best course was to have that knowledge available to you at any time, but to introduce it into your conversation with male persons so unobtrusively that the male persons got the impression it was theirs and not your own. This was known as feminine diplomacy. She would admit that such an ingenious yet very womanly approach, one that was indeed, in the last resort, profoundly humane, called for the utmost tact and delicacy of feeling, but if we acted in accordance with her guidelines we would not have the slightest difficulty in winning the heart and love of at least one of those male persons, and winning the heart and love of a male person, so that he would enter willingly into the contract of a respectable marriage, was essential to the members of the female sex. For if a member of the female sex did not succeed, through the diplomatic conduct described above, in inducing a male person to take this step, indispensable for well-regarded members of our society, then her life would be extremely difficult, as we could easily observe from the example of her own, Fräulein von Roth-Rothenhorst's, existence. Women who failed in the unremitting pursuit of this elementary feminine task, who for lack of guidance by their teachers or because of their own blindness had not understood early enough that the sole happiness of their sex consisted in the role of wife and mother, must resort to a way of life obviously much thornier than the opportunity thus offered of a fulfilled and comfortable domestic existence: either a life of privation as a servant or governess, like herself, or one of sacrifice and service in one of the Christian orders. There was another alternative, although it was more than dubious, and she would tell us about it at some later point in time.

Fräulein von Roth-Rothenhorst taught us not only literature, history and languages, but also the skills of embroidery and playing the piano. We learned to use rectangular and round embroidery frames, and practised fillet stitch, satin stitch, netting stitch, hemstitch, broderie anglaise and tapestry stitch, and as for the piano, we got as far as the hesitant performance of simple waltzes by Chopin, a composer of whom the governess was very fond, since first she considered him a romantic figure, and second he had visited Marienbad and left the spa in a state of emotional turmoil over his difficult relationship with a young Polish woman, Maria Wodzynska. The governess said she had searched the standard biographies in vain for confirmation of her belief that Chopin had immediately given himself up to the creative process in the post chaise, expressing his grief at the Polish woman's faithless conduct by spontaneously noting down a piece of music, but she thought it extremely likely.

And my expulsion from Paradise continued. On my return from church on Sunday with my mother, she suggested that I occupy myself reading one of the little Reclam edition books in the garden because she didn't feel well, and was going to spend the rest of the one half-day off she had in her working week to lie down for a little. I did as she told me, and sat down on the white-painted wrought-iron bench under the pergola, but my reading was soon disturbed by Helene and Marie, who didn't like to see me still busy with my lessons on a Sunday. They accused me of overweening ambition, told me I was nothing but a servant's brat trying to raise myself above my humble position and ingratiate myself with Fräulein von Roth-Rothenhorst, snatched the little book from my hand and threw it high in the air and over the garden wall. Once I had succeeded in breaking free of the pair of them as they tried to hold me fast, pull my hair, scratch and bite me, I ran weeping through the garden gate to look for my little book. An elegant, dark-bearded man wearing a black frock coat and a top hat, probably one of the visitors to the spa, was standing on the gravel path on the other side of the gate, leafing through the little volume with interest. I addressed him, saying shyly that the book in his hands was my property, whereupon the man looked at me, pinched my cheek, smiling, handed me the book, and as he did so declaimed the following lines from Goethe's *Marienbad Elegy*, which it contained: 'Then follow me, with cheerful courage still / Seize on the moment, and do not delay! / Make haste to meet it with a right good will.'

With my little Reclam book in my hand I climbed the stone staircase, the wooden staircase, and finally the narrow spiral staircase to our servant's bedroom to escape the spiteful attentions of Helene and Marie. I opened the door, and in the bright light of that Sunday morning falling in through the attic window I saw clearly and with my own eyes what had previously, so my mother assured me, gone on only in my nocturnal visions or nightmares. The shadowy figure of the Deputy Director was not shadowy any more, but the Deputy Director himself, in flesh and blood, sharing my mother's narrow bed, with his white back covered with dark hair, his broad shoulders, sturdy neck and round head with its tousled black hair between me and my beautiful young mother as I stood there in the doorway. I could see part of her face, one blue eye staring upwards, her mouth half open with its corners turned down, like the face of the statue of the Madonna of Lourdes beside the bed on the enamel washstand. I turned and raced downstairs. On the landing between the narrow spiral staircase and the rather broader wooden stairs I ran into the Deputy Director's wife, who was standing there motionless, one hand on the banisters, her gaze turned upwards like my mother's, although less steadily, in the direction of the attic above.

The Deputy Director and my mother had not noticed me. I don't remember exactly how old I was at the time of this incident, but I was probably about eleven or twelve. What I had seen, curiously enough, did not help remove my doubts about what I had been seeing, but instead cast me into an abyss of uncertainty. Since it was out of the question for my beautiful young mother, upon whom I relied and who protected me, not to have told the truth, I must inevitably conclude that the hallucinations which until now had haunted me only at night under cover of darkness were now plaguing me in the full light of day, for it was not possible that what I had seen so clearly before my eyes that Sunday morning could have been real, it was too absurd for that. Why in the world would people force themselves to act in such a ridiculous way?

My deep insecurity and self-doubt were made even worse by the spiteful behaviour of the Deputy Director's wife and two daughters, which badly undermined my confidence. What was happening to me, what evil forces were distorting my powers of perception, confusing the five senses which had done me good service in the past, giving me a clear, unambiguous view of the world and everything in it? I sought an explanation, and I found one.

While my mother and I worked in the kitchen together, she had always dwelt on the inexhaustible kindness, the boundless goodness of the Madonna of Lourdes and other female saints to those who were true believers and persons of good will. However, she said, there were other powers that worked against these good female saints, wicked and malevolent beings called witches who would lead you into temptation, and if you weren't strong enough to resist that temptation they could ruin you entirely. You must always be on your guard against these demonic creatures who were in league with the Devil and met him at accursed places to pursue their godless pleasures, for they would seize on the slightest human weakness to win people over to them, grasping at them with their claw-like fingers and bringing them as prey to the Evil one, their lord and master.

Could I have come under the influence of these beings, could they, with their sinister powers, have sent me the hallucinations that distorted my sight and hearing, showing my dear mother performing incomprehensible actions which couldn't be in her true nature?

One day, when my mother was in the kitchen plucking a pheasant that the Deputy Director had shot when out hunting in the Kaiserwald with the Spa Director, the chairman of the imperial-and-royal Spa Medical Council and the managers of the Weimar and Star Hotels in Marienbad, I asked whether you could protect yourself against the wiles of the witches she had mentioned to me, and if so how. My mother stopped plucking the bird, looked at me, and said, well, yes, you could certainly protect yourself, for instance by taking care not to wear dirty shoes, always washing your hands carefully in the morning, and putting a little salt in your shoes or wearing it in a small bag around your neck. If I felt those wicked creatures were threatening me in any way she wouldn't hesitate to make me a small bag of that kind and fill it with salt, but first she would sprinkle a few grains from the imperial-and-royal saltworks at Ischl in my shoes; in any case it could do no harm when someone was prone to illusions of all kinds, like me. She rose to her feet, opened the wooden lid of a pretty blue and white porcelain container fixed to the wall and bearing the word *Salt*, took a pinch out of it, removed my shoes – old shoes that Marie had outgrown – and sprinkled the grains of salt in them. This gesture soothed my fears, and so did the little bag of salt I was soon wearing around my neck, but neither of these measures made any difference to the nocturnal shadows that continued to haunt our servant's bedroom.

During the weeks that followed, my mother fell sick. She fainted twice at work in the kitchen, once when she was descaling a large carp caught by the Deputy Spa Director during a fishing competition at a pool in the Kaiserwald with the Spa Director of Music, the Abbot of Tepl Monastery, the landowner Baron von Klingenstein and the authorized agent of the Viennese Stock Exchange, and the second time when she was skinning the legs of a hare caught by the Deputy Director out on a battue in the company of the above gentlemen, in order to prepare Jugged Hare Iglau Style from Magdalena Dobromila Rettigova's recipe. She found it difficult to get up in the morning, and she could keep down almost nothing she ate. The Deputy Spa Director's wife showed no concern for my mother's poor state of health; on the contrary, ever since I'd seen her standing on the landing between the narrow spiral staircase and the rather broader wooden staircase, her eyes full of concern as they looked upwards, she had treated my mother worse than ever, and gave her so much work that she was seldom in bed before midnight, and had to rise again around five in the morning to get everything done.

One morning my mother packed a bag, put on her flowered hat and said she had urgent business in Eger, she was going there by the post coach and would be back next day, meanwhile I was not to disgrace her, and I could sleep in her bed if I liked. I felt that her absence, however short, was ominous, for as far back as I could remember I'd never spent a night without her. In the evening I knelt down as usual in front of the enamel washstand and the Madonna to say my prayers, and then I put on my white linen shift and got into my mother's bed, feeling sad and anxious. I was woken in the middle of the night by the sound of footsteps on the spiral staircase, and next moment the outline of that nightmarish apparition with which I was so familiar entered the room, moving towards me. I dared not move, not even when the nightmare put back the covers, but when its whole dark weight lay down on top of me and its hands groped under my linen shift I bit its ear, which happened to be right in front of my face, with all my might, whereupon the nightmare let out a shriek, jumped off the bed and ran out of the room. That was the last time I ever saw it. I put my sudden boldness down to the little bag of Ischl salt, which I kept around my neck at all times, and had therefore been wearing during this alarming incident.

When my mother came back from Eger I was terrified, for she was deathly pale and could hardly keep on her feet. After she had been lying exhausted in her narrow bed for two days, the Deputy Director's wife climbed to our attic bedroom and shouted that she, my mother, was to get back to work at once, she, the Deputy Director's wife, wasn't throwing her husband's hard-earned money out of the window paying a cook who had no intention of cooking, who was a lazy idler and malingerer and thus typical of the Bohemian ethnic group among whom she, the Deputy Director's wife, was obliged to live because of her husband's profession, being bound to follow him wherever he went, as ordained by the New Testament. It was lucky for her, my mother, that she enjoyed the good will of her, the Deputy Director's wife's, kind and far too lenient husband, because if she didn't then she, my mother, would long since have been dismissed by her, the Deputy Director's wife, and for all she cared could take me, the regrettable consequence of her dissolute way of life, and embark on a career of begging or the prostitution to which we, my mother and I, would gravitate anyway on the grounds of our natural disposition and innate inclination. She, my mother, had better get up at once, go down to the kitchen and make the marinade for the roast saddle of venison to be served at her table on the occasion of the imminent visit by the Deputy Spa Directors of Karlsbad and Franzensbad and their wives, because she, the Deputy Director's wife, wasn't about to give the complicated preparation of that marinade her personal attention, what did she employ a cook for, after all? And I, Rosa, had better make myself useful; she wondered why she went along with the privileged treatment accorded to me, Rosa, solely on the grounds of the undeserved good will of her husband, who was much too generous and unfortunately was easily influenced; she wondered why she stood by watching me, Rosa, born in shame and unmistakably sprung from a vulgar clan of Bohemian smallholders, being educated by a distinguished governess from a noble old Viennese family, along with her own two beautiful talented daughters; yes, she really did wonder why.

My mother was too ill to react appropriately to the insulting remarks of the Deputy Director's wife, and when the latter went over to her and tried to pull her out of bed she offered no resistance. She dressed, dragged herself down to the kitchen, and began chopping the root vegetables she needed for the marinade. I helped her as best I could, and that evening I told her how sad and anxious her wretched condition made me and asked why we stayed in a house where they starved and scolded us, and what was more, a house with an attic haunted by ghosts. My mother recoiled and asked how I could say such a thing, how could I say anything against a family that was providing me with the kind of education usually enjoyed only by the upper classes, and even among them only by the sons of the family, how could I complain of a diet which, while she would admit there wasn't much of it, was always highly nutritious. As for the occasional harsh remark, I must keep the life of Our Lord constantly before my mind's eye, for what the Deputy Director's wife and her daughters said to us now and then in their weaker moments was as nothing beside the insults and injuries suffered by Our Lord. Then what about the phantom, I cried, what about the dreadful apparition that visited us night after night, I couldn't understand why she'd never tried to defend herself against that nightmare figure. My mother stroked my hair and smiled. Oh, Rosa, she said, oh, my Saturday child, my Leap Year child, what strange things you do see!

During the next few months my mother went into a rapid decline, a circumstance that by no means prevented the Deputy Director's wife from requiring her to do as much work as before she fell ill. When I came back one day from running an errand for my mother I found her being carried out of the kitchen, unconscious, by the maidservants, the Deputy Director's wife and the Deputy Director's hunting companion, the chairman of the imperial-and-royal Spa Medical Council. I stood there silent in the corridor, hearing the voices of the doctor and the Deputy Director's wife as if from a great distance. The word 'haemorrhage' was mentioned several times. My mother was carried up to the attic and put to bed. I moved the chair to the head of the bed, sat down on it, and spent hours gazing at her face, from which all the colour had drained away. I didn't move from the spot over the next few days. I remember that a servant girl brought up a plate of potato soup several times, and my mother ate it, and I remember a visit from the chairman of the Spa Medical Council, the Deputy Director's hunting companion, who told me to leave the room while he examined my mother, and I remember how shortly after that visit the Deputy Director's wife climbed the three flights of stairs again and told my mother that the chairman of the Spa Medical Council had pronounced her as fit as a fiddle and she, the Deputy Director's wife, didn't think it could have done her, my mother, any harm to be without the little bit of blood she had lost, for the lavish table enjoyed by the servants in her house meant that she, my mother, had been rather too full-blooded anyway, and she could get back to her work again now. My mother nodded faintly.

After the Deputy Director's wife had gone I begged my mother to tell me what I could do to help her. She said quietly that we must submit to God's will, and as it was obviously God's will to take her to him rather sooner than he took most believers, we shouldn't interfere, kicking against the pricks and ignoring that divine will. The one thing that could give her comfort and support her in her faith would be some holy water from Lourdes, but holy water from Lourdes was unlikely to be obtainable in Marienbad. I wasn't going to leave anything untried, so I went straight to find Father Bohumil, who got up in the Church of the Assumption on

Sundays to deliver those impressive sermons, the content of which coincided, apart from minor deviations, with my mother's own views, and who adopted such an awe-inspiring stance in the pulpit, for it seemed to me that a man so favoured by God and the saints would undoubtedly be able to get my mother the miraculous water from Lourdes very soon, and thus make her better.

Father Bohumil was not particularly pleased by my unannounced visit, since I disturbed him in the consumption of a dish of steamed ox tongue, but after I had waited half an hour in the cold sacristy I was allowed to make my request. He was silent for a while, and then said it was true that he had several small phials of the valuable liquid, a fortunate circumstance arising from his friendship with Father Method Jelinek of Vienna. Then his gaze rested on me for some time, and he added that unfortunately my mother, while an upright and industrious character at heart, had done very wrong in the course of her admittedly arduous life, she had committed an indiscretion that marked, so to speak, the very beginning of my existence, a serious misdemeanour that made it impossible for him to let her have one of those little phials. In a case like this he must give preference to those who had not made such very understand-able mistakes, women who had succeeded better than my mother in obeying the difficult task of remaining on the straight and narrow path of virtue. He was sorry, but he could give me no other answer. God in his boundless loving kindness would protect my mother and, after all, we lived in a town where healing springs welled up from the earth everywhere, everything that existed was God's creation and therefore miraculous, why shouldn't my mother be cured by the sulphurous water of the Marienquelle where, after all, there was an image of the Mother of God too, the Madonna was the Madonna, the Mother of God was the Mother of God, it was a sign of little faith to connect the miraculous aid of the Virgin Mary in all its fullness with certain geographical locations alone. And now I must forgive him; he had to go to a christening in Baron von Klingenstein's private chapel.

My mother lived three more days. An hour before she died in our attic, she beckoned me over with her powerless fingers and said, in a barely audible voice, that now her departure from this disappointing world was imminent, and she was about to leave it for what she believed would be a considerably more satisfactory existence in the next world, now that the heavenly Jerusalem, a land flowing with milk and honey, and the fields of the blessed seemed near enough to grasp, she felt she ought to give some advice to me, her only child, since I must make my way on through life without her, my mother. Of course her possessions, that is to say her clothes including the flowered hat, and the printed books that she could call her own, would pass to me as her rightful heir. She asked me to treat the statue of the Madonna of Lourdes, her prayer book and the *Housewives' Golden Treasury* by my name-sake Rosa Lindenmeyer with particular respect. In addition, before she passed away she wanted to unburden her conscience and reveal something she had hitherto kept from me because of my tender years and my childish, carefree nature. She had never felt that the absence of a second parent oppressed me excessively, indeed it had struck her that I never felt that absence, but she wouldn't hide my father's identity from me, and even though it was quite possible that I would not know what to make of the information just yet, she believed I'd be grateful to her for the revelation at some later point in my life. The fact that the Deputy Spa Director always lavished loving attentions on me and, as an educated man, had seen that I received a good education, did not spring merely from Christian love of his neighbour but from the fact that he had engendered me nearly thirteen years ago, in this very attic where we now were. Being scarcely seventeen years old at the time, she hadn't known how to resist a mature man's stormy persuasions either then or later, so fate took its course, a fate that had been much kinder to her than to most other girls of her own age, sex, class and profession, who in similar cases were immediately dismissed or obliged to get rid of the fruit of the womb with

85

the help of godless female persons, a practice which I knew nothing about and she hoped I never would. Because of her delicate and indeed childlike physique, no one had noticed her condition at all, a fortunate circumstance in her situation, but she thought that the Deputy Director's wife had always guessed the truth of the matter through feminine intuition, although naturally her husband had never told her. That also explained the humiliations we had suffered at the hands of Frau Gerstner and her daughters, who were under her influence, but my mother herself was convinced that one must not rebel against one's fate, and it would be pointless to pursue certain persons who had an influence for the worse on that fate with boundless resentment, inexhaustible hatred and never-ending bitterness, God had created us to exercise forbearance and patience, mercy and forgiveness, and I had never given her any reason to doubt my readiness to follow these simple and sensible Christian principles.

I sat beside my mother, the person I loved most in the world, holding her left hand in my right. What she had just told me was shattering, since it revealed her, of whose integrity I had always been convinced, as a deceiver and a liar, one whose untruths and distortion of the facts had cast me into fear and doubt, and indeed made me sure I was under a witch's spell.

My mother fell silent, exhausted. I pressed her hand.

So he was the phantom, I asked, feeling the tears run down my cheeks, he was that ghostly nocturnal figure?

With what little strength she had left, my mother stroked my hair. The hint of a smile lit up her pale face.

Oh, Rosa, she said, oh, my Leap Year child, my Saturday child, what phantom are you talking about?

Then she closed her eyes.

TWO

No one stood beside my mother's open grave except for the Deputy Spa Director, Father Bohumil and myself. The Deputy Director's wife had excused herself, saying that a migraine of unusual ferocity, which she put down to the sudden change in the weather and which was accompanied by dizziness and a numb feeling in her face and limbs, made it impossible for her to leave the matrimonial bedroom. Helene and Marie had gone out with Fräulein von Roth-Rothenhorst on an expedition to Gablonz on the Upper Neisse, where the glass beads regarded as fine craft items and known as Bohemian diamonds were manufactured. They were hoping to see replicas of various pieces of Empress Elisabeth's jewellery while they were there, particularly a copy of the flowering tendrils made from diamonds and emeralds that she wore in her beautiful chestnut-brown hair at parties, a copy of the broad black velvet choker set with diamonds and large rubies that she had worn round her slender neck in 1873 on the twenty-fifth anniversary of her husband the Emperor's accession to the throne, and a copy of the famous diamond stars made by the Viennese court jeweller Köchert which sparkled in her hair on very special occasions.

Father Bohumil's funeral oration was rather short, but as impressive as his Sunday sermons. He emphasized the fact that my mother had been an industrious, modest and God-fearing woman, who for years conscientiously carried out her tasks as cook to the Gerstner family, a family that was so popular and so highly regarded in Marienbad, and who had found the fulfilment of her unfortunately brief existence in the quiet and ever-attentive service of her neighbour. Her faith in the holy Madonna of Lourdes, he added, had given her strength in the days of her last illness, and she had also constantly endeavoured to pass that faith on to me, her only child. At this point Father Bohumil turned to me and said that my mother's estate, namely the statue of the holy Madonna of Lourdes, the *Housewives' Golden Treasury,* the four cookbooks and the little prayer book were deeply symbolic items through which my mother, never a woman of many words, was pointing me the way to a future in which I might follow her example, a future of happy service to my fellow men performed in the sober awareness that trying to rise above one's station was tantamount to rebelling against God. He would allow himself to keep back only the *Dream Book of the Pharaohs,* since such reading matter placed an unnecessary strain on a young girl's impressionable mind. He didn't mention the flower-trimmed hat. After this oration Father Bohumil stepped up to me and made the sign of the cross on my forehead, a distinction which embarrassed me so much that, casting my eyes down, I stepped aside and almost fell into the open grave. Then Father Bohumil looked at the Deputy Spa Director and said that his family, so highly esteemed in and around Marienbad, had always shown humane benevolence, indeed benevolent humanity, towards its servants, and he, the Deputy Director, had been like a father to me, for which God would reward him. Then he picked up a small iron spade, threw some earth on the coffin with the spade held at the end of his long arm, and put it into my hand, but I didn't use the spade, instead digging my hand into the soil and letting a handful of it fall on the coffin. Father Bohumil did not notice me throwing a pinch of Ischl salt on the coffin together with the earth, for my mother had said that graveyards were mysterious places haunted by all kinds of dreadful creatures, witches included, and I wanted her to rest in peace.

Very soon after the funeral it became obvious that the Deputy Director's wife didn't want me in the house any more and was planning to turn me out into the street. I was defenceless, and it was only owing to the influence of my father, who didn't know that my mother had told me about our blood relationship, that matters took a less disastrous turn. I was sent away to the nuns in Prague, although without the hat with its pretty trimming of orange and violet pansies which was my mother's legacy and my rightful property.

I put the blue notebook down on the lid of the chest beside me. My eyes were hurting because the cramped little Sütterlin script was difficult to decipher, and there were no lights in my room, or rather Wilma's, except for the lamp with the brass stand and the shade of pleated fabric with white roses on a yellow background. Aunt Pia had several times complained of the ever-rising cost of electricity, calling the employees of the Vienna Municipal Electricity Company cut-throats, taking the last penny from her pocket. She said the only way of defending yourself against the ruthless methods of those bandits was to use very little electric power, not just because of the horrendous price per kilowatt but also, since like Schwechat natural gas this form of energy was by no means entirely safe – not that you got the same danger of explosions as with gas, but those electric currents and the magnetic fields involved seemed to her very suspect – also because she thought this invisible source of energy very injurious to health, and she'd already wondered whether her partial deafness might not be the result of electromagnetic influences rather than a perforated eardrum and defective middle ear, as claimed by her doctor of many years' standing, a nice man if not very perceptive, with a large practice and consulting rooms in Wollzeile. At any rate, it was her opinion, and she was sure I shared it, that a medium-sized room was adequately lit after dark by a thirty- or forty-five- watt bulb. If you wanted to read or do some kind of handicraft you simply had to get as close as you could to the source of the light.

I wondered how the autobiography of Rosa Havelka, who like my mother's side of our family came from northern Bohemia, had found its way into my relation's chest. Aunt Pia might be able to tell me, but I had reservations about asking her, for it was quite possible she might not like my rummaging around in her personal effects without her express permission.

John called around eleven in the evening. Oh, my cross little chocolate bun, my sweet Sachertorte, my sulky chocolate éclair, he whispered when I started straight in on describing my situation and telling him about my decision to leave Vienna. Oh, how I long for you, my little Bohemian poppy-seed cake, my little Viennese coffee cream. I said please would he stick to the subject, this was serious, the singing teacher supposed to be so highly gifted was a physically, intellectually and spiritually debilitated character whose teaching methods were totally outdated and who didn't keep his appointments, and no good could be expected of him. Look, I said, New York was full of really dynamic singing teachers from all over the world who could teach me a great deal more than this pathetic mother's boy minus his mother to whom my unworldly great-aunt had sent me.

John replied that while he didn't quite see how I could speak of outdated methods in the same breath as a Viennese singing teacher, and I must surely realize that in the birthplace of the immortal works of Viennese Classicism people set out from musical assumptions not at all like those prevailing in the hectic atmosphere of New York, a place exposed to every eccentric artistic movement and way-out musical whim, every creative mood however fantastic, still, though he couldn't really follow my arguments just now and wouldn't and indeed couldn't make me change my mind once I was sure of it, human beings were free agents, and far be it from him to force me into doing anything alien to my innermost nature. Anyway, he'd already been wondering whether he could justify it to himself and his conscience to ignore a young actress's obviously deep-seated artistic preference for the man who was certainly the greatest of all dramatists, diverting her career into channels which might be and undoubtedly were very promising and could bring great success, if they went against her original intentions. As chance would have it, only yesterday he'd gone into the McDonald's right beside his office and made a discovery there, for he was served by an interesting young woman from Haiti who admittedly had no stage experience but whose charisma he thought made her not unsuitable for the role of Anna Freud, in fact in some ways just a tad more suitable than me, since she was a little shorter and moreover, as he'd found out by chance, was a natural lyric soprano, so there was no need to look for one of those New York singing teachers who were usually so wickedly expensive.

I'd been expecting John to do his best to dissuade me, as usual, and it took the wind out of my sails to find him ready to give me up, just like that, for someone who didn't know the first thing about the stage. Rather sheepishly, I said I hoped he didn't misunderstand me, I was very keen on the part and hadn't the slightest intention of letting him down, not now, not with the preparations already well advanced, I was only anxious to continue my voice training with a teacher who'd have a better understanding of my individual artistic needs that Herr Horvath and do it in my native New York, where my talents could develop better than in the cold city of Vienna, a place that was far from hospitable to foreigners, indeed was obviously extremely hostile to them. Well, so far as that went, said John, unfortunately my wishes couldn't be granted, he'd already mentioned the vertiginous fees demanded by New York singing teachers, they would place far too great a strain on his budget, which he'd already overshot by quite a long way. Moreover the little Haitian, who seemed to be not only charming to look at but also to have an amiable and pliable character, had already said she herself was prepared to pay for the few lessons she'd need to refresh her voice and adapt her untrained lyric soprano to public performance, something to which she was unaccustomed. He didn't need to emphasize that he was anxious to continue our collaboration, which had proved harmonious in more ways than one, but I must surely see that it wasn't in his power, or even that of his father, the highly regarded producer John F. de Luca Senior, whose credit was good everywhere, to draw on unlimited sources of money. I was an artist, he couldn't expect me to have a sense of what was practical and feasible or any understanding of complex financial transactions, but he was appealing once again to my feeling for an artistic construct inspired by communal effort, for creative activity that might involve some sacrifices, in short, for a sense of artistic responsibility.

I realized I was defeated.

Yes, very well, I said yet again, I'll stay.

5

I was relieved to realize that my health was improving. I was
scarcely suffering at all from breathlessness any more, and my
attacks of coughing were less frequent. Before I left home to visit
the Dorotheum, the Viennese state auction house in Dorotheergasse, I decided to knock on Fräulein Haslinger's door to give her a
chance of felicitating me on my convalescent state. She was busy
using crayons chosen at random to colour in the outline of the rose
window of Chartres Cathedral, copied from a book about the
architecture of the Gothic cathedrals of France entitled *Nearer, My
God, To Thee!* which she thought a valuable aid to meditation. She
was pleased to hear that my general health was improving, but
begged me not to be rash, and to go on taking a level teaspoon of
her cough syrup from the Bucklige Welt country area three times a
day. Before I left she pressed a copy of the outline of the maze of
Chartres Cathedral into my hand, suggesting I try finding my way
to the heart of it, an original way of training one's powers of
concentration, but if I didn't succeed in solving the puzzle she
could let me have a copy of the maze of Reims Cathedral, which
wasn't quite so complicated.

Before leaving the building I exchanged a few words with the
receptionist in the death chamber, whose originally rather strained
relationship with me had now become an almost friendly one,
something I ascribed not least to our shared enthusiasm for
knitting and crochet. She was busy with the thumb of a mauve

woolly glove, and I stopped briefly and looked over her shoulder, since I was planning to knit myself a pair of mittens to match the colour of the Resi Hammerer loden coat. On the way to Kettenbrückengasse underground station I met the friendly florist, who was carrying a date palm about a metre high and asked me who that striking dark-skinned lady who had visited me the other day was, a pupil, she supposed, my fame seemed to have spread beyond Vienna and Austria, even beyond Europe, all the way to Africa. I confirmed her supposition, and seeing that she seemed rather exhausted carrying the palm I hastened to assure her that in normal circumstances I'd have been happy to take it from her and carry it to the flower shop, but although my bronchial catarrh was almost better I still had to take care of myself, the Viennese weather was so unpredictable, you always had to beware of a relapse.

I got into the underground train going towards Heiligenstadt with the old lady from 14 Kettenbrückengasse. She had to go to the vet in Abraham-a-Sancta-Clara-Gasse, she said, her spaniel was suffering from an advanced cataract and kept bumping into people and things in the street, which wasn't really surprising considering that he would complete his twelfth year of life next 24 December, a day when, as it happened, that pro-Hungarian agitator the Empress Sisi had also been born. He'd probably need an operation, and she was wondering how she was to afford it out of her tiny pension; her late father, the retired stipendiary councillor, always said you wait and see, Hildegard, you wait and see, the time will come when the decent people of this country go hungry, and as usual her father had been right.

I got out at Karlsplatz underground station and decided that before I went to the Dorotheum I'd pay a brief visit to the crypt of the Capuchin Church, the last resting place of many of the Hapsburgs and one of my very favourite places in Vienna, along with the Central, the Grinzing, Hietzing and St Marx Cemeteries, the Cemetery of the Nameless and the grounds of the psychiatric hospital on Baumgartner Höhe: an oasis of peace in a metropolis where the hectic and thoughtless pace of life is perceptibly gaining the upper hand. On a weekday morning I was often the only visitor to the great vault, and could view the sarcophagi in the crypts of Charles VI, Maria Theresia, Emperor Francis, Ferdinand, Franz Josef and Leopold and the Toscana crypt at my leisure, along with the talon-like feet of the sarcophagi of Empress Anna and Emperor Matthias, the skulls wearing helmets and imperial crowns to remind us that even the mighty are mortal, the mysteriously veiled girls' heads at the four corners of the sarcophagus of Empress Elisabeth Christina, and the double sarcophagus of Empress Maria Theresa and her husband Emperor Franz.

As I stood beside the sarcophagus of Empress Elisabeth, adorned as usual with a great many wreaths and bunches of flowers, I thought of Miss Brown, a curious mental connection between two women who had nothing at all in common with each other. I tried to think of some possible link, and discovered that it must be to do with the moment when Miss Brown stood at the baby grand in a position that was typical of my mother, singing 'The Trout' in a mezzo-soprano reminiscent in its colouring of my mother's voice. And it had been my beautiful mother, not Miss Brown, who resembled Sisi. As for Miss Brown, I didn't think her appearance very attractive; she was far too thin, and she dressed in a rather peculiar way. So far as I could remember, both in the cemetery and on her visit to my apartment she had worn very tight black trousers, an equally close-fitting rib-knit pullover, and black boots with chunky high heels, a style that is neither feminine nor elegant. I was grateful to her for making my tea and preparing my inhalation, but all the same I'd felt there was something over-assertive about her manner, particularly in her tactless assumption that I was an alcoholic, and while the fact that she played percussion might be explained by her ethnic origins, it still contravened those delicate feminine instincts for which, according to my mother, any sensible man should be on the lookout. I wasn't familiar with that type of female; the women I usually met — Fräulein Haslinger the pastoral assistant, the florist, the pharmacist, the lady in the tobacconist's shop and the receptionist in the death chamber — were all considerate, calm and composed. Miss Brown's nature was alien to me, and consequently I was surprised that she had so unexpectedly sprung to my mind in connection with Empress Sisi and my mother. I stood in front of the white-gold sarcophagus of the Empress who had been so shockingly assassinated, and continued to reflect on this phenomenon. As someone who, on account of his congenitally weak health, finds it vital to register every somatic prompting, every psychophysiological change of mood and every organic vibration, however apparently insignificant, it had struck me that there'd been a noticeable improvement in my condition since she called on me. At the moment I couldn't think of any explanation for this odd but indisputable state of affairs.

I left the Capuchin crypt, not without stopping for a little chat with the kind old lady, an expert on the history of the House of Hapsburg and Hapsburg-Lorraine, who often sat at the cash desk and was there today, discussing with her the relationship between Leopoldine, later Empress of Brazil, and Archduke Johann's wife Anna Plochl, and then I went on my way to the nearby Dorotheum, the famous Austrian pawnbroking and auctioneering firm, a place with a long tradition behind it, and it wasn't a way that I found easy to tread. The fact that chronic bronchitis had confined me to my sickbed several times over the last six months had not been without its consequences. Three of the six pupils I was teaching had left me, which was unfortunate but understandable considering the tender age of those pupils and the impatience natural to youth. Including Miss Brown, a new arrival and thus very welcome, I therefore had only four pupils at the moment, and the fees they paid weren't enough for my keep. Apart from the considerable fall in the number of my pupils, the expense of medicines and visits to the doctor was also eating into my savings at an alarming rate. Since I've inherited my mother's sensitive and easily upset nature, not only had my nightmares about her death cost me a great deal of sleep during the past few weeks, but so had the thoughts that went through in my head in the dark, revolving constantly around the subject of my financial problems and refusing to go away — a vicious circle, since insomnia in its own turn undermined my health. I felt bad about owing the proprietors of the Café Anzengruber for three Kaisermelange coffees and three brioches, although both husband and wife showed great understanding for my temporary inability to pay. I was also behind with payment for the medicaments I'd bought over the last few weeks at the St Mary Magdalene Pharmacy, and for the beef to make broth which I got from an Anatolian butcher in the Naschmarkt. These debts really preyed on my mind, since my mother had always brought me up to be honest and upright and had drummed it into me that never, in any circumstances, was I to owe anyone money. That's the beginning of the end, Josef, she used to say, debts are the beginning of the end. And now I found myself obliged to pawn something she had left me, an item valuable both in itself and for sentimental reasons, something that she had treasured all her life and which was also extremely dear to me, a portrait of Schubert by his friend the painter Kriehuber, a very fine likeness with a written dedication to the composer Franz Liszt, showing Schubert leaning on the back of an armchair with his left hand placed on his right. The master had put his signature at the bottom of the portrait, which naturally added a good deal to the value of the picture.

I entered the palatial building of the Dorotheum, passed through the tall entrance hall with its glass display cases of jewellery and other valuable items, and then turned left up the broad staircase. I could see my mother's grave face before me the whole time. She would consider what I was about to do a betrayal of music, but I could see nothing else for it. I spoke to one of over seventy valuers and experts in the Old Masters department, who sent me off to a different part of the building, where yet another of these awe-inspiring authorities turned his attention to me. I showed him my picture, pointing out that it was a rarity, my mother, who was Hungarian by birth, had once come upon this portrait of Schubert in an antique dealer's in Budapest, more precisely in Ofen, and she accounted for its having travelled so relatively far from its place of origin to the city where she found it by its dedication to the Hungarian composer Franz Liszt and by Schubert's visits to the Hungarian estates of prince Esterhazy. The valuer and expert looked first at me and next at the portrait, which he examined for some time with the aid of a magnifying glass. Then he said the lithograph I'd shown him was certainly very attractive but worth practically nothing, and collectors knew there to be several hundred copies of it in circulation. I replied that this was impossible, he must be wrong, the Hungarian antique dealer had given my mother written confirmation that the picture was unique and I would be happy to show him this certificate of authenticity, which was in a chest of drawers in my apartment in Vienna 4, I didn't want to hurt his feelings but he could be wrong, after all to err is human, and I'd be grateful if he would consult another of the firm's valuers, known as they were even beyond the frontiers of our own country for their profound understanding of art and the accuracy of their judgement. Here a sudden change came over the expert's previously rather phlegmatic attitude, and he asked indignantly just what was I suggesting, next February would mark the twenty-fifth anniversary of his career as a valuer in the Dorotheum, a very creditable record, his eyesight was perfect, as good as ever, he'd discovered forgeries that had never been spotted by valuers at either Drouot's in Paris or Sotheby's in London, and it was hardly his fault if gullible females travelling abroad let shady antique dealers of Hungarian origin palm worthless rubbish off on them. I couldn't let this malicious slur on my dear mother pass without protest. I asked him to take that remark back at once, he might be an experienced valuer but as a human being he lacked civility, perhaps he'd kindly give me back my masterpiece at once, I was sure they'd have a better opinion of it in the small but distinguished private auction house a little way off in Bräunerstrasse, how typical that even today, even in the Dorotheum, Schubert was exposed to the dismissive neglect he'd encountered throughout his life from the supposedly art-loving population of Vienna, I wasn't going to tolerate such slights from so-called experts a moment longer, and as Schubert couldn't defend himself I would protect him from such defamatory statements on the part of a firm that might once have deserved its high reputation but now obviously and indiscriminately acquired works of poor quality. So saying I snatched my picture out of the hands of the valuer, who looked at me without making any reply, turned, went downstairs again, left the building through the entrance into Spiegelgasse and set off towards St Stephen's Cathedral, where I was to meet my former Choral Tutor, who had kindly pulled strings and got me two tickets for Mass in the Court Chapel next Sunday. I thought it important for Miss Brown to see the imperial chapel in the Schweizerhof of the Hofburg Palace, with its long historical tradition and its close connections to the rise of Viennese Classicism, and after the lesson we had fixed for Thursday I was going to suggest taking her.

It was some time since I'd seen the Tutor, and since we hadn't been able to agree at once where to meet on the telephone we had decided to look for each other by the figure known as 'Christ with Toothache' behind the cathedral and then decide on a coffee house that we would both like. I had to admit that I was looking forward to our meeting with a certain emotional excitement because our former friendship had been so close, and since I grew up without a father, the Tutor, several years older than me, had been not only an intimate friend but a father figure whose advice I was happy to take and whose instructions I followed without question. As I wrapped my scarf more closely round my neck, since you always have to reckon with gusts of wind coming from all directions as you cross the Stephansplatz, particularly near the ground plan marked in red cobblestones of the Chapel of St Mary Magdalene that burned down in 1781, a very exposed area, I remembered that it had been the Tutor who discovered and encouraged my talent for playing female parts, a talent that finally brought me the role of Bastienne in Mozart's opera buffa *Bastien und Bastienne*, in which I was always very successful. I turned the corner by the Haas & Haas tearoom, and there stood the Tutor, absorbed in contemplation of the emaciated torso of Jesus emerging from the capital of a column. Whenever I saw him I was struck again by his physical presence. He was a tall, slender, ascetic-looking man who held himself very upright, and in some circumstances could give an impression of severity, even brusqueness, to those who didn't know him as well as I did. Today this purely superficial effect was somewhat mitigated by the soft jacket of red-brown fox fur he was wearing. He seemed glad to see me, kissed me on both cheeks, and suggested going to the Frauenhuber coffee house in Himmelpfortgasse, an idea to which I readily agreed. We went down Churhausgasse, Liliengasse and Rauhensteingasse, where I took the opportunity of buying two nut macaroons in Huschka's bakery as a little gift for Fräulein Haslinger, and where the Tutor stopped for a moment outside one of the display windows of Alexander's, the exclusive gentlemen's outfitter on the corner of Rauhensteingasse and Ballgasse, to admire a silk scarf in delicate, iridescent shades of pale grey, pale orange and pale pink.

As usual, it was pleasantly quiet in the Café Frauenhuber, and the waiters served us courteously and without haste. There was a good smell of coffee, freshly baked pastries, floor polish, perfume and plush upholstery. The Tutor chose a large coffee with milk and one of the chocolate cakes known as a Mohr im Hemd, while in view of my present financial embarrassments I contented myself with a small mocha, an economy which made the Tutor, who was familiar with my habits and knew that I usually like a Kaisermelange coffee and a brioche at this time of day, ask whether I was short of pupils. I said that as he knew more about the musical life of Vienna than anyone else, he'd be aware of the difficulty of keeping one's head above water professionally in a city that produced such a superfluity of singing teachers. I could say that again, he replied, all those music teachers, most of them inadequately trained, whose deficiencies passed unnoticed by the troops of ignorant little Japanese girls wanting to learn to sing the Queen of the Night, were pushing up prices in an alarming way, at this rate Vienna would very soon lose its reputation as the world capital of music, a reputation already endangered anyway, former bastions of musical life such as the Golden Hall of the Musikverein, the Konzerthaus and the Vienna Chamber Opera were already crumbling. When he thought of the wonderful concerts the Vienna Boys' Choir used to give when I was still in it – ah, did I remember the applause that broke out in the Golden Hall after that remarkable performance of Gustav Mahler's E Major Symphony for which we'd rehearsed so long, or the happy atmosphere in the dormitory that evening! He took a small spoonful of the chocolate sauce that had been poured over his cake, and smiled at me. Indeed I did, I said, nodding, indeed I did, I remembered that evening as if it was yesterday.

Not only the musical life of Vienna but the life of the Konvikt boarding school in the Augarten Palace and the atmosphere in the dormitories had changed, said the Tutor, regretfully, the boys were not what they used to be, their vocal abilities weren't so good, few were interested in belonging to the Vienna Boys' Choir these days, no, the membership of an Austrian institution which had always been a great honour to those who belonged to it no longer seemed worthwhile. And no sooner did a boy join the choir than he left again, voices broke so early these days, it was a shame, this early maturing and the premature breaking of boys' voices. You might be delighted to have a soprano with a clear, bell-like voice come along, glad to have a velvety alto join the choir, but you'd be rejoicing too soon, for the minute the new boy opened his mouth his voice would begin to break, the clear soprano turned to a hoarse croak, the velvety alto to an ugly mutter. A promising lad would be given his first sailor suit in the Augarten Palace, and next thing you knew his voice was changing and he'd have to move to the Josefstöckl building. The number of applicants was falling and the number of boys with their voices breaking was constantly rising, there were yawning gaps at the Augarten Palace, while the boys with breaking voices thronged the Josefstöckl. Well, he asked me, and how were you supposed to teach the boys hand-kissing, saying grace at table, all the conduct so essential to the smooth running of the Konvikt boarding school and to perfection in public appearances? Much as he had enjoyed direct contact with the boys, in view of all these regrettable changes he was glad not to be so closely concerned with them now, since he had worked in the organization's administrative department for some time. To avoid getting completely out of touch with the practice of singing, he placed his own baritone at the disposal of the St Augustine Choral Society every week, and he must say it gave him great pleasure to be a part of that internationally known church music ensemble, had I ever thought of joining it myself?

Here the waiter, who had approached our table to clear away the Tutor's empty coffee cup, joined in our conversation and said goodness, was the Tutor really a member of the St Augustine Choral Society, please accept his congratulations, as a lover of Mozart's Masses he tried to hear as many of them as possible, an expensive hobby when you remembered how the price of concert tickets in Vienna kept on rising. The St Augustine Choral Society's interpretation of the *Great Credo Mass* was incomparable, not even the chorus of the Vienna Musikverein had such intense feeling for the work. The Tutor said he was glad the waiter had noticed that, he wouldn't like to cast aspersions on the reputation of the chorus of the Musikverein but in his view its quality was rather over-estimated. And the *Sparrow Mass*, said the waiter as he moved away, the musical interpretation of the *Sparrow Mass* had brought tears to his eyes, an emotional experience he hadn't know since his father's cremation.

The Tutor gave me the two tickets for the Hofmusikkapelle and asked who I was planning to take to Haydn's *Missa Dolorum*, to be performed by the Vienna Boys' Choir next Sunday. I said I had a new pupil, a young woman from New York whom I was preparing for a part in the music theatre there, it was obviously a very modern work and set in Vienna. So I thought it my duty, since my pupil came from a different kind of musical background, to acquaint her to some extent with the city's cultural heritage.

We left the coffee house. Before we parted, the Tutor clasped my left hand, held it for a while and said he sometimes missed the long conversations we used to have in the dormitory of the Augarten Palace, and then after my voice broke in the Josefstöckl, not to mention the walks we took in the vineyards and up to the Gloriette when I had left the boarding school. Did I ever think of that afternoon in the Palm House at Schönbrunn? He had the liveliest memory of that afternoon, the humid temperature, the condensation on the panes of glass, the thickets of plants, the soft twittering of birds, indeed he sometimes dreamed of it. He could hardly imagine anything he'd like better than to spend such an afternoon with me again. I said I couldn't really see any objection to another visit to the Palm House, although its artificial tropical or subtropical climate did entail certain risks for me, because it was such a sudden contrast to the temperature and air humidity outside that I might easily contract a severe chill, he mustn't forget that my physical constitution, always delicate, had not become any stronger over the last few years, far from it. The Tutor seemed rather disappointed when we parted outside the Donnerbrunnen in the Neuer Markt.

Towards evening I decided not to wait until Thursday to tell Miss Brown I had two tickets for the Hofmusikkapelle. I was sure she'd be glad to have the information a little while in advance, so that she could prepare more thoroughly for the performance. I telephoned her.

Her reaction disconcerted me slightly. She said she'd meant to go running in the Prater on Sunday morning; these last few days her hostess had been feeding her dishes – well, a single dish, really – which obviously made you gain weight fast. She was used to running, and even if the Stadtpark wasn't exactly Central Park, New York, she wanted to keep the habit up in Vienna. Moreover, just now she was busy reading something that also occupied some of her time, but very well, if I insisted she could go to this chapel with me since I obviously thought so much of it, well, yes, why not? Now, please would I excuse her, she was expecting an important phone call from New York. Before she could hang up I quickly asked if the name Empress Sisi meant anything to her. The Empress Sisi? she said. No, never heard of her. And now she really must ring off.

6

A loud knocking on the door of my room woke me from a dream in which the beautiful doll with the china head and hair made of mohair sitting on the desk in her black velvet hat trimmed with real feathers and her long, high-necked black satin gown rose, moved to the edge of the desk, jumped down to the floor and came over to my bed, getting larger all the time. She bent over me until the black plumes touched my forehead, smiled and said her name was Wilma, she'd always wanted to meet me, she was sure I'd like to know more about the details of her death. With these words she leaned close to my left ear, so that the gleaming feathers covered not only my forehead but my eyes too, and whispered something I didn't hear, for at that moment Aunt Pia knocked on the door and called that we'd run out of beechwood logs, and hadn't I promised to go down to the cellar and bring up more firewood instead of the Bosnian caretaker's husband who demanded an indecently high price for rendering the smallest service?

I got up, made my way past the dolls and pulled back the curtain with the pattern of little pink roses on a white background. It was Sunday, and drops of water were streaming down the window pane so that you could barely see the plane tree in the courtyard – weather that wrecked my plan to go running in the Prater. It had been raining almost uninterruptedly since I arrived in Vienna, I thought crossly, and I was sorry I'd accepted my singing teacher's

105

invitation, for the prospect of going out in this downpour carrying my relation's large purple umbrella with its sunshine-yellow border, and without suitable footwear, skipping over puddles as I made my way through the Inner City to the chapel in the Hofburg Palace and then listening to a Mass in that melancholy oddball's company was anything but enticing. Josef Horvath, Aunt Pia and Vienna all depressed me, and I longed for my old job waiting tables in the off-Broadway theatre, my little room in St Mark's Place, and most of all for John. The singing lesson last Thursday, interrupted by Horvath's attacks of coughing, had not been calculated to bring me out of my depression either, particularly as we began with a song from Schubert's *Winterreise* going on about the sad and gloomy world, snow-covered paths, darkness and stray dogs, two lines of which, so my singing teacher confided in me, were inscribed on his late mother's gravestone. When I asked whether she was the woman in the photograph standing on the baby grand, Horvath said, oh yes, that was indeed a portrait of his beautiful mother, who when alive had been credited, not entirely unjustly, with some similarity to the assassinated Empress Sisi, one of the most radiant creatures of her time, and I looked into the thin, long-nosed woman's piercing eyes, thought it better not to make any reply to this remark, and concentrated on the correct tension of my soft palate and on conscientiously curving my pharyngopalatine arch upward. We worked on this song, 'Good Night', for about twenty minutes, and then Herr Horvath clutched his breastbone and asked me to be kind enough to go the short distance to the St Mary Magdalene Pharmacy and ask for a little bag of the herbal tea mixture for coughs which the extremely obliging pharmacist there made up specially for him and always kept in stock, I had only to mention his name and she'd know what I wanted. When the pharmacist had told me she was so glad someone was looking after poor Herr Horvath at last, I went back to the Death House and found my teacher sitting in a wing chair, taking a hot foot bath in a rather battered white enamel basin. He glanced up and asked me to make the tea for his chesty cough and then leave him alone, the inclement autumn weather was giving his bronchial tubes a good deal of trouble, we'd see each other on Sunday, and meanwhile I mustn't forget to get the Schubert album for singing voice with piano accompaniment from Doblinger's music shop in Dorotheergasse. On the way home I decided to go to the music shop straight away, and while the sales assistant went off to find the sheet music I wanted, I picked up a little mallet with a felt-covered head and tentatively struck a very beautiful East Asian gong of indeterminate pitch, consisting of a round, slightly vaulted bronze disk with a curved, narrow rim, which was hanging on the showroom wall, thus producing a deep, long-drawn-out note, and then, acting on a sudden impulse, I slipped the little mallet into my pocket.

Aunt Pia knocked at my door again, shouting that the fire in the tiled stove was about to go out any moment, she supposed I didn't want to freeze, and perhaps I'd finally go and bring up some wood as I'd promised, whereupon I dressed, put Rosa Havelka's autobiography, which was lying on my bedside table, back in the chest, went to the kitchen and drank a cup of coffee, while my relation pressed the cellar key into my hand and said, chuckling, that as I'd see, that cellar was old, very old, it had belonged to the convent that once stood on the site of this building, many of the old vaults under the buildings of Vienna 1 were linked by underground passages, who knew how many murders had been done down there, how many bodies had mouldered away. I picked up the basket, went down the stone stairs and past a fat, elderly woman with untidy long hair dyed raven black, wearing slippers on her bare feet and a bright pink knitted pullover that was too tight for her, beneath which her rolls of fat and her large white bra clearly showed. She was just wiping down the steps with a wet cloth. I went through an iron door on the ground floor and reached another stone staircase, leading down to a poorly lit vault with walls made of old brick, from which I climbed on down into an even deeper, darker cellar with a cold, trodden-mud floor and walls glistening with moisture, smelling of rotten fruit, old potatoes and mould. I paused, and was suddenly overcome by an oppressive feeling that this wasn't the first time I'd been down here. When I had suppressed the fear rising in me, and continued going the way Aunt Pia had described, I entered a dark, narrow passage, and let out a cry when I saw myself suddenly facing a man's shadow. Next moment a light went on in the cellar, and the stocky, grey-haired man with the weathered face who stood in front of me, holding a jagged axe with a wooden handle, contorted his mouth into a grin, showing two gold teeth, and asked what I was so scared of, it was only him, the caretaker's husband. I breathed a sigh of relief, gave the man my right hand, and said that apart from my Aunt Pia, for whose tiled stove I'd come down to get some logs, I didn't know any of the people who lived in the building, but I was glad to meet him anyway, whereupon the man's grin faded and he said what was all this about then, hadn't Frau von Hötzendorf asked him to do that job? Since he and his wife, sad to say, were Bosnian refugees they depended on the few coins the good lady paid him, two people couldn't live on an Austrian caretaker's wages, perhaps I knew that an Austrian caretaker's wages barely kept you off the breadline, this had to be some kind of misunderstanding, and once he'd finished chopping sticks for the stove in the yard he'd come up and discuss the matter with the good lady. So saying, the man turned and made his way up the stairs with a heavy tread.

A little later I was about to set off for the chapel in the Hofburg Palace, but when I opened the apartment door Aunt Pia came up to me, inspected me from head to foot and said she hoped I wouldn't mind her speaking frankly, but my attire seemed to suggest that I didn't entirely appreciate my good fortune in being invited to one of the Court Chapel Sunday services, good heavens, I was wearing the same close-fitting black things I wore every day, garments which emphasized my alarming thinness unbecomingly.

Perhaps I didn't know that people came from all over the world to
hear Mass performed so inimitably by the Vienna Boys' Choir, she
herself, alas, hadn't enjoyed that privilege even once in her life,
and she was now over eighty, but she imagined that the audience
went dressed in their best, whatever would young Herr Horvath, a
man of good family who, she supposed, would be wearing a frock
coat, think if I, Magnolia, showed myself so indifferent to this
solemn occasion? In the last resort it was she, Pia von Hötzendorf,
who would be blamed for such an insult to Viennese customs, so
would it be asking too much if she urged me to take off my
American outfit and put on one of her late daughter's pretty
dresses, as good as new thanks to the mothballs she had used to
preserve them for the last forty-three years. I thanked Aunt Pia for
her offer, but pointed out that I had my own style, and apart from
the umbrella which she was kindly lending me I wouldn't make
any inroads on either her wardrobe or Wilma's. To this my relation
said sharply that I must do as I thought fit, and I needn't be
surprised if this was the first and last invitation I ever had from
Herr Horvath, one of the most eligible bachelors in Vienna.

When I entered the Burghof through the Schweizertor my
singing teacher was already waiting for me with a big black
umbrella, and we went into the chapel together. I was pleasantly
surprised by his appearance, for so far I'd seen him only in either a
shapeless loden coat and an unbecoming fur hat, or a shabby
salmon-pink dressing-gown and grey felt slippers, but today he
wore a dark suit which, if a little threadbare, was decidedly
elegant, and a clean if not very carefully ironed white shirt, and his
thick curly hair was properly combed. Before Sunday Mass began
he greeted several acquaintances, men of his own age whom he
introduced to me as former members of the Boys' Choir, and who
inspected me surreptitiously. Then we took our seats in one of the
Baroque galleries. During the performance by the Vienna Boys'
Choir I glanced sideways at Josef Horvath now and then, and I
thought that though his profile with its domed forehead, slightly

tip-tilted nose and round chin was rather childlike, it was very appealing, even though I felt somewhat irritated when several times he took a thermometer out of his coat pocket, shook it briefly, and popped it into his mouth for a few minutes. At the end of the service my teacher said that whenever he went to Sunday Mass in the Hofburg Chapel he felt overwhelming nostalgia for the days when he had been a chorister himself, there was nothing like boyish friendships, such pure emotions are rare between the sexes. Then he put up his big black umbrella and added that he was glad to have shown me this place, rich in tradition as it was and founded by Emperor Maximilian, where Joseph and Michael Haydn had made music and Bruckner had been organist, and he had been meaning to ask me to lunch afterwards at the Three Picks Inn, but he realized how badly his organism would react if he stayed out of doors any longer, so he'd better go straight back to the Death House. I made haste to say I entirely agreed, and I was planning to spend some time in my room at Aunt Pia's reading that afternoon.

After I'd tried calling John from the telephone kiosk in the Stephansplatz, without being able to reach him, I went back to the apartment on the corner of Blutgasse and Domgasse where Aunt Pia was busy working on a broad-brimmed blue crochet hat for her doll Serena, made in Coburg in 1920 by the Johann Walther & Son porcelain factory, and eager to learn more about the life story of the now motherless Rosa Havelka, who like my own family on the maternal side came from Bohemia, I took the blue notebook out of the chest and went on reading.

Three

'O praise the Lord with joyful song,' we sang day in, day out, in the courtyard of the Ursuline boarding school, which was surrounded by a high brick wall. It must be clear as a bell, clear as a bell, said Sister Perpetua the choir mistress, jabbing her left forefinger into the right cheek of a soprano who had not succeeded in achieving the requisite pitch and purity of intonation. Clear as a bell, or what will our dear Lord Jesus think of us?

The Ursuline choir was the nuns' pride and joy. On the occasion of its successful participation in several imperial-and-royal choral competitions, its fame had spread not only over the high brick wall but beyond the borders of Prague and Bohemia, out into the adjoining crown territories and to the capital of the monarchy itself. I too was one of those likely to have their hair frequently pulled by Sister Perpetua, or their ears tweaked, or to be pinched in various parts of the body, for although I was naturally endowed with an alto voice in the middle register and of only average quality, she had taken it into her head first to make a mezzo-soprano of me and then, circumstances permitting, even transform me into a soprano. Rosa, you look like an angel, she said, giving my left pigtail a brief tug, and you're going to sing like an angel too. 'O praise him, praise his power and might,' I sang, turning my eyes heavenward so that in that respect at least I could come closer to the angelic creature of light she'd mentioned and the pure, bell-like sound she wanted. 'Praise, praise him, O my soul!'

I didn't enjoy singing. I preferred to go off to some corner of the convent library and read one of the old, leather-bound books describing in what seemed to me a manner that was both instructive and entertaining the lives and deaths of the saints of the Catholic Church. These accounts reminded me of my dear mother's stories, of the *Life of the Devout Maidservant Katharina*, and thus of the Paradise from which I had been so suddenly expelled. That child will ruin her eyes, sighed Sister Immaculata the librarian when I came to ask her for the heavy, dark-brown volume with gilt-edged pages containing the pathetic story of the life of St Ursula, patron saint of our order and according to the legend the daughter of a British king, telling how she and her eleven thousand virgin companions were massacred by the Huns in the year 452 on their way back from a pilgrimage to Rome. At heart, however, the sisters were quite pleased with my interest in the holy and dangerous activities of the martyred servants of God. They secretly hoped that at a later date I would join the Ursuline Order and enrich the edifying literature of Catholicism with hagiographic contributions of my own. Sister Immaculata already saw me as the convent's future chronicler and author of a new life of St Ursula, and stroked my hair when she saw me sitting immersed in the *Acta Sanctorum*, the *Legenda Aurea* of Jacobus of Voragine, or the *Martyrologium Romanum*. The child is so eager to learn, I heard her whisper to Sister Perpetua, such a spiritual nature, a thoroughly contemplative character. And her handwriting, so neat, she has a real gift for writing. We may expect great things of Rosa. An enchanting voice too, agreed Sister Perpetua, nodding, unusual vocal limpidity, positively crystalline. Just made to sing the motets of Palestrina and Orlando di Lasso as soon as her pitch and head-voice are fully developed.

'God is our light, in God we trust,' we sang from morning to night in the courtyard of the Ursuline convent in Prague. I felt strange in my new surroundings, and took little notice of them, for my mother's death had upset me so much. In my imagination the small statue of the Madonna of Lourdes standing on my bedside table took on her likeness, and whenever I had a chance I knelt down in front of it and conducted silent conversations with her, a habit that did not escape the notice of the girls who shared the dormitory with me. Whereas I had suffered before from the insults and ill-treatment of Helene and Marie, who despised me for my Bohemian origin and descent from a family of smallholders, my fellow pupils here, most of them the daughters of distinguished German-speaking civil servants of the Austro-Hungarian monarchy, called me a hypocritical goat, a sanctimonious goose and a bigoted cow, and avoided me as far as they could, conduct which did not cause me much pain, since I had withdrawn into a world they could not enter, a world entirely dominated by memories of my dead mother and, in direct relation to those memories, my edifying reading matter, which was largely confined to the lives and legends of saints. Whenever grief at the loss of my mother threatened to overcome me I made haste to think of the far greater torments suffered by St Sebastian when he was shot full of arrows and then clubbed to death, I thought of St Catherine and her terrible end, broken on the wheel, of St Barbara, beheaded by her own father, of the stoning to death of St Stephen, and finally of the martyrdom of St John of Nepomuk in Prague, the city where I was now living.

'How bright the light of heaven doth shine,' we sang incessantly in the courtyard of the Ursuline convent, and the wind carried our voices over the convent walls and out into the city streets. Sometimes it bore other sounds back into the square courtyard above which old chestnut trees towered, sounds we girls couldn't explain to ourselves, a crying and bawling that frightened us. When we asked the nuns why people were making this noise they would give no precise answers, and we had to be content with mysterious allusions and vague hints. We were told it was all to do with bad characters who didn't respect the order established by God and Emperor Franz Joseph, who wanted to shake it and finally

113

topple it; they were criminals to whom nothing was sacred, who thought they could ignore the boundaries fast rooted in nature and religion and claimed rights to which they were in no way entitled, persons of the worst kind who called themselves Young Czechs, they wanted to replace our euphonious German language by another, Slavonic tongue, and to undermine the union of our monarchy, firmly founded as it was in history and law, by boldly proposing what they called Fundamental Articles; in short, they were troublemakers and agitators who wanted to spread the godless chaos in their own minds to the rest of society, infecting their fellow citizens with some nebulous political feeling called Bohemian national awareness, blaming the Emperor and the fatherland for their own discontent, and making the harmonious social order of our empire the target of their destructive radical frenzy. When we asked the nuns to tell us more about these dangerous characters, they adjusted the snow-white bows at the necks of our blouses and said that young girls like us, delicate female creatures in the midst of their spiritual, physical and mental development, had no business with such questionable matters but must devote our minds entirely, with the active support of themselves, the nuns, to developing qualities pleasing in the eyes of God, such as a sweet temper, modesty, decorum and humility. For the time being, anything that distracted us from this common task was inappropriate. So we refrained from asking any further questions and struck up the next verse of the hymn. 'This fair light will never fail us,' we sang, trying to drown out the disturbing sounds that reached our ears from an outside world of which we knew next to nothing.

The nuns were obviously very anxious to air the subject of the qualities of modesty, humility and sweetness of temper, and the notion of decorum, for which they also used the alternative terms purity, innocence and chastity, seemed to play a leading part. Once again, however, they didn't express themselves very clearly when it came to defining these terms more precisely, but indulged in mysterious expressions, concealed hints, confusing turns of phrase and meaningful comments, often couched in the imagery of flora and fauna. Fiddling with the folds of our dark blue skirts, they spoke of buds nipped by the frost, of roses plucked before their time, of snow-white lilies broken by the storm when they had scarcely come into bloom. They mentioned tender doves falling victim to evil-intentioned birds of prey, guileless fawns entrapped by unscrupulous poachers. They emphatically stated that every female creature's most precious possession and finest ornament was her virginity, and consequently this greatest of all goods must be defended with determination against all unseemly attacks, more especially because it was a treasure that, once lost, could never be recovered. I wondered what such expressions meant, and whether they might in some way be connected with the nocturnal phantom whose appearance had cast such a shadow over my childhood, but I never gave myself up to such thoughts for long, since they revived ideas of my past, a past that made me fearful and anxious, and apart from my cherished memories of my mother I preferred to forget about it.

'O love, thou wilt awaken me,' chanted the choir in the courtyard of the Ursuline boarding-school building. In front of me stood Olga Zuckermann, the seventeen-year-old daughter of a Jewish furrier from Krakau who had converted to Catholicism. 'O love, to thee I come,' we sang. She had put up her black hair, and when we were doing voice exercises and practised the *appoggio*, that long, hovering sung note, my breath stirred the wispy tendrils of the hairline at her neck. Olga's neck was short, slender, white and beautifully rounded, and I liked looking at it while Sister Perpetua tried to teach us to sing an Italian *legato* with a broad, curving vocal line. I thought Olga was the prettiest of my fellow pupils. She was small for her age and delicately built, and moved with grace. Dark down grew on her forearms and calves. Her lashes were long and thick, her eyes large and almost black beneath broad, straight eyebrows, her forehead was low, and on

115

her left cheek she had a violet birthmark running from below her cheekbone to the root of her nose. I would unobtrusively place myself close to her in the gym, because she smelled nice. Once, when I was on my way to the refectory, she came up to me and asked why I kept staring at her, hadn't I ever seen a person with a cavernous haemangioma before? Before I could reply she quickly took my right hand, laid it against her birthmark and said I'd better touch it, it was perfectly safe and felt interesting. Well, didn't it? she said, when I had cautiously felt the spongy growth that protruded slightly above the skin. She'd have preferred a dark cherry red, she added, but unfortunately no one gave her any choice in the matter of colour. I asked Olga how long she'd had the mark, and she said since birth, her mother believed it was wished on her as a four-month-old embryo in the womb by a Bulgarian gypsy woman because she, Olga's mother, had refused to give the beggar woman money. And when the gypsy cast the spell, some of her magic powers must have been transferred to her, Olga, because she could make cows calve prematurely when she wanted to, stop clocks and get people to commit suicide. So I'd better watch out, she said, tugging at the leather lace round my neck until the little bag of salt I always wore came into view. Salt, she said, well, well, how did I know about that, how did I know salt protects you from travelling accidents, dark thoughts and the evil eye?

This sealed our friendship. I showed her the books I'd inherited from my mother: the *Housewives' Golden Treasury*, the prayer book and the four cookbooks by Dobromila Rettigova, and I told her about my veneration of the Madonna of Lourdes and the profound respect I felt for the resolute conduct of St John of Nepomuk. Didn't I know that the oldest statue on the Charles Bridge was a figure of that saint, asked Olga, and when I said no, she said that on the next of the few outings we were allowed she'd take me to see the statue. Then she added that while she under-stood and approved of my admiration for the saints of the Catholic Church she couldn't share my high regard for them, indeed as a

Hasidic Jewess born she felt a deep aversion to the Christian Church, its hierarchy and its rites, which was particularly regrettable and difficult for her because seven years ago, when her father had a dream full of significance in which St Teresa of Avila appeared to him naked and covered with stigmata against a background of midnight-blue damask embroidered with stars, that patriarchal and despotic figure had decided to convert to the Roman Catholic faith along with his whole family, and to have himself and his household baptized after the example of Christ's baptism in the Jordan, that is, by immersion and not just infusion, a ceremony performed by the Archbishop of Krakau in the bend of the River Vistula. She, Olga, who had been afraid of water since birth, was nine years old that March and vigorously resisted immersion in the cold waters of the Vistula, an essential part of the ritual, scratching and biting the Archbishop's waxen hands as they performed the ritual, so with the best will in the world she couldn't imagine that the ceremony was valid and had made her a full member of the one holy Catholic and apostolic church. Anyway, she continued to regard herself as belonging to the mystic Hasidic movement, and if I, Rosa, thought the book carefully covered with pale brown paper, which she, Olga, read at least as often as I, Rosa, read the *Legenda Aurea* and the *Martyrologium Romanum*, was a copy of the Bible, then I was wrong. It was not the Old Testament and most certainly not the New Testament she held in her hands, but the Cabbala. And if I, Rosa, had previously been of the opinion that the Christian hymnal was the source of the tunes that she, Olga, sang quietly to herself before going to sleep in her hard, narrow iron bed in the dormitory not far from my, Rosa's, bed, then I was wrong again. The songs she hummed came from the traditional Hasidic collection of mystic melodies, and were far more moving than those boring Catholic hymns with their stupid words that Sister Perpetua was always making us learn.

Olga's revelations upset me. How could she deceive the nuns so, I asked, those pious women who had nothing but our welfare at heart, and how could such conduct be reconciled with the stipulations of the Christian Ten Commandments? To this Olga said pious women my eye, she found my naivety touching, those nuns were the most spiteful, horrid creatures imaginable, and what did I mean, Christian commandments? Distressed, I asked if she wasn't afraid the nuns might find out what kind of reading matter that pale brown cover concealed, what sacrilegious songs their charge struck up every evening, and didn't she fear that if her secret was discovered she'd be expelled from the boarding school on the spot? So what if she was, said Olga, she felt like a prisoner in this school anyway, things could hardly get any worse than they were already. Furthermore, while the nuns might be spiteful and horrid they were also of limited intelligence, which made any discovery of her, Olga's, secret practically one hundred per cent unlikely. And if the worst did come to the worst, the golem would help her. When I asked Olga who this curiously named helper might be, she smiled, and said perhaps she'd tell me on our planned walk to the Charles Bridge.

'O love that loves me ever,' we sang during the next few days in the convent courtyard, 'O love that ransoms me.' My vocal apparatus was mastering the higher registers with less difficulty than usual, something I ascribed to my feeling more cheerful since the beginning of my friendship with Olga. She kept her word, and on our next free afternoon she took me to see the statue of St John of Nepomuk. We looked up at the stone saint, and I said to Olga it was a pity we weren't allowed to leave the boarding school after dark, since in broad daylight the five stars around his head inscribed with the letters t, a, c, u and i were of course invisible. T, a, c, u and i, repeated Olga, *tacui*, meaning 'I kept silent', why *tacui*? I told her that besides being priest of the Church of St Gall in the New Town of Prague, St John had been confessor to King Wenceslas's wife Johanna, and the King had urged him to betray what his wife said in the confessional. When he refused he was imprisoned, tortured horribly with pitch flares, the King personally taking a hand in the torture, and then dragged through the streets of Prague before finally being thrown off the Charles Bridge into the River Vltava with his hands and feet bound. Olga shivered and said I obviously had a peculiar taste in men, she herself was more inclined to admire a powerful character like the golem. I objected that after all, St John of Nepomuk was one of the most revered saints of the Catholic Church, reliably providing assistance to the innocent who were wrongly suspected and in danger of drowning. What's more, when his tomb was opened several centuries after his burial, his tongue was found still entirely unputrefied. Olga shuddered again and said unputrefied, what a word. Then she took my hand, led me away from the statue of the martyr and over the bridge to the Old Town, exclaiming that she could no longer stand the incense-laden air of the boarding school, our monotonous singing under Sister Perpetua's direction, or the lying, sadomasochistic legends of the Catholic Church, she felt drawn to surroundings that suited her nature better, and would find them in the Jewish quarter and the Jewish cemetery, even if those places were in the ghetto of Prague and not of Krakau, where she had grown up. I tried to withdraw my hand from hers and cried that she must be out of her mind, as pupils of the Ursulines we couldn't go wandering around a Jewish cemetery, if the nuns ever heard of it we could expect instant expulsion, and the boarding school might not be a very exciting place but unlike Olga I had been born in humble circumstances, and it enabled me to get a thorough, wide-ranging education based on the solid foundations of Christian humanist teaching. But Olga wouldn't let go of my hand, and drew me on down Karlova Street and Husova Street, right across St Mary's Square into Valentinska Street and Siroka Street, and so through the great gate into the old Jewish cemetery. I stopped resisting and let her lead me past the crooked old gravestones until she stopped in front of a tomb. This was the tomb of Rabbi Löw, she said, the learned man who had made the golem. She sat

119

down on the ground in front of the tomb and waited for me to sit beside her. I looked all round me, in case anyone saw us sitting there among the Jewish gravestones in our school uniform of dark blue pleated skirts ending ten centimetres below the knee, our knitted jackets, also dark blue, with the school emblem showing St Ursula holding an arrow, sewn to the breast pocket, our long-sleeved, high-necked white blouses, our white cotton knee-length socks, our flat black patent-leather shoes and our dark blue straw hats with their turned-up brims, but except for a little old man with a tall black hat and a lock of hair like a corkscrew in front of each ear, who was standing not far off by one of the gravestones and scribbling something on a piece of paper, ignoring his surroundings, there was no one to be seen.

Rabbi Löw was a very clever man who dabbled in mysticism and alchemy, Olga went on. He had made a human figure out of clay, brought it to life by reciting a combination of letters taken from an old Jewish book of magic, and called it a golem. The golem was tall as a giant, mute and very ugly, and in general he was kindly disposed and came to the rabbi's aid when he was wanted. And when the rabbi recited another set of letters the golem lay down and went to sleep. It was all perfectly simple, except that you mustn't forget the letters or mix them up, for then the golem ran out of control and could turn violent. Olga looked at me and said that years ago, by pure chance, she'd discovered an unauthorized reprint of that book of magic, entitled the *Book of Creation*, in her family's library in Krakau, and out of boredom she began experimenting with different combinations of written characters until, believe it or not, the golem appeared and made gestures clearly informing her that he was at her service. Since then she had felt safe from every danger, even the spite and malice of the nuns. You do believe me, don't you, she added, glancing at me sideways. I thought for a while and then said the story certainly sounded most unlikely, and my late mother, whose opinion I almost never questioned, would undoubtedly have dismissed it as the distorted

120

product of a growing girl's lively imagination, but I had had some very strange experiences myself in a similar field, in connection with a nocturnal phantom which had also appeared to me in human form, or to be more precise in the form of a grown man, so I didn't think such phenomena entirely impossible. Olga laid her little head on my left shoulder, sighed, and said she was so relieved to have found someone who took her seriously at last, as if it wasn't difficult enough living with a cavernous haemangioma. What's more, I must have noticed that the other girls thought she was crazy and called her moonstruck, and unfortunately she couldn't be sure it was safe to dismiss what they and the nuns all claimed, saying that she'd already gone sleepwalking several times at full moon, walking past the two long rows of beds in the dormitory, her eyes closed and her arms outstretched. If she really had behaved in this strange way, which wasn't perfectly certain, then in her view it could be accounted for, like her birthmark, by the witchcraft of the Bulgarian gypsy she'd already told me about. I replied that such a thing was perfectly possible, ages ago my mother had told me about the wiles of certain demonic female creatures who strove to lead other, right-minded people astray, or even ruin them entirely. I'd happily lend her the little bag of Ischl cooking salt that I always wore round my neck for a little while, in cases like hers it could only be useful. Olga thanked me for my kind offer but said she trusted the golem to protect her, the golem had never let her down yet. Then we stood up and went back to the boarding school arm in arm.

'O love that wilt not let me go,' we sang on sunny days and cloudy days alike in the school courtyard. I blew my warm breath at the nape of Olga's neck as she stood in front of me. Her company became dearer to me every day, and we spent a great deal of time together. Our friendship was closer and more intimate than anything I'd ever known before, apart from my relationship with my late mother, and every evening as I lay in my narrow iron bed I thanked God and the holy Madonna of Lourdes for sending

me Olga. One night, however, not very long after my daily prayer
of thanks, I was woken, as I thought, by a sound, and on opening
my eyes I saw a shadow leaning over me and groping for my
blanket. All at once the Marienbad phantom came into my mind,
and I got ready to bite. But as soon as the shadow had slipped into
the narrow iron bed beside me I realized that this was not the
heavily built nightmare of the attic bedroom, but my delicate and
slender bosom friend. Before I could react suitably to this surprising approach she said, low-voiced, that she was quite beside
herself with fear; for reasons she couldn't explain she had recently
found herself unable to remember a single one of the characters
that, if arranged in the correct order, would send the golem to
sleep, and he'd already visited her twice in the middle of the night,
standing there before her mightier than ever, making intimidating
and threatening gestures. Olga began crying quietly, and so dear
had she become to me within a short time that I couldn't help
taking her in my arms to comfort her. I felt her loose hair against
my cheek, and the warmth of her body under the calf-length
school uniform nightdress, and I was suddenly transported back to
my early childhood, before the uncanny phantom began paying
nocturnal visits to my mother, before I had been banished to the
straw mattress at the foot of her bed. Overwhelmed by the
unexpected return of a past from which I was trying to distance
myself, I involuntarily pressed close to Olga, and it seemed to me
as if I was once again breathing the fragrance of fresh bread and
cake and eau de Cologne that used to emanate from my mother.
Then my friend drew me to her and began touching me as no one
had ever touched me before, in a way that had nothing at all to do
with the protective tenderness of my mother's embrace, and was
far from evoking the sense of comfortable security that I had felt in
her physical presence, but produced completely different sensations, sensations whose novelty alarmed me. But when I tried to
pull away from Olga's hands and Olga's mouth, she whispered that
I surely couldn't reject a person who turned to me for help, a

person who, as must be clear to me even if we couldn't see our hands in front of our faces, was in a state of acute psychic crisis and so terrified she didn't know what to do. Could she really count on the firm friendship I'd promised her, swearing the most solemn of oaths? Ought she to have believed my assurances and promises as naively as she did? Olga's whispering grew louder and louder, and when the girl in the bed on my left audibly sighed, and the girl on my right turned over in her sleep, I desisted slightly from the defence I was putting up, fearing that one of them might wake and see something that it would be very difficult to explain to the nuns. Hereupon Olga immediately continued the loving manipulations in which I'd tried to interrupt her, and when I held her hands fast she began to sob, yet again causing my resistance to slacken a little, since the girl in the bed opposite uttered a long murmur in an undertone. And when Olga whispered, in tears, that I couldn't mean to force her into even more frantic behaviour by my hard-hearted refusal to show true sympathy for her fear and confusion, behaviour which the nuns might in certain circumstances misinterpret, I gave up, and abandoned myself first reluctantly and then willingly to her caresses, until she ceased first to weep and then to murmur.

'O holy pleasure, deepest awe,' we sang next morning, and I looked straight past Olga's slender neck in embarrassment, to right and to left, since the sight of it reminded me of those events of the night before that I would have preferred to erase from my memory. After choir practice Olga came up to me as if nothing had happened, put her arm round my shoulders and said why didn't we spend our next free afternoon in the Old Town of Prague again, the Old-New Synagogue where Jehuda Löw ben Bezalel had been rabbi was a very special place, she hoped the rabbi's spirit, which surely still lived on in those old walls, would appear and tell her the combination of characters she needed to appease the golem. I pushed Olga's hand away and said that though she herself might not have managed to base her life on a firm belief in the

Trinity and the saints and blessed souls of the Catholic Church, she could still be kind enough to refrain from pestering other people with the difficulties inevitably caused by this fundamental error of faith. I didn't have the leisure to go into the problems she obviously imagined she had, I intended to spend my next free time not in the Prague ghetto with her but studying the exemplary life of St Teresa of Avila, who had so miraculously led her, Olga's, father to Christianity if not, unfortunately, Olga herself. So saying I turned, went to the convent library, and took a volume with pictorial reproductions of the saints and martyrs off the shelves, in order to divert my attention from Olga and the unsettling sensa- tions, as intense as they were hard to define, that her nocturnal presence had aroused in me. I tried to concentrate as hard as I could on the appearance and attributes of the saints, but I wasn't entirely successful, since after a very short period of contemplation the faces of those female miracle-workers all began to look curiously like Olga's. No sooner had I immersed myself in the sight of the countenance of St Anne, the kindly mother of the Blessed Virgin, than Olga's features were superimposed on it, and the face of St Clare equally quickly assumed my friend's expression, while the physiognomy of St Elisabeth became hers as well. In my incomprehensible state of restlessness and emotional agitation I closed the book, and decided to calm my spirits by writing a little hymn of praise to the qualities desirable in God's servants, the kind of thing the nuns liked.

I found paper, pen and ink, and began to write. I had chosen as my subject the steadfast constancy of my favourite saint, St John of Nepomuk, but when I read through the first two verses I couldn't help seeing, to my surprise, that there wasn't a word on my piece of paper about his strength of character and admirable silence even under torture, only some lines concerned with Olga's beguil- ing physical charms, gracefulness and affectionate nature which might have come straight from the *Song of Solomon*, a work that Fräulein von Roth-Rothenhorst had read with us in the Gerstners' house, for she was of a romantic and secretly passionate disposition and knew, as she said, how to appreciate a religious poem which, she explained to us, made use of extremely erotic metaphor. In my regular reading of Holy Scripture at the boarding school, I had noticed that the *Song of Solomon* was missing from all available editions of the Bible. It wasn't hard to see that the pages in question had been cut out with scissors, and I supposed that this action could be accounted for as the work of the nuns, with their constant emphasis on the supremacy of innocence even above all other Christian virtues. The lines now before my eyes, very obviously written by myself, called Olga a lily among thorns, her eyes were compared to doves and her temples to pomegranates. The verses stated that the smell of her garments was like the smell of the spices of Lebanon, that her lips dropped honey and her love was better than wine, and that she had captured the heart of the lyrical 'I', as Fräulein von Roth-Rothenhorst called the narrator, with one glance of her eyes. They also mentioned the removal of a dress, and a sister, a spouse who was like a garden enclosed, a spring shut up, a fountain sealed. Was it possible that such expressions were the work of my own hand, and I had written these phrases down as if in a trance? I remembered that Olga had claimed to possess magical abilities from the womb because of the spell cast on her by the Bulgarian gypsy. Could she have been guiding my pen as I wrote this description? I put the pen down, crumpled up the sheet of paper, threw it out of the open window and hurried out of the library and along the arcades of the cloisters, past the refectory and into the dormitory, empty at this time of day, where I threw myself on my narrow iron bed and buried my head in the pillow.

'With joy, with pleasure, with delight,' we sang in the boarding-school courtyard under Sister Perpetua's musical direction. But the satisfaction she had expressed only a few days ago at the fact that my voice was steadily developing and getting higher, which like my interest in hagiography aroused great hopes in the nuns, had been replaced by an irritable and cross temper. Was I out of my mind, asked Sister Perpetua, treading on the big toe of my left foot with her medium-heeled black lace-up shoe, what about the breathing techniques she'd been so patiently and laboriously teaching us, had I forgotten them overnight, couldn't I make my diaphragm oscillate in the right relaxed way any more? What other explanation could there be for the sudden forced, even hoarse tone of my voice, rendering me unable to produce the delicate head-notes that it had given her and the other sisters so much aesthetic pleasure to hear? She was sorry, but if my voice hadn't regained its former quality within a certain period, she would have to suggest that I gave up my place among those singing the praises of our Creator to another pupil, at least for the time being. I could think of no reply to Sister Perpetua's reproaches, and cast my eyes down. 'Love divine, all loves excelling,' chanted Olga, right in front of me, with a slight vibrato in her voice.

I avoided Olga after that incident in the dormitory. If I was sitting reading my psalter in the convent garden, and she quietly sat down on the bench beside me, I would stand up, muttering some excuse, place the Old Testament in her lap, and go back into the building. If she offered to carry my school books from the refectory to the classroom I would thank her but refuse, and would turn to talk to another girl. And if she crossed my path as if by chance as I walked down one of the long corridors in the convent, I avoided her gaze, stepped aside and went on. I was all the more surprised when there was a repetition of the incident about two weeks later, and I woke up around midnight to find Olga lying beside me. I recoiled, and whispered that I realized she had a difficult relationship with the golem, but if she was ever to put adolescence behind her and become a mature human being, she must overcome her fear of the ghostly presence, which was what I took it to be, just as I'd mastered my own fear of the nightmare in the attic bedroom. My patience was exhausted, and I told her to go away immediately and get back in her own bed. She replied in a drowsy murmur, asking what I was talking about, as far as she knew she was in her bed already, and anyway the golem had obeyed her every word again since her last visit to the Old-New Synagogue, when Rabbi Löw's voice had told her the spell essential for commanding the giant. After I had pointed out as quietly as possible that she, Olga, was lying beside me, Rosa, she woke up properly and whispered that it wasn't possible, she couldn't explain such a thing, not unless the white light of the full moon that had been shining through the thin curtains since the previous evening had sent her on this little excursion. For as Sister Modestia had told her, she was one of those unfortunates who are prone to the phenomenon of sleepwalking, or somnambulism, and on nights brightly lit by the moon, under the influence of that inconstant heavenly body, perform complicated actions which they can't remember at all later. Surely I could imagine how terrifying it always was, waking up after acting in this incomprehensible way, and she knew I would show suitable sympathy for her present difficult situation and her illness, for an illness it was, and would lead her carefully and tenderly back to the real world with which she had obviously lost all contact for a while. So saying she pressed close to me, trembling, and for the second time I could do nothing but embrace her like a sister and soothe her with gentle caresses. Her anxieties were instantly relieved, she breathed more freely, and began to return my affectionate gestures so impetuously that I found myself unable to keep her vehemence within the proper bounds, and gave myself up to her passionate assurances of gratitude hesitantly at first, but finally without resisting.

These first two visits were not the last. On every subsequent bright moonlit night Olga would turn up in my narrow iron bedstead, insisting that she had no idea how she had got there, for the full moon upset the balance of her mind entirely. When, after a week during which I had not ventured to turn her out of my bed, I pointed out that with a brief glance at the sky she could assure herself of the indisputable fact that Lady Luna was clearly on the wane, her voice rose to an alarming volume. What was I getting at, she whispered in agitation, to the best of her knowledge there was to be a total eclipse of the moon in a few days' time, and with her unusual sensitivity she could already feel the approaching phenomenon, one that was awaited with excitement and alarm, and had been observed with the utmost interest since ancient times, a total eclipse of the satellite when it entered the shadow of the earth, as Sister Modestia had so graphically explained to us, was no small thing, or did I disagree? So as not to disturb the rest of the other girls sleeping around us I gave way, and allowed Olga's fingers and lips to do as they would with my body again, at first reluctantly but then without resistance.

'From the pleasures of this earth,' we were singing one morning not long afterwards in the school courtyard, and I looked over Olga's round little head and up to the tops of the chestnut trees. 'Joy and bliss for ever more,' I heard her voice chime in. After choir practice Sister Perpetua summoned the pair of us and told us to come with her to see Sister Constantia, the Mother Superior and headmistress of the school, without giving any reason. On the way she didn't say a word to us, but quietly sang a tune to herself. I caught the line, 'The spirit would not leave the flesh', and a few more words, 'All fleshly lusts subdue'. We entered Sister Constantia's office, and I noticed to my surprise that all the nuns to whom our education was entrusted were present, gazing gravely at us across the long table. Olga and I were told to sit down facing them. Sister Constantia rose to her feet and called first on St Ursula and the founder of the order, St Angela Merici, asking them to help the meeting reach a just verdict. I cast a brief glance at Olga, sitting beside me, but the expression on her face suggested that she knew no more than I did why we were there.

The Mother Superior then went on to praise the merits of the Ursuline order in the education of young female persons, and emphasized the importance of ensuring that tender young plants were encouraged to thrive, were planted in the fertile ground of the Word of God and watered by the light of the Holy Spirit, so that they might grow and mature, becoming strong, evergreen growths and living witnesses to the beauty and diversity of God's creation. The regrettable case upon which they must adjudicate here showed very clearly that this process of growth could never be too carefully supervised. Two pupils, one of whom had doubtlessly shown signs of certain developmental problems, although they did not seem insoluble, while the other had aroused the highest expectations with her musicality and her love of Catholic literature, something that made her conduct all the more reprehensible, had been observed engaging in the most appalling of practices, activities to which a stop must be put at once and in no uncertain manner, for they were in stark contrast not only to the principles of the boarding school but to the standards of moral conduct binding on one and all. So saying, she held up the piece of paper that I had crumpled up and thrown out of the library window and that had now, as I could see, been smoothed out again. Could I deny that I had written what was on this piece of paper, asked Sister Constantia, looking sternly at me. I cleared my throat and said no, I couldn't, and would she be kind enough to explain why I *should* deny it, since it contained nothing but a small poetic exercise, modelled on the *Song of Solomon*, intended to be in praise of creation and consequently of the Creator. Sister Constantia's reply was cutting. How, then, could I explain the fact that this shoddy piece of work was addressed not to God, Jesus Christ, the Virgin Mary or any other saint, but bore the title *Ode to Olga*? To this I replied that a person's inability to explain certain things ought not to be immediately taken as evidence incriminating that person. God's ways were inexplicable, as they themselves, the nuns, had taught us. I had written the poem in a subconscious or only partly conscious state of mind, and I didn't think it was fair to call me to account for such an action, performed subconsciously or only partly consciously, particularly as I couldn't remember a single word of my little poetic effort. At this Sister Immaculata stood up and told me angrily to stop splitting hairs, the *Ode to Olga* was not the only evidence of our disgraceful behaviour, the proof was overwhelming, it would be easy for her to call in at least four other girls who had both seen and heard me and Olga indulging in unnatural practices at night, but she wished to spare us such a humiliating interrogation. She would merely ask me how I, whom she had taken to her heart more than any of the rest, could have brought myself so treacherously to disappoint her hopes of both my capacity for ethical development and my gift for hagiography. And that wasn't all, added the refectory supervisor Sister Prudentia, intervening at this point, as if it wasn't bad enough for us to ignore all the fundamental rules of decency and morality, cheerfully committing the dreadful sin of unchastity, one of us was also a wolf in sheep's clothing, a person who had appeared to embrace the true faith while really adhering to the heretical confession of those who had nailed Our Lord Jesus Christ to the Cross, a girl with so little conscience that she pretended to be reading the Bible while in fact she was studying the writings of the arch-enemy of every honest Catholic soul. With these words she triumphantly brandished the evidence in the air above our heads: the Cabbala, now stripped of its brown paper cover. An indignant murmuring arose among the sisters and grew louder and louder. I could make out the words inexcusable, blasphemous, abnormal, and finally Sister Modestia said that she didn't know what more there was to discuss, the situation was perfectly clear, the offence cried out to Heaven, and they should proceed directly to a vote, she herself was calling not only for the irrevocable expulsion of the miscreants from the Ursuline boarding school with its long and honourable tradition, but for a categorical ban on either of them ever attending another religious educational institution in the territories of the Austro-Hungarian monarchy. Here Sister Perpetua said, in a quiet voice, that naturally our misdemeanours could hardly be excused, but one must be careful not to judge too harshly, she would remind them of the forgiving loving kindness of Our Lord, which of them would cast the first stone, after all, the accused were of an age when one easily strays from the path of virtue, it wouldn't be right to forbid us any chance of returning to it, many of those present would surely remember the aberrations and confusions of their early years, judge not that ye be not judged, those were Our Lord's words. She would also remind them that for all our sinful conduct we had regularly attended choir practice, raising our clear girlish voices in the praise of God, willingly if not always with virtuoso skill. In a word, she was pleading for us to be allowed to stay on at the school. As a confused babble of voices rose again, we were asked to leave the room, and told that we would shortly be informed of the outcome of the vote. Olga had maintained a defiant silence in the face of all accusations, and she still remained silent as we stood outside the double door waiting for the verdict.

The nuns decided to expel Olga from the school, since she represented a danger not only to the virtue of the other pupils but to the purity of the Christian faith, and I, whom they obviously regarded as a soul not entirely beyond salvation, was to be allowed a period during which I would have an opportunity to prove myself worthy of continuing to stay at the convent. Olga showed no emotion at all when Sister Constantia imparted the tribunal's decision to us.

'Confess thy sin, O child of man,' we sang next day under the chestnut trees, and I was spared having to avoid looking at Olga, for Olga no longer stood in front of me but was busy packing her trunks and preparing to leave. 'Let us fight with sin, our foe,' I sang in a husky voice. Nor was Olga allowed to go out to Mount St Laurence with the rest of the pupils that evening to see the total eclipse of the moon. On our return in the dark we did not immediately notice that Olga was nowhere to be seen. Only when the dormitory lights went out and she still wasn't in her bed did I begin to feel uneasy, and then I went all over the building in my nightdress looking for her, afraid that under the influence of the

131

eclipse she might be wandering down the long corridors in her sleep. I couldn't find her, and returned to the dormitory. On an impulse, I went over to the window nearest to her bed and looked down into the courtyard. The dark outline of a human figure could be made out on the cobblestones in the light of the street lamp near the gate in the convent garden. I flung the window up and called Olga's name, and several of the other girls ran downstairs and out of the house to find out what had happened. I stayed where I was by the window until they came back.

Next morning the girls were officially told that Olga had fallen from the second-floor window and had broken her neck in the accident, which in all probability was connected with her tendency to somnambulism. The dead girl's mortal remains would be sent home to Krakau, where a funeral Mass would be celebrated in the Church of St Mary. No one was to blame.

The following period remains in my mind as a long series of monotonously identical days. I said almost nothing and ate little, which the nuns were pleased to interpret as a clear sign of repentance. Sister Immaculata stroked my hair kindly again when she passed me, casting a fleeting glance at the life of St Birgitta of Sweden, which I happened to be reading, and murmured something about remorse and reflection, taking stock, purification and sincere penitence, and Sister Perpetua took me aside after choir practice, stroked my cheek and said I couldn't think how glad she was that with the aid of the heavenly steersman, Our Lord Jesus Christ, my little barque of life hadn't been wrecked on the dangerous rocks of sexual entanglements, that I'd put a stop, just in time, to a temptation that could have had a permanent and devastating effect on my life in general and my voice in particular, capable as it was of such fine development. She put her arm gently round my waist and said, oh Rosa, how good that you've stepped out of the dark thickets of fleshly desire into the sunny clearing of the pure and fervent love of God. Then she drew me carefully to her, kissed me quickly on the mouth and whispered Rosa, oh Rosa, how well I understand you, we all have our moments of weakness. I was glad when Sister Prudentia came into the room.

In fact my lack of appetite had nothing at all to do with a desire to fast, and there was no self-imposed commandment of silence behind my unwillingness to talk. Instead, it was as if, curiously, I now missed Olga's advances, although I had tried to fend them off as best I could when she was alive. And when we sang 'How blest are they who turn from sin' under the chestnut trees in the morning, I wondered whether I was really so happy not to have my sleep disturbed any more, or be exposed to the complicated but interesting sensations that Olga's nocturnal visits brought with them. For although Olga was dead and buried, the memory of our encounters seemed to grow more vivid every day, manifesting itself in the form of mental images that oppressed me constantly and everywhere, so that it cost me a great effort to keep them under control, and as a result I took little notice of my surroundings and understandably enough lapsed into silence. My loss of appetite was also linked to these fantasies, which I could hardly resist and which could be so demanding that they made it difficult for me to join in our communal meals, and I cut them short as far as possible. I gradually developed a dislike for the boarding school, where thoughts of Olga tormented me everywhere, but I saw no chance of removing myself from the place where I now was, since I was sixteen years old, with no financial means and no experience of life.

One day, when my thoughts of my friend who had perished so strangely threatened to overwhelm me, I decided to turn to the stone saint on the Charles Bridge and ask him to lend me just a fraction of the steadfast resolution he himself had shown. It turned out that I was not the only one hoping to get help from the saint's likeness, for as soon as I was standing there in front of him in my school uniform, hands folded, a young man came up beside me, took off his hat, clasped his fingers over it and began praying out loud in Czech. I asked this petitioner, whose clothing was

133

rustic, to keep his voice down a bit as he made his request or I wouldn't be able to concentrate, whereupon he looked me up and down and asked what a little boarding-school miss like me was doing here anyway, I'd better go back to the school for upper-class girls from which I had obviously run away and refrain from pestering the Czech patron saint with my German-Bohemian demands. I dropped my hands, which had been raised in prayer, and said what did he mean, German-Bohemian, my mother had been baptized with the good old Czech name of Libussa and came from a family of Czech smallholders living in the Pilsen area, I knew Czech as well as he did, and my current presence in the Ursuline convent had come about without my own involvement and independently of any personal wishes of mine. The young man was still looking at me suspiciously, and he said true patriots stuck together and didn't fraternize with monarchically minded German-Bohemians, even when advantage might be derived from the connection. He, for instance, was here to ask St John of Nepomuk to bless a journey to Vienna on which he meant to set out in a few days' time. Not that he liked the idea of going to the capital of the monarchy and mingling with Austrians, who oppressed the Czechs whenever they could, but the economic situation in the Bohemian Forest where he had been born and bred was so bad that he saw nothing for it but to look for work in Vienna. He wasn't the first in his village to decide on this step, he said, over the last few years the Emperor had needed a large labour force for the grand buildings he was erecting at the cost of his poorer subjects, nor would he be able to manage without them in the future either. His elder brother had found work in one of the brick kilns near Vienna, and would get him a job too. When I said I wished him luck in this venture, for unlike him I longed to leave the place where I was at present, and I envied him the exciting trip on the Emperor Ferdinand Northern Railway, he said ha, Northern Railway, I must be joking, and if I thought he could afford a train ticket I was much mistaken. He was going by a very different form of transport. Besides teaching me to despise Czechs in my posh boarding school, they'd certainly have informed me that St John of Nepomuk was not only the protector of the faithful against slander, patron saint of father confessors and those in danger of drowning, but also interceded for travellers in general and boatmen and raftsmen in particular. And as he didn't suppose I knew much about conditions in the Bohemian Forest, he'd probably have to explain further and tell me that a canal had been built between the upper Vltava and the Mühl, and during the warmer months of the year large quantities of lumber were floated along it in rafts to the Danube, and were then sent on to Vienna. Since he was a woodcutter by trade, like his father, his grandfather and the rest of the male members of his family, he intended to get to Vienna that way, riding on the tree trunks they had felled. Then he stopped, and said he wondered why he was telling all this to a spoiled girl from a social class with which he, as a sympathizer with the Young Czechs, had nothing to do, nor did he want anything to do with, so perhaps I'd be good enough to stop bothering him in his prayers to the saint. So saying he folded his hands again, gazed at the statue and moved his lips silently. I too pretended to be deep in my supplications once more, but in fact my thoughts were no longer concerned with the extreme steadfastness shown by St John of Nepomuk and my own lack of it, but with the person of the young man whom fate had just brought my way, and with whose help I might be able to give more concrete shape to my previously rather unfocused endeavours to get away from life in the boarding school, where the nuns imposed their will on me, my fellow pupils excluded me, and memories of Olga kept coming back into my mind.

When the young man had finished his prayer and turned to go, I asked him to listen to me for a moment, a request with which he rather reluctantly complied, and then, in broad outline, I described my situation. I began by expressing my surprise at finding that supporters of the Young Czechs, described by the

LILIAN FASCHINGER

nuns teaching in the convent school where I reluctantly rather than voluntarily found myself as extremely dangerous forces undermining the constitutional state that rested on the two pillars of the Catholic religion and the Empire, nonetheless obviously included such hard-working and God-fearing young men as himself. Furthermore, I was sick of the nuns and their constant admonitions, and was looking for a way of leaving convent life behind me. Like him, I cherished a wish to lead a free, independent life and earn my living through honest labour. So saying, I looked him in the eye and asked if he could understand that. He nodded and said of course he could, he now saw that I felt the same way as he did, and he apologized for misjudging me at first on the grounds of mere outward appearances, such as my school uniform. With these words he offered me his right hand and said his name was Milan, Milan Havelka. I took his hand and said my own name was Rosa Tichy, and I'd been an orphan since my mother's death two years ago, a death of which the Austrian bourgeoisie opposed by him and the Young Czechs was not entirely innocent. At this remark Milan grew quite angry and said not a day passed by without his coming upon another victim of the German-speaking upper classes, it was high time I developed an awareness of my political, historical and linguistic identity as an oppressed Czech and began to oppose the prevailing conditions, an endeavour in which he'd support me. I swiftly said that if he really meant to help me, then perhaps he would give me the chance of going to Vienna with him.

This request seemed to take Milan aback. Vienna, he cried, a young orphan in Vienna, how did I see myself managing, I probably had a totally inaccurate notion of Vienna, a romantic picture that in no way reflected reality, Vienna wasn't the city of music, literature, painting and architecture it was misleadingly represented as being, his older brother had written to him saying Vienna was a witches' cauldron, a huge city of workers where people struggled for survival, where you slaved until you collapsed

136

in return for starvation wages and had to be careful you didn't end up pretty quickly in an asylum for the homeless, Vienna was far too dangerous a place for me, a gently reared young girl, what did I think I'd do there, how was I going to earn my bread, no, he most decidedly would not advise me to go to Vienna.

I let Milan Havelka have his say and then replied, well, for instance, I could work as a maidservant in a middle-class household, maybe even as an assistant cook, my late mother had worked as a cook and imparted some knowledge of cookery and housekeeping to me, and in the right circumstances I might make use of that. And who knew, perhaps someone would even engage me as a governess, since for various coincidental reasons, some fortunate and others less so, I'd enjoyed the privilege of an excellent private education, and as nature had also given me a very good memory I hoped I had remembered all I learned and could pass it on if necessary. Milan still seemed unconvinced, and slowly shook his head back and forth. Then he said that several girls had left his village in the Bohemian Forest and gone into service in Vienna, and they'd all come home again discouraged and worn out, utterly exhausted, all except two, and one of those had died of tuberculosis while the other had been found stabbed to death in the water meadows by the Danube. Did I, he asked, want to end in the same way? I said no, of course not, I felt confident that the Madonna of Lourdes and St John of Nepomuk would protect me. The mention of the patron saint softened Milan somewhat, and after brief thought he said, well, at bottom no one could be preserved from misfortune, not even an orphan, and as there was obviously no dissuading me he was prepared, although not without reservations, to take me by water to Vienna with him. However, he must warn me that the Schwarzenberg Canal was no Emperor Ferdinand Northern Railway, it was quite a risky artificial watercourse to navigate. But anyway, he intended to set off for southern Bohemia early next day with his brother-in-law and the brother-in-law's horse and cart, and I could meet him at five in the morning at the foot of the Vysehrad, the old fortification on the right bank of the Vltava in the south of Prague, and wait for the cart to arrive.

Milan's instructions shook me slightly, since this meant I had only twelve hours to prepare and execute my escape from the boarding school. However, I showed no dismay but said calmly he could rely on me, I'd be at the appointed place at the appointed time, and I said goodbye. Then I went back to the convent, sat down in the library and opened a volume of the *Acta Sanctorum*, so that on the pretext of reading that work I could think, without being disturbed, about how to get away. After the lights were put out in the dormitory that evening, I kept myself awake by imagining my new life in the big city, an active life of cheerful service to my neighbour, in line with my dear mother's last wish for me. As soon as I heard the crowing of the rooster that belonged to the old lady who lived in a dilapidated old cottage behind the convent, I got up, put on my school uniform, took the little statue of the Madonna of Lourdes from my bedside table, groped my way in the dark to the cupboard where my few possessions were kept in a little cardboard case, opened the cupboard door carefully, took out the case and left the room. I went down the dark stairs to the ground floor, climbed out of a window that the nuns always left open at the warmer times of year and into the school courtyard. Then I ran to one of the chestnut trees growing beside the red-brick wall, some three metres high, which surrounded the building, put the little statue of the Madonna into the cardboard case and climbed the tree with it. I let myself down to the top of the wall from a stout, horizontal branch, and in the process my dark blue straw hat slipped off my head and fell into the grass under the chestnut tree. I threw my case into the bushes on the other side of the wall and jumped after it, spraining my right ankle as I hit the ground. I got up and limped in the direction of the Vltava. The dawn chorus was beginning, and there was a broad strip of grey sky and a narrow strip of greyish-pink light visible on the horizon. The cart was already there on the narrow path between the fortress and the river, a simple rustic rack wagon with one black horse and one brown horse between its shafts, and once Milan's brother-in-law had taken off my left sock and used it to bind up my right ankle, we set off southwards.

7

The thoughts going through my head as I crossed the grounds of the psychiatric clinic on Baumgartner Höhe and climbed up to the church were not pleasant. I wrapped my pure wool scarf more tightly round my neck, for although the sun was shining for the first time in days, which was why I had decided to get on the 46A tram outside the Volkstheater and go to Steinhof, there was a nasty wind blowing and I didn't want to run any risk of inflaming my mucous membranes again. That morning the proprietor of the Café Anzengruber had pointed out very civilly, when I ordered my breakfast from him, that in times when trade was slow he couldn't afford to go on giving credit to his regular customers, of whom I was certainly one of the most faithful, and he'd have to ask me to settle my small bill within the next few days, a sum scarcely worth mentioning, for the consumption of several cups of Kaisermelange coffee and various brioches, together with a couple of pairs of frankfurters with mustard and horseradish and a portion of scrambled eggs. I went back to Kettenbückengasse through the Naschmarkt in a rather gloomy frame of mind after that, and as I was passing the stall of the Anatolian butcher where I bought meat for my broth he came out from behind his counter, detained me by holding the sleeve of my loden coat, and said I still owed him for a kilogram and a half of best beef and three large marrowbones, and he didn't want to offend me, but as he was obliged to send a not inconsiderable amount of money home to his family on the shores

141

of Lake Van every month he couldn't really do without that sum, small as it might be. To make matters worse, when I looked in at the St Mary Magdalene Pharmacy to replenish my stock of violet-leaf tea, the pharmacist pointed out that I was rather behind in settling the bill for my medicines, and she must ask for payment of this debt, however small, in the near future, there was always competition, I'd be aware that there were several other pharmacies quite close to hers, and what was more, her assistant had been asking for a rise for months now.

These demands had moved me, shortly afterwards, to go off to the Dorotheum again with a legacy inherited from my mother, namely a manuscript by Gustav Mahler, or more precisely three poems by Friedrich Rückert transcribed in Mahler's hand on a double sheet of lined paper, poems that the composer set to music as the first three of the *Kindertotenlieder* during two weeks of his summer holiday in Maiernigg on Lake Wörth in the year 1901. My mother had pressed the double sheet of paper into my hand not long before her death, telling me that by a lucky chance she had come upon this unique document in an antique dealer's shop in Klagenfurt, and urging me to revere the composer's manuscript and in no circumstances ever to sell it, for to make money out of such a gem could lead to nothing but disaster. With a guilty conscience, I made my way to the Autograph Manuscripts department and placed my double sheet of paper before the appropriate expert, who looked at it, left the room with it, came back and said quietly that I had only the forbearance of the head of the department to thank for the fact that the old auction house, which had a reputation to maintain, wasn't going to bring charges of deception. The lined double sheet of paper came from a school exercise book made in a paper factory in Frantschach in the Lavanttal in the 1950s, and the writing on it was that of a left-handed child of about seven using one of the inks containing methyl violet dye typical of the same period. In the whole course of his career to date as a manuscripts expert I was the first person who had ever had the outrageous impertinence to show him such a blatant forgery. When I objected in dismay that this was impossible, my mother, a pianist who had died as the result of a medical error on Holy Innocents' Day three years ago in Vienna General Hospital, and who during her lifetime was well known in and around Vienna as an authority in everything to do with the great composer, couldn't have been so mistaken, the manuscripts man asked menacingly how I dared tell him, a recognized expert, such lies, and if I didn't want him to forget himself I'd better leave the building that moment and never darken its doors again.

Shortly after my return from this distinctly unsuccessful transaction I had a phone call from one of my pupils to say that during the six months he'd been taking singing lessons from me he had in fact only been given nine lessons in all because of my constant poor health, and as that was not enough he had decided to continue his training in singing with a different teacher.

By now I was outside the Church of St Leopold am Steinhof, on the steps leading up to the four columns of the church entrance, crowned by angels, and I turned round and looked over the extensive grounds of the psychiatric clinic, where patients were moving among the buildings. Flocks of crows flew overhead, settling with a loud cawing on the bare trees and television aerials. Then I entered the church, which has walls faced with white marble and large glazed windows, and sat down on a bench in front of the main altar with its fine gilded canopy. The church interior, flooded by light, raised my spirits, and my thoughts turned to the only pleasing item which had come up in my life during the last few weeks, namely Magnolia Brown and her voice.

During Miss Brown's first singing lessons, when we studied several songs chosen from Schubert's *Winterreise*, I had quickly realized that she had a fine natural voice with a wide range, as well as great musicality, and needed only to stabilize her larynx and develop a sense of the remarkably small amount of breath you need for singing to ease her way towards the cultivation of a soprano register. The more confidently Miss Brown made her way up to the high notes, the more attractive she seemed to me, and as she stood there beside my mother's portrait on the baby grand, beginning to resemble her more and more even outwardly, I felt a curious excitement that remained with me long after she had left the apartment, and reminded me not only of the mother who had brought me up but also of the delightful if contradictory sensations accompanying my intellectual, spiritual and ultimately physical encounters with the Tutor. After the end of the last singing lesson I asked her to stay a little longer and drink a cup of violet-leaf tea with me, an invitation she did not refuse. In the course of the animated conversation which then developed I felt moved to tell her about my passionate relationship with the Tutor, dating from the very beginning of my membership of the Vienna Boys' Choir, an affection that I had never mentioned before to another living soul, for it must be said that it went far beyond the usual limits of friendship between fellow singers. Magnolia listened attentively and smiled slightly when I told her about the afternoons when the Tutor gave me extra coaching in his room, when I spoke of those nights on which, a half-grown boy in my striped school pyjamas and clutching my pillow, I left my bed in the dormitory and, driven by impulses as confused as they were irresistible, sought the Tutor's nocturnal presence like a sleepwalker. Encouraged by her under-standing, I even admitted that my passion, for such it was, had sometimes led me to bitter self-reproaches, distressing me so much that I'd toyed with the idea of going to the Prater on one of my free afternoons, buying a ticket for a ride on the giant wheel, and then opening the door of the carriage in which I was sitting alone when I had been carried up to the highest point of the wheel's rotation, and throwing myself down to the depths below. Before Magnolia left that day she said she had the impression I lived in the past too much, what did I think of the idea of going for a run with her in Schönbrunn Castle park one day soon, there was nothing better than a little sporting activity for shaking off painful memories and anchoring you more firmly to the present.

Two days later we met at eight in the morning by the Fountain of Neptune in the castle park, a moment I'd been looking forward to ever since my pupil made her suggestion. Miss Brown smiled at me and asked if my clothing wasn't going to hinder my movements, and was I sure my shoes were suitable for running, and I looked at my pale grey jacket and dark grey flannels with their neatly pressed pleats, then down to my brown lace-up shoes, and then I looked at Magnolia's close-fitting black running outfit under her jacket, the broad hairband holding back her little plaits, and her fashionable black trainers with white stripes, and said in some embarrassment that I'd never tried this kind of activity in aid of physical fitness before, so I wasn't quite sure what the right equipment was. As we moved off at a run along the damp, sandy paths, Magnolia kept talking about some book she was in the middle of reading, but I could hardly make out what she said, since I was having difficulty with my breathing and kept lagging behind her, whereupon she turned and called out that we'd meet in half an hour at the coffee house up on the Gloriette, but when I arrived there, absolutely exhausted, I looked for her in vain and finally sat down at a small round table to wait for her. About ten minutes later she came limping into the bright, high-ceilinged room, cautiously sat down on a chair beside me and said she'd sprained her right ankle, which didn't really matter, it was only a minor injury and was sure to be better again long before the premiere of the musical. We drank coffee and then went down to the Fountain of Neptune and took the underground back to the city centre together, and before I got out at Kettenbrückengasse station I told Magnolia that while the run had tired me at first I didn't feel any ill effects to my breathing passages, which was amazing in the middle of November, the most dangerous month of all in that respect, to which she replied that if I liked we could go running again as soon as the swelling on her right ankle went down. From the platform I could see Magnolia standing in the train as it set off, strap-hanging

145

with one hand, and I thought that in spite of her excessively slender figure she really looked very feminine in her black tailored jacket with its little fur collar and her elegant wide headband.

That afternoon I took the 71 tram to the Central Cemetery, since I felt impelled to tell my mother about my new acquaintance. Without making my usual detour past Schubert's tomb I went straight to her resting place, sat down on the little mica slate wall round the grave, looked into the serious dark eyes gazing back at me out of the medallion, and told her at once that just over a week ago a person of the female sex had entered my life, and one I'd first seen in this cemetery too, although I had entirely misjudged her at the time, in fact it had actually been here by her own grave that I met her, a young woman who I was afraid wasn't entirely the type she had always recommended me to look out for. Although it was obvious to me that an artistic nature like hers, my mother's, would not suffer from prejudice, I could imagine that it was just possible she might not like the colour of Magnolia's skin, for Magnolia was the young woman's beautiful name, a rich, velvety dark brown skin verging on a golden hue in good light, or the fact that her father was an Afro-American, which explained this skin colour. I would not conceal from her that for some days past Magnolia, a good musician and most important of all an outstanding singer with a voice exactly like her own, had aroused feelings in me that I had never yet felt for anyone except her, my mother, not least on the grounds of this vocal similarity, and that I found these feelings rather disturbing. Since to my alarm I thought that at these words my mother's beautifully arched eyebrows drew closer together, expressing displeasure, that her gaze, lovingly turned on me, clouded over, I made haste to add that it was unnecessary to assure her that no one else could take her place in my heart, but I'd be greatly relieved to have some sign that she wasn't against this friendship, for it was no more than a friendship. Here I looked intently at my mother's face, but the expression of annoyance in it did not go away, so after a few minutes I said goodbye to her and

146

went despondently back to the tram stop.

I was so deep in these thoughts of Magnolia and my mother that I jumped when a visitor to the church passed me with ringing footsteps and knelt before the altar, and I decided to leave the house of God and set off for home. By now the sun had sunk, but flocks of crows were still flying up and settling on trees and rooftops to spend the night there.

8

When I went to fetch my burgundy-red shoe from the cobbler in Postgasse and asked how he could justify the high price he demanded for repairing it, he said it was an American shoe, not a European shoe, he'd needed special nails to fix the heel in place, little golden nails obtainable only from a place selling specialist equipment in Grosse Mohrengasse in Vienna 2, I'd understand that he must charge me for his journey to Grosse Mohrengasse and back, his cobbler's workshop was one of the last of its kind in Vienna, competition was always a threat when people didn't mind about the quality of the work, these days you could have a heel glued to the rest of the shoe in any department store, and he would repeat *glued*, for naturally those shop assistants, and he would repeat *shop assistants*, shrank from the painstaking work of carefully nailing a high heel into place. And how, he then asked, was dear Frau von Hötzendorf, the good lady had been deaf as a post ever since her sudden acute loss of hearing as a result of her daughter's tragic death, and she left the building less and less often these days, and when I told him that as far as I knew the cause of my aunt's deafness was a perforated eardrum, the cobbler shook his head and said, oh no, that was out of the question, it had been an acute loss of hearing directly after Wilma's death by suffocation, he remembered it as if it were yesterday, the poor dear lady had never recovered from the death of her only child, especially since it was partly her own fault that the flue gases had escaped from the

Biedermeier tiled stove, heating a place with Viennese Biedermeier tiled stoves was one of the trickiest things imaginable, flue gases quite often escaped through cracked tiles, he knew from a reliable source that the proper repair of two cracked tiles had seemed too expensive to the good lady at that time, and so the accident happened. I said, oh dear, that was terrible, whereupon the cobbler smiled at me, handed me my burgundy-red shoe over the counter, and said yes, of course it was terrible, life in general was terrible, and did I know that Wilma's spirit could find no rest and was still haunting the building at the corner of Blutgasse and Domgasse, the Bosnian caretaker, one of his customers, had recently seen her, poor old maid, for Wilma had indeed died an old maid on account of her good mother's grasping nature. Then he pointed to a small wooden stool and asked me to sit down on it and tell me a little more about myself, his life didn't have much variety in it and people from other countries seldom made their way to his work-shop.

So I sat down, and while the cobbler made holes in a child's shoe with a rotating punch and then fitted the holes with eyelets, using a machine for setting in eyes, hooks and press studs, he asked me questions about my origins, which I willingly answered. Among other things, he wanted to know how my mother, who he knew had forebears from northern Bohemia, had come to meet my father with his black African ancestors, and I explained that my mother, born in the state of Minnesota, had studied political science at Columbia University, New York, and in the middle of the sixties, she had told me, was taking part in one of the demonstrations demanding equal rights for black Americans, a demonstration that had degenerated into a street fight, in the course of which she collided with a young black jazz musician, more precisely a saxophonist, indeed even more precisely an alto saxophonist, in fact my future father who was part of the same mass demonstration, and this collision had given her a bad nosebleed, so my future father put his arm around her and led her away from the demo and into nearby Central Park, where he made her sit down under a magnolia tree, lean against its trunk and keep her head held up. As my mother had also told me, she had followed this advice and looked up into the crown of the magnolia tree, whereupon the nosebleed very soon stopped, a fortunate circumstance which the black musician, who was a few years younger than she was, took as an opportunity to make love to her under the magnolia tree, an act based partly on the irresistible physical attraction my mother had instantly exerted on him, nosebleed or no nosebleed, and also on the fact that this was not only the period of the American civil rights movement but also the initial phase of what's known as the sexual revolution, when progressive young people seized every opportunity of giving offence to their elders, who for the most part were not just older but more conservative, by making love as often as possible in general and by having sexual relations with people of different colour in particular. And that was how I, Magnolia Brown, was conceived one late spring afternoon in Central Park, New York, in the shelter of the canopies of the trees near the obelisk between Belvedere Lake and the Reservoir. The cobbler, who had listened attentively with his red cheeks getting redder than ever, said at the end of my brief account, why, that was incredible, to which I replied of course it was incredible, all life was incredible, and I left the cobbler's workshop in Postgasse.

On the way to St Stephen's Cathedral, which Aunt Pia had urged me to go and see, I passed a young man with a purple birthmark on the left side of his face from the cheekbone to the root of the nose, and I thought of the description I had read in Rosa's autobiography yesterday evening of her friend Olga's cavernous haemangioma, which must have looked just the same. I would have liked to ask the man if I could touch it. My right ankle hardly hurt at all any more, and I was looking forward to running in Schönbrunn Castle park with Josef Horvath again soon. He had said that next time he'd show me the butterfly house next to the palm house in the grounds, the butterfly house was something really special, as I'd see, he wasn't promising more than he could perform, the butterfly house always amazed people, he had been interested in butterflies ever since suffering severe viral influenza, one of those nasty infections that spread all over Europe like an epidemic at regular intervals and are difficult to combat, since the virus adapts to local conditions with extraordinary speed and the infection inevitably sets in with fatigue, headache and rheumatic pains; well, because this attack of flu when he must have been about eight made it necessary for him to be isolated in his nursery for weeks on end, his mother had given him his first display case of butterflies to pass the time. His butterfly cases still hung in his bedroom, where of course I hadn't been; they contained such specimens as the Red Pierrot, the Great Eggfly, the Postman, the Owl Butterfly and the Orange Emigrant, and to this day he liked looking at them before he went to sleep. I said I'd very much like to go to the butterfly house with him, for I had noticed that every time I met Josef Horvath I liked him better; his awkwardness, which had irritated me at first, was beginning to touch and even amuse me, and when, encouraged by my consent to this idea, he suggested a walk to Nussdorf to visit the Heuriger there, one of those inns selling new wine, I said we'd see.

As I came out of Schulerstrasse into the Stephansplatz, making for the telephone kiosk from which I planned to call John, I thought of young Rosa Havelka and her courage in running away from the convent by night and setting off into an entirely unknown future, and the fearless way in which she had entrusted herself to a man who was a perfect stranger. I compared those qualities with the faint-heartedness that left me stuck in an unsatisfactory relationship with a married man who had three school-age children, and I turned away from the telephone kiosk I had been about to enter, making the elderly man waiting behind me step backwards in surprise, passed the horse-drawn cabs standing beside the cathedral, and went through the huge entrance and into the building.

As soon as my eyes were used to the dim light I looked round, rather bored because I'd never been particularly interested in churches, noting the tall columns, the vault, the altarpiece showing a saint being stoned to death, and the statues standing in the niches. A black-bearded Christ hung on a wooden cross in a chapel, and a little moon-faced nun in a brown and white habit, standing beside me with a rosary in her hand and reciting a prayer under her breath, stopped praying and told me the beard was real hair, it was trimmed every year on Good Friday and always grew back again, and then she asked if I had seen the window-gazer yet, no visitor to the cathedral ought to miss the window-gazer, and when I replied to her question in the negative she took my hand and led me to the pulpit, carved in filigree-like stone, with stone lizards and toads crawling along its balustrades. She walked round the pulpit with me and pointed to a sculpture at its foot, showing a long-haired man looking out of a window, wearing a cap and holding a pair of compasses, and she said this figure was known as the window-gazer and was a self-portrait of the man who carved the pulpit, Anton Pilgram, he had come from Brünn to Vienna to be the architect of the cathedral and was immediately persecuted by the local stonemasons' fraternity with typical Viennese xeno-phobia, which incidentally and fortunately did him no harm. There was a story to be told about almost every statue in the cathedral, she added, leading me on to a statue of the Virgin standing at one corner of the main nave with her child in her arms. This was the Madonna of the Servants, said the little nun, impelling me closer to the statue, and while I looked at the friendly faces of mother and child I had a feeling, as distinct as it was ridiculous, that I had stood before this statue before. The Madonna used to stand in the domestic chapel of a rich countess who accused her maid one day of stealing a pearl necklace, said my companion, and when the girl, who was innocent, prayed to the statue for help, the necklace turned up in a glove her mistress had carelessly removed, where-upon the countess was sorry she had accused the girl wrongly, and donated the statue to the cathedral. I looked at the face of the Madonna of the Servants with its delicate smile again, and it seemed as if she was smiling not at her baby but at me.

When I got back to Aunt Pia's apartment she asked me to fetch the steps from the lumber room, rather than calling in the caretaker's husband who usually did such jobs for her but, as she had already mentioned, demanded a shocking price for them, and change the bulb of the ceiling lamp in the hall, the bulb was too strong and it was not a good idea to waste energy like that. So I fetched the steps, climbed up them and set about unscrewing the round bulb from its holder, but suddenly I seemed to see the tired, pale face of young Rosa Tichy doing something to an ochre velvet curtain, and I felt dizzy and almost fell off the steps to the star-patterned parquet hall floor. Aunt Pia, who was standing at the foot of the steps and saw me swaying, said that my weak state didn't surprise her in the least, considering the way I kept refusing to eat the nourishing soup she made specially for me.

That evening I went to my room early, picked up the blue notebook, lay down on the bed with the scarlet crochet cover, and re-entered Rosa's life. Aunt Pia knocked at the door when Rosa had just met the apprentice waiter on the little island in the Danube, and said the gentleman with the lovely deep voice was on the phone, but I asked her to tell him I wasn't in.

Four

The journey to Vienna is still vague in my memory, a succession of arduous and exhausting days. The rack wagon was unsprung, and my sprained ankle hurt at every jolt. Near Budweis we said goodbye to Milan's brother-in-law, changed to a new cart which with several others was accompanying the consignment of timber, and then later to one of the great rafts into which the tree trunks, after floating separately down the upper Vltava and passing several dams, were lashed by the woodcutters and raftsmen with whom Milan was working, subsequently to be drawn downstream along the Mühl and then the Danube by horses negotiating the narrow towpaths on the river bank. Between Klosterneuburg and Vienna the rafts were moored to the banks while preparations were made to take the timber overland to a large sawmill nearby, a job with which Milan was going to help before seeking out his brother, who worked at a brick kiln in the south of Vienna. I myself was anxious to get to the city and find a position as quickly as possible, so in spite of the objections put forward by Milan, who said I ought not to set off into such a large metropolis unprotected, quite apart from the fact that my hasty departure deprived him of the chance to convince me of the merits of the Young Czech cause, I took my case, wished him good luck, and set off for Vienna on foot, although the swelling on my right ankle hadn't entirely gone yet.

I walked along beside the Danube, and when I felt tired I

crossed a narrow wooden bridge leading to a bare little island not far from the bank to have a brief rest there before continuing on my way. I put my case down on the coarse sand by the river bank, sat on it, and watched the dark grey waters of the river, with the freighters slowly passing in the evening twilight. After a while I noticed a boy of my own age standing some ten metres away from me, wearing a white shirt and with a long white apron over his trousers, throwing stones into the water in so low an arc that they sometimes bounced off the surface five or six times before sinking. When he saw me watching him he came closer and asked what I was doing here all alone, with my case and my bandaged ankle. I told him I came from Prague and was on my way to Vienna to look for work as a housemaid, and then I asked whether it was much further to the city, because I was exhausted and hungry, my ankle hurt, and moreover it was getting dark. The lad looked at me for a while and then said that if I liked I could spend the night at the nearby inn where he was employed as a piccolo, and go to Vienna with him in the morning, his employer sent him there once a week to make purchases in the various Viennese markets, and he could use the opportunity to take me to the domestic service employment agency, because looking at me he had a feeling I scarcely knew such a thing existed, let alone where it was. I said he was right, I knew nothing about any such employment agency, and would he be kind enough to tell me what a piccolo was? A piccolo, he said, well, a piccolo was an apprentice waiter, someone ordered about by the innkeeper and his family, not to mention the other waiters and the guests, blamed if not actually beaten for the slightest misdemeanour, and made to perform the most menial tasks. The humiliating treatment that he had to put up with uncomplainingly, he said, sometimes made him feel so bad he lost all pleasure in life and toyed with the idea of putting an end to his existence, in fact he would admit that when he was pursuing his favourite occupation, playing ducks and drakes with flat pebbles and skilfully making them jump several times on the surface of the Danube at the spot where we happened to be at present, he had often had to fight an impulse to wade out into the river until he could no longer feel any ground under his feet, and as he was a non-swimmer he would then perish in the water. This revelation alarmed me, and I asked how he could even think of doing anything so sacrilegious, he mustn't commit such a sin, he should be proud of the way he earned his bread, a servant's existence was a life pleasing to God, the service of man was the service of God, hadn't his parents and parish priest told him that, didn't he know that every one of his helpful actions would be rewarded a thousandfold in the next life? The apprentice waiter looked at me in surprise and said he wondered first who had told me such nonsense, a servant's existence was a wretched one and the service of man was sheer slavery, and second why I was looking for a position as a housemaid when I was dressed so finely. So saying he let his eyes wander from the bow at the neck of my blouse over my dark blue jacket and pleated skirt to the tips of my black patent-leather shoes. I stood up and said there was no need for him to bother about that, outward appearances were often decep-tive, but anyway I'd be happy to accept his offer, perhaps he'd be kind enough to carry my case to the inn where he worked, it wasn't heavy, and after all the stress and strain of the last few days I was already looking forward to spending the night in a soft bed. Here the piccolo looked rather embarrassed and said it wasn't quite as simple as that, of course I couldn't expect to get a bed with clean sheets for nothing, even he didn't sleep in a bed like that but rather, like many Viennese waiters and above all waiters' apprentices, in what they called a bunk bench or flea chest, a piece of furniture that was closed up in the daytime so that guests could sit on it. He could offer me one of these benches to sleep on, since the other piccolo, who usually spent the night in the bunk next to his, had vanished without trace three days ago, which to be honest didn't surprise him considering the treatment the poor boy got at the inn. The bunk was certainly far from comfortable, and probably not long enough for someone of my height, but if I drew my knees up I'd fit into it all right. In any case, a young girl like me couldn't possibly spend the night out of doors, we were on the outskirts of the capital of the empire, and as everyone knew, such outlying areas were full of shady customers, the suburbs of great cities were dangerous places, that was general knowledge. The piccolo took my case and told me to follow him, and we crossed the bridge and then went along a road lined with cottages and walnut trees until we came to an inn with a sign saying 'The Bunch of Grapes' over its door, which was painted dark green. My companion asked me to wait outside the door, he would have to ask the landlady's permission first, the landlady was a softer touch than the landlord, he didn't think she would have any objection to my spending the night in the bunk bench.

So it was that I spent my first night in Vienna, or on the outskirts of Vienna, in a wooden box like a coffin where I couldn't get a wink of sleep all night, since the bunk was not only too short for me but full of fleas as well. I was also tormented by hunger, since the boiled rice that the fat landlady with the dirty white pleated apron, double chin and countless little red veins on her cheeks had put in front of me, muttering something about work-shy little tramps bent on nothing but turning a young fellow's head, was almost cold, and also covered with a layer of semi-translucent greenish mould, so I thanked her but refused it, saying I'd eaten already, whereupon the woman said beggars couldn't be choosers, this was what you got for your charity, ingratitude was the only return for a person's kindness of heart. I was freezing too, since the only cover I had was one of the red and white checked tablecloths that were spread on the tables in the inn. When it began to get light outside, beyond the drawn curtains which were also of red and white check, my eyes finally closed, but then the piccolo jumped up from his own bunk, shook me, and said I must get up, it was time to leave. After we had drunk leftover fig coffee from badly washed, cracked white porcelain bowls, the piccolo took a large wicker basket, and we set out. We walked along past the walnut trees, and the waiter's apprentice told me this village was called Nussdorf after the walnut trees, and the Viennese liked to come out to it because of its many inns and the nearby vineyards. When an almost empty tram drawn by horses and gliding along rails came round the corner and went on in the same direction as ourselves I asked why we didn't get in, since the tram seemed to be going to the city. This made the piccolo smile, and he said the likes of him couldn't afford the tram, you could buy a whole kilo of bread for the price of a ticket, and he had to work for several hours to earn that much.

After a while we arrived in a more built-up area where the streets were wider and more crowded, the buildings taller and finer. We went on following the tramlines until we came to a boulevard lined with handsome buildings and maple and lime trees, with many two- or four-wheeled horse-drawn carriages driving down it. The piccolo said this was the Ringstrasse, where the Emperor was having a whole series of palatial buildings erected – theatres, museums, concert halls, hotels, residences for the rich – while the city was full of folk who had nothing but a straw mattress or a plank bed on which to sleep for a few hours, full of the homeless who didn't know where to lay their heads, but camped out in the tunnels of the underground canal and sewer system, under the bridges and in the boats and boathouses along the Danube, because they didn't even have the money to spend the night in one of the cheap hostels. It was true that he often railed against fate for bringing him into the world so poor, but compared to these wretches he was well off, on his wages he could afford an expedition to the Wurstelprater once a month to ride on the grotto railway or the boat carousel, see Rosita the Giantess, Romanov the Human Torso, Konrad the Strong Man and Miss Lily the Lion-tamer, and visit Präuscher's Panopticum or the waxworks show. I assumed that this place mentioned by my new friend must be some large pleasure garden, but before I could find out more about it he pointed to huge excavations on our right and said this was where the two court museums were going to be built, one a picture gallery and the other for the wonders of nature. He shook his head. Incredible, he added, they'd put up buildings to house pictures and the wonders of nature but not people, sometimes he wondered if the Emperor really was bent on the welfare of his subjects all the time, as was generally claimed. We turned off the Ringstrasse and went down several narrower streets and alleys, until the piccolo stopped outside a large white building and said the domestic service employment agency was on the ground floor, to the right. Then he paused, and asked if I had enough money to pay the agency fee if I was offered a suitable position. I replied that all I had in the world was five gulden, and he laughed and said I'd better make sure I found work soon, then, because I wouldn't live very long on that. But now he'd have to hurry, the best bargains in the produce market on the Tiefer Graben were soon snapped up. I gave the waiter's apprentice my hand, but before I could thank him for his help he had turned his back and was marching away with his big basket.

I pushed down the handle of the tall, heavy front door and leaned against it until it opened. All was quiet on the ground floor, although about fifty women and girls, most of them poorly dressed and unhealthy-looking, were sitting or standing crowded close together in the corridors, waiting for their turn. Some of them leaned against the wall with their eyes closed, others were standing in the middle of the corridor looking fixedly into space, others again sat on the stone floor, their legs drawn up and their foreheads on their knees. I looked from one to another, and it struck me that I wasn't the youngest there, that some of the girls seeking employment looked no older than twelve or thirteen. I joined the back of the queue.

When the thin, bald man with the black button eyes, moustache and slightly grubby white handkerchief in the pocket of his pale grey waistcoat, before whose desk I finally stood with my case in my hand, had taken my particulars and asked what I wanted, and when I had replied that since circumstances had allowed me an extensive education I thought I would be not unsuitable for a post as a governess, he smiled slightly and asked whatever made me think that, a governess's post was one of the greatest responsibility, a governess was in charge of her pupils' sound intellectual development, and I must forgive him, but I was far too young and inexperienced for such work. And when I said I had cookery skills as well, and perhaps they might come in useful, he replied that just now there were no vacancies for cooks or even assistant cooks, positions for assistant cooks and cooks were rare and much in demand, and anyway, looking at me standing there, he couldn't think I would be capable of providing meals for a bourgeois Viennese family of several persons, perhaps many persons, day in, day out to their satisfaction. When I said nothing, feeling despondent, he placed his ringed hands on the top of the desk, fingers splayed, leaned forward and told me not to look like that, he had just the thing for me, a place as parlourmaid in the family of Regional Postal Manager Lindner, who lived in the Inner City, to be more precise in the Neuer Markt. The Lindner family employed only Bohemian servants on principle, so that was lucky, and if I liked I could go there to apply at once, that was to say after payment of the ridiculously low registration fee of just two gulden.

The man in the employment agency told me the way to the Neuer Markt, and I made the journey confidently and with a spring in my step, trusting that with the aid of God and Our Lady I would find myself among good folk whom I would serve to the best of my ability. The sun was shining, the streets were full of elegant carriages and well-dressed people, the façades of the buildings and the many churches were adorned with statues, golden balls, reliefs and coloured frescoes. When I had crossed the Ringstrasse I passed a very fine building that, judging from the description of the man in the agency, must be the Court Opera House, and then a church with a niche in front of it containing an impressive statue of a monk holding a cross aloft, and finally I reached the rectangular square of the Neuer Markt, which was surrounded by handsome buildings and had a large round fountain in the middle of it. There were dark statues of men on the little wall around it, and a statue of a woman with four little angels at her feet stood at the centre. I found the number of the building where I had been told to go, entered the well-maintained house, which had a pale grey façade, went up the broad stone stairway with its shallow steps and wrought-iron banisters, and wielded the knocker shaped like a lion's head on a tall double door on the third floor, which had a plate bearing the inscription 'Regional Postal Manager Roman Lindner' fixed to it.

The pretty plump lady who opened the door to me, with her nut-brown hair pinned up in a coronet and wearing a high-necked burgundy dress, struck her hands together when I gave her the employment agent's brief note. A first job, she cried, how could Prohaska dream of sending her someone who had never worked in a household before, a pigtailed adolescent, half a child still, as anyone could see, an anaemic creature who couldn't be expected to carry the heavy carpets left to her by her aunt Agneta from Bukovina down to the yard to be beaten and back upstairs again. She skimmed the letter. Still, a Bohemian girl, she added, in rather milder tones, at least a Bohemian girl wouldn't have the barefaced cheek to make the outrageous wage demands one got accustomed to in Austrian domestic servants. She lowered the letter and looked at me. Apart from my obvious delicacy my outward appearance was all right, she murmured, and considering the frightful shortage of trained staff, what was a person to do, she wondered, what would become of the monarchy if things went on like this. After another short pause for thought, the lady asked me into the apartment, and I carried my case over the threshold into a small, dark entrance hall. Then the mistress of the house, for this must be she, preceded me into the kitchen, sat down at the big square table, its wooden surface smooth and pale with much scouring, and told me to sit down too. She opened the drawer of the table and took out a thin leaflet. This, she explained, was an excerpt from the Viennese Rules for Domestic Staff of 1 May 1810, the contents of which she would briefly outline for me insofar as they concerned the conditions of service into which I was about to enter. She paused, and glanced at the pages. First, she said, I was bound to strict compliance with everything my employers, in the present case her husband the Regional Postal Manager and herself, thought right for the maintenance of order in their home. I was obliged to do without protest everything that could be understood to be part of the performance of my duties according to the nature of my service, and I must at all times be at the disposition of my employers, that is her husband the Regional Postal Manager and herself. If I did not perform the tasks I was given properly, or actually refused to do them, my employers, being her husband the Regional Postal Manager and herself, had the right to administer discipline which might range from a simple warning to refusal of leave to go out or to actual corporal punishment, not exceeding the bounds of what was right and proper. On Sundays and feast days I was entitled to go to church, and over and beyond that I was in principle allowed to go out for several hours every other Sunday. In return for my services I would get board and lodging and an appropriate monthly wage. Regional Postal Manager Lindner's wife put the pamphlet back in the drawer, stood up and looked at me. My monthly wage would be six gulden, she said, more than enough for a girl of my age. What with the cramped living conditions of Vienna in general and the Inner City in particular, of course she couldn't give me a room of my own, but she would part, although reluctantly, with the valuable divan covered with finely embroidered tapestry depicting an impassable landscape scene in the Carpathians which had been standing in the ironing room, and I was to push it into the corner of the light and spacious entrance hall opposite the kitchen door, an ideal and comfortable place for me to sleep. Well, I could begin on my duties at once, and first I was to clean the beautiful star-patterned parquet floor in the sitting room, a task never satisfactorily performed by my predecessor, a person from the Erzgebirge who had turned out only too soon to be an impudent hussy, and whom she had been obliged to dismiss after several unpleasant incidents. With these words the Regional Postal Manager's wife briefly left the room and came back with a shabby dress and a rather yellowed white apron. Before I started work, she said, she was officially handing over my housemaid's uniform, a black dress of the best Styrian cloth, good as new, and the white apron of starched, bleached, home-woven Galician linen that went with it, both of which I must of course conscientiously care for myself and replace if they were damaged. I could change in the bathroom and push the case with my belongings under the divan later, luckily a young person didn't need much room. But first I had better go back to Herr Prohaska, pay the agency fee and get my copy of the servant's book.

At the employment agency Herr Prohaska came towards me with outstretched arms, shook hands with me, and said he was glad I had found work so quickly, and he was sure I would understand that because of the rapidity with which my affairs had been settled the agency fee would be four gulden instead of the usual three. When I whispered, in embarrassment, that unfortunately all the money I had in the world was no more than three gulden twenty-four kreuzers, the agent's tone changed, and he said brusquely that it was always the same, young women today didn't know how to be thrifty, might he ask me what he was supposed to live on, the profession of employment agent was one of the most precarious imaginable, since it was constantly subject to the fluctuations of the economy. However, he would be generous enough to accept the three gulden twenty-four kreuzers, but he'd expect me to make up the outstanding sum immediately I received my first monthly wages. When I had handed him the contents of my purse, he took a book out of a drawer in his desk and said this was the so-called servant's book, which all domestic servants received on taking up their first position and in which all the references provided by their employers testifying, to the best of the employers' belief, to their industry, loyalty and morals, would be subsequently entered and must be shown to any new employer. I took the book, said goodbye, and left Herr Prohaska and the employment agency.

Half an hour later I was wearing the black dress, which was too big for me, kneeling on the parquet floor of the huge living room and scrubbing it with hot soapy water to which, as instructed by the Regional Postal Manager's wife, I had added a little ammonia. I wasn't used to such work, and even rolling up the thick carpets and pulling out several pieces of furniture had exhausted me, but Frau Lindner said that would soon wear off, the exercise would make me stronger. I was not familiar with housekeeping, except for a certain knowledge of cookery acquired from helping my mother, but luckily I could always consult the *Housewives' Golden Treasury*, which was in my cardboard case. Once the floor was dry my employer told me to rub it down with steel wool to make it sparkling clean. The ammonia had risen uncomfortably to my nose, and now I kept coughing the whole time, since this process raised a great deal of dust which I couldn't help breathing in, and sharp fragments of steel wool penetrated the thin gloves the Regional Postal Manager's wife had given me and cut my skin. Finally, I applied the floor polish made of yellow wax and turpentine which I had previously softened in a container of hot water, and when the polish was dry I brushed the floor until it had a regular gloss all over. My hands were hurting, my eyes were streaming and my back ached, but when I finally rose and thought I would go to the kitchen to drink a glass of water my employer said I might put myself to the trouble of working a little faster, the parquet floors of the dining room and her husband's study were waiting to be waxed and polished as well.

It was about eleven in the evening of that first day working as a humble housemaid for Regional Postal Manager Lindner's family, and after a supper consisting of a plate of spinach and two boiled potatoes, when I sank on the narrow, sagging divan I had moved from the ironing room into the hall. I could feel its defective springs in my back. However, the excitement I felt at the beginning of my new life in Vienna wouldn't allow me to drop off to sleep at once. I certainly hadn't imagined that my work would be quite such a strain, nor did Frau Lindner entirely match the image of a kindly, understanding employer I had secretly pictured to myself, but I thought of my dear mother and the guidelines to proper conduct that she had impressed upon me, and decided to quell the slight disappointment I felt and go on doing my best. It was worth putting up with a few small inconveniences for the privilege of being in Vienna, indeed the very centre of Vienna, that brilliant capital city. With these and similar reflections passing through my mind, I finally fell into an uneasy slumber.

I hardly seemed to have slept for ten minutes when I was aware that someone was unlocking the front door of the apartment. Opening my eyes, I saw the vague outlines of a figure in the doorway. The figure came into the hall, bumping into my divan in the dark, and to judge by the voice that now began cursing and swearing it must be a man. I immediately remembered the nightmare in the attic, and reached in alarm for the little bag of salt hanging round my neck, but when the figure approached my bed, leaned over me, and blew its gin-sodden breath into my face, I calmed my fears, for this could only be the Regional Postal Manager himself, having allowed himself a glass or two in a nearby inn in the company of a few colleagues after a gruelling day's work at the imperial-and-royal Main Post Office. In relief, I turned to face the wall, and heard the figure open another door and move off, muttering to itself.

I was woken at five by the sound of the alarm clock set by the Regional Postal Manager's wife, which was standing on the window sill. I tumbled out of bed, washed in the bathroom, put on the black dress and the white apron, ate the breakfast laid out for me by Frau Lindner the evening before – a roll and a cup of weak coffee – and went to the kitchen balcony, where the family's shoes were ranged in a long row, waiting to be cleaned in accordance with the mistress of the house's instructions. First I rubbed down the fabric shoes with a rag dipped in ethyl alcohol, then I wiped them over with a dry cloth and conscientiously treated them with finely powered pumice. Then I moved on to the many pairs of black and brown leather shoes which I had first to brush with a soft brush, next applying egg white and finally rubbing them over with a mixture of six dessertspoons of skimmed milk and two dessertspoons of turpentine. Last of all I removed the dirt and dust from several pairs of patent-leather shoes with a woollen cloth, carefully rubbed a piece of hard wax over the cracked places, washed the shoes with a little milk, let them dry, then wiped down the patent leather with the cut surface of an onion and polished it with a soft cloth. My glance happened to fall on my own black patent-leather shoes, and as they had clearly suffered from the arduous journey to Vienna by water and land I took them off and gave them the same treatment. As I was just rubbing the patent leather with the cut side of the onion the Regional Postal Manager's wife stepped out on the balcony in a long silk nightdress, with her hair down, and as soon as she saw what I was doing she asked crossly what I thought I was up to, looking after my own wardrobe during working hours, after all I had plenty of free time at my disposal, and of course there could be no question of my squandering food belonging to my employers for this purpose, let alone such basic foodstuffs as milk and onions, everyone knew that times were hard and the professional position of officially appointed Regional Postal Managers had never been as precarious as it was just now. And as for the expensive education of her talented son Georg, intended for the military profession and the offspring of her over-hasty and therefore unhappy first marriage to a second cousin from Chernowitz, the capital of Bukovina, I had no idea what it cost. Then Frau Lindner bent over the shoes, carefully examined them pair by pair, and said I had carried out my task in a far from satisfactory way, but in view of my youth and inexperience she would make allowances. Now I was to set out at once for the market in the Judenplatz and collect the sack of potatoes, the two turkeys and the ham she had ordered a couple of days ago from the nice farmer's wife from the Waldviertel countryside, second stall on the left as you entered the square from Jordangasse.

The sack of potatoes weighed about twenty kilos, and the bag with the turkeys and the ham another ten, and I found I had to put them both down on the pavement every few metres. The Viennese pedestrians smiled at me in a friendly way, particularly the men, but no one offered to help me. By the time I was approaching the building where the Regional Postal Manager lived I was near tears. Utterly exhausted, I put the sack and the bag down on the pavement once again, and my glance fell on the façade of the church with the statue of the monk outside it. Then a little old woman dressed in black, leaning on a stick and with a black scarf round her head, came towards me, shook her head and asked who had given a delicate little thing like me such a load to carry, how cruel people were, such a frail creature wasn't made to carry so heavy a burden, and she would ask the life-sized statue of the Virgin of Lourdes standing in a grotto on the high altar in the Capuchin church to make my life easier. I pricked up my ears at this, and asked the old woman if it was true that there was a Madonna of Lourdes in the church, I was new to Vienna and for certain reasons connected with my late mother was interested in everything to do with the miracle-working Madonna who had appeared to the child Bernadette. Of course, cried the old woman, of course it was true, not only were a large number of members of the royal house set over us by God's grace and ruling with his aid buried in the crypt of the Capuchin church I saw before me, but thanks to Father Macarius it had very quickly become a centre of the Lourdes cult, why, there had even been a pilgrimage from

Vienna to the south of France recently. On the spur of the moment I asked the old woman to keep an eye on my sack of potatoes and my bag for a moment, saying I would be back directly. I went through the open doorway of the church and up the nave to the high altar, fell on my knees before the statue and begged her to give me a humble and obedient disposition so that I could carry out my duties as a servant satisfactorily and without complaining. I looked up at the statue, and it seemed as if she was smiling at me and inclining her head, just as the Madonna had smiled and nodded to the child Bernadette.

Over the next few weeks I worked daily from five-thirty in the morning until eleven at night. I turned out the rooms, washed and ironed the laundry, did the easier sewing and mending, carried wood and coal up from the cellar and did the shopping. And when I lay down on the shabby divan in the evening exhausted, and covered myself with the felted, scratchy, grey-brown blanket given me by Frau Lindner, who adjured me to take good care of it and not neglect my personal hygiene, as many Bohemian girls were unfortunately inclined to do, a product made from the unusually fine wool of Bukovina sheep deserved respect – when I was on the divan and had finally fallen asleep I was sure to be woken every night by the noise of the Regional Postal Manager opening the front door of the apartment just after Viennese closing time, usually not entirely steady on his legs. He would look down at me, swearing quietly, or even sit down for a moment on the edge of my bed and mutter something incomprehensible before continuing on his arduous way to the matrimonial bedroom. However, I congratulated myself on the speed with which I had found a position in a city swarming with the unemployed. And on Sunday morning when, dressed in my boarding-school uniform, I had devoutly attended the Capuchin church, where Father Macarius conducted divine service as impressively as Father Bohumil did in Marienbad, when I had stood before the priest with my eyes closed and my mouth open to receive the body and blood of Our Lord, I never forgot to offer up a little prayer to the life-sized statue of the Madonna of Lourdes before leaving the church, thanking her briefly for allowing me to be numbered among those inhabitants of Vienna who were permitted to devote their lives to honest labour, and asking her to give me inexhaustible strength to perform it.

I was happiest when I was allowed to clean the piano. The Lindner family had a black grand piano made by the Leipzig firm of Blüthner standing in the middle of the sitting room, on which my employer accompanied herself every afternoon as she performed two songs, always in the same order: first 'The Trout' and then 'The Linden Tree'. Since the music album containing these songs always stood open at the same place on the folding music stand, I knew they were composed by Schubert. I loved both songs, and sometimes sang them to myself in my head, for the Regional Postal Manager's wife liked her domestic staff to be silent. She had told me to rub the piano keys with a little diluted spirit every time she finished playing, to keep them from turning yellow too quickly. Every Tuesday I zealously cleaned the keys with powdered bone and cheap olive oil, and now and then I bleached them with a mixture of two parts of fresh chloride of lime to ten parts of water, strained through a clean cloth. I rubbed any troublesome fly specks off the keys and the black lacquer with half a juicy onion, then washed them with lukewarm water, and polished the piano until it shone, using a few drops of lavender oil. Once, when I was touching the keys, oblivious to all else, my hands began to play a Chopin nocturne as if of their own accord, and Frau Lindner burst into the room wanting to know whether I was out of my mind, had I entirely forgotten my station in life? When I guiltily asked her to forgive me, but the sight of the grand piano had suddenly transported me back to a very happy era in my life, a time when I was sometimes allowed to play a mahogany pianino that stood in a bay window looking out on a beautiful park, she said sternly not only did I show more and more negligence in going about my duties, not only was I clearly becoming increasingly disinclined to concentrate and keep my mind on my work, I was now beginning to tell lies into the bargain. She had already been wondering whether she had done right to take me into her home, and if I didn't soon get a grip on myself she wouldn't hesitate to replace me with another Bohemian girl, there were as many young, willing Bohemian girls in Vienna just longing to work in a well-ordered household like hers as there are fish in the sea. Thus reprimanded, I said quietly and in a faltering tone that I was sorry, but as I was working on average seventeen hours a day, and since I was woken every night by the noise Herr Lindner made when he came through the hall and usually couldn't drop off to sleep again at once, I probably wasn't having quite a good enough night's rest. At this Frau Lindner asked what on earth I was getting at, after all I hadn't taken service with her to spend my time asleep, half-grown girls like me didn't need much sleep, in fact she had recently read in the *Viennese Householders' Journal*, to which she and her husband had subscribed for years, that too much sleep was decidedly injurious to the youthful organism. And she hoped I wasn't suggesting that her husband the Regional Postal Manager, holder of an official appointment in the imperial-and-royal Post Office and valued by one and all in and around the Neuer Markt, was the kind of man who frequented inns, taverns and coffee houses and didn't know when it was time to go home. I was to go to the bathroom where she had laid out a bodice of genuine Brussels lace immediately, wash it carefully in unboiled lukewarm milk, rinse it in sugar water and iron it while still damp on a soft surface with a moderately hot iron.

In the course of time the brief pauses made by Regional Postal Manager Lindner beside my divan in the hall became longer pauses, and his indistinct muttering became clearer. He would lower himself laboriously to the foot of my bed, breathing gin-laden fumes in the direction of its head and muttering complaints, to the effect that he saw more clearly every day what

an inexcusable mistake he had made, at his mature age, in
marrying a woman twenty years younger than himself, and one
who craved pleasure at that, always wanting to go to the theatre in
Vienna to see the latest operettas, or Raimund's *The Spendthrift*
and *The Peasant as Millionaire* with that fop Alexander Girardi in
the leading role, all the women in Vienna seemed mad about that
dandy even though he was involved in one scandal after another.
And in addition his wife was a beautiful woman who naturally
wanted to emphasize her looks with appropriate clothing, expensive corsets, hats, furs, lace, frills and furbelows and God knows
what else, always pestering him to buy her pearl earrings, garnet
brooches and amber necklaces, and how was he, an ordinary civil
servant in the imperial-and-royal Post Office, to pay for all that,
she'd end up sending him off to the pawnbroker's in Dorotheergasse to pledge his valuable family heirlooms, oh yes, his wife was
quite capable of such a thing. He should have listened to his
mother, a war widow with whom he'd lived harmoniously for
decades in an apartment in the Fleischmarkt, right next to the
imperial-and-royal Post Office where he worked, and who, when
he introduced her to his future wife, had taken him aside and
warned him, Roman, she had said, and he remembered every
single word, Roman, women from Bukovina, women from the
steppes of Bessarabia, witches of the steppes as you might say,
were sly as the devil and had been known to ruin good-natured
men like him in short order, he'd better come to his senses before
it was too late and not be stupid enough to marry a woman who
already had a child; a child meant another mouth the feed, a wife
and child meant two more mouths to feed, two mouths that would
gobble up his salary as a Regional Postal Manager in no time at all,
just let him wait and see, and then he'd remember what his mother
said. I wondered whether my employer was actually aware of my
presence during these nocturnal ruminations. Anyway, I pretended
to be asleep, and he took no further notice of me.

One Sunday Frau Lindner told me early in the morning that I

must do without my time off that day, since she had invited guests to dinner, influential civil servants of the Austro-Hungarian monarchy who might perhaps help her husband get promoted to Inspector in the imperial-and-royal Post Office, a promotion he had long deserved, these guests being Sectional Manager Dr Hübl and his wife, Principal Manager von Kaunitz, Administrative Director Hohenberg-Unschlitt, and Deputy Dean Professor Blittersdorf-Magenschab and his fiancée. She didn't suppose I had any objection, it looked to her as if I didn't know what to do with my generous allotment of free time as it was. In any case, at around eleven in the morning I was to lay the Biedermeier table in the dining room with the openwork embroidered tablecloth, set it for eight persons and serve at table; the cook who came in daily knew all about it and would tell me what to do, as usual on such occasions there would be soup with vermouth, fish with white wine, a roast with side dishes and red wine, a sweet with champagne, dessert, coffee and finally liqueurs. Still half asleep, I went into the kitchen and tried to remember everything the daily cook told me: I was to set a small dessert plate for rolls on the left of the flat fish plate, a knife with the blade facing inwards on the right, fish knife beside it, spoon on the outside of the setting. Rather indistinctly I heard her tell me to put the meat fork on the left of the place setting, with the fish fork outside it, and as if from a great distance I learned that the glass for the vermouth went on the outside, the white wine glass beside it, just above the tip of the fish knife, then the glasses for red wine, sparkling wine and water, in that order. I was to serve the food from the right, remove used plates from the left, and fill glasses from the right.

Lethargic with fatigue, I laid the table, and when the guests had sat down to eat and the Regional Postal Manager's wife gave me a sign, I went into the kitchen as if in a trance to fetch the big tureen of soup and liver dumplings. As I was coming back into the dining room, sleep overwhelmed me for a split second and I let the tureen drop, pouring some of the hot soup over my feet, and I woke up with a scream. The Regional Postal Manager's wife jumped up and pushed me into the bathroom, hissing that this was too much, letting her and her husband down like that, we'd talk about it later, but now she must go back to her guests. So saying she closed the door, and I stood there, looking down at my insteps, where the skin was swelling and turning red, and only now beginning to hurt. I took off my shoes and ran cold water over my feet until the pain had lessened, and then went to the kitchen, painted my insteps with salad oil, took the container of iodized Ischl cooking salt from the hands of the astonished cook, who was just seasoning the Hungarian carp with it, and sprinkled plenty of salt on my scalded feet.

When the guests had left, my employer took me to task, saying she hoped I was aware that I might have severely damaged her husband's career, she'd had to summon up all her presence of mind and charm to mollify Professor Blittersdorf-Magenschab's fiancée in particular, a frightful, disagreeable woman who none-theless had great influence on the Dean, and to prevent her from leaving early. She warned me that she wouldn't tolerate another such lapse on my part.

For the next few nights my need for sleep remained unsatisfied, since the Regional Postal Manager continued to sit at the end of my bed complaining at length and in slurred tones about his young wife and her desire for the pleasures of life. The accident that brought my service with the Lindner family to a sudden end happened on a Thursday afternoon. I was about to take down the ochre velvet sitting-room curtains, for my employer had told me to rub them with warm, fine, dry bran and then stretch them over steam, reverse side down, so that the vapour would raise the little velvet fibres, thus refreshing the fabric. So I fetched a ladder from the lumber room, leaned it up against one of the tall windows and climbed it. When I had opened the first of the ring-shaped clips from which the velvet curtains hung on their poles, so that I could take the heavy lengths of fabric down, weariness overcame me

174

again, everything went dark before my eyes and I fell from the ladder to the star-patterned parquet floor that I had brushed and polished so carefully. As I landed I finally lost consciousness.

Some time later, how long I didn't know, I heard an angry voice, first at a distance and then closer to me. I was dazed, my head hurt, and I felt sick. When I had half opened my eyes to look around me, with difficulty, I realized that I was lying on my divan with Frau Lindner and the daily cook beside me, and the angry voice was my mistress's. Dazed as I was, I still understood the gist of what she was saying, to the effect that this was too much and I was dismissed without notice. Then I sank back into unconsciousness.

I returned to my senses in a hospital ward where every bed was occupied. I asked the nurse leaning over me where I was and what had happened, and she told me not to worry, I was in the care of the medical and nursing staff of the imperial-and-royal General Hospital, known for their conscientiousness in and beyond Vienna, my employer had sent me here in a cab with a small cardboard case, my reference, my servant's book and my wages for the last month, I had suffered severe concussion after a fall and must have complete bed rest for several days.

Once my pain had ebbed, my pulse had picked up speed and I was breathing regularly again, I asked the nurse on duty where they had put my reference, and she took a sheet of paper from the drawer of the metal bedside locker and put it in my hand. The document said that I had been dismissed on the grounds of my unstable and refractory character and for incurable indolence.

When I heard how much a day in the imperial-and-royal General Hospital cost, I was alarmed, did a quick sum, and came to the dismal conclusion that even if I left the hospital at once, although I wasn't entirely better yet, so as to spare the expense of a day and a night, I would have only sixty-three kreuzers left. And even if I went straight to Herr Prohaska and was lucky enough to find a position again immediately, I would have to owe him the agency fee, quite apart from the fact that he might not be ready to allow me to pay late a second time. But in that case what was I to do? I had heard there were bed-women who would rent you a bed for the night, but with the sum at my disposal I couldn't contemplate going to one of them for more than a night or two, and I had to eat something as well. When the nurse on duty came over to my bed to take my pulse, I gave her a radiant smile and said I had enjoyed a wonderful sleep, I was feeling very well now, entirely cured, and I didn't suppose anyone would mind my leaving the hospital at once. The nurse said, rather dubiously, that so far as she knew I wasn't expected to be discharged until next day, whereupon I made haste to tell her that on his early rounds the assistant doctor had expressed his surprise at my remarkably good state of health, and had no objection in principle to my discharging myself at once.

So it was that I left first the building and then the grounds of the hospital in my boarding-school uniform, carrying the cardboard case which now also contained my reference, my servant's book and my last month's wages, with a white bandage round my head, and feeling rather weak I made my way to the employment agency. When I had been walking for about ten minutes I decided to make a small detour and visit the life-sized Madonna of Lourdes in the Capuchin church. I went up to her, put my case down, looked into her eyes and explained that in all probability this would be my last visit to her since, as she could see from my bandage, neither she nor the miniature likeness of her imported from Paris by the Capuchin vicar Father Method Jelinek had given me that minimum support which might be expected from a saint of her standing. So saying I opened my case, took out the little replica with its eyes turned to heaven, placed it at her feet, closed the case again, picked it up, turned and left the church.

As I was waiting for my turn at the employment agency I looked surreptitiously at one woman after another, and among the expressions reflecting hopelessness, disappointment and desperation I noticed the face of a young woman who was reading a journal, but looked up now and then to inspect her companions briefly: a face with dark down on the upper lip, black eyes and a low forehead, a face full of defiance and fighting spirit. The young woman noticed my own gaze, pointed to my bandage, smiled and said my employers didn't seem to have treated me very well, and I made haste to tell her it was no such thing, I had been working for employers who were correct, if slightly demanding and not easily satisfied. I'd fallen off a ladder, that was all, pure carelessness on my part. Well, said the girl, she hoped I didn't mind her asking, but in our job all kinds of things happened that really ought not to be allowed, and it was a shame that the one journal for those in our walk of life, the *Domestic Servant*, which she was sure I knew, advertised positions but never said a word about the iniquitous treatment to which almost all servants were exposed, our working conditions were impossible and we ought to organize ourselves, demand sick pay, old-age pensions and accident and invalidity insurance. She held up the journal, and a murmur rose from the women present, getting louder and louder, until you could make out words like trouble-maker, agitator, sedition-monger and wild idealist. An older, work-worn woman standing beside me asked sharply how she could say such disrespectful things, making unreasonable demands and calling for such radical changes, she must be aware that her own feminine nature abhorred reversals and upheavals of all kinds, preferring to maintain, to preserve, to support and make secure, did she want to overturn the order ordained by nature and pleasing to God, did she unthinkingly want to destroy it? That was right, cried another haggard job-seeker, who was carrying a thin baby, how dared she deny the existence of the mutual liking and respect which, with a few unfortunate exceptions, marked the relationship between employers and their domestic staff, it wasn't for the servant class and still less for the feminine sex to make demands, our employers would add further privileges of their own accord to those we already had when the right time came. To serve was to command, cried a third woman, who showed the signs of consumption and had two small, circular red spots on her pale cheeks, hadn't she understood that profound Christian truth, the first would be last, but we last would be first. Then she was shaken by an attack of coughing, and Herr Prohaska opened the door and summoned the young woman with the *Domestic Servant* weekly journal into his office.

When I was standing in front of his desk about half an hour later he said not a word about my bandage, but frowned and remarked that he was surprised to see me, I hadn't been very long in my first position with the estimable Lindner family, and please could he see my reference. When I had handed him the piece of paper, my eyes lowered, and he had taken it and skimmed the contents, he looked at me gravely and said that naturally getting such a bad reference at the end of my first job greatly decreased any prospect of my obtaining a second position with an equally respectable employer, indeed made it practically impossible. Since he had to think of the reputation of his business, which he had now been running for twenty-seven years to the benefit, he might venture to say, of a whole generation of domestic servants, he must suggest that I sought out another of the employment agencies in Vienna, there were plenty, even if they were less efficient than his. He would merely enter in my servant's book the reference undoubtedly given not without much thought by the Regional Postal Manager's wife, a Viennese citizen known for her integrity, just so that everything was in order and potential employers could get an unprejudiced idea of my character.

I left the white building, feeling depressed, and wandered aimlessly around Vienna with my cardboard case. Soon the lively bustle in the streets distracted me slightly from the cares weighing me down, my mood became more cheerful, and the confidence natural to me began to revive. There was no denying that the Madonna of Lourdes, of whose remarkable abilities my late mother was so sure, had failed me. But that didn't mean that in this great city with its many churches, where countless statues of saints stood and hundreds of pictures of them hung over the altars, there might not be some other saint to take pity on me and help me in my hour of need. So I decided to visit St Stephen's, the cathedral at the centre of the city, which I had passed quite often while running errands for the Regional Postal Manager's wife, for such a huge church must contain several of these intermediaries between God and man.

When I entered the interior of the cathedral through the gigantic gateway, adorned with many reliefs and statues, it took my eyes some time to become accustomed to the dim light. Then I went slowly through the side aisles, past the Chapels of St Catherine and St Barbara, past the high altar and the Chapel of St Eligius. A smiling Madonna with a crown on her head and a sceptre in her hand stood on a plinth set into the wall of the Chapel of St Eligius. The hunchbacked old verger who was just removing the stumps of candles told me she was called Keeper of the Gate of Heaven, brought to the cathedral from a nearby convent after giving clear evidence of her miraculous gifts, like three other figures of the Virgin whose active miracle-working was equally uncontested. He took the arm of my jacket and drew me on, over to a picture painted on wood in a costly frame, showing the Virgin with the baby Jesus in her arms. This was the greatest miracle-worker of all, he said, she came from Pötsch. If, as he assumed, I wanted a cure for my injured head, she was just the one. And the next, said the old man, propelling me on, the next was the Madonna of the Protective Cloak, a very nice saint indeed. He pointed to a charmingly curvaceous statue of the Madonna on a column, her cloak outspread to receive the faithful, and said she was the one her personally loved most, although the Madonna of the Servants had many admirers too, the statue of the Madonna of the Servants was very popular among the faithful. At the mention of this name I instantly pricked up my ears, and asked the old man where this statue was and what he knew about it. He hurried a few steps on and beckoned me over to the pulpit in the nave, near which a Madonna of cheerful appearance stood with an equally happy-looking Child, his right hand on the brooch fastening his mother's garment over her breast. This statue, said the verger, once belonged to Countess von Ramshorn, a rich Viennese noblewoman who one day accused her maidservant of stealing a pearl necklace. The maid had gone on her knees to the Madonna, begging her to prove her innocence. Sure enough, the necklace had soon been found in the possession of a groom who confessed to its theft, and in remorse for her unjustified suspicions the countess had made a present of the statue to the cathedral chapter. I thanked the hunchbacked verger very much for this information, and unhesitatingly let him sell me a long, white wax candle, which I lit and placed in one of the holders for votive candles at the saint's feet. I had found the ideal intercessor at last, a Madonna who specialized in the problems and sufferings of domestic maidservants. Suddenly I was not afraid of my uncertain future any more.

9

On my way to the Sigmund Freud Museum in Vienna 9 I passed a grey building in Alserstrasse with a plate on it bearing the inscription 'Provincial Court', and I realized that this was the building where Rosa Havelka had written her autobiography while she awaited execution. The more I learned about her the more I sympathized with that affectionate, obliging, honest and exploited creature. I turned into Berggasse, walked down the street to No. 19, went through the entrance and entered the well-tended stairway, with windows providing a view of the building's attractive internal courtyard, and then I opened the door with an iron grille inside it to the museum, formerly Sigmund Freud's consulting rooms, where he had worked for decades and had treated Dora, the Wolf Man and the Rat Man. I bought a ticket, went round the rooms and looked at the furniture and pictures in what had once been the waiting room, and saw part of Freud's collection of antiques on show in a display case, with other items of his personal possessions including his doctor's bag, a large black umbrella, a hat and an old chest. I hadn't really come for his sake but for his youngest daughter Anna's, since she had also lived in this house, practising as a children's analyst, and was taken away for interrogation by the Gestapo on 22 March 1938, before the family fled to England, but they released her the same day. This was the woman I was to play in John's musical based on the life of Freud. In the museum shop I leafed through several books, finding several photographs of Anna Freud as a child, and then as a young, middle-aged and very old woman, and I spent some time looking at a portrait of her in her youth, which I liked very much and which showed her smiling, but with sad dark eyes, a dark beret pulled down over her forehead, and a necklace worn under a shiny lightweight coat. Before I left, the young man at the cash desk suggested I might like to support the Sigmund Freud Society with a subscription of five hundred schillings a year, and since it was a private academic association every member was a great help; my subscription would allow me to visit the museum as often as I liked with my friends and acquaintances, and in addition I would receive the Society's newsletter four times a year, as well as invitations and reduced entry to the events it arranged, and I could use the library.

After visiting Freud's house, something John had told me I must on no account omit to do, I decided to go to my next singing lesson in the Death House on foot, since the sun was shining, there was no wind, and my ankle no longer hurt, so at last I could wear my high-heeled burgundy-red shoes again. I went through the Volksgarten, and when I passed the statue of a beautiful woman who, as I gathered from the inscription on its plinth, was Elisabeth of Austria, the same Empress Sisi whom Josef Horvath had already mentioned twice and who also surfaced several times in Rosa Havelka's story, I went closer to the stone sculpture, examined her features, and couldn't see the faintest resemblance to the portrait of my singing teacher's mother.

On the stairs leading to Josef Horvath's apartment I met his neighbour Fräulein Haslinger, to whom he had now introduced me, and she stopped and said she was really delighted to see that poor Herr Horvath had found someone to look after him, and I must know that his late mother, of whom he always spoke in tones of the greatest respect, had by no means shown herself deserving of this touching veneration while she was alive, she'd been a mediocre and rather unattractive pianist who had tyrannized poor Herr Horvath all his life, a very ordinary person who thought herself something special but who had really been too mean to buy medicine for her sickly child, too egocentric to look after him as he needed if he was to thrive. And as for his father, added Fräulein Haslinger, lowering her voice and bringing her small, round mouth close to my ear, as for poor Herr Horvath's father, on whom he had never set eyes in all his twenty-nine years of life, it was rumoured that the pianist herself couldn't have said for sure which of the men with whom she used to consort merited that description, on account of the wild life she led for years travelling in Austria, the eastern Burgenland district and western Hungary as part of a Hungarian touring musical ensemble, but if the identity of the child's father couldn't be established for certain she herself, the pianist, had spread the story that he was a famous violinist who appeared in the top concert halls of the United States this side of the Mississippi, the son of an illegitimate daughter of Gustav Mahler conceived while he was guest conductor at the Metropolitan Opera House, New York. However she, Fräulein Haslinger, was more inclined to think poor Herr Horvath's father had been a juggler in a small Croatian circus which the aforesaid touring ensemble had met on its travels, but she supposed no one would ever know the truth of the matter. And if, as she assumed, I too was concerned for poor Herr Horvath's physical well-being, she would be happy to lend me *The Priest's Housekeeper's Cookbook*, a collection of recipes from Catholic presbyteries, and she could let me have a jar of lime-flower honey from her brother-in-law's apiary now and then; she would recommend me to sweeten the dishes I made with this natural product, the very best thing for Herr Horvath's susceptible bronchial tubes.

As I went on up the stairs I wondered if Josef Horvath was really only twenty-nine, because I'd put his age as considerably older. To my surprise, when he opened his door he was not, as usual, wearing his salmon-pink dressing-gown but jeans and a blue roll-neck pullover, which really did make him look rather younger, and as I stood by the baby grand singing, 'Ah, now I know why from your sparkling eyes / Such dark flames flashed, dark flames that met my own. / Our eyes met! Our eyes met!' I studied my singing teacher accompanying me on the piano, and thought the colour of the pullover suited the blue-grey of his eyes. I had felt lately that I was making some progress and my vocal tensions were resolving themselves, I enjoyed singing, particularly singing a duet, and every time I left the Death House I felt more relaxed and less tense. And when Horvath claimed that the voice was a metaphysical instrument, a miracle, when he said you could think of song as a cipher, the cipher of cosmic order, when he spoke of the floating architecture of the upper regions, I no longer found this kind of language as extravagant and difficult to grasp as I had at first.

We had fallen into the habit of drinking a cup of herb tea at the end of the singing lesson, and on one of these occasions I mentioned the handwritten autobiography I had found in my relation's chest and asked if he had ever heard of someone called Rosa Havelka, née Tichy, who was executed for murdering her husband around the turn of the century by an executioner called Josef Lang, a question he answered in the negative. Then he added that he thought he remembered there actually had been an executioner of that name, but as far as he knew no woman had ever suffered at his hands, to which I said that very likely the story was all pure fiction, but I was moved by the fate of the orphan girl so shamefully exploited by her employers, a family called Lindner living in the Neuer Markt. Here Horvath put a hand to his brow and muttered Lindner, Lindner, he knew some Lindners who did live in the Neuer Markt, a family whom he envied because of the grand piano that had been in their possession for decades, made in Leipzig by the firm of Blüthner; he had given their youngest daughter lessons on it some years ago, whereupon I said that was amazing, Rosa Havelka described a piano just like that in her story, what a strange coincidence, and I poured my teacher a cup of violet-leaf tea.

When I went back to the apartment on the corner of Blutgasse and Domgasse late that afternoon, Aunt Pia was sitting in front of the television, and she said the set, which she and the Major had bought in 1964 from a specialist shop in Mariahilferstrasse, worked as well as ever but the picture was a little blurred, couldn't I adjust it to make it sharper, she could hardly hear a thing anyway but now she was having great difficulty making out young Romy Schneider in all her beauty in that wonderful film *Sisi, the Young Empress*. After I had tried in vain to improve the picture quality I sat down beside my relation in front of the black and white set and made do with following the movements on screen of the indistinct outlines of Sisi, her imperial spouse and her mother-in-law, while Aunt Pia told me the plot. It had been love at first sight, she said; over tea in Ischl, Karlheinz Böhm had fallen head over heels in love with the tomboy that was Sisi at the time, and she pointed to the light, bell-shaped patch on the screen and said that must be the gossamer-fine silk dress with its wide crinoline, worn with a white lace mantilla, in which Romy Schneider, destined for so tragic a fate, had gone by steamer to meet her fiancé, just imagine, leaving that funny little court for the great wide world, and never mind the enthusiastic welcome she received everywhere the steamer put in between Straubing and Nussdorf, it could never have turned out well, Sisi's death by suicide in Paris, the assassination of Romy Schneider by an Italian anarchist in 1898 had been a threat looming all along, just like the disastrous end of her own little Wilma, there was nothing you could do about the dispensations of Providence.

That evening my mother phoned to ask how I was, and I said after a few initial problems adjusting to the place I was fine, I was getting accustomed to deaf Aunt Pia and my singing teacher now, in spite of the bad weather which hardly ever let up I quite liked Vienna, and by the way, in Aunt Pia's apartment I'd chanced upon a servant girl's autobiography from the turn of the century, did she by any chance know the name Rosa Havelka, née Tichy? Here my mother said nothing for so long that I was beginning to think we'd been cut off, but then she said, Rosa Havelka, not as far as she knew, and anyway I ought not to abuse Aunt Pia's hospitality by rummaging around in her chests.

Just as I had put the receiver down and was thinking, chests, now why did my mother say chests, I never said a word about any chest, the phone rang again, and this time it was John asking how his bitter-sweet little songbird was, how did his nut-brown nightingale feel, and when was I planning to fly back, he could hardly wait to see me, to which I replied that I was in sedate Vienna and not hectic New York, things went to their own rhythm here and it wasn't a good idea to hurry them along, my teacher, a typical Viennese whose qualities as a singing teacher I'd rather underestimated at first and whose character I had also mistaken, couldn't be pressed too hard, and as we, my singing teacher and I, could give of our best only if we had enough time at our disposal, going too fast wouldn't be a good idea. John protested, saying he didn't entirely understand, after all I was the one who'd been wanting to cut my visit to Vienna short, and when I said that I now realized how arduous and difficult the way to the vocal heights was, he replied, well, maybe, but he'd like to remind me that rehearsals for the musical would soon be beginning, the timetable was already fixed, and perhaps I'd remember that Anna Freud was a starring role, I couldn't just skip the rehearsals, to which I said casually we'd see how it all turned out, but now I had to go on reading something that had been occupying a good deal of my time for the last few days, and we'd speak again in the foreseeable future.

Five

When I emerged from the cathedral into the open air I passed a woman sitting in the doorway begging, with her hand outstretched. I gave her a kreuzer, as I did so glancing at her face, which was half hidden by a scarf, and to my surprise I recognized the young woman who had recently spoken up so resolutely in the employment agency for the rights of domestic servants. I greeted her, and she smiled at me and said she supposed Prohaska hadn't found me a position either, and that would be why I'd turned to the saints for help, a step frequently taken by domestic servants, particularly when their situation was desperate, although she doubted its efficacy. When she was out of work she'd rather beg, although you had to be on the watch for the police, who were just waiting for an excuse to send people like us to the house of correction. She'd had a very good position with the Honourable Herr von Schreyvogl's family at 18 Stubenring, but the lady of the house had dismissed her for reasons of economy before they went away on their summer holiday. However, it was possible that the von Schreyvogls were back in Vienna from their visit to their country house in Altaussee by now, and I might try them, you never knew, perhaps I'd be in luck.

I thanked the girl for this hint, and said I'd follow it up at once and go straight off to see the family she recommended. She called after me not to expect too much, she herself had come to Vienna from Maribor by the Southern Railway six months ago to look for work, since when her life had been one long round of disappointments, and I had better be wary of the Viennese, their superficially agreeable manner was deceptive, most of them were mean, sly people who exploited and oppressed their servants whenever they could, there was no other city known to her where domestic servants had fewer rights than here, and by the way her name was Lyuba, Lyuba Zupan, and perhaps I'd remember her.

The building at 18 Stubenring before which I was standing ten minutes later was grand and palatial, and its magnificent exterior overawed me so much that at first I didn't dare to enter it in my school uniform, which by now looked rather threadbare and not entirely clean, and carrying my shabby cardboard case. But then I told myself I must seize the unexpected opportunity Lyuba had offered me, went in, and was immediately stopped by a fat woman in slovenly clothing with untidy grey hair, who was sweeping the stairs and asked what I thought I was doing in this building, begging and peddling were strictly forbidden here. I said I had no intention of doing either, I was looking for the Honourable von Schreyvogls' apartment, having heard that the family needed a domestic servant. The fat woman stopped sweeping, leaned on her broom, inspected me thoroughly and then said disparagingly that they did indeed, but she could hardly imagine that elegant and remarkably charming young gentleman, son and partner of the silk manufacturer Hugo von Schreyvogl, and his beautiful and amiable wife, born Baroness von und zu Purgstall-Wohlleben, entrusting their enchanting little twins to the care of some girl from heaven knew where in search of a job. Then she added that nonetheless, the delightful young family had finally parted with that unruly, sly-looking Slovenian girl who kept making eyes at the young master, and whom she personally wouldn't have trusted an inch, you never knew with Slovenians, they were unruly and sly by nature, it was a racial characteristic. At this point I cautiously set my foot on the bottom step of the stairs, and said I wondered if I might make bold to ask if she'd be kind enough to tell me which floor the family lived on. Reluctantly the fat woman, who was probably the caretaker, moved her broom out of my way and said abruptly they were at No. 6 on the mezzanine floor.

I went up the stairs, pulled the brass bell hanging beside the door of No. 6, heard footsteps approaching, and finally the door was opened and a very tall, very thin and very pale pregnant woman with her black hair in a bun and nickel-framed glasses on her nose repeated what the caretaker had already told me, to the effect that begging and peddling were strictly forbidden in this building, no exceptions. Before she could shut the door in my face I said quickly that I'd heard there was a domestic position vacant in her home, and I'd like to apply for it. The woman thought for a moment, sighed deeply, and said that was true enough, she was urgently in need of a nursemaid, looking after twins of eleven months old called for nerves of iron and was more than she could possibly manage on her own, it took all her strength, strength she must save for the new life which, as no doubt I could see, was growing within her. Her summer holiday at Altaussee, which always used to give her boundless energy and from which, unfortunately, they had been obliged to return three days ago, had been anything but restful this year, she was absolutely exhausted, and I might as well come in, for goodness' sake, and show her my servant's book. I handed her the book, and the lady read what the Regional Postal Manager's wife had written and murmured, unstable, indolent, not much of a recommendation there. Then she looked at me and said she really had hardly any choice in the matter, she had no time or strength to go looking for someone more suitable, she'd try me, although she couldn't possibly pay me more than three gulden a month, the income from the little silk factory in Vienna 7 belonging to her husband's family was losing business rapidly.

I spent the next few hours in the Volksgarten, where my new employer had sent me with her twins Tassilo and Klaus Maria. The children of prosperous Viennese families, little girls in white pinafores and boys in sailor suits, played hide-and-seek, catch and marbles and skipped with a rope in this park, supervised by nursemaids and nannies. Frau von Schreyvogl had impressed it upon me that I mustn't allow any contact at all between her twins and common children who mingled with the offspring of the upper classes in the playground, one couldn't entirely prevent it, you could hardly be sure of sticking together with your own kind at all these days. I played with the two little boys, talked to the other nursemaids sitting on the steps of the Theseus Temple for a while, then put the babies back in the twin pram and pushed it home to the grand apartment on Stubenring, where Frau von Schreyvogl told me to feed her sons, bath them and put them to bed. When Tassilo and Klaus Maria were in their cots, the young mother said she had prepared my room, well, not really a room but a roomy walk-in wardrobe next to the smoking room which was hardly ever used, it was a very pretty place, tall and airy, with valuable silk wallpaper made in the Schreyvogl and Sons factory which, as they had been assured by the imperial-and-royal court contractor Schimmerling, with whom they were on friendly terms, perfectly matched the colour and pattern of the blue Lyons silk that had covered the walls of Emperor Franz Joseph and Empress Elisabeth's matrimonial bedroom on Schönbrunn Palace since their wedding in 1854, and she was sure I'd be very comfortable there. Frau von Schreyvogl led me through the large, handsomely furnished sitting room and the smoking room with its tall bookcases, heavy, dark brown leather armchairs and a billiards table covered with green baize, and into a windowless cubby hole measuring about two by two metres, with worn strips of blue fabric hanging from its walls. Apart from a mattress on the floor it contained no furniture except for a rickety washstand with a flaking enamel basin and a battered white enamel jug, a chair with a sagging seat, an old chest of drawers with a half-burned candle in a candlestick standing on it and a piece of murky mirror glass with a diagonal crack across it leaning against the wall. Frau von

Schreyvogl pulled out the top drawer of the three in the chest of drawers, with some difficulty at first because it stuck, took out a black dress, a creased white apron and a little white cap, and said this was the outfit worn by Lyuba, her charming nursemaid from Maribor who, unfortunately, had left a month and a half ago. Lyuba had been a little smaller than me, but she was sure this smart uniform would suit me very well too.

Our conversation was interrupted by the appearance of the master of the household. I turned, and saw a good-looking man with curly dark hair, a well-tended beard, a stiff collar and a top hat, who wore a black frock coat and seemed curiously familiar to me. After kissing his wife on both cheeks he turned to me, and when I failed to move, since I was still wondering where I could have seen him before, Frau von Schreyvogl dug me in the ribs with her elbow and whispered that I was to bob a curtsey. I made the deep curtsey that Fräulein von Roth-Rothenhorst had taught Helene, Marie and me, telling us it was the court curtsey as performed by ladies-in-waiting at the imperial court, and the Honourable Herr von Schreyvogl took my hand, smiling, and drew me to my feet. Then I suddenly knew who he was: by one of the remarkable coincidences that were to continue occurring in my life with amazing frequency, the man before me was the very man who had stood on the gravel path outside the Gerstner family's house in Marienbad, leafing through the little edition of Goethe containing the 'Marienbad Elegy' that my half-sisters had thrown over the garden wall. I guessed from his expression that, unlike me, he did not remember that brief encounter.

When I lay down on my mattress that first evening in the Honourable von Schreyvogls' walk-in wardrobe, after eating my supper, a not very generous portion of cabbage, and washing in the water left over from the babies' bath by the express wish of the lady of the house, who said one had to cultivate habits of economy and the admittedly excellent water from the Viennese mains was getting more expensive all the time, I let the exciting events of the

191

past day unroll once more before my mind's eye. I considered myself lucky to have found a place again so quickly, this time with an aristocratic family living in a palatial building in one of the streets on the Ring, a family that did seem to be rather thrifty where its domestic staff were concerned, but otherwise appeared delightful. After a brief prayer of gratitude to my new patron saint, the Madonna of the Servants in St Stephen's Cathedral, I blew out the flickering flame of the candle that illuminated the walk-in wardrobe, at least after a fashion, turned my face to the wall and immediately fell asleep.

Next morning I put on the dress left by Lyuba, which was too tight and too short for me, and as instructed by Frau von Schreyvogl the previous evening I went out to the baker's in Wollzeile at six to get fresh white rolls, brioches, poppy-seed rolls and croissants for the young couple's breakfast. Then I boiled two large eggs, made coffee, laid the Augarten porcelain coffee set, ivory white with a delicate pattern of pale green tendrils, on a large silver tray, poured the fresh, fragrant coffee into its pot and place that on the tray too, together with the eggcups containing the soft-boiled eggs, the little basket of crisp rolls and pastries, farmhouse butter, amber-coloured honey and strawberry jam from Altaussee. I knocked on the bedroom door, as I had been told to do, entered when I heard Frau von Schreyvogl's voice telling me to come in, cast a quick glance at the young couple in the wide bed with its embroidered hangings and velvet canopy, put the tray down on the cream-coloured Rococo bedside table, and left the room. I was hungry, but I wasn't allowed to have my own breakfast, a slice of bread and butter and the remains of yesterday's leftover coffee, before nine o'clock. I took the von Schreyvogls' dirty washing out of the big laundry basket, sorted it into bedclothes, table linen and personal clothing, removed all the buttons and hooks and eyes so that no rust marks would be left after washing, put the laundry into three cotton bags and took them down to the big laundry room in the basement of the palatial building.

About three hours later, feeling rather weary and very hungry, I returned to my employers' apartment, where Frau von Schreyvogl had already put the twins in their pram. She said the weather was unusually sunny, the constitutions of Klaus Maria and Tassilo were not as strong as they might be, something she attributed to a rather unfortunate hereditary tendency as the result of intermarriages in her family, the Barons von und zu Purgstall-Wohlleben, and they badly needed fresh air and sunshine, so I could go out at once to take the children for a walk in the Prater, my breakfast could wait a little, I'd have more time to enjoy it when I got back.

So I pushed the pram down Stubenring and along the Danube Canal, crossed the canal by the Radetzky Bridge, and was soon in the Hauptallee of the Prater, a long, straight avenue full of people and carriages, and lined with cafés and restaurants outside which customers were sitting eating and drinking at wooden tables in the open air. I was feeling hungrier and hungrier, and was tempted to buy a sandwich, but I didn't have so much as a kreuzer of my own left, and the coins Frau von Schreyvogl had counted out into the palm of my hand were the exact price of a ride on the Calafati carousel, a steam-train roundabout, she had told me, with the outsize figure of a Chinaman in the middle of it, where the Viennese in general and her twins in particular loved to ride round and round in the genuine steam that the locomotives puffed out. So with one twin under my right arm and the other under my left arm, and my stomach rumbling, I got into one of the cars, placed one twin on my right knee and the other on my left knee, and sat through their squealing as I longed for the end of the ride, since the circular movement made me feel sick, probably because it was so long since I'd eaten. Then, when I had pushed the pram past several sausage stalls where people were eating hot sausages with fresh rolls, mustard and horseradish, and then past more coffee houses and inns with shady gardens where all-female musical ensembles were playing and people were drinking beer and eating goulash, roast veal and fried chicken, and after being approached by several men of various ages, I decided to turn home, feeling weak with hunger and enticed by the prospect of my bread and butter and coffee.

On the way back the crowd of people grew denser and denser. They were standing by the roadside, craning their necks, and seemed to be waiting for something. I felt curious, and in spite of my ravenous hunger I stopped too. Next moment there was cheering, and several elegant carriages drawn by horses with plumes on their heads trotted by at a smart pace, among them a closed black coach with horsemen in silver helmets riding beside it. I stood on tiptoe to get a glimpse of the inside of the coach, and for a brief moment I saw the outline of a profile behind a dark veil, with a black fan being waved in front of it by a black-gloved hand. Then the coach had disappeared from my sight. A young woman in a pale dress, who had put up a little white parasol to shield herself from the sun and was eating sweets out of a bag, turned to me and said the Empress was getting more and more peculiar in her old age, she never showed herself on public occasions any more, and when she drove through Vienna she was always heavily veiled. When I asked whether the dark figure of the lady in the coach had really been Empress Elisabeth, that beautiful young woman whose trousseau on her arrival in Vienna in 1854 had contained four ballgowns, seventeen party dresses with trains, fourteen silk gowns, nineteen summer dresses and sixteen hats, not to mention three dozen nightdresses and ten bedjackets made of batiste, twelve embroidered nightcaps and twenty-four ker-chiefs for night wear, six dozen piqué and flannel petticoats, twenty-four make-up capes and three bathing dresses, a hundred and thirteen pairs of shoes, two fans and two umbrellas, three large and three small parasols, as well as three pairs of rubber galoshes and a box of hairpins and ordinary pins, ribbons and buttons, the woman took the soft golden-brown caramel into which she had just bitten out of her mouth, held it between thumb and forefinger, stared incredulously at me for a moment and said, well of course, what did I think, her beauty was all gone, diet as she might, it did no good, what a shame we were landed with an Empress like that, a woman who kept leaving the poor Emperor on his own instead of standing by him, as natural propriety and Holy Scripture ordained for the female sex, a person who went travelling round the world at her subjects' expense, buying expensive horses and doing no end of harm to her husband's reputation, not to mention that of the imperial-and-royal Austro-Hungarian monarchy and its people. So saying, the young woman put the bitten caramel back into her mouth, twirled her pleated white parasol and went off.

When I got back, the Honourable von Schreyvogls were sitting in the dining room eating lunch, and as I made haste to the kitchen to have my own breakfast, since of course I wasn't allowed to eat with my employers, I was able to see, from a swift glance at the table, that they had reached dessert, a fresh apple strudel, and judging by the bones left on the plates which had not yet been taken away, their main course had been roast chicken.

I soon became used to my new job, and learned to know Vienna better and better on the walks I took with the twins in the various city parks, the one I liked best being the Prater with its old trees, wide expanses of grass, and all its many opportunities for diversion. My work was less strenuous than in the Regional Postal Manager's household, for looking after the children was not very difficult, and I was allowed a rather longer night's rest, although it was often interrupted when the sound of my own rumbling stomach woke me. Frau von Schreyvogl kept telling me about the difficult situation of the silk manufacturing industry at present, saying that a small firm like Schreyvogl and Sons simply couldn't compete with the increasingly large and numerous textiles factories using the latest modern machinery in and around Vienna, the only way of warding off the threat of destitution was to economize in certain areas. She was sure I would understand if she asked me to light the candle in my room as seldom as possible, paraffin for a lamp would be far too expensive, and anyway not using one spared

the expensive silk wallpaper exposure to traces of soot, so injurious to its delicate, light fabric. As for my board, I must realize that
it couldn't be too lavish, what with the present price of food, but
we should remember that over-substantial dishes quickly led to
obesity, and thus to various diseases of the organism, so a less
lavish diet confined to natural, tasty food was preferable for the
good of one's health anyway, she was sure I wanted to maintain
my strong constitution, and the human frame in general, especially
in youth, could manage on much less nourishment than was
commonly assumed. In difficult times we all had to pull together,
and undoubtedly I would realize that I must put my own wants
second to the welfare of her family.

I certainly found this an illuminating argument from a young
housewife anxious to run her household on economical lines, but
hard as I tried to think of the food allotted to me as adequate, I
simply could not feel satisfied by my breakfast of a thin slice of
bread and butter and a dish of the weak, barely drinkable coffee
which was brewed every few days for the staff – including besides
myself a cook and a chambermaid who didn't live in – and which
was sometimes several days old by the time I drank it, or by the
leftovers from my employers' lunch, or by my usual supper of a
small plate of cabbage or spinach. I couldn't buy myself anything
to eat on my walks with the twins, my employers having kept back
more than half my first month's wages, since the Rules for
Domestic Staff allowed them to deduct money to the amount of
any damage done by an employee. And as I had little experience of
housekeeping and so was sometimes rather clumsy, I might
occasionally break something, or let the blue bag leave a mark
while I was doing the laundry. In addition, the black dress I wore,
which was much too tight for me, soon had a long tear down the
back because I had to bend so often that the threadbare fabric
finally gave way, whereupon Frau von Schreyvogl commented that
those expectations one might legitimately have of a domestic
servant included a certain grace and flexibility of movement, a

harmonious manner of working which would preclude such clumsiness, and the dress was made of calico in perfect condition, although not impervious to tearing, so it was obvious that I must either get the damaged article of clothing repaired at my own expense or buy myself a new one. Accordingly I spent the other half of my first month's pay on having the tear mended in a small alterations workshop run by a Slovakian dressmaker on the corner of Wollzeile and Postgasse.

While Frau von Schreyvogl's original amiability gave way to a rather impatient attitude over the weeks, something only too understandable in her condition, the master of the house proved from the very first day to be a courteous, generous and lenient employer, who took my part more than once and showed himself worthy in every way of the aristocratic title of Honourable. I admired his sophisticated manner, both reserved and decided as it was, his attractive appearance, and not least the tender consideration with which he treated his young wife, and I could well understand that she sometimes cast a jealous sideways glance at the pretty parlourmaid who came in five times a week, although as far as I could tell Herr von Schreyvogl never gave her the slightest occasion for such anxieties, particularly as the silk manufacturing business made many demands on him, and he was seldom home before eight at night.

One evening – it must have been towards the end of August – I was lying on my mattress in the walk-in wardrobe, unable to sleep because I was tormented by hunger after facing a plate of scraps of fat beef at midday, cut from the joint by the cook, fried up quickly and set before me, only half of which I had been able to eat because of their unappetizing appearance, while my supper had been a bowl of thin potato soup. And since Frau von Schreyvogl had commented in some annoyance yesterday that in spite of her admonitions my candle had grown two centimetres shorter within a very few days, I dared not get one of my edifying works or cookbooks out of my case and take my mind off that tormenting feeling by reading. In my mind's eye I kept seeing the chestnut gâteau which had been served to my employers for dessert at lunch and now, only a quarter eaten, was standing under a glass cover in the kitchen. The children were fast asleep, Herr and Frau Schreyvogl had gone to bed as well, and since both the bedroom and the nursery were some way from the smoking room and so were remote from my own quarters, it would have been easy to get up, make my way through the smoking room and down the corridor unnoticed, enter the kitchen, take a knife, lift the glass cover, cut a small slice of chestnut gâteau, put the glass cover over it again, wash the knife and put it away, and return to the walk-in wardrobe with the slice of gâteau in my hand. I realized that such an act would be theft, would amount to the abstraction of movable property that was not mine to take, with the intention of illicitly appropriating it, as Fräulein von Roth-Rothenhorst had taught us, and the almost tangible image of the chestnut gâteau consequently gave way to a picture of my late mother looking at me sadly and shaking her head. And theft was not only a crime, a deliberate offence against my employers who gave me board and lodging and paid my wages, but also a sin, if a venial sin which, as far as I could remember from Sister Immaculata's teaching, because of its objective triviality could disturb the soul's relationship with God but not cause a complete break with him. In the grip of this temptation, the temptation to do evil, according to Sister Immaculata, being rooted in mankind's sinful instinctive nature, and permitted by God in order to put our morality to the test, I tossed and turned on my mattress until my powers of resistance began to weaken as my imagination pictured that chestnut gâteau more and more vividly, adding hallucinations of smell, flavour and taste, and I jumped up in my calf-length linen nightdress from the Ursuline boarding school and pushed open the smoking-room door, determined to carry out the illicit act. There in the gentle light of a standard lamp with a pleated sunshine-yellow fabric shade, wearing a dark-blue silk housecoat, sat Herr von Schreyvogl in one of the heavy brown leather armchairs, smoking a cigarette.

I was cast into such confusion by this entirely unexpected sight that I immediately stepped back into the walk-in wardrobe and was about to close the door, but Herr von Schreyvogl took the cigarette holder and the cigarette it contained out of his mouth, smiled at me, and told me gently not to be so timid but to come and sit with him for a while, he couldn't sleep, any more than it seemed I could sleep myself, and my presence would distract him a little from the anxieties that went with the slow but steady decline in the silk factory's ability to compete in the market. So saying, he indicated the armchair next to him. I looked down at my linen nightdress and my bare feet, and whispered that I'd be happy to keep him company but I must put something on first, an idea that Herr von Schreyvogl waved away, saying oh, that wasn't necessary, the situation in which we found ourselves was perfectly casual and informal, anyway it was unusually warm for the end of August when the first signs of early autumn normally began to show themselves, and he wouldn't ask me to sit beside him in my dark, high-necked nursemaid's uniform, much as it suited me. Since I dared not disobey my master's orders, I timidly lowered myself to the very edge of the seat of the armchair, and sat there in silent embarrassment. Herr von Schreyvogl drew deeply on his cigarette, blew a smoke ring, and said I must forgive him, he knew I had a right to rest without being disturbed and he never usually sat in the smoking room, but probably because of those problems he'd just mentioned he felt he wanted to smoke for the first time in a long while, simply in order to relax, and so he had come to sit in here. His wife had been asleep for hours, in her present condition she obviously needed extra sleep, and she slept more deeply than usual too. And by the way, he'd like to take this opportunity of telling me that whenever he came home from the factory my presence in his household, the sight of such a fresh young creature, cheered, encouraged and really uplifted him. I whispered shyly that I myself felt lucky to be able to serve him and his family, whereupon Herr von Schreyvogl put the hair I wore loose at night back from my forehead with his free hand and asked how old I was. I said I'd been sixteen last February, and Herr von Schreyvogl sighed and murmured quietly, sixteen, what a wonderful age, a girl of sixteen was like a rosebud still furled, a snow-white lily, a tender dove, an innocent fawn, he very much hoped the child his wife was expecting would be a girl. I looked into his face, surprised to find him using exactly the same botanical and zoological terms as those employed by the nuns in the convent when they wanted to impress upon us their idea of chastity and the difficulties of maintaining and defending it. Then Herr von Schreyvogl raised his hand and tugged playfully at the little white bow tying my linen nightdress at the neck, undoing it, a gesture which also reminded me of the way the nuns involuntarily moved their hands as they spoke of the dangers to which we growing girls were exposed. Embarrassed, I tied the bow again, rose, and by way of retrospective justification for leaving my bed said I had been going to the kitchen to drink a glass of water. Herr von Schreyvogl, whose cigarette had now gone out, rose too and said that when the opportunity offered he would very much like to continue our stimulating conversation, which had made him quite forget the problems of the silk factory.

When I was lying on my mattress again my hunger, my vision of the chestnut gâteau, and with them my intention of committing the crime of stealing food, had dissolved into thin air. Instead, I saw in my mind's eye the winning features of my employer, his understanding glance, his kindly smile, his manly beard, and I felt deep gratitude to him, for by his mere presence he had kept me from doing very wrong. I decided that by way of thanks for this intervention I would be at his disposal whenever he wanted, an attentive partner in conversation and above all a good listener.

Next morning the twins were not well; they were coughing and their eyes were sore. Two days later a rash spread over the skin of their little bodies, they ran a high temperature, and the doctor who was called diagnosed measles and said they must stay in bed for two weeks. I gave the babies compresses for their cough, rubbed their chests and backs with ointment made with thyme which was also good for coughs, and made sure they did not get cold. Frau von Schreyvogl was cross, and blamed me for letting her sons come into contact with nasty common children in the various playgrounds I took them to, thus making it more likely they would catch something, and for not protecting them well enough from the Viennese wind. Klaus Marie and Tassilo recovered remarkably quickly, but I myself caught the disease seven days later, never having had measles as a child, and it left me feeling very weak, since Frau von Schreyvogl accused me of faking the symptoms to get out of working and wouldn't allow me time to convalesce, so that I also contracted a painful inflammation of the middle ear and couldn't get that treated either, with the result that I am rather deaf in the left ear to this day.

I was upset by the obvious deterioration of my relationship with my mistress, which as far as I knew wasn't my fault, and which also had unfortunate consequences in that Frau von Schreyvogl, who in any case was far from generous in the provision of food for her servants, gave me even smaller portions that before, and that in turn had a bad effect on my physical constitution, so that my weakened resistance caused me to run a high temperature. At this she said, angrily, that she wished I'd stop faking, she now wondered why the sight of the white bandage I was wearing round my head when I came to her door looking for work hadn't immediately told her that she was dealing with a sly malingerer pretending to be in physical pain so as to arouse sympathy and play on a young housewife's guileless, trusting nature, and thus get a position as nursemaid by devious means. And now I was to make preserves from the fruit stored in the pantry and brought back from the garden of their summer residence in Altaussee, it was high time too, or did I want those fine gooseberries, pears, currants and plums to go rotten?

After I had seen to the twins I went down to the cellar, shivering with fever, to fetch the preserving jars. I felt hotter and hotter all the time I was boiling the redcurrants, and since this sensation of heat took my mind off what I was doing I forgot to put silver spoons in the empty jars before pouring in the redcurrant jelly, to attract heat and keep the jars from cracking. So two of the full jars broke, and when Frau von Schreyvogl came into the kitchen to inspect my work the hot, thick liquid was running over the edge of the table and dripping on the floor, where it spread into a red puddle. My mistress was overcome with fury at this sight, she wrung her hands and cried that she didn't know what unlucky star had sent me to them, what stroke of fate had made her open the door when I knocked on it, first of all I'd made her children sick through my irresponsible negligence, now I was trying to drive her mad too, how dared I break that expensive jar, make such a mess of the solid walnut table top and the irreplaceable unglazed tiles from Friuli with fresh redcurrant jelly, still liquid, and leaving fruit stains which I'd know, if I had a spark of common sense, would be there generations later. She was at the end of her tether, and if she didn't have a genuine angel for a husband she'd have been driven to despair long ago by her problems with two demanding sons, a lazy cook, a slovenly parlourmaid, and now to cap it all a mendacious and useless nursemaid. So saying, she dismissed me from the kitchen and told me to get out of her sight, until further notice from her I was to stay in the comfortable little room allowed me by her generosity and go without my supper, the slices of nourishing black bread and the medium-sized healthy white radish she had intended for me, a supper like that had to be earned.

I obeyed my mistress's orders at once, walked unsteadily through the smoking room to the walk-in wardrobe, feeling entirely disorientated because of the rapid rise in my temperature, and dropped on my mattress, where I soon fell into a restless, feverish sleep through which long rows of jars of strawberry, raspberry, plum, gooseberry, bilberry and blackberry preserves made their way in procession, and from which I woke, after some indeterminate period of time, feeling hungry. All was quiet, nothing stirred, so I concluded that it was night and the von Schreyvogls had gone to bed. The fever that had attacked me so violently had died down slightly, but now that my eyes were open I still saw the countless jam jars from my dream before me. My hunger increased, and this time, after Frau von Schreyvogl's unjust treatment of me, I didn't have to struggle with myself for very long before I rose and made my unsteady way, my legs still weak, to the kitchen to look for something edible. The glass jars of redcurrant jelly were still on the table, and I quickly removed the waxed paper from one of them, picked up a coffee spoon, dipped it into the jelly, which had now set, and let its delicious sweetness melt on my tongue. I had intended to stop after two or at the most three spoonfuls, but my ravenous hunger and weakened constitution made me lose control of myself, and I went on until the jar was empty. Since I didn't suppose Frau von Schreyvogl knew exactly how many jars there were, I simply threw it out of the window, and it flew in a high trajectory over a low wall and into the yard next door. Then I lay down on my mattress again and fell asleep.

Next morning, when I entered the kitchen rather later than usual but feeling considerably better, to eat my bread and butter and drink my weak coffee, I was surprised to find Frau von Schreyvogl standing by the kitchen table, her outstretched finger pointing accusingly at the jam jars. Where, might she ask, she said, was the thirteenth jar of redcurrant jelly? The thirteenth jar of redcurrant jelly was missing, you could never be too careful where domestic staff were concerned, so of course she had counted the jars.

I instantly decided to resort to a lie, a deliberate falsehood designed to mislead, something which Fräulein von Roth-Rothenhorst had taught us all ethical systems agreed in condemning, since it undermined both the mutual confidence of human beings in each other and the self-respect of the person telling the lie, and as I well knew from my regular reading of the Bible in the old days, it was also utterly condemned in *Ephesians* Chapter 4, verse 25, and *Matthew* Chapter 5, verse 37, but it could be excused in certain circumstances with what is known as a mental reservation as a necessary lie, a serviceable lie, or a conventional lie. I decided that this was a case of a necessary lie, and said calmly that of course I too had counted the jam jars before bringing them up from the cellar, out of a sense of duty, and there had been a dozen, twelve jars, no more and no less. Frau von Schreyvogl took a deep breath and cried that the impudence with which I lied in her face took her breath away, my true nature, which I'd managed to conceal quite well until now, was becoming visibly evident, she saw more and more clearly that she had been dreadfully mistaken in me and I was not, as she'd thought at first, an unfortunate creature who was good at heart and deserved help, oh no, my surface appearance of being willing and needing help concealed a prime example of underhand mendacity, I was a positively crim-inal character which she could hardly take the responsibility of sheltering under her roof any longer.

For the first time my inner being revolted against what I considered a rather biased description of my personality, and I defiantly decided to add the shocking offence of perjury, a deliberate false oath, to the moral misdemeanour of lying. I raised my right hand and said so help me God, I swore I hadn't made away with any of the jars, I called to witness the Madonna of the Servants who stood in St Stephen's Cathedral and made it her business to protect our often unjustly treated class, if madam insisted we could go straight to the cathedral, which wasn't far, and visit her, and I was sure she wouldn't refuse us a small sign in proof of my innocence. Here my mistress wanted to know what I meant by denying my impudent theft and calling on the name of Our Lady, she had a good mind to call a police officer from the station on the corner of Wollzeile and Riemergasse, Frau Navratil the caretaker would certainly be ready to go the short way there for the sake of justice. This threat alarmed me, and in fear of the loss of my job and possible punishment by the police I resorted, I must admit, to the shameful device of slander or false accusation, and said quietly but firmly, well, perhaps I could help madam by giving her a little hint, quite by chance I'd seen the parlourmaid bending over the jars in the kitchen late last evening, a sight that had surprised me, since first she didn't often come into the kitchen, and second she usually went home much earlier, but then I explained her presence to myself by thinking that perhaps madam had asked her to write the labels for the jars of jam. At this Frau von Schreyvogl stopped shouting, looked at me thoughtfully and said, hm, yes, the parlourmaid, she'd believe anything of the parlourmaid, who would have to give an account of herself in this unfortunate matter the moment she arrived.

At this moment the Honourable Herr von Schreyvogl came into the kitchen and asked for an explanation of our loud and agitated conversation. Curiously enough, all the fury and indignation seemed to drain away from Frau von Schreyvogl at once. She pressed close to her husband, smiled at him, and said there was no need for him to get worked up about nothing, there had just been a small misunderstanding between her and the nursemaid, which was now cleared up. Then she left the kitchen, humming a little tune. As I was about to follow her to fetch the butter from the larder, the imposing figure of Herr von Schreyvogl almost entirely filled the doorway, making it impossible for me to get past him.

Herr von Schreyvogl looked kindly and a little sympathetically down at me and said his wife had told him I wasn't in the best of health, and he was really sorry. At the same time, however, he hoped the fact, rather painful to him, that since that conversation of ours which he remembered with pleasure I hadn't been back to the smoking room although he had often enjoyed a cigarette there, was connected with my indisposition and not any shyness or embarrassment on my part, or even some dislike of him. I made haste to assure him that I really had been unwell, but I felt much improved this morning, in fact almost completely better. Here my employer pinched my right cheek gently and said he was glad to hear it, really glad, and now that the circumstances had changed I mustn't deny him another meeting in the evening, it was positively my duty to cheer up an overworked, melancholy and fundament- ally lonely man entangled in a network of obligations like himself with my company, which did him a great deal of good, why not soon, why not this very evening, he'd expect me in the smoking room. I dared not refuse, and nodded my consent, whereupon he stood aside and let me slip through the doorway beneath his outstretched arms.

Over the next hour, as I saw to the twins and then went into the kitchen to top and tail the gooseberries from Altaussee carefully, pricking each with a pin and then steeping them in water in which I had dissolved a little alum until they rose to the surface, I couldn't get that brief conversation in the doorway between the kitchen and the corridor out of my mind. And as I took the gooseberries out of the water and dried them with a cloth, meanwhile picturing my employer's dark, curly head, his well-shaped nose and his high, broad forehead, I was overcome once again, to my surprise, by a kind of daze, a sense of weakness that began in my head and spread to the whole of my body. When I put my hand to my forehead and cheeks to check my body temperature, my skin was burning hot. I couldn't explain these strange processes inside me, any more than I could explain the gooseflesh and the trembling of my hands that came over me the next moment, but I guessed that this time the cause was not some childish ailment caught later in life, but my elegant and masterful employer.

The loud voices of Frau von Schreyvogl and the parlourmaid, perfectly audible and obviously emanating from the sitting room, suddenly broke into my anxious reflections and emotions. I heard the Baroness the Honourable Frau von Schreyvogl saying it obvi- ously wasn't enough for her, the parlourmaid, a good-for-nothing tramp whom she, Baroness the Honourable Frau von Schreyvogl, had rescued from misery, to keep pestering her, Frau von Schreyvogl's, husband, to whom she had been bound before God and man by the holy sacrament of marriage for eight years, with her tasteless and futile attempts at seduction, lying in wait for him everywhere so that the poor man couldn't take a step without coming into the parlourmaid's vulgar presence, oh no, she, the parlourmaid, had now been brazenly misappropriating the family's property, thus trying to undermine their very subsistence, which could be described as endangered in any case, and she ought to be well and truly ashamed of herself. I then heard the parlourmaid replying angrily that this was pathetic, she must be joking, if they were going to talk about attempts at seduction then might she beg to point out that it was by no means Herr von Schreyvogl who had to be on his guard against her, the parlourmaid, but the other way around, and she, the parlourmaid, was at her wits' end trying to avoid that ladykiller. If she reached up for a jug on one of the top shelves in the kitchen he'd slip his arm round her waist unexpectedly, skirt-chaser that he was, if she bent down to brush the fringes of the carpet, he'd be right there behind her as if he had popped up out of the ground, touching her where he shouldn't and taking his time over it, and if she lay down on the floor to get at the underside of a chest of drawers and dust the cobwebs off it, she'd suddenly feel his lecherous hands under her skirts. As for the theft of the jar of jam of which she was accused, she didn't need to consume her employers' preserves, she came from the Wachau area, famous for its orchards, and her mother sent her fruit both fresh and preserved by the kilo every fortnight, delivered by a cousin who worked in an iron foundry in Vienna and went home every other week. After this self-justification I heard nothing for a while, but then the cold, calm voice of Frau von Schreyvogl spoke. She had no intention, she said, of defending herself and above all her husband against the monstrous slanders of a common parlourmaid, all she could say was that she, the parlourmaid, was dismissed on the spot, and would have to work her mischief in some other family.

As I put the gooseberries in preserving jars, covered them with sugar and steamed them for about ten minutes, I let what I had involuntarily overheard run through my head. Although Frau von Schreyvogl had been far from amiable to me recently, I was on her side, since it was impossible for her husband, that refined gentleman and good employer, to have behaved in such a disgraceful way as the parlourmaid said. Her malicious insinuations against Herr von Schreyvogl aroused my sympathy, and I determined to be particularly friendly and understanding at the meeting we had arranged in the smoking room.

That evening I washed myself as I generally did, carrying the twins' bathwater into the walk-in wardrobe in the old enamel jug and pouring it into the basin, though I was slightly surprised to notice that I was paying rather more attention than usual to my personal hygiene, passed the flannel more frequently over my breasts, stomach and thighs, cleaned my teeth more thoroughly with powdered diluvial chalk and brushed my hair a hundred times instead of the usual fifty. I put on my linen nightdress, lay down on the mattress and covered myself with my nursemaid's uniform, for Frau von Schreyvogl had said she was sure I wouldn't object to her taking the pretty quilt away for the time being, its rustic diamond pattern went so well with the bedroom furnishings in their summer residence in Altaussee, and I listened for sounds from the smoking room. Suddenly there was a knock on my door, and before I could answer, it was opened, and there stood Herr von Schreyvogl, smiling. He bent, for the door to the walk-in wardrobe was low, and came in. Much embarrassed, I tried to cover myself up with the nursemaid's uniform as best I could, and courteously returned his greeting.

He'd just thought, began Herr von Schreyvogl, he'd just thought he could spare me the short journey to the smoking room, since I must certainly be tired in the evening after doing housework and looking after his sons, who as he knew were a remarkably lively pair, so he thought he would come to me instead, he hoped I didn't mind, and he must say he liked my room very much indeed, the furnishings were both attractive and functional, and the mattress seemed to have just the right amount of give in it. So saying he came closer, leaned over me, and tested the sagging seagrass mattress several times by pressing it with his slender but powerful hand. Then he sat down at the far end of my bed and placed one hand lightly on my left shin, under the nursemaid's uniform. Wasn't I cold, he asked, the fine late summer days were over now, it was getting cool, and those of us who had an opportunity to keep each other warm could count ourselves lucky. Since a curious shudder had run through me when he touched my shin, I said truthfully, yes, I was in fact shivering slightly, whereupon he slipped his hand under the nightdress, began massaging my calves and said I'd soon feel warmer. Sure enough, all of a sudden waves of heat swept over me, and I admitted in some confusion that he was right, perhaps it was the candle flame that warmed the little room so nicely. Then my employer slipped under the nursemaid's uniform beside me, sighing, Rosa, oh Rosa, could he be my little stove and keep me warm, just for an hour or so, just for a minute, and he put his large but slender hands around me. In alarm I groped for the little bag of salt I was wearing round my neck, but halfway there my hand fell powerlessly on Herr von Schreyvogl's shoulder, for I was almost paralysed by the weakness that overcame me, which must certainly have been the result of the illness from which I'd only just recovered and the lack of food from which I had recently been suffering. The Honourable Herr von Schreyvogl noticed my gesture, smiled, took the ribbon with the little bag from my neck, placed it beside the candle, and said, there now, that wouldn't bother me any more. Then he blew out the candle.

Next day Frau von Schreyvogl was in a better temper than usual and said that even if her days were unpleasant and trying, at least her nights were refreshing, for she was naturally blessed with a capacity for deep, relaxing sleep, in fact she slept like a top, a characteristic of almost all members of the von Purgstall-Wohlleben family. Perhaps when I'd done the sweeping and dusting, duties that I would of course have to undertake after the extremely unedifying departure of the parlourmaid, I would be good enough to take Tassilo and Klaus Maria to the Volksgarten, it was exceptionally still today with no wind at all, very unusual in Vienna. But she must impress upon me that unknown children and adults who looked as if they were of the middle or lower-middle classes, and in particular those who seemed to belong to the working class, must be kept well away from the pram, more especially if they appeared to be friendly, which was the most suspicious thing of all. You never knew, the most extraordinary things could happen, quite apart from the fact that such people lived in far from hygienic conditions, their own fault in most cases, and spread bacteria wherever they went, which could lead to an outbreak of dangerous, indeed life-threatening diseases. She was warning me: if Tassilo and Klaus Maria fell sick again, even if they only caught a harmless chill, she would hold me responsible and wouldn't hesitate to declare our contract of employment null and void, particularly as our relations had not been especially harmonious from the first.

As I pushed the pram past Christ with Toothache at the back of the cathedral, I thought I would pay a brief call on the Madonna of the Servants and ask her to forgive me for the sins I'd committed since I last saw her. Outside the huge entrance I came upon Lyuba, begging, who said, oh, so I'd got the job then, happily took the twins out of the pram and hugged and kissed them, and I seized my chance and said since she knew Tassilo and Klaus Maria, could I ask her to look after them for a moment, I wanted to light a candle for the soul of my mother, who would surely have gone straight to heaven after her death without having to spend time in purgatory first. Then I went over to the plinth on which my new patron saint stood, knelt down before her and confessed that since my last visit to her I had committed theft and told lies, and moreover I had done certain other things, I didn't know quite what to think of them because of my lack of information and experience, but they might possibly be thought a dreadful indiscretion very closely connected with the sin of unchastity, a sin which I had hitherto known little except by hearsay because I found it so difficult to work out what it really meant. I was also in a state of doubt because up till now I had believed that you felt uncomfortable about sin even as you committed it, but that was fully true only with my lying, partly true of my theft, and not at all true in the case of the third offence as I had just described it to her; on the contrary, those activities had aroused distinctly enjoyable feelings comparable to the consumption of delicious food or the pleasure of the tender caresses lavished on me by my mother and later by a dear friend of mine. Anyway, I was most fervently asking her to forgive me and not withdraw the favour she had already so kindly shown me by allowing me to find another position at once. I looked imploringly up at the Virgin, and thought to my alarm that I saw a different expression on her kind face and on the face of her son, who usually looked so cheerful: an angry, indeed a hurt expression. As I lit one of the slender, tapering white candles laid out for sale near the plinth of the statue I remembered the twins, and turned to hurry back to the entrance. In turning, I stopped for a moment, reached out quite involuntarily for the candles, hid three of them in the apron of my uniform, and left the cathedral.

Lyuba and several men, some of them of rather disreputable appearance, were standing around the pram, amusing the twins by picking them up and petting them in turn, and when I went over to the party Lyuba waved a hand at the men and said could she introduce her dear friends, some of them unemployed like her and passing their time with an occasional bet on the horses in the Prater, some of them directly involved with those noble beasts as so-called waterers, the indispensable assistants of the cabbies, who gave their horses water, groomed them, and polished their harness to a high gloss, and in any case they were all good, honest fellows. I greeted the company rather shyly, and looking into one face after another I thought I saw a striking likeness to Milan Havelka in the features of the man who was holding Tassilo, wore a brown peaked cap and had a brown cravat at his throat. I quickly took Tassilo from him and Klaus Maria from Lyuba, put them both back in the pram and said I was sorry, but I was in a hurry and must be off, I had important things to do.

From where I stand today, with the end of my earthly existence so close that I can judge matters rather more objectively, I count the following weeks among the happiest of my life, despite the fact that, as I now know, they were full of morally dubious activities and feelings, and even though the price I had to pay for that happiness was disproportionately high.

Herr von Schreyvogl got into the habit of coming to the walk-in wardrobe late every evening, and then to the seagrass mattress, where he initiated me into sensual pleasures that, as a more or less ignorant Bohemian girl, I wouldn't have dreamed were possible. Within a very short time he succeeded in breaking down the initial half-hearted resistance I put up to his dynamic and purposeful actions, convincing me by both words and deeds that it was all to my good for me to entrust myself to his expert guidance and comply obediently and swiftly with his tenderly whispered directions, since they reliably bore me up to the dizzy heights of a pleasure I had never known before. My employer reinforced his actions, performed with both vigour and deliberation, with words that flattered me and made me feel even more anxious to be of service to him in this new field as well as in others. They were expressions that reminded me strangely of the phrases I myself had used in my half-consciously composed *Ode to Olga*, for he said my figure was like a slender palm tree ready for him to climb, he said my eyes were like deep pools, my thighs like jewels, my neck was as a tower of ivory and the smell of my breath like apples. He put his mouth to my ear and whispered that there were threescore queens, and fourscore concubines, and virgins without number, but I, his dove, his undefiled, was but one, there was no flaw in me, I was fair as the moon and clear as the sun. Surprised and captivated, I listened as he asked me softly to let him come into my garden and eat my precious fruits, for I had enchanted his heart. Once, when I asked him if he knew the *Song of Solomon,* he said no, he didn't, the silk factory left him little time to devote to music.

After a while, however, I realized with some uneasiness that Herr von Schreyvogl was visiting me only every other evening. I went to great pains to satisfy him, to read his every wish in his eyes and dispel his business worries, but he became more and more monosyllabic, his gestures were more and more perfunctory and his visits shorter and shorter. When I asked at what seemed to me a good moment for some explanation of this change in his conduct, he replied rather impatiently that he didn't know what I meant, he was just the same as usual, I was imagining things, unhealthy fancies like that, remote from reality, were typical of my sex. I indicated hesitantly, but persistently, that recently he had not called on me daily but only every other day, to which he said crossly that a relationship like ours couldn't be summed up in purely arithmetical terms, he hadn't expected such a petty, calcu- lating approach from me, did I think feelings could be weighed and measured like goods for sale in the Karmelitermarkt, he must admit he was rather disappointed by this aspect of my personality, only now coming to light, when it was my yielding and selfless loving and giving qualities that had attracted him, and in the circumstances he thought some further curtailment of his visits advisable. So saying, he rose from the seagrass mattress, put on his dressing-gown, and concluded by saying that anyway his wife, whom he loved with all his heart and who, as I knew, was in an interesting condition, needed his attention and support more than ever now, I had no idea how happy the growth of new life made one feel, it was a happiness that could be only very approximately compared with any other. Then he stooped and left the walk-in wardrobe.

Herr von Schreyvogl allowed me to welcome him to it three or four more times and then finally withdrew his interest. Because the number of his visits, in which I had found such fulfilment, had been drastically reduced within so short a time I developed severe withdrawal symptoms, and the strange physical sensations – hot and cold shivers, feverish attacks and fits of faintness – caused first by an inadequate diet, then by illness, and finally by my passionate feelings for my employer returned, stronger than ever. These symptoms went hand in hand with an increase in my appetite, which I couldn't satisfy because of Frau von Schreyvogl's meanness. I no longer dared creep into the kitchen or the pantry by night, since I knew now that she kept a close check on the quantities of foodstuffs in her household. One place, however, was an exception, the cellar, for both the cook and she herself had an insurmountable fear of going down to that old, vaulted and rather eerie place, full of rats and mice as it was, and since Herr von Schreyvogl never concerned himself with household affairs, I was the only one who ventured into the depths of the building to fetch up wood, coal, potatoes and other provisions stored there, for I wasn't afraid of cellars, it was attics I feared, no doubt because of my rather unpleasant experiences in the Gerstner family's attic bedroom. When my appetite increased enormously with the withdrawal of Herr von Schreyvogl's love, and on the orders of the mistress of the household the cook gave me supper of a cold white bread dumpling left over from my employers' midday meal, I felt perfectly justified in saying I'd eat the dumpling in a moment, but first I had to go down to the cellar for a jar of pickled Znaim gherkins, she, the cook, knew how our mistress craved Znaim gherkins in her pregnancy, she always had to have Znaim gherkins within reach, we didn't want to risk a premature birth, did we, still less a miscarriage? Then I went down to the old vaults and indiscriminately ate anything edible stored there. I picked fragrant apples off the boards where they lay and bit with relish into their juicy flesh, delved into the wooden tub where tasty walnuts and hazelnuts were stored in sand to help them keep longer and cracked them impatiently with my teeth, dipped my forefinger greedily into jars of dark woodland honey from the Altaussee apiary, hungrily explored the tins of delicious gingernuts and other biscuits, swiftly opened the metal clips on jars full of red, green and yellow Hungarian peppers, stood on tiptoe to dig my teeth into the hams and sausages hanging from the vaulted ceiling by iron hooks, and tasted an extensive assortment of jams and fruit compôtes. And if I felt particularly hungry I would put my hand into the round container of eggs floating in isinglass, take a beautiful white egg out of the almost opaque liquid, and suck its contents. Then I would find a jar of Znaim gherkins, go slowly upstairs and back to the kitchen feeling well fed, and if the cook asked where on earth I'd been all this time, the dumpling had gone cold, I was quick to say that Frau Navratil the caretaker had asked me to read her a short piece about Georg Ritter von Schönerer from the newspaper, her eyes were getting worse every day, and anyway I wasn't hungry.

Some time later I found myself afflicted with increasing frequency by an unpleasant sense of nausea in the mornings, which at first I explained to myself by my secret feasts in the cellar and which led to a sudden diminution of my appetite and a deterioration in my general health. I kept wanting to vomit, my legs felt curiously heavy and I was tired all the time. I soon began to wonder if these ills were a punishment sent by the Madonna of the Servants for my recent more than dubious way of life and above all for the theft of the three wax candles, a crime that I had committed before her very eyes and that had surprised me myself, and I decided to give her back the two candles I hadn't yet used. On my next afternoon off I put on the new dress made by the

Slovakian dressmaker who did alterations in her place on the corner of Wollzeile and Postgasse, at a low price to which she agreed with the comment that we Slavs living in Vienna ought to stick together, obliged as we were to place all our abilities at the disposal of the Viennese bourgeoisie, receiving poor treatment in return, and I went off to St Stephen's Cathedral in it. It was a lovely pale lilac dress, with violet lace inserts at the throat and shoulders, long, full sleeves and pleated trimming at the hem, and since thanks to the dressmaker's solidarity I still had some of my first savings left, I had gone to the milliner's on the corner of Annagasse and Seilerstätte and bought a hat to match, which I had trimmed with orange and violet silk pansies in memory of my dear departed mother. When I had put the two candles back where they came from, I knelt down before the Madonna of the Servants, folded my hands and said quietly I realized that she couldn't just overlook the error of my ways, my theft of the candles which were there for the sole purpose of being lit in her honour and placed before her was a misdemeanour which couldn't easily be made good, although it had happened almost entirely without my conscious volition. Of course I had earned a reprimand, and I was ready to say an unlimited number of Paternosters and Ave Marias, she could decide how many for herself, but I wished she would do something to stop the almost intolerable nausea that came over me early in the morning every day. Apart from that, I thanked her heartily for the kindness she had shown me up to now, thanks to which I could come to see her in my new outfit. Then I stopped talking and looked hard at Our Lady's face to see if it showed any reaction at all to what I had just told her, but she seemed to be ignoring me and devoting her attention more assiduously than ever to her child, smiling lovingly at him, which at least suggested a kindlier frame of mind than her angry glance after my last visit.

As I turned from the Stephansplatz into the Graben, to amuse myself a little and mingle with the people out walking, Lyuba came towards me with outstretched arms and cried was this possible, why, I looked quite different in my delightful new outfit. I said it was true that I had nothing to complain of in that respect just now, but I had some health problems. When Lyuba took my arm in her free and easy way, propelling me through the crowd and saying I'd better tell her all about it, perhaps she could help, I began describing my complaints, and after a few minutes she stopped, looked at me gravely and said my ignorance was not just incredible, it was positively criminal, and the symptoms were only too clear: I was expecting a baby.

At this I asked Lyuba to sit down with me on a bench, because what she said had rather upset me. When we had found one I went on, saying that was impossible, how could it have happened, whereupon Lyuba clasped her hands in the air above her head and asked if no one had ever told me the really important facts of life. I replied no, not straight out, for while the nuns had a good deal to say about flowers untimely plucked and the fruit of the womb, they'd never gone into the subject in more detail, and when I started my bleeding, the nuns, sighing and looking up to heaven, had given me clean white cloths and told me a new part of my life was now beginning, pain was woman's lot, and I was to soak the bloody cloths in slightly salted water before washing them. Lyuba said I must go and talk to the man responsible for my condition immediately, of course he would have to marry me, and when I said he couldn't because he was married already and had been for the last eight years she cried, oh no, the Honourable Herr von Schreyvogl, she might have known it, that fine gentleman would chase any skirt inside and outside the Ring and the Linien ramparts, naturally he'd tried it on with her too, but unsuccessfully, whereas I, naive little lamb that I was, had obviously been easy prey. Anyway, once I had medical confirmation of my suspected condition I must have a straight talk to him, of course he'd have to meet the costs of my confinement and pay maintenance for the child. Rather doubtfully I said I wasn't sure he would be willing to do that, because he had to meet the costs of his wife's

217

confinement and the maintenance of their legitimate child first, it was to be born very soon, and Lyuba shook her head and said good heavens, was there no limit to my stupidity?

On the way back to the building at 18 Stubenring I kept thinking of my mother's fate, and with alarm I realized that I was in a fair way to following in her footsteps. The doctor Lyuba had recommended, who didn't inspire much confidence and had his shabby consulting rooms in a dark, narrow alley near the Southern Railway station, did indeed confirm that I was in my second month of pregnancy. It proved difficult to engineer a situation in which I could speak undisturbed to the Honourable Herr von Schreyvogl, since he was avoiding me whenever he could. But one day when Frau von Schreyvogl gave me a briefcase and said I was to go to the silk factory in Vienna 7, her husband had left this file with the double bookkeeping accounts at home, and no wonder, he'd been sitting over them for hours last night so that he was tired and absent-minded this morning, I seized my chance to visit him in the little office where he sat at a desk in front of a great many rolls of silk, and put him in the picture.

Herr von Schreyvogl leaned back in his armchair, said nothing for a while, and folded his hands over his pale grey silk poplin waistcoat. Then he said surely I didn't think he was going to believe this fairy tale of mine, I was far from being the first girl who had tried to fleece him like that, cases of servant girls embarking on relationships with their masters with ulterior motives of this nature were only too familiar, the overwhelming majority were flighty, greedy girls who did as they fancied with men of their own station on their afternoons off, and then if there were consequences brazenly tried to lay the blame on their employers and capitalize on their plight. Unfortunately, he was obliged to recognize this calculating streak in me too, I was obviously no exception. When I said I didn't know what he was talking about, I wasn't acquainted with any men in the city at all except for a piccolo who had been helpful to me when I arrived in

Vienna, very kindly finding me a bed for the night, Herr von
Schreyvogl cried, aha, there we had it, a piccolo, a bed for the
night, well, that said it all, and in any case he'd concluded from
my extremely free and easy conduct during our brief, insignificant
liaison that I was no little innocent. I'd better go and settle this
tiresome business with the waiter to whom I had given myself so
casually and immodestly in that obscure bed for the night, if
indeed, and it was by no means certain, there was any truth in the
story I was trying to palm off on him, in his office at that, where
God knew he had more important things to think about. However,
if I was really expecting, naturally I couldn't stay on in his
household, one pregnant woman was quite enough, as he was sure
I would see. I quietly said I didn't understand why he suddenly
sounded so different, didn't he remember the pet names he had
whispered in my ear in the walk-in wardrobe, but here Herr von
Schreyvogl brusquely interrupted me, saying pet names, what pet
names, he never called anyone by pet names except his wife, what
on earth put such a thing into my head, he was a married man and
a happily married man at that, and didn't need to think up pet
names for some chance-come maidservant. And now would I
please go away, I was taking up his valuable time, I'd better get
back to the Stubenring and give his wife his dear love, he was
looking forward to the leg of venison *au naturel* she had promised
to serve for dinner in the evening.

On the way back from the silk factory I was nearly run over
twice because I wasn't looking where I was going, first at the
junction of Siebensterngasse and Stiftgasse by a man riding a
velocipede and taking the bend at breakneck speed, then on the
corner of Parkring and Himmelpfortgasse by a one-horse carriage,
the driver of which, avoiding me, clipped his vehicle roughly
against the kerbstone and angrily requested the devil to take that
wretched woman. I let the scene that had just taken place in the
Honourable Herr von Schreyvogl's office sink into my mind as
slowly as possible, so as not to be utterly overwhelmed by what

had happened. Realizing how critical my present situation was, I tried to calm myself by imagining my mother's face and remembering the last words she had spoken to me, her only child, when she adjured me to continue acting in accordance with the Christian principles she had taught me. I must show forgiveness and pity, mildness and submission, and bow to the will of the Almighty, she had said, there was no point in being consumed by anger and hatred for others. And not only she but the nuns, Father Bohumil and Father Macarius had emphasized the fact that the meek would inherit the kingdom of heaven, if someone struck you on one cheek you must offer the other, and you were to love your enemies. What right did I have to examine such commandments critically, where could I turn in my hour of greatest need if not to the teachings of those who brought me up? I wouldn't condemn Herr von Schreyvogl, it wasn't my place to do so, vengeance is mine, saith the Lord, that's what the Bible said. I would bring my baby into the world and God would look after us, the way he looked after the lilies of the field and the birds of the air and everything else.

Back at No. 18 Stubenring I went in search of Frau von Schreyvogl at once to deliver her husband's message, and found her reading in the sitting room. Before I could open my mouth she closed the book, while I caught a fleeting glimpse of the title on its cover, *The Miracle of New Life*, drew herself up to her full height, adjusted her glasses and asked icily how I had the nerve to defy her express directions in such a shockingly thoughtless and irresponsible way. No sooner had she impressed it upon me, for very good reasons, that Tassilo and Klaus Maria must on no account come into contact with strangers than I took the twins off to the Stephansplatz, where I mingled with a gang of vagabonds, ruffians and crooks known to the police who were loafing about there, and let them pass those poor defenceless children from one pair of arms to another. When I objected that as far as I knew they were not the kind of people she described but friends of a girl I

220

knew, serious-minded people who worked with horses, more precisely racehorses, jockeys and breeders and so forth, my employer told me I was a born liar, she would rather take the word of Frau Navratil, who had never once told her anything but the truth in all these years, and Frau Navratil would be taking the twins for their walks now, I must realize that a nursemaid who represented real danger to the existence of those who were dearer to her, Frau von Schreyvogl, than anyone else in the world except her husband couldn't be tolerated in her home any longer. She would immediately pay me my wages for the coming month, let no one say she didn't treat her staff fairly, and she would expect me to remove from the wardrobe my personal possessions, apart of course from the nursemaid's uniform and the apron that went with it, and leave a family towards which I had conducted myself with anything but loyalty. She had already written my reference and it was lying on the chest of drawers.

10

After another pupil, a talented coloratura soprano, had told me at the end of a singing lesson that she had decided to continue her studies in Rome, I began to ask myself how I was going to earn my living over the next few months, and wondered which of my possessions I could take on the discouraging way to the Dorotheum this time. For fear of annoying my mother even more, since she already seemed rather displeased with my liking for Magnolia, I decided not to dispose of any of the items I'd promised her to keep and venerate, but instead try selling some of the photographs from my time in the Vienna Boys' Choir, for surely such genuine contemporary documents, recording the activities of a world-famous choir, would have their value. I confidently entered the auction house, and as I didn't know exactly which department to look for I showed a person at a window on the ground floor, who looked like an expert, four of the photographs taken by the Tutor with an Olympus camera and framed by myself, and asked him politely to direct me to the appropriate place. This person looked briefly at the photographs and then at me, and asked what I thought I was doing here with these amateur shots of half-grown boys, I surely didn't think this famous auction house, with its several subsidiaries in the Federal Republic of Germany and Prague and further branch offices in Brussels and Tokyo, had pederasts among its customers, to which, rather offended, I said there was no need to adopt that disparaging tone, couldn't he see that the young men in their well-cut sailor suits in the photographs were members of one of the most famous choirs in the world, the Vienna Boys' Choir, invited to perform before kings and emperors and received by the most powerful heads of state? When the person, not sounding much impressed, pointed out that Vienna was full of photographs of the Vienna Boys' Choir, you saw them on every other CD displayed in Vienna's audio shops in Kärntner-strasse, on the Graben and in the Kohlmarkt, they grinned down at you from every advertisement hoarding in the Inner City, he was sick of the sight of their milky-skinned angel faces, red mouths wide open and eyes hypocritically raised aloft, I replied that he, the person, might try for a more courteous means of expressing himself, after all at this very moment he had a former member of the Boys' Choir before him, it was a famous Austrian institution and such invective practically amounted to treason. The person made a weary gesture, shook his head slowly and said, treason, I must be joking, he wondered how much money that pre-pubertal association cost the Austrian state, and when I replied in some annoyance that the four choirs, each consisting of twenty-four boys, with two of the choirs always on tour, needed no state support, they financed themselves entirely out of their own funds, he said he wondered what on earth had induced him to enter into this tedious discussion with me, what was my idea, the Dorotheum sold works by world-famous photographers like Man Ray, Andy Warhol, Cindy Sherman and Prince Philip, I could try my luck with my photographs at the flea market held rain or shine on Saturdays between Rechte and Linke Wienzeile, but if he were me he wouldn't get too hopeful. At this moment the manuscripts expert who had given such an unfavourable opinion on the double sheet of lined paper in Mahler's handwriting came down the stairs and said, oh no, this was too much, after the impudent attempt at fraud for which I'd been banned from the house, here I was back again, venturing into the halls of the Dorotheum, and I'd better get out if I didn't want to be arrested, whereupon I quickly picked up my photographs and left the building through the door into Spiegelgasse.

After this unpleasant altercation I decided to raise my spirits with a little walk in the Prater and take a light lunch there, since there wasn't a cloud in the sky and the air could almost be described as balmy. I love the Prater, but I can never visit its extensive terrain with all those trees, shrubs and grassy expanses in spring or early summer, because although the warmer temperatures do to some extent protect me from colds and chills I'm particularly vulnerable at that time of year, that's to say I react to flower pollen with violent sneezing, considerable swelling of the mucous membrane of the nose and nasal secretions, along with conjunctivitis and sometimes even swelling of the spleen, facial oedema, nettle rash and hives. My attempts to combat this allergy with full baths, hip baths, affusions to the thighs and going about barefoot have not yet been successful, nor has rinsing out my nose with a decoction of horsetail, whereas the homoeopathic medicaments *arsenicum* D6, *sabadilla* D4 and *aralia racemosa* D3 can provide some temporary amelioration of my condition. I was about to go into a restaurant in the Hauptallee of the Prater to order roast veal and camomile tea when I remembered the dismal state of my finances and decided to have a pair of frankfurters at a sausage stall instead, with mustard, horseradish and a nice crusty roll, although unfortunately I never actually consumed these items since the sausage seller who, as it transpired in the course of the argument developing between him and myself, was also the proprietor of the stall, on being asked politely whether he was sure the processed meat of the frankfurters he had boiled and was now selling was perfectly all right, because the rather artificial pink colour worried me slightly, and whether the roll he had given me was today's, because it did feel a little soft, and whether the horseradish had really been grated within the last ten minutes, seeing that the fibres of freshly grated horseradish are usually white and this looked a little grey, replied in a surprisingly angry tone that he'd been running his sausage stall for seventeen years now, when the *Kronenzeitung* newspaper did a gourmet survey of the sausage stalls of Vienna his own had achieved an excellent position right towards the top of the middle ranks of those assessed, the article he'd clipped from the *Kronenzeitung* about it was stuck to the wall of the sausage stall to my right and I could read it any time I liked. Then he removed the rectangular paper plate holding two frankfurters and the mustard and the horseradish from one of my hands, and the roll from the other, and said my morbid suspicions were insulting and would I kindly go and eat at another licensed sausage stall, so far as he knew there were over two hundred of them in Vienna.

So I strolled on, sat down on a bench not far from the giant Ferris wheel, and tried to cheer myself up after this second unpleasant incident of the day by thinking about Magnolia. A few days earlier we'd gone out from the Schottentor to Nussdorf on the D-line tram, walking through the vineyards, which were wet with rain, in the direction of Heiligenstadt, since I planned to go to the Mayer am Pfarrhof Inn for some Heuriger wine, but when we were passing the old and not very inviting tavern called the Bunch of Grapes, Magnolia insisted on going in there for a drink, which turned out not to be a very good idea, since the double-chinned fat landlady with many little red veins on her cheeks and a dirty white pleated apron who served us was very unfriendly, and the white wine in the glass jug she put down on the red and white checked tablecloth was tart. However, Magnolia seemed to enjoy this rest, the dry, tart wine went to her head, she said it was amazing, time seemed to have stood still here, and after we had left the inn and walked a little further she suddenly took my hand, made me stop, and laid her head with all its little black plaits on my shoulder. Once again those sensations made up of my feelings for my mother, the earlier and passionate emotions I had felt for the Tutor and something entirely new came over me, the same sensations as I felt when Magnolia stood by the baby grand and sang, and I put my arm around her waist and looked down at the two big dark cubes of the General Hospital below emerging from the haze that covered the city.

While I was unlocking the front door of my apartment in the Death House after this expedition, Fräulein Haslinger, having heard me approaching, came up to me looking rather flushed and holding an open Bible, and said she had just been reading in the *Song of Solomon*, she found the *Song of Solomon* most impressive, why didn't I spend this rainy late afternoon immersing myself for a while in that incomparable religious poem with which I would certainly be familiar, although Catholic circles in Vienna didn't by any means all agree in their moral assessment of it, and when I said she was wrong there, I'd never heard of the *Song of Solomon*, Fräulein Haslinger, looking flushed, pressed the Old Testament she was holding into my hand, her head briefly resting on my shoulder as she did so, then straightened her neck, looked up at me and said, her eyes half closed, 'Let him kiss me with the kisses of his mouth,' wasn't that just lovely, I could bring back her copy that evening, she didn't mind if it was quite late in the evening.

Feeling rather surprised by Fräulein Haslinger's unusually forthcoming behaviour, I sat down in my armchair and began to read, and to my surprise I realized that the writer was describing exactly the afternoon I had just spent in the late-autumn vineyards north of Vienna. 'My beloved spake, and said unto me, Rise up, my love, my fair one, and come away,' I read. 'Let us get up early to the vineyards; let us see if the vine flourish.' 'He brought me to the banqueting house,' the writer continued, 'and his banner over me was love.' Then came the line, 'His right hand doth embrace me.' I leafed through the work. 'I am black, but comely, O ye daughters of Jerusalem, as the tents of Kedar, as the curtains of Solomon. Look not upon me, because I am black,' it went on, and later, 'Thou art all fair, my love; there is no spot in thee.'

When I had finished reading the poem I got up, went over to the telephone and called Magnolia. Her great-aunt answered and said, oh, it's young Herr Horvath, for a moment she'd thought it was the foreign gentleman with the lovely deep voice again, no doubt I'd like to speak to the child, who was reading as usual, she'd ruin her eyes. Then she brought Magnolia to the phone. Magnolia, I said, Magnolia, have you ever come across the *Song of Solomon*? Her voice when she answered told me that she was smiling. Oh yes, Josef, she said, oh yes, I know the *Song of Solomon*. Now do let me go on with what I'm reading.

Six

And so it was that half an hour later I was walking towards St Stephen's Cathedral with my cardboard suitcase, hoping to meet Lyuba, who was so much cleverer and more experienced than me, and might be able to help me. I did in fact find her outside the main entrance, in conversation with an unemployed governess who had found work paid by the hour sorting feathers in a small millinery accessories business in Mariahilf, and a likeable if slightly intoxicated chambermaid currently working in the Prater as third girl assistant to the famous conjuror Anton Kratky-Baschik, who had owned his own magic theatre on the Fireworks Field since 1864, so she told me, I really must visit it. Lyuba pointed to my case and said my services as nursemaid to the von Schreyvogl family were obviously no longer required, and when I could do no more than nod, since my eyes filled with tears, she put a friendly arm round my shoulders and said I should be glad of it, good riddance to that miserly beanpole of a baroness and her honourable husband the shady seducer. What's more, there was something to celebrate: a few days ago she and the other two here, with a few more like them, had founded the *Maidservants' Clarion*, a radical monthly journal for female domestic servants, a step of which great things might be expected. By a lucky chance they had found a young unemployed typesetter who had expressed her willingness to print eight hundred copies a month in a basement, unfortunately rather a damp one, in the Margareten district on a small hand press, worn but still serviceable, which she, the typesetter, had acquired through her connections in the printing trade. Of course the number of copies a month could rise and with luck would, depending on demand. Lyuba wanted me to join this struggle for the rights due to us, all volunteers were welcome, particularly women like me already used to expressing themselves in writing in one form or another, and even if in my own case my written works, as I'd told her, were contributions to the history of the Catholic saints, a subject remote from the fight for freedom of the servant class if not actually hostile to it, well, one couldn't pick and choose, and the movement was only in its infancy. I wiped a tear from the corner of my eye, cleared my throat and said I felt honoured by her confidence in me, but as she could imagine just now I was so absorbed in the purely personal problems which we'd been discussing not long ago that I was hardly even capable of thinking clearly, let alone writing revolutionary articles, but I promised to support her work as soon as I had found at least a partial solution to those difficulties. Lyuba thanked me and suggested a little visit to the landlord of the Merry Vintner tavern on the Brillantengrund, to drink to the favourable reception of the first issue of the *Maidservants' Clarion*.

Except for my brief stay at the Bunch of Grapes in Nussdorf I had never been in a tavern before, for when my mother visited public places she confined herself to churches, the nuns had given me hardly any chance to move freely on my own in Prague, and my work in Vienna had kept me from knowing any of the places open to the public apart from playgrounds and produce markets. So I was not a little surprised when we stepped through the doorway of the smoky taproom from which singing and laughter surged out to meet us. The room was crowded with male and also, to my surprise, female customers, standing close together at the bar, drinking to one another and talking at the tops of their voices, while other visitors to the inn sat cheek by jowl at the few simple

wooden tables, swaying back and forth and singing. The landlord
was obviously pleased to see Lyuba, called out something in a
language I didn't understand, came round from behind the bar,
hugged her, found us room at a table and placed four bulbous
glasses with a ribbed, dark green foot and an etched pattern of
grapes in front of us, filling them with golden-yellow wine. Lyuba
said there was nothing like having a fellow countryman around,
this was Primož, a neighbour from Maribor, who had left Slovenia
a little while before her to try his luck in Vienna, and as we could
see had done very well in a very short time; also, being cleverer
than most, he had steered clear from the first of the displeasing
upper classes of Viennese society, a possibility seldom open to
women like us who came to the city, since most of us were obliged
to go into service in some bourgeois household. Then the three
women clinked glasses so vigorously that the wine slopped out,
drank, and insisted on my doing the same. Apart from the
Communion wine at Mass I had never drunk wine before, and a
shudder ran through me as I swallowed the tart liquid. But Lyuba
and her friends kept urging me to drink, and soon the taproom
seemed to me a bright and friendly refuge where I felt safe and
well among the noisy crowd of drinkers.

Suddenly a hush fell in the taproom, there was a whispering and
a buzzing, and we looked around to discover the reason for this
change in the atmosphere. The feather-sorter excitedly pointed to
a stocky man with a red face and a thick moustache, wearing
check trousers, a black velvet jacket and waistcoat, a white-spotted
blue cravat and a half-height top hat with a narrow brim, who was
in the company of several other persons, all obviously in cheerful
mood, and she whispered Bratfisch, that was Bratfisch, the cabby
Bratfisch and his colleagues had just come into the inn, what an
honour for the landlord, Bratfisch the cab driver was Crown Prince
Rudolf's personal cabby, everyone knew the Crown Prince was a
very sociable character and liked to mingle with the people when
he was driven out by the cabby, with whom he was on friendly

terms, in her opinion Crown Prince Rudolf was the best of the members of the imperial house by a long chalk, a pity he and his father didn't agree on matters of government. Here the conjurer's third girl assistant dug her in the ribs with her elbow and told her to shut up, Bratfisch was probably going to sing a song or two, and Lyuba, turning to explain to me, said Bratfisch was not just the Crown Prince's personal cabby but also gifted in singing and whistling, and would entertain us with the most delightful popular songs if we were lucky and he was in the mood, for he liked whistling something to the company on his nightly visits to the inns of Vienna. Sure enough, a little later Bratfisch swung himself up on a little platform beside the bar, and after a couple of humorous remarks to the guests, the meaning of which I didn't understand, he pursed his lips and whistled tune after tune. I listened, enchanted, and it seemed to me that apart from the songs 'The Trout' and 'The Linden Tree', which the Regional Postal Manager's wife used to sing in the afternoons, I had never heard anything so wonderful in my life. Stout and clumsy as the man was, the notes he whistled through his thick, pursed lips, his tongue flicking back and forth, rose light and lithe into the air, he twittered, warbled and trilled so charmingly that although I had enjoyed walking in the grass of the park at Marienbad when it was wet with dew, I couldn't remember ever hearing a bird sing anywhere near as well. After a while it struck me that Lyuba and her friends were looking at me, and I realized that while an hour ago I had been weeping in wretchedness and despair, the tears were now running down my face out of emotion and a vague yearning.

Since I had nowhere to spend the night, Lyuba suggested going back with them to the bed-woman's where the feather-sorter, the conjuror's third girl assistant and she had been sleeping for the last week. There would be a mattress vacant in their room at midday, she said, the place was reasonably clean and the bed-woman, a widow who was hard of hearing, didn't mind when you

232

came in and went out. So we set off in the dark, on foot and singing, to make the long journey back to Leopoldstadt on the banks of the Danube, where the bed-woman lived in an unattractive hut. Tired but far from depressed, I dropped on the mattress, which was stuffed with maize straw, and after praying to the Madonna of the Servants and thanking her for not abandoning me in my hour of need but instead sending me three good fairies, helpful, cheerful members of her sex and mine, I wondered briefly why the mattress was going round and round in circles, taking me with it, and then I fell asleep.

Next morning I looked in my case for the reference which I had picked up from the chest of drawers in the von Schreyvogls' walk-in wardrobe without really reading it. It said I was not at all suitable to have the care of children, particularly babies and toddlers, since my moral standards left much to be desired, and I was not only a notorious liar but had a dreadful tendency towards theft which, it was to be feared, might get even worse; besides, wilfully mingled with bad company, even taking with me those entrusted to my care and thus endangering them too. As I was reading this devastating condemnation Lyuba, who had come up behind me, looked over my shoulder and uttered a brief whistle. She could already picture me in some dark textile workshop in a musty basement in Vienna 6 knotting fringes, she said, or a *demi-mondaine* walking the Stadtpark on the lookout for cavaliers, because with a reference like that it was going to be next to impossible for me to find another position in a Viennese household. Then she bent down to me and whispered that in my present state she hoped I'd already looked around for an angel-maker, and I had better tell her which one I'd picked, she knew quite a number of them and might be able to tell me if my choice had fallen on someone who knew her job or not, you had to be careful with such women, they had quite a few girls who'd trusted them on their consciences. I turned round and asked her to tell me what she was talking about, I didn't know what a *demi-mondaine* was, or an angel-maker either, she must remember I wasn't Viennese-born and was still only very superficially acquainted with the customs of the city. Lyuba rolled her eyes and murmured, honestly, this child had to have everything explained to her, adding that a *demi-mondaine* was a kind of high-class prostitute who walked the parks looking for custom, and when, in some embarrassment, I interrupted her by admitting that I didn't know what a prostitute was either, she sighed and said there was no end to my naivety, a prostitute did what I had done with the Honourable Herr von Schreyvogl, but for money, and an angel-maker got rid of the consequences such activities entailed if you were unlucky, in short she destroyed the fruit of the womb. At this I rose from the wobbly, dirty kitchen table of the bed-woman's hut where I was sitting, straightened my back and asked Lyuba what she was trying to talk me into, my late mother had warned me on her deathbed about the criminal practices of such wicked women, even if she hadn't told me about them in detail – her own experience had been the same as mine, but despite suffering the greatest adversity, she'd had the courage to bring me, the fruit of her own womb, into the world, and surely she, Lyuba, didn't think I would go against my mother's principles; furthermore when I looked at her, Lyuba, she suddenly appeared to me Antichrist in person, she'd better get out of my sight and try tempting other girls away from the straight and narrow with her more than dubious propositions.

Here Lyuba cried that that was enough, and I might thank God that he'd brought a sensible person like herself across my path, a person who lived in the real world, unlike me, and had enough experience of life to know what was best to be done in a tricky situation. It was high time I took a good straight look at the extremely difficult predicament in which I found myself as the result of what could only be described as hair-raising gullibility and incredible stupidity, it was time I made use of my bird brain for the first time in my life and *did* something. Did I really think the world was just waiting for the illegitimate proletarian children of the likes of us, for a servant girl's brat, did I want to offload my mother's sad fate and my own pitiful lot on some poor little creature who never asked to be brought into the world by a helpless maidservant like me? How was I going to earn a living with such a millstone round my neck, who'd take a housemaid with a baby into service, I'd have to get the child looked after and that cost money, more money than I could earn, that amount of money could be found only if I went looking for custom in the Prater, she knew plenty of female servants who had been dim enough to give in to some kind of vague maternal instinct and were now either prostitutes registered with the police and working in brothels or common streetwalkers, many of them in the process of dying wretchedly of syphilis, it was on the official records that a good half of the prostitutes of Vienna had once been maidservants, and the percentage of unofficial working girls who originally belonged to that class of society was about ten times as high. Well, there we were, that was the way of the world, the real world wasn't that fine house in the park at Marienbad where I'd grown up, the world was a sink of iniquity, a ladies' boxing ring like the one in the Prater where people smashed each other's faces in, and when was I going to get my mind around that fact? I'd better go and see Black Sophie in the Lobau before it was too late, that would be best, not only was Black Sophie well versed in midwifery and knowledgeable about love charms and curses, tinctures and potions of all kinds for man and beast, she was also the best angel-maker in Vienna and wouldn't ruin my health like some others in the same line. And once I'd got rid of what was still a tiny burden, rather than waiting until it was a millstone, I had better look for proper work again, or else put my abilities to good use in lightening the yoke borne by the servant class, myself included. So saying, Lyuba turned on her heel and left the bed-woman's kitchen and her house.

This outburst of anger from my only friend in Vienna had made me feel so uncertain of myself that I decided to take a little walk along the banks of the Danube, since I had noticed that I found a solution to my problems more quickly and easily in the immediate vicinity of large expanses of water than anywhere else. Sunk in deep gloom, I walked along the path on the bank, for the cheerfulness I had felt last night after my unaccustomed consumption of wine had vanished when I woke in the early morning, leaving nothing but a dull headache behind. After a while I came to a little tongue of land projecting out into the Danube, where the kinds of trees found in water meadows grew, and at the very end of this small promontory I found a little hollow containing several rows of low, grass-grown mounds next to a small hut, with crosses of wood or wrought iron on them and shaded by alders and willows. I slowly walked down the gentle slope and looked at one of these unadorned burial places after another, but except for one plaque with faded wording that I couldn't decipher I found no name, no year, no picture, no funerary inscription, nothing to tell me anything about the dead lying here in this strange place. Since the quiet spot matched my own sad mood so well, I sat down on the grass of the slope, clasped my arms round my knees, laid my forehead on them and gave myself up to the thoughts that were circling around in my aching head, unable to find any way out.

Suddenly a hoarse, feeble male voice broke into my brooding. Another visitor at last, said the voice, a person could sometimes feel really lonely in this peaceful but secluded spot. I looked up and into the suntanned face, criss-crossed by a grid of countless fine, very fine lines, of a little old man with long, thin white hair, holding a sickle in one hand and a rake in the other. Now what brought a young girl like me here, he inquired, had I lost my way, I wasn't of an age to feel drawn to the dead, let alone those whose names, with a few exceptions, no one knew, since they had sought and indeed found their deaths in the water and were washed up here by the eddying Danube. In alarm I asked the old man if he was talking about drowned bodies and he said yes, yes, drowned bodies, he had been looking after their graves for years, didn't get a penny in return, it was a kind of pastime of his, you might call it a hobby, he lived in a dreary rented place not far from here and he'd always wanted a garden, so now he had found his garden, a little graveyard garden, a garden for the dead, he was sure the poor drowned people wouldn't mind his looking after them, mowing the grass, pulling the weeds out of their grave mounds and straightening the crosses when the Viennese wind knocked them askew, making sure everything didn't get overgrown, I had no idea how quickly everything seeded itself out here in the water meadows, corncockle, stinging nettles, thistles and bindweed would be smothering everything before you knew it. He brandished the sickle above his head and laughed. But as long as he lived, he announced, yes, until Gustl Papuschek joined his dead charges underground, everything would be kept in order here. Then he looked at me. I didn't look very cheerful, he said, and yet I was a neat, pretty little thing, I ought to be having a good time with others like me, why wasn't I at the five-kreuzer dance in the Prater, that was where I belonged, on the dance floor and not in the graveyard, though there was something to be said for graveyards. Youth passed so soon, the skin wrinkled like a winter apple, your hair turned white and fell out, you lost your teeth, you ached all over, just look at him, Gustl Papuschek, he'd been a handsome fellow himself in his time though you'd hardly believe it now. He leaned on the handle of his rake and let his glance wander over the grave mounds. Then he looked at me again and said he could imagine how young girls like me, girls who hadn't recovered from their first lovesickness, women expecting an illegitimate child and unable to deal with the situation, might do something desperate in poverty and need, lonely folk with no one they could turn to for help, oh yes, such things had happened, of course, and always would, but you couldn't just fling your life away like that, there was always some way out if you were only patient for a while, wasn't there? When I heard the old man talk like that, heard him describing my own fate, I buried my face in my hands and began to weep. Then the old man came closer, sat beside me, put his rake and his sickle down on the grass, patted my head and said, there, there, why so sad, such a lovely child, pretty as a picture, a blonde angel, it couldn't be as bad as all that, I'd soon see, I'd soon see, everything would be all right by the time I married. The old man's company did me good, and I wept and wept until I thought I had no more tears to shed, while the old man talked and talked. He had buried some of these unfortunates himself, he said, the police brought them along, and a pretty sight they were after lying in the water for days or weeks on end or even longer, as I could imagine. Anyway, he laid them out on the table in the hut and cleaned them up, carefully, because a finger or an arm could easily drop off a drowned body like that, it was all sodden, of course, bound to be after so long in the water. It wasn't pleasant work, no, it certainly wasn't, and he admitted that of an evening he felt afraid, really scared, but that was part of the job, and in the last resort he loved them all, all his poor dead folk, each as much as the next.

After I had pulled myself together I stood up, said goodbye to the gravedigger, and climbed the slope again. Souls, rest in peace, / sweet slumber ye have found, / your woes now cease / laid in this quiet ground, Gustl Papuschek called after me in his thin voice, waving, and then he had disappeared from sight in the hollow.

As I went back along the path by the bank I thought of the people who had drowned in the Danube and found their last resting place in that little hollow, and I couldn't help admiring their resolution, for it must take a great deal of courage to make up your mind to such a death. On the other hand the nuns had taught us that respect for the life given us by God precluded suicide, and that it was a terrible sin against the fifth commandment unless you were voluntarily giving your life for the sake of others. I stopped at a sandy place on the bank, and standing there thoughtfully I found myself trying to throw smooth stones over the water in a shallow arc. I wondered how the piccolo was getting on, and hoped he hadn't taken the terrible step he contemplated, although I could understand him better now than when we had met on that little island in the river, and the idea of walking on and on into the water until I was submerged in it and rid of all my troubles at a stroke began to seem seductive. Deep in such thoughts, I returned to the bed-woman's place, where the feather-sorter was waiting for me and told me we would have to share two straw mattresses between the four of us now and occupy them as our working hours dictated, because the bed-woman had raised the price per night. She was just off to Vienna 6 to sort feathers, she said, and then she was going to see Lyuba in the temporary editorial office of the *Maidservants' Clarion* in the basement in Margareten, so if I liked I could rest on her mattress meanwhile. I said I wasn't tired and would walk around the city a little; I had a few things to think over, and you thought better on the move.

I set off towards the Inner City without any clear idea of where I was going or what I planned to do. The sun was shining, and I decided to take the route through the Prater with its expanses of grass and fine old trees and walk past the Rotunda, the great building erected by the Emperor for the World Exhibition in 1873, which impressed me deeply whenever I set eyes on it. I hoped to be able to afford a ticket some day, so that I could go up to the roof in the hydraulic lift, climb still further up stairs and ladders to the lantern at the very top and touch the copy of the imperial crown that stood above it, over five metres in height and weighing four tons. Sadly, I thought that my dismissal had made any hopes of the fulfilment of that wish almost as unlucky as my mother's longing for the pilgrimage to Lourdes on which she never went. On my way I passed through a pretty little wood with a simple inn standing in a clearing in the middle of it, a place where you could go in and drink a glass of beer or wine. A man and a girl were sitting at one of the rustic wooden tables outside the inn, and when I came closer I saw that the man was the Honourable Herr von Schreyvogl, whose slender but strong hands were caressing a pair of small, rather plump hands that were extremely familiar to me, the hands of the dismissed parlourmaid. I passed the two of them, pretending not to see them, but out of the corner of my eye I noticed the parlourmaid withdrawing her small hand from beneath the Honourable Herr von Schreyvogl's and running it through his dark, curly hair, whereupon the Honourable Herr von Schreyvogl caught hold of the small hand and covered its firm back with a number of little kisses. I was almost out of the clearing when I distinctly heard him telling her that she alone was fair and without spot, her skin smelled sweeter than cinnamon and myrrh, her hair was softer than the fleece of a flock of goats on Mount Gilead, and when I cast a quick glance back before turning off along a little path through the woods, I saw him bending to lift the hem of the parlourmaid's skirt and gently massage her left shin.

How I reached the Rotunda I don't remember, I only know that by the time I set eyes on the huge cupola, the tall pillars and the gallery twenty-three metres high I had made up my mind. I would go to see Black Sophie in the Lobau that very day and get rid of the thing growing inside me, which once born might look just like the Honourable Herr von Schreyvogl, might be his living image, even though I knew that my mother, the priests and the nuns would never forgive me for taking such a step. Nor do I remember exactly why I suddenly and irrevocably came to that decision, but it was something to do with the way the Honourable Herr von Schreyvogl bent down to lift the hem of the parlourmaid's dress, a gesture that I can see clearly before my mind's eye to this day, although I caught only a fleeting glimpse of it from a distance.

I made my way straight to the editorial basement in Margareten, where Lyuba was sitting at a little desk writing by the light of an oil lamp, and asked her to tell me exactly where the angel-maker she had mentioned lived, because I proposed to go and see her as soon as possible. Lyuba looked up, startled, and said she was surprised and pleased that I'd changed my mind so completely in such a short time, and if I liked she would come with me as soon as she'd finished her work, which consisted of writing the leader for the first edition of the *Maidservants' Clarion*, dwelling on the unusually high suicide rate among female servants, a long overdue revelation, for the cases in which maidservants jumped out of windows, poisoned themselves with lysol, turned on the gas tap or threw themselves into the water were increasing at an alarming rate. And since I with my convent education was certainly better at spelling than she was, would I cast a quick eye at it over her shoulder and correct any mistakes? While I was doing this the conjuror's third girl assistant came down the short flight of steps into the basement, stood behind Lyuba too, skimmed through what she had written so far and said the article was much too dry, Lyuba must remember that most maidservants were uneducated and in the evening felt utterly exhausted after their work anyway, what servant girl wanted to hear about percentages and statistics, it was real people they needed, true-to-life characters, young girls like themselves with whom they could identify, desperate, intimidated, downtrodden creatures who stood freezing on the banks of the Danube on foggy evenings in late autumn with a merciless war between the fear of death and the knowledge that there was no way out being waged inside them, a struggle in which hopelessness would win the day, and they would pick up their skirts and walk slowly, very upright, into the black river, until the icy water came first to their knees, then to their waists, then to their breasts and up to their necks, finally closing gently over their heads and flowing quietly on, through the Marchfeld and on through Hungary, until it came to the Black Sea. Lyuba turned, looked at the conjuror's third assistant in surprise, and said did she really think so, yes, she had to agree that didn't sound bad at all, perhaps her friend was right, why didn't she sit there instead of her and write down what she'd just said straight away, and then she and I could go off without delay on an errand that couldn't be postponed.

Late in the afternoon, after a long and tiring walk, we crossed to the opposite bank of the Danube and went on to the little cottage where Black Sophie lived in the isolated stretch of country, overgrown with undergrowth, between the Natterfleck and Zigeunermais areas. Lyuba knocked at the front door, hanging off its hinges and bleached and battered by the wind and weather of Vienna, wind and weather from which this desolate, flat region on the other bank of the river is not as well protected as the areas on the right bank of the Danube, and immediately we heard an unpleasantly shrill, harsh voice call out from inside asking who was there, she wasn't expecting anyone and her consultations were always without exception in the morning, but when Lyuba had given her name the door opened and a bony middle-aged woman with pitch-black hair, deep-set dark eyes close to each other, a narrow mouth turning down at the corners and a prominent chin stood there before us in a long black dress. When the pair of them had held a brief discussion in a language I didn't understand, although I took it to be Slovenian, the woman looked keenly at me and beckoned us into the cottage. We left Lyuba in a kind of waiting room with bare, unwhitewashed, stained walls and a mud floor, with nothing in it except a couple of rickety chairs and a dark metal crucifix in one of its four corners, and I went further on with the angel-maker into a small, overheated little room with a great many bunches of dried plants hanging from the ceiling, and a glowing iron stove with a long stovepipe before which a plump black cat with glossy fur and a triangular white patch on its forehead was curled up asleep.

The woman, in slightly broken German, told me to undress and lie down on the plank bed that stood in one corner and had a tattered brown coverlet on it, and she would examine me. After she had palpated my stomach at length both internally and externally with her hard, pointed fingers, fixing me with her piercing eyes the whole time, while the cat, which had jumped up on the end of the bed, licked my toes, she nodded quickly several times and said no problem, no problem, luckily I was in rather poor physical shape, and in addition my reproductive organs were so underdeveloped that nothing very drastic would have to be done, a medicine made of various plant and animal substances would be enough to kill off the unwanted life within me. She had stocks of this mixture, its recipe was strictly secret, taken from an old manuscript she had inherited from her mother who came from the Karst, which to the best of her knowledge didn't exist in any other copy, but she would tell me that among other ingredients it contained cress, cuckoo flower, hare's droppings, gunpowder and powdered hyacinth, a gem that had done good service even in ancient times in getting rid of the fruit of the womb, and she would give me some of it: I was to pour boiling water over a dessertspoon of the mixture three times a day, let it stand for ten minutes, and then drink the decoction in small sips. She said she wanted three gulden from me, cash down, before she gave me the mixture.

Black Sophie's mixture did its work within a few days, and I should have been glad and relieved to be spared the fate of a destitute single mother as described to me so cogently by Lyuba. Curiously, however, I felt far from relieved and liberated, and sat heavy of heart and monosyllabic on the maize-straw mattress in the bed-woman's hut on the bank of the Danube while my three friends went about their various occupations. The feather-sorter asked me why I didn't go to the millinery accessories business in Mariahilf with her, she'd be happy to let me do a couple of hours' work instead of her, sorting feathers wasn't very arduous, you could talk to the other girls while you worked and it was really entertaining, that way at least I'd earn a few kreuzers a day. Or why didn't I introduce myself to the conjuror Anton Kratky-Baschik, said the conjuror's third girl assistant, she'd heard him say he needed a fourth assistant and I seemed to her just the girl to hand him his magic implements while wearing a pretty sequinned dress, that would give me a taste of show business, a world all to itself and an exciting one too. And Lyuba said crossly I ought not to let myself go like this, I wasn't the only girl in the world to have

243

had an abortion, and such an easy one too, what did I want, I had a roof over my head, a bed, something to eat and company, and she'd like to know what prevented me from putting my convent education at the service of the maidservants' struggle against their bourgeois masters and getting down to work at the desk in the editorial basement in Margareten. I either said nothing in reply to such suggestions, lying on the straw mattress and turning my face to the wall, to which large numbers of the midges which found ideal living conditions near the Danube still clung in a squashed condition, or I said my dear late mother had been a cook and thus a servant, and had brought me up to spend my life in the service of others too, if they were my friends how could they expect me to change my nature and work in surroundings that were entirely alien to me, and as for Lyuba, she even wanted me to rebel against my origins, turn my back on the values I had always revered and be a traitor to my class. I was sorry, but I just couldn't do it. At this my three friends turned their eyes heavenward, sighed and left me alone.

My despondency also affected my relationship with the Madonna of the Servants, who I felt had let me down, I being a member of that class of society which she had pledged herself to help, and one day I told her so. As I was kneeling before her, expressing my displeasure at her lack of support under my breath, while she listened without any change of expression, I was interrupted in mid-sentence by a tall old lady dressed in black with a lace mantilla on her head. I must forgive her, said this lady, for unceremoniously breaking into my appeal to the Holy Virgin, but in passing she had heard fragments of my prayer without meaning to. I looked at the lady in some surprise, and she smiled and reached out her two hands, attired in black gloves of lacy crochet work, which I involuntarily took. When she had drawn me to my feet she said one mustn't overtax the saints, perhaps I had expected too much of the Madonna of the Servants, and maybe I ought to turn to one of the many other Virgins in the various churches of Vienna: Our Lady of Victory, for instance, whose icon had been miraculously recovered from the ruins of Strankowitz Castle in Prague, although with its eyes put out, or the Thrice-Miraculous Madonna in the Chapel of St Mary in Jacquingasse, or the Immaculate Heart of Mary, very popular among the Viennese, Our Lady of the Bowed Head in the Church of the Discalced Carmelite Nuns in Leopoldstadt, the Rosary Madonna in the Church of Maria Rotunda, or the Suffering Madonna, revered in various parts of the city for the many miracles she had worked. As I could see, added the lady, taking me by the elbow and gently propelling me out of St Stephen's Cathedral, there was a wide choice, and who should know that better than she did, for it was her custom to go to at least one church service a day, and she knew the churches of Vienna better than many another inhabitant of this unfortunately not very God-fearing city.

So said the lady, and a very devout lady she seemed, as she guided me the way she wanted me to go with light but purposeful touches to my elbow, and I yielded to her guidance and answered her many questions readily, so that by the time we had crossed the Ring, had walked some way along beside the Vienna River and then turned left into Kettenbrückengasse, finally stopping outside the building at No. 7 in that street, she knew that I was of Bohemian origin and had grown up in Marienbad, that I had been given a good education by the Ursuline nuns in Prague, and that I was now trying to make a living as a servant in the capital. All alone, she cried, such a young creature, all alone in the big city, would I like to pay her a little visit and give her the pleasure of drinking a cup of rosehip tea with her? I thanked the kind lady and said I would be happy to accept her invitation, I wasn't used to meeting such amiable folk in Vienna, my experiences with the local population to date had been somewhat negative and made me feel rather downhearted and indeed afraid of them. How well she understood me, replied the lady, she who had been widowed three times, we women were particularly vulnerable, delivered up

245

defenceless to the evils of the world, but a cup of tea made from rosehips, a fruit known to be rich in valuable vitamins and plucked by herself from the wild rose bushes growing in the immediate vicinity of Schönbrunn Castle, would certainly help me to forget the unkindness of the human race for a little while. Before we entered the house the hospitable lady pointed to the building opposite and told me that was where Franz Schubert had died, Schubert the great composer, too early, much too early, she seriously wondered whether his death might not have been postponed for a considerable time if only he had acquired the habit of drinking rosehip tea regularly, for that beverage was generally known to prolong life. When I cried, oh yes, Schubert who composed those two lovely songs 'The Trout' and 'The Linden Tree', the lady looked at me rather sternly and said she didn't entirely care for his songs, songs were too worldly for her, and in her opinion his unfortunate tendency towards the things of this world had contributed not a little to the composer's early death. If he had confined himself from the start to composing organ works and Masses, or at least religious tone poems, he would have lived to a ripe old age, she was sure of it, for like rosehip tea, a frame of mind bent on the next world contributes to longer life. As she opened the door of her apartment on the third floor she went on talking, saying unfortunately organ music had been of secondary importance in the period of Viennese Classicism, but in her own case the years in which she had been able to play the organ in the nearby Church of St Joseph were the best years of her life. The remark that slipped out of me to the effect that I knew what she meant, I myself could think of nothing more enjoyable than playing a little mazurka by Chopin on a well-tuned piano, earned me another cool glance from the lady, who said, a piano, oh, what a piano, a piano was nothing compared to an organ, just as there was a suspect kind of worldliness about Schubert's songs, a piano was a thoroughly worldly and thus a dubious instrument, and as for that decadent Franco-Polish consumptive Chopin, she would ask me never to mention his name again within these four walls, which we had indeed now entered.

The pious lady's first names, she told me, were Dora Vittoria, and following the death of her three husbands she had, after some hesitation, resumed her maiden name of Galli, for her parents had been Italians who had left their native Trieste in their youth and came to the capital of the Austro-Hungarian monarchy. Her apartment was full of a conspicuously large number of ticking clocks, and an equally large number of paintings in heavy gilded frames in which, to the lady's surprise and pleasure, I immediately, because of my still fairly recent enthusiasm for hagiography, recognized the martyrdoms of saints of the Catholic Church. On all the tables, chests of drawers and shelves, on all the seats of the chairs, upholstered armchairs and sofas, were ornamental covers, all of them embroidered with motifs showing the Cross. Frau Galli, seeing me look at them, said that she thought the Cross, the Tree upon which Our Lord had died for us, giving up his life to save us sinners, was the finest of all ornaments and a symbol of endless diversity. While my hostess made the rosehip tea, I carefully sat down on a swastika done in zigzag stitch, the centre, as I could see, of a cover embroidered with a fillet-work pattern in old rose-pearl cotton on a natural fifty per cent linen fabric and placed over the seat of the Thonet chair which I had been offered. Then the lady brought a plain Greek gold cross out of the bosom of her dress and said that on her deathbed her mother, Renata Maria Galli, née Croce, had taken this cross from her own neck and placed it around her daughter's with the last of her strength, whereupon I eagerly showed Frau Galli my little bag of Ischl salt and said that this too had been a legacy from my own mother, who died young. Frau Galli put her hand out, felt the little bag suspiciously and asked what was this, it seemed to be an amulet, one of those godless items of which people increasingly made use these days, in her view they were nothing but works of the devil removing mankind ever further from God, such practices would merely hasten the end of the world as announced in the *Revelation of St John*, an event which she hoped to survive unscathed, since unlike most people she made every effort to do penance, only penitential exercises could yet save mankind. I nodded eagerly and told her that the nuns in Prague always said so too: only through penance, fasting and prayer, giving alms and going on pilgrimage could the disruption of the relationship between man and God be made good, to which Frau Galli thoughtfully replied that she hoped so, she fervently hoped so. After a short pause she asked whether I could do embroidery, and when I said that as it happened good fortune had allowed me to familiarize myself with the principles of that craft as a child and to increase my knowledge with the Ursulines in Prague, she asked if I would care to stay in her apartment, in return for board and lodging and a salary that could of course not be very high because her miserable widow's pension was always being cut back by the imperial-and-royal government, and I could render her a few small services such as reading to her from the Bible and doing a little light embroidery, her eyes were not as good as they used to be, and in addition she must admit that since the death not so long ago of her third husband, a retired clockmaker, she had felt a little lonely, although the ticking of the clocks he had left behind had to some extent alleviated the silence in which she lived. The apartment, which was inherited from her first husband and had a total area of a hundred and twenty-four square metres and five rooms, all of which she used, was not very spacious, but she could offer me the airy bathroom to sleep in, and she was sure I'd sleep well in the big, solid and seldom-used bathtub of galvanized cast iron. Frau Galli stopped and looked expectantly at me.

I thought of the mattress stuffed with maize straw that I was sharing with the feather-sorter, and the way it rustled when you turned involuntarily in your sleep and kept waking you up, I thought of the few kreuzers I still had to my name, my sparse wardrobe, the boarding-school uniform which had been worn so often that it was now shabby, and the pretty pale lilac dress which was also beginning to suffer from my recent rather irregular way of life, and I decided to accept her invitation. The grave and dignified bearing of my new acquaintance inspired me with confidence, and I felt reconciled to the Madonna of the Servants, who had brought such a mature and respectable person to cross my path, and said, 'Yes, madam, I'll stay if you like.'

So it was that a few days later I packed my cardboard case and moved into Frau Dora Vittoria Galli's apartment at 7 Kettenbrücken-gasse, where the widow immediately put a well-read copy of Holy Scripture, containing both the Old and the New Testaments and left to her by her prematurely deceased second husband, into my hand and asked me to select passages dealing with punishment and repentance, for as she had said, the subjects of repentance and punishment were those she found particularly interesting and instructive. While she sat in a comfortable armchair, eyes closed, her head with its sparse grey hair resting on the centre of an antimacassar with a cross of St Andrew embroidered on it in herringbone stitch, I crouched on a stool at her feet and read from *Jeremiah*, Chapter 25, verse 29. 'Ye shall not be unpunished: for I will call for a sword upon all the inhabitants of the earth, saith the Lord of hosts.' When I noticed that my new employer had fallen asleep I put down the Bible, picked up an embroidery frame, and continued working on the Maltese cross in tent stitch which was the centre of the cover for a book and which Frau Galli had asked me to do, telling me to use a blunt needle and a thread that was not too long, and work from the centre out.

Days went by, the many clocks that it was one of my duties to wind in the morning ticked, and I began to get used to the peaceful life of the Widow Galli's household and appreciate the advantages that came with it. She neither made me work until I was ready to drop, like the Regional Postal Manager's wife, nor did she starve me like the Honourable Frau von Schreyvogl, and every day it seemed to me increasingly pleasant that there was no man in the place to disturb my sleep in any way whatever. I did find it rather a drawback that Frau Galli would come into the bathroom where I slept whenever she liked and without knocking to see to her toilette, and it was also a nuisance that every night I had to wait until she had finished her evening wash, which could take a long time, so that I was often so tired I fell asleep at the kitchen table. Then, when my employer abruptly woke me, I had to go to bed in the windowless little room, now full of steam, without a chance to read a little from the books I had inherited from my mother, since I could see almost nothing because of the steam. The books also began to suffer from the almost constant humidity in the room; their pages buckled or stuck together, and I saw traces of mould on their bindings. But I told myself that first, high humidity was good for the skin, and second, it would be mean-spirited of me to take exception to such little things when I had found a new home with a good Christian lady who was kind enough not to ask to see my references and obviously had my welfare at heart. I tried to repay her kindness not only by doing embroidery for her as faultlessly as possible but also by surprising her with new motifs, which I thought up in my bathtub at night, and one day, when I presented her with a spectacle case made of cream cotton-linen with a coarse weave on which I had embroidered a decorative crown of thorns, my benefactress, to my great satisfaction, showed that she was pleased and touched. Encouraged by this reaction I proceeded with my independent creativity and began decorating pillowcases and wall hangings with biblical texts which I thought would appeal to my employer, and which I did in rustic cross stitch using pastel-coloured medium-thick matt embroidery thread. Frau Galli was impressed on the day I gave her a narrow runner for a linen press on which I had embroidered *Job*, Chapter 42, verse 6: 'Wherefore I abhor myself, and repent in dust and ashes.' And I saw her smile, for the first time since she had drawn me to my feet with her black-gloved hands in St Stephen's Cathedral, when I put up a hanging on the wall over the living-room chest of drawers on which I had embroidered in beige embroidery yarn the text from *Revelation*: 'As many as I love, I rebuke and chasten.'

The Widow Galli wanted me to accompany her to church frequently, if not daily, since in her view a girl like me with her faith just developing must become familiar with the churches of Vienna and their saints, although I preferred to pursue my new enthusiasm for embroidery. After she had allowed me to stay at home one morning, while she set off to the church of the Elisabethine nuns on Landstrasse to pray to the head of St Elisabeth of Thuringia which was kept there, St Elisabeth being the patron saint of our Empress Sisi, my eye fell by chance on one of her plain shifts of coarse and rather yellowed linen which was lying in the bathroom, and the idea of adorning this rather unattractive item of underwear with a text from the Bible came to me. This time I boldly decided to choose a text to my own taste, and I hit upon St Paul's saying, 'Follow after love!' and immediately embroidered it round the square neck of the shift in pale pink cross stitch. My employer's reaction to this little attention of mine rather disappointed me, for she frowned and said she was glad I was occupying my mind with Holy Scripture, but she wondered why I hadn't chosen a text from the Old Testament for my work and why I didn't stick to the subject of punishment and penance, which was of much greater importance than the sometimes rather ill-considered and superficial remarks made by the writers of the New Testament on love, remarks occasionally suggesting positively worldly connotations with which she did not always agree. And as for the colour of the embroidery silk, she would have preferred a dark brown. Then she told me to leave her alone in the bathroom, the bathroom was the best place for certain penitential practices which her confessor Father Peregrin, the priest of St Peter's, had told her to perform. During the next half-hour I thought I heard whistling noises, sighs and suppressed shrieks coming from the bathroom, but now that experience had taught me to be cautious about interpreting the impressions of my senses I supposed they were an acoustic illusion.

Next Sunday, an unusually warm and sunny late-autumn day, I decided to wear my pale lilac dress, put on the hat trimmed with pansies, and use my afternoon off to go for a walk in the Prater. When Frau Galli saw me in this outfit she clasped her hands above her head and said I couldn't possibly go out so lightly clad, the weather in late autumn in Vienna was most unpredictable, you could leave home in bright sunshine and as soon as you were out in the street it might begin to rain and blow, even snowfalls couldn't be ruled out. So saying, she hurried into her bedroom and came back with a long black cape which she handed me saying that this black warp-pile velvet cape with its shimmering effect, given to her by her second husband for her mother's funeral in Trieste, was ideal for the weather today, and she would lend it to me, but I must take good care of it. With these words she placed the cape around my shoulders and propelled me out of the door.

On my way to the city centre and on towards the Prater I stumbled several times over the folds of the fabric billowing around my feet, since the cape had been made for the Widow Galli's stately height and was too long for me. Moreover, I was getting definitely warmer, for in spite of my employer's fears there was no sign of rain or stormy winds, and the heavy black velvet absorbed the warm sunshine, but I dared not disobey her by taking off the cape, so that finally I sank down, tired and hot, on one of the benches outside the Rotunda, and could only nod when a young man in a pale suit with a straw boater on his head asked if he could sit beside me. I was about to close my eyes when the young man looked hard at my face and cried in surprise, what a coincidence, it was the girl from Prague he'd met on the banks of the Danube, didn't I remember him, the piccolo who had taken me back to the Bunch of Grapes Inn? All of a sudden my exhaustion was gone, for I was delighted to recognize the apprentice waiter who had helped me, and I said of course I remembered him, in fact I'd often thought about him and wondered how he was getting on. He smiled, and said he'd been lucky, through the good offices of a member of the Hornischer ladies' music ensemble which played in the Café Eisvogel in the Prater he had found a job as a waiter in that establishment, where he was much better treated than in his old position, and better paid too. He was here today because he wanted to go up to the roof of the Rotunda in that wonderful invention the hydraulic lift and see the copy of the imperial crown, and hoped he could invite me to join him on this little expedition. I looked at him in amazement and said it had long been my dearest wish to touch the crown, but my financial situation hadn't allowed me to indulge that wish yet. The waiter gave another broad smile, cried out that this was capital, jumped to his feet and pulled me up from the bench. Then he stopped, looked at my outfit and said I looked absolutely exhausted and no wonder, wrapped up in a shapeless black cape on such a fine day, and he was sure I wouldn't mind if he relieved me of that item of clothing for a while. And before I could object he had liberated me from the cape and hung it over his arm, and was looking me up and down with his head on one side. Much better, he said appreciatively, what an enchanting hat, what a pretty girl, he hadn't remembered me as so pretty, why, I looked just like Empress Sisi in all her photographs and paintings, except that I was blonde and blue-eyed, not dark like Her Majesty.

A little later I was over a hundred metres above ground level, standing on the roof of the Rotunda with the former piccolo, whose name I only now discovered was Hans Holzer, and at last I was able to place my hand on the gilded imperial crown set with precious stones and pearls. He touched the metal with his own right hand, and when, in the process, it briefly made contact with my fingers I felt a sharp pain, like a long, thin needle going through my heart.

I remember the rest of the afternoon as a series of colours flowing into each other, a shimmering play of light and shade, the alternation of warm air and cooler air, a number of lively movements, the echo of cheerful voices. Hans Holzer took my hand

and led me from the slide to the roundabout, from the grotto railway to the waxworks display, he took me into the pavilion with the lady snake-charmer, into the booth with the fat lady and her trained cockatoos, into the tent with Pepi the incredible elephant and the dancing dogs, and he stood with his arm around me in front of a camera with a black cloth draped over it in the snapshot booth. When I finally said in some alarm that it was getting dark and I must go back to my place of employment in Kettenbrücken-gasse, Hans looked shyly away from me and pressed into my hand the photograph showing us standing in front of the clumsily painted backdrop of a mountain landscape, a souvenir, he said, adding quietly that he hoped he wouldn't lose sight of me again for as long as after our first meeting. For the second time that day the long, thin needle went through my heart, and I looked at the ground and whispered that I hoped so too, whereupon he suggested that we could meet again outside the Rotunda next Sunday at three in the afternoon, and he carefully put the cape around my shoulders, saying it had turned a little chilly. I held the cape together at my throat with my left hand and set off, and after a few steps I looked back at Hans, saw him watching me go with his arms by his sides and his straw boater tipped on his head at an angle, and I called out that we'd see.

When I came into the Widow Galli's living room she was reading aloud under her breath from a large book, and didn't notice me. I came closer and caught some words in rhyme, which I took at first to be biblical texts until I clearly, and to my great surprise, made out the lines, 'Good is bad and bad is good / Help my witchcraft, witch's brood!' And when I came up behind her and cast a quick glance at the book I saw that it couldn't be the Bible, since this folio volume contained curious diagrams and strange signs such as I had never seen anywhere. Before I could decipher at least a few words of the writing, which was difficult to read, the widow shut the book with such a bang that a cloud of dust rose from it, stood up suddenly, and ran her eyes over me.

Where had I been all this time, she asked, it wasn't like me to stay out until dark, and with my hair down too, my face flushed, and the flowers trimming my hat all crumpled. If she had any mirrors in the place, those items in which vain folk were always admiring themselves, then I would be able to see my dishevelled state for myself. When I murmured apologetically that I had been stretching my legs a little in the Hauptallee of the Prater she raised her voice and cried, the Prater, worse and worse, everyone knew what went on in the Prater, its concealed little lawns, its dark little woods were sinful spots, the scene of shameful and disgraceful practices, places of the deepest depravity, what was I thinking of going to such a place, she had supposed I was taking a little walk through the Inner City to improve my knowledge of the cultural shrines of Vienna, for instance the Church of Maria am Gestade, the Ursulines' church, the Church Am Hof, the Capuchin church and many more, but no, far from it, I felt attracted to the Prater to mingle with a pack of rogues, rabble who feared the light of day, it really left her speechless. Such a lapse on my part must be punished, no doubt about it, and she was going to deprive me of my usual rosehip tea and any bedclothes for three days, goodness knows three nights lying in the hard bare bathtub was not a severe punishment for my transgression.

That evening I lay in the galvanized cast-iron bathtub, shivering with cold and trying to work out why my hitherto kindly mistress had reacted so violently to my harmless walk in the Prater. I could find no answer to the question. I decided to try even harder than before to win her approval and regain her favour. While the Widow Galli was at church the next day, I made haste to embroider the rather frayed hem of one of her mildew-spotted petticoats with a verse from that work I liked so much, the *Song of Solomon*, choosing the words, 'Behold, thou art fair, my beloved, yea, pleasant'. These affirmative sentiments worked in glossy pale blue embroidery silk would surely soften her mood, if not bring her round entirely. I confidently awaited her return, but when, commenting that my sense of tidiness and order had recently left something to be desired, she had picked up the petticoat from the living-room sofa, where I had left it on purpose so that she would see it at once, and when she had read the text in sky-blue cross stitch, she asked indignantly what on earth this meant, was I making fun of her with this verse from the *Song of Solomon*, of all the books of the Old Testament the *Song of Solomon* was the one she couldn't abide because of its shocking worldliness, and perhaps I would kindly rip out the embroidery at once. Despondently, I withdrew into the bathroom with the petticoat, wondering where I had gone wrong this time.

The closer Sunday came, the more restless I felt and the louder seemed the ticking of the clocks, although I had scarcely noticed the sound of them before. And once again I heard that curious whistling and cracking, groaning and wailing in the bathroom, but once again I put it down to my imagination, just as I had explained a similar sighing and wailing years ago in the attic bedroom in Marienbad, just as I accounted for the sight of the curious book that had been in the widow's lap and her recitation of the verse that sounded like a magic spell, by supposing that I had been mistaken in what I heard and read.

Sunday dawned overcast and rainy, and Frau Galli, who was now in a rather better mood, said she supposed I wouldn't want to go out on my afternoon off in weather like this, no doubt I would rather drink hot rosehip tea and read aloud from the *Revelation of St John*. Resorting to a deliberate falsehood, not for the first time in my life, I said swiftly that I had told Father Peregrin I'd go to the presbytery and help him put together some little Advent gifts for the poor of the parish of St Peter's, to which my mistress replied that it was a praiseworthy project and in the circumstances she would happily forgo my company, good works naturally came first, and she would also lend me the velvet cape from Trieste again. Weighed down by both the heavy velvet and my lie, I set off for the Rotunda, where Hans was waiting for me in his straw boater, holding an umbrella and a little bunch of autumn crocuses, which he handed me saying he'd thought the colour of the flowers would match my dress nicely. Then he asked if I liked to dance, because he was passionately fond of dancing himself, and when I told him that a governess of noble birth had taught me the basic steps of the Viennese waltz back in the past, and later I'd danced to the rhythm of a mazurka with a Polish girlfriend now and then, but beyond that I had no familiarity with the skill, Hans said that a few steps of the waltz and a few steps of the polka would be quite enough for the five-kreuzer dance floor, and we'd go straight off to the Dead Mosquito tavern in the Prater and join the dancers there.

Half an hour later I was whirling around with Hans on the tavern's raised dance floor of plain spruce boards to the sound of music played by a quartet of four old gentlemen, and I don't remember being happier ever before or since in my life, one that can be described as a failed life and in the very near future, with almost one hundred per cent certainty, as a short life too. Hans, who had taken off his coat and was dancing in shirtsleeves, had his arms firmly around my waist, and I leaned confidently back, my hands clasped behind his neck and abandoning myself to the swirling movement. Washerwomen, soldiers, waiters, milliners and servants, all the common folk of Vienna, danced with us. When a waltz by Lanner or Strauss, a polka by Ziehrer or a Viennese popular song came to its end they went back to their tables or strolled around in a circle, arm in arm with their partners, until the violinist, guitarist, flautist and clarinettist struck up another tune. My feet moved as if of their own accord in the lively two-four time of the polka and the more leisurely three-four time of the waltz as, with my right hand in my partner's left and my left hand placed lightly around his neck, I saw his smiling face before me, his flushed cheeks and the little beads of perspiration on his forehead. Never in my life had I given myself up to someone else's lead so yieldingly, with such pleasure, and I could see from my partner's face that he too was enjoying the harmony of our physical movements as he skilfully steered us through the crowd of other dancers, guiding me to one side and back again to avoid colliding with them. I don't remember now how long we danced like that; I remember only that at some point we left the inn and walked in silence along a narrow path between hazel bushes, that Hans, who had put up his umbrella because of the slight drizzle, suddenly stood in front of me and, barring my way and thus forcing me to stop, slipped his free hand under my cape, drew me firmly to him, and pressed a kiss on my lips. The needle pierced my heart and again I wriggled out of his embrace, startled, cleared my throat and said I must get straight back to my mistress, who would certainly be expecting me by now. When Hans had made me promise to meet him again at the same time and same place next Sunday I ran away from him, holding up the cape with one hand and clutching the hat with the pansy trimming and the little bunch of autumn crocuses in the other, making for the Inner City.

On entering the Widow Galli's apartment, and assuming that since she was nowhere to be seen she had gone to church, I opened the bathroom door to wash my hot face. Then I recoiled, distressed by the sight that met my eyes: my benefactress was standing with her back to me, whimpering quietly, her withered torso bare and sprinkled with brown liver spots, in the act of scourging herself with a leather whip. Her grey-white strands of hair, all wet, fell over her shoulders, and the yellowish skin stretched over her very visible ribcage was covered with weals, some of them scar tissue, some fresh and bloody. When a small scream escaped me she whirled round, turning towards me her flaccid breasts and her face, which was both surprised and distorted with pain. I stood there, my hands to my mouth, my eyes wide with horror, and then her lips, though pressed together with pain, distorted into a grotesque smile, and with flickering eyes she cried out that we were sinners all, all of us were sinners before the Lord and must do penance to the end of our days for fear of being cast into eternal damnation, I too, I above all must chastise the desires of my young flesh if I was to avoid suffering all the torments of Hell, she ordered me to do so. With these words she picked up a dark brown hair shirt from the black and white tiles and handed it to me, also presenting me with the handle of the whip. I slammed the door, ran to the furthest corner of the apartment and crouched on the floor there, my heart beating wildly. Soon afterwards the Widow Galli left the bathroom in her usual black dress with its white lace collar, her hair pinned up in a knot as she always wore it and, holding herself very erect, put the kettle of water on the stove for rosehip tea, took the Bible off its shelf and asked me to read her Chapter 13 of the *Revelation of St John.* I opened the Bible, and began: 'And I stood upon the sand of the sea, and saw a beast rise up out of the sea, having seven heads and ten horns.'

When I was lying in the bathtub that evening I kept looking at the leather whip standing in a corner of the bathroom and the hair shirt lying over the edge of the tub. I now realized that my ears had not deceived me, and it had been the widow sighing and moaning under the lash of the whip with which she chastised herself. The scene I had observed made me profoundly uneasy. My mother, the nuns and the priests had also emphasized the necessity of doing penance, but I had taken that to mean a set of Our Fathers and Hail Marys, or perhaps going without a meal on occasion, not the terrible humiliation to which Frau Galli subjected herself. But perhaps my transgressions of the sixth, seventh and eighth commandments really were so bad that I could atone for them only by punishing myself in such a way. Furthermore, my mother had always drummed it into me that the orders of one's employers, however strange and absurd, must without exception be obeyed. I stood up, took off my linen nightdress with the little bow at the neck, and put on the hair shirt, shrinking. I tossed and turned all night and couldn't sleep, for the rough material scratched my body and made my skin sore, and in my half-sleep the afternoon passed before my mind's eye again, Hans whirled me round faster and faster, his mouth open, and then thrust the long, thin tip of his umbrella into my heart, so that I fell down dead.

I slept in that shirt for the next few nights too, and curiously enough a certain sense of satisfaction at this manner of self-denial soon set in. When the Widow Galli entered the bathroom late one evening without knocking, as she usually did, and saw me lying in the tub in that garment, she smiled and said I seemed to have reflected on her words, she valued my good sense, and if I liked she would bring me a cup of hot rosehip tea sweetened with genuine flower honey. Happy to hear any friendly remark from a grown woman to me, a motherless girl, I nodded in agreement and blushed for joy to think that my benefactress looked kindly on me again. Next evening, determined to do my utmost to ensure her future favour, I took off the shirt, picked up the whip that was still standing in the corner, and let the lash fall on my back, gently at first. Then I drew back my arm rather further so that the leather lash, which had sharp little bits of metal set into it, struck my skin harder, and I felt a pang that reminded me of the sweet pain my heart had felt in the presence of Hans Holzer, inducing me to repeat the blow several times, striking rather harder each time. The harder I struck, the more vividly I seemed to see the waiter's cheerful, open face, and I went on whipping myself until I uttered a low scream and desisted. Frau Galli, who had heard the sound, came into the bathroom, stroked my back gently, making me flinch, and then said that such suffering was good in the sight of the Lord, I had understood and was well on the way to turning aside from the path of sin. At this I laid my forehead on her shoulder and wept, and she murmured soothing words and pressed a tender kiss on my tangled hair.

Once again the timepieces left to my benefactress by her third husband, the master clockmaker, seemed to tick and strike louder and louder the closer Sunday came. This time I found it remarkably difficult to put on the pale lilac dress and the hat trimmed with pansies and go off to the Prater, and only the promise I had given Hans induced me to set out in time. Before I left, the Widow Galli placed the velvet cape around my shoulders, tied the black ribbons at its neck, kissed me gently on both cheeks and said I shouldn't neglect to attend evening service at Mariahilf Church after my walk, she had heard from Father Peregrin that the Catholic girls' choir was planning to perform an extraordinarily interesting setting of a text from the Psalms composed by a Jesuit brother from Innsbruck.

The sky was blue, but a chilly wind was blowing, and the Hauptallee of the Prater was covered by a carpet of rustling, brightly coloured leaves. Hans saw me from a distance and ran to meet me, so that the little rucksack he was wearing over his coat bumped up and down, but I avoided his embrace and said, with my head bowed, I didn't have very much time, my mistress had given me a complicated piece of Madeira work to embroider on coarse-weave cotton-linen and I was behind with it, and when Hans tilted my chin up with his right index finger, looked carefully at my face and asked what was the matter, because I didn't seem the same as usual, I said he was wrong, I just felt a little overtaxed by the Widow Galli's demands, that was all. Who was this widow anyway, asked my friend, I'd told him nothing at all about the circumstances in which I was living, whereas he hadn't concealed from me the fact that, after the landlord of the Bunch of Grapes Inn had thrown him out for alleged cheek and before he had found his new job as a waiter in the Café Eisvogel, he had managed for a while by setting up the skittles in suburban taverns, selling cigarettes in coffee houses and delivering milk and newspapers, and honest work might be a tribulation but it was no disgrace. I said the Widow Galli was a very devout lady, and kind to me if a little severe, I had a great deal to thank her for, and felt obliged to her, and now would he please stop interrogating me. At this Hans placed one arm around the cape to lead me along the path, and asked if I'd like to go out in a boat on the Heustadelwasser, you could hire rowing boats quite cheaply at a place on the bank, and he liked the idea of going out with me on the little lake, and I looked up at him and said yes.

A little later I was sitting in the bows of the boat, one hand trailing in the water, watching Hans as he propelled us forward with powerful strokes, driving the flat blades of the oars vertically into the surface of the water. As I tied my hat firmly under my chin so that the fresh autumn wind wouldn't blow it away, it struck me that we had first met beside water, and I asked him if he still entertained such gloomy thoughts as he did then on the little island in the Danube, at which he shook his head, its dark blond curls dishevelled by the Viennese wind, and said by no means, those dismal notions belonged to the past, after all fate had been kind to him since then, not only leading him to decent employers but bringing me to cross his path a second time – a second time, just think of that, what a happy combination of circumstances, and this time I wouldn't shake him off so soon! I smiled and playfully splashed him with water, and he let the oars hang loose in the rowlocks, bent over to me, clasped my hands firmly and kissed them. Then he steered the boat towards the bank, brought it ashore in an isolated, sandy spot surrounded by weeping willows and aspens, and gave me his hand to help me climb out. Next he removed my cape, spread it on the sand and with a charming and sweeping gesture invited me to sit on it. When I had done so he took cold roast chicken, potato salad and a bottle of wine out of his rucksack and said, smiling, that he'd taken the food from the kitchens of the Café Eisvogel with the cook's permission, so I was to make myself comfortable and tuck in. I propped myself on my elbows, picked up a chicken drumstick in my fingertips and carried it to my mouth, for meat was never served in the household of the Widow Galli, whose opinion it was that all evil had come into the world with the slaughtering of animals for human consumption, but the very first mouthful reminded me pleasantly of the hearty dishes my mother used to make in Marienbad, and I decided to enjoy it, even if my benefactress might consider that relishing such earthly pleasures brought me dangerously close to those sinners who indulged in gluttony, nor did I refuse the heavy Hungarian red wine that Hans poured into generous round glasses. Soon I felt light at heart and merry, I forgot about the widow and our penitential practices and gave myself up entirely to the present moment. We ate and drank and then lay down on the cape, I was happy for Hans to trace the contours of my cheeks with a blade of grass, and I lay still while he leaned over me, covered my face with tender kisses, and one by one slowly undid the little bead-shaped violet buttons that ran close to each other all down the top of my pale lilac dress. I closed my eyes and felt his hands on my bodice, but when he put an arm behind my back, touching the wounds I had inflicted on myself with the leather whip, all of a sudden I was no longer there in his affectionate company in that idyllic little bay but back in the bathroom with Frau Galli, and I cried out in pain and pushed his arm aside. At this Hans said he'd known there was something wrong, I must show him my back that minute, it was a well-known fact that some employers thought they had a right to beat their servants, and he tried to hold me firmly and turn me over. I resisted as hard as I could, scratching and biting until I finally managed to free myself, jumped to my feet, did the little violet buttons up again with trembling fingers, clutched the cape to me and ran away without looking round.

When I opened the door of the Widow Galli's apartment she was standing very upright there in the corridor, holding her right hand behind the full skirt of her shiny black taffeta dress and looking sternly at me. Not only, she cried, not only did the state of my attire, or more precisely my missing hat, dishevelled hair, badly fastened buttons and the creased and dirty Trieste cape, clearly indicate the indecent acts in which I must have been engaging, but while I was out, and by pure chance, she had come into possession of further evidence of the depravity of my black soul. So saying, she brought her right hand out from behind her skirts and triumphantly held up the sepia ferrotype taken and developed in the snapshot photographer's booth, showing Hans and me in front of the Alpine background. Plucking up all my courage, and in a choking voice, I began asking how she could reconcile it with her conscience to search the cardboard case in which I kept the photograph and which was my private property, but Frau Galli cut me short and said private property, what did I mean, private property, if our Lord Jesus Christ, who had always spoken out against selfish promptings of this nature, had not risen again but were still in his grave then he would turn in it to hear me talk like that, and what's more she was forbidding me this minute to say any more, I was guilty of promiscuous conduct with a person of the male sex, and she required me to go to the bathroom and remove my upper clothing, for I must understand that she couldn't allow such behaviour on my part to go unpunished.

Soon afterwards I was moaning as I flinched under each of the ten lashes slowly inflicted on me by the Widow Galli, counting them out loud, while tears came to my eyes and dropped on the black and white tiles of the floor. Then she ordered me to thank both her and the Almighty for my correction, which had been for my own good and my benefit, and told me that in my own interests I must expect chastisement of the same or a similar extent every evening until next Sunday. And of course I was forbidden to leave the apartment until further notice.

This entirely unexpected turn of events upset me so much that I could scarcely form a coherent thought, and fell into deep depression. I couldn't understand how the same woman who had drawn me to my feet with her hands in their black lace gloves before the Madonna of the Servants, who had seemed to rescue me from my difficult situation, a fine and educated lady who played that royal instrument the organ and knew large parts of Holy Scripture off by heart, could be one and the same as the woman who beat me with a leather whip. My mind was in confusion, and when she was out I began walking from room to room of the apartment, pacing restlessly back and forth. I neglected my appearance, took my daily meals without noticing that I was eating at all, and submitted apathetically to the promised beatings, conduct that filled the Widow Galli with satisfaction, since she took it for a sign of remorse.

Next Sunday I was allowed to go out for the first time to make my confession. Eyes lowered, I went along Schönbrunnerstrasse, keeping close to the walls of the buildings, and did not look up even when a man overtook me. Only when he stood in my path did I raise my head in surprise, for it was the waiter Hans. I was about to cross quickly to the other side of the street, but he took me by my upper arms, shook me, and said would I for heaven's sake tell him what had happened, he had followed me last Sunday and now he knew where I was living with that horrible pious hypocrite, I looked absolutely distraught, the light in my eyes had quite gone out, and he urged me to come away with him, I mustn't stay with that witch a moment longer. At that moment the new organist of the Church of St Joseph, a native of Regensburg, came round the corner, and I took the opportunity of wishing him good day, whereupon he approached me and Hans was forced to let go of me and walk on. But when I arrived at the entrance of the building at 7 Kettenbrückengasse after confession, there he was again, begging me once more not to go back to the Widow Galli but to follow him to the Café Eisvogel, the Hornischer ladies' ensemble urgently needed a zither player, and as he knew I had once played the piano and in his opinion would very soon master the zither he couldn't understand why I still hesitated. Without answering him I opened the front door, and when he tried to detain me I tore myself away and ran up the stairs.

One day soon afterwards, during my restless wanderings through the Widow Galli's large apartment while she was out, my eye fell on the big book I had seen her reading, which was now lying on the bedside table in her room. I sat down on the edge of the bed, which had the words *Memento mori* carved into its heavy wooden headboard, and opened the volume at a page which, to my surprise, contained a printed recipe, with comments and additions in the Widow Galli's handwriting, for an ointment made from the juice of such poisonous plants of the nightshade family as belladonna, henbane and thorn apple, and which when applied under the armpits would enable a person to fly and to turn into an animal as witches did, those evil beings of whom my mother had told me. Choosing another page at random I came upon a passage dealing with the evil eye and its magical power to make men and beasts fall sick, even kill them. Beside it, a comment in the widow's tall, pointed, cramped handwriting read: Obviously works, R. showing less and less will of her own. Breathlessly, with trembling fingers, I leafed through the book and found passages about incubi and succubi, evil spirits with whom the witches had nocturnal intercourse, and once again Frau Galli had written under them: I. must be set upon R., see *Hammer of Witches* p. 52. I did not understand exactly what these mysterious comments meant, but I felt there was something wicked afoot that threatened my life itself, and the hairs on my lower arms stood on end of their own accord. Next moment I heard the sound of a key turning in the lock of the apartment door, closed the book and quickly left the room, and when the Widow came into her living room I was sitting on the Thonet chair with the swastika cover, the Bible open on my lap, pretending to be immersed in reading it.

My condition deteriorated in the days that followed, but although I was now aware of the Widow Galli's evil intentions, and knew her appearance of piety concealed a state of mind that could be described only as mad, possessed by the influence of demonic ideas and bent on my destruction, I couldn't manage to escape her power and leave her apartment; she was no longer keeping me confined to it, and indeed encouraged me to start going to church again, but as soon as I was a certain distance from her apartment at 7 Kettenbrückengasse a mysterious force seemed to draw me back. I knew no way to help myself except to discover more about the Widow Galli's secret arts and thus counter her pernicious influence over my mind. As soon as she left the apartment I would hurry to her bedroom to read the big book, and so I learned that you could indeed fall victim to witchcraft, but there are ways to protect yourself against it, for instance by turning your shift and stockings inside out, wearing odd shoes or placing them with their toes turned towards your bed, hanging a sprig of mistletoe or a piece of the inner bark of the linden tree or some peony seeds around your neck, and burning juniper wood. The evil eye could be warded off too, among other things by amulets with an eye painted on them, the rope that had hanged a man, certain precious stones, and above all by wearing salt about your person. I now realized why Frau Galli had been so scornful of my little bag of Ischl salt, and some time ago had ordered me to take it off and put it in my cardboard case, but when I was about to take it out in secret and put it on again, she caught me in the act and, saying my superstitions were obviously more deeply rooted than she had supposed, threw it into the fire on the hearth, whereupon I lost courage entirely and lapsed into lethargy, realizing that her action had robbed me of the protection of my dear dead mother, and I was now delivered up to the widow even more helplessly than before. I rebelled against what seemed my inevitable fate only once again: while Frau Galli was out I took my cardboard case, put on the cape, and left the apartment. But the widow met me on the stairs, and I stopped in mid-stride, unable to set one foot in front of the other, and without the slightest resistance allowed her to take my case from me and lead me back to the bathroom, where she suddenly let her mask of piety drop and said, with a contemptuous grin, that like her three husbands, all of them good-for-nothing weaklings and not worthy to share their lives with a strong and talented woman like her, I myself, at least their equal in cowardice and depravity, would be unable to withdraw from her influence and would be bound to her until the end of my days, which she fancied, remembering the fate of her husbands, would not be so very far off. At this, desperate and worn down as I was by now, I lost control of myself, rushed panic-stricken out of the bathroom, into the corridor and then the living room, ran to one of the tall windows, flung it open, and clambered out in the velvet cape on to the window sill, intending to jump from the third floor to the paving stones below and put an end to my life. But before I jumped I heard someone calling my name, and I stopped and looked down in the direction from which the call had come. Below me on the paving stones, face turned up to me, arms raised and with my hat in one hand, was the waiter Hans. Cast into confusion by this sight I hesitated, stood there on the window sill, and saw more and more people assembling in the street and looking up at me. I don't know how long I stood like that, I only know that at some point powerful arms came around me, lifted me off the window sill and held me fast, and I felt a long, thin needle piercing the inside of my left elbow, whereupon a pleasant lassitude spread through my body and I closed my eyes in relief. As if through a mist, I realized that I was being put on a stretcher and carried downstairs, and then the stretcher was placed in a large cart drawn by two black horses.

11

I put the blue notebook down on the grey and white speckled marble top of the bedside table, then switched off the lamp with the brass stand and pleated fabric shade with white roses on a yellow background. I was sorry that Rosa's sufferings were not yet over but seemed to be getting even worse, so much worse that she had seen no way out but suicide, and I did hope someone well disposed to her would finally cross her path again. Then I fell asleep.

Next morning I went on foot to Kettenbrückengasse underground station to meet Josef Horvath and go running in Schönbrunn Castle park. I waited for him outside the Marktamt building, and it wasn't long before I saw him come out of the St Mary Magdalene Pharmacy and walk towards me. He apologized for being late, he said he'd been buying a little bottle of eucalyptus oil from the pharmacist with whom, as I knew, he was friendly, and in the course of a very interesting conversation into which they had spontaneously entered about the various forms of chronic bronchitis he'd quite lost his sense of the time. I looked at Josef, whose hair curled over his ears and forehead, and thought of the expedition to Nussdorf we had made recently, during which it had become clear to me that I was well on the way to falling in love with my singing teacher, remote from reality and in need of help as he was, being both a mother's boy and unsuccessful, and I wondered what unfortunate combination of genes, what sin of omission unknowingly committed by my parents in my upbringing was to blame for my feeling attracted to this peculiar person. During the past two weeks I had noticed that he was beginning to pay more attention to his appearance, dressed a little more trendily and on the whole made less of a sickly impression, a change for the better which I put down to our walks in the fresh air and most of all to our running together, for the purpose of which he had bought himself a sky-blue flannel training suit from Sport Dusika in Mariahilferstrasse. I was pleased to find that his breathing was getting easier, he no longer lagged so far behind me as at first and he had lost a little weight, and when we came back to the city centre by underground there was a faint pink glow in his usually pale cheeks, his weary glance looked rather livelier and the dull greyish blue of his eyes rather bluer.

When we had run from the Roman ruins to the Fountain of Neptune, from the Fountain of Neptune up to the Gloriette and then down through the wood again and past the zoo to the palm house, Josef stopped and said, gasping, here we were, today he was going to show me the butterfly house, and he made for a small glasshouse on the edge of the park. We bought two tickets to go in and entered a tall, warm space full of assorted tropical trees, shrubs and flowers, with butterflies of all sizes and colours fluttering among them, now and then settling on the plants and on the visitors. I must watch out for the dwarf quail, said Josef, if you kept looking at the butterflies, which meant looking up, you were in danger of treading on one of the dwarf quail which ran around on the ground hidden by the branches of the trees and shrubs, he didn't know for sure just how the quail had got into the butterfly house in the first place, probably rearing them as well as butterflies was a hobby of the lady who looked after the butterfly house. Looking down, I really did see a small bird with brown plumage striped yellow and black on top and with a yellow stripe on its head in front of my running shoes; it immediately disappeared under a camellia bush. When I looked up again there was a beautiful blue-black butterfly sitting on Josef's left shoulder, and when I pointed it out to him he carefully turned his head, looked sideways and down and said, oh, a Striped Blue Crow, a butterfly found in Malaysia, South China and the Philippines, the butterflies in the butterfly house were very tame, and if you didn't know that it would damage their wings you'd be tempted to stroke them. I mustn't move my head, Josef added in a whisper, a beautiful Monarch had just settled on my head, a pale brown butterfly found in North and South America and Australia, it was a migratory butterfly too, a strong flyer that could travel amazing distances. I said I admired his knowledge, unfortunately I knew very little myself about these insects, you hardly saw them at all in Manhattan, it was very unusual to see even an ordinary Cabbage White, Brimstone Yellow or Common Blue flutter past you. Look, look, cried Josef, drawing me behind a tall banana plant, which made the Monarch fly away, and pointing to a banana leaf on which a large dark red butterfly with three small white spots on each back wing had settled, the Red Helen, the Red Helen, a very rare specimen, and then the Red Helen rose in the air and settled on my plaits, and in the shelter of the banana plant and the warmth of the glasshouse Josef put out his left hand, gently touched first the butterfly and then my plaits, brought his mouth close to my lips and kissed me, then withdrawing first his mouth and next moment his hand in alarm, clearing his throat briefly and saying that the butterflies pupated inside a cocoon they had spun, when they emerged the imago broke the head and breast sections of the sheath of the pupa and pressed blood and air into the still limp wings so that they expanded and within four to seven hours had hardened, and the butterfly could fly.

On the way back to the Death House where we were now to have my singing lesson Josef Horvath was unusually silent, and as I was not sure of the reason for this taciturnity and didn't want to annoy my teacher, who seemed more attractive to me every minute, I took care to put great feeling into my performance of

Schubert's song 'Dream of Spring', closed my eyes and sang, 'I close, I close my eyes once more, / My heartbeat still I hear. / When will the leaves turn green again / When will I hold my dear?' and before I opened them again the piano had stopped playing, two rather limp arms came around me, and the soft lips I had felt behind the banana plant were laid on mine again. But when I began to react to these caresses in a way far from unusual in a thirty-three-year-old woman, of childbearing age and in excellent health, when I opened my eyes, took Josef's hand, led him towards the bedroom and asked if he would show me those display cases of butterflies he'd mentioned and tell me more about the metamorphosis of a larva into a pupa, he clutched his throat and whispered that it was a funny thing, but he suddenly felt another attack of his breathing difficulties coming on, a typical problem in sufferers from bronchial asthma caused by catarrhal inflammation and constriction of the tracheal branches, although he hadn't had one for days, and it had come on unusually strongly too, he must sit down in the armchair at once and ask me to brew up that herbal decoction made of equal parts of coltsfoot, sundew and corn poppy immediately, which I conscientiously did before leaving the Death House and taking the underground to the Danube Island, where I walked along the riverbank going over what had just happened in my head, since I had noticed that I found a solution to my problems more quickly and easily in the immediate vicinity of large expanses of water than anywhere else. I was furious with Josef and furious with myself, and to soothe my fury I picked up pebbles from the ground and threw them into the water as hard as I could. As soon as my anger had died down a bit I started throwing them into the river in a shallow arc, trying to make them bounce on the surface of the water as often as possible, and then I suddenly stopped, because all of a sudden I felt as if I had stood on this bank once before.

When I climbed the stairs to Aunt Pia's apartment a little later the Bosnian caretaker, for that was the woman with the long, pitch-black hair and the too tight bright pink crocheted sweater, was engaged in removing cobwebs from the corners of the stairwell with a long broom, and as I passed her she put the broom down on the ground, looked me up and down, and asked if I'd heard that an extreme right-winger had attacked and raped a young Vietnamese nurse in the Stadtpark last night, and he didn't even shrink from calling Wipplingerstrasse police station after committing this crime and explaining his reasons, saying that slowly but steadily the number of persons of racially inferior blood in the country was rising above the count of pure-bred Austrians, and since the authorities responsible couldn't bring themselves to deport these foreigners then people like him, who loved their country, had to resort to self-help. Here the caretaker cupped both her hands under her heavy breasts in the white bra that was visible through the intricate crochet pattern of her sweater, raised them, let them drop again, leaned over to me and whispered that she was aware of the danger these racists represented to her and her husband as Bosnian refugees, but people didn't notice that they belonged to a non-Austrian ethnic group as clearly as they did with me, and in my place she wouldn't venture out of the building after sunset, even better, I should go straight back to my black African homeland where I really belonged after all, she hoped I wouldn't mind her saying so.

Next moment I was entering Aunt Pia's living room, where she was sitting in front of her black and white TV set crocheting a burgundy-red shawl for a Käthe Kruse doll, and when she saw me she asked where on earth I'd been all this time, I must be starving, luckily there was a pan of freshly made chopped lights, lungs and heart on the stove, and I must join her as soon as I'd satisfied my hunger, she was just watching the film of *The Third Man* yet again, its zither theme tune was world-famous. She watched this film, set in Vienna under the occupation of foreign powers, my own country included, every time she got the chance, for it reminded her of the happiest years of her life, spent in deep harmony with the Major and Wilma, she was familiar with every take and every cut, she knew the dialogue off by heart, so she wasn't particularly bothered by the fuzzy picture on her set. The dark round spot moving there to the right of the screen was Orson Welles, of course, it was amazing how such an outstanding actor could be such a thorough villain too, we human beings really were contradictory creatures.

That evening I took the blue notebook out of the chest again, and after opening the window a crack because it was so hot in the room I sat on the chest and read the first page of the seventh chapter, in which, after the torments she suffered in the Widow Galli's household, Rosa comes back to consciousness in a place that she cannot at first identify.

Seven

I woke up in a huge room with bare walls painted pale lime green, containing a great many iron bedsteads. I felt sick, and couldn't see very well, and when I tried sitting up in the bed where I lay I found that my arms were crossed over my breast and I couldn't move them. When I had kicked off part of the grey blanket that covered me I saw that I had been put in a jacket of white canvas closed down the front and with very long sleeves, the ends of which were obviously tied behind my back. Alarmed by my inability to move, I began shouting, whereupon two women dressed in grey took me out of the bed, out of the ward, through a room where a great many other grey-looking women were sitting on chairs or the floor or walking about, and then into a large shower room with plaster peeling off the walls, where they took off the jacket, leaving me naked, and turned a jet of icy water from a brick-red hose on me. This cold shock made me scream even louder and flail about, whereupon the two women forced me back into the canvas jacket, pushed me down a narrow corridor into an empty little room without any window, and shut the door. It was cold in the little room, and I crouched in a corner, weeping and wondering in despair where fate, which seemed to have had it in for me for quite some time, had brought me now. After a while the door opened and a man in white with slightly greying, wavy dark hair and blue eyes behind round glasses, who immediately aroused my confidence, came in carrying my hat. I asked him to tell me what had happened to me and where I was, and he put the hat on my head, smiled and said in a calm voice that I need have no fear, I was in a safe, peaceful place, Vienna's largest public imperial-and-royal lunatic asylum in District Nine, known as the Alsergrund, where I would very soon be cured of my illness. When I replied with due respect that as far as I knew I wasn't ill, he smiled again gently and said I must leave it to the professionals to decide that, but in any case I had tried to throw myself out of a window in the third-floor apartment of my employer, a lady well known in and around Vienna for her charity and love of her neighbour, and that was not the conduct of a mentally stable person. I protested that I had originally shared his own opinion of the Widow Galli, but experience had shown me that her love of her neighbour and charity were only a sham, as had become clearly evident when she first beat me with an oxhide whip, a punishment the consequences of which he could see for himself by examining the weals on my back, and second had tried to deprive me entirely of my free will be putting the evil eye on me, whereupon the white-clad man held the upper and lower lids of my left eye apart with the thumb and index finger of his right hand, asked me to move my eye first up and down and then from left to right, and while I complied mentioned in passing that Frau Galli had convinced the staff of the imperial-and-royal lunatic asylum, himself included, that the little scratches on my back, which were no cause for concern, had been inflicted not by her hand but my own, since I was obviously addicted to excessively austere penitential practices, a habit that did not suggest robust mental health either but a pathological tendency to autopunition, a term he didn't intend to explain more fully just now. When I asked how he had come by my hat, the doctor, as he obviously was, said that a young man who had been among the onlookers during my suicide attempt, for that was what it had undoubtedly been, claimed to know me and had given it to the orderly at the imperial-and-royal lunatic asylum, asking him to convey it to me with best wishes from Hans Holzer and to assure me of his love which, as the orderly had told him, the doctor, and therefore as the young man must have told the orderly, would of course not be diminished by our temporary separation, the light in which he saw my admission to the imperial-and-royal lunatic asylum, his love could only grow. Then, when the hospital cart into which I had been put on the stretcher set off, the young man who at first, so the orderly had told him, the doctor, seemed perfectly reasonable, had surprisingly tried to jump into it too and was prevented by the onlookers, whereupon the young man went berserk and began to flail around him, so it was decided to bring him in as well and place him in the men's section of the asylum, which, as I would understand, was strictly separate from the women's section. I asked the doctor what this cell was that I had been shut up in, and why I had been placed in bonds, to which he said he wouldn't describe the little room where I was at present by the rather derogatory term of a cell, nor the admittedly not very comfortable item of clothing which had been put on me for good reason as bonds, if I was shut up and in bonds, as I put it, these were merely measures adopted to soothe and moderate my state of mind, and anyway he was going to get the nurses to take me straight back to the ward now, this little room here was not at my personal disposal, the asylum was overcrowded and there were a great many people just waiting to be allowed to retire to this room.

The next few months linger in my memory as a monotonous succession of days and nights, since I spent them for the most part with nothing to do and in the company of the insane, epileptic, imbecile or alcoholic women inmates of the huge wards and prison-like yards of the imperial-and-royal lunatic asylum in Vienna 9. Since the asylum was indeed overcrowded, the doctors, nurses and male orderlies usually gave their attention to an individual patient only on arrival, and after that most of the inmates were left more or less to their fate, unless they disrupted routine by violent behaviour, which was checked by even more violent measures of restraint. I sought in vain to find out if Hans Holzer was still in the men's section. I was allowed to read the books from my cardboard case, and after a while I knew the *Housewives' Golden Treasury*, the prayer book and the four cookbooks by Dobromila Rettigova almost off by heart, and developed the habit of walking back and forth for hours on end reciting recipes, prayers and household hints out loud to myself, a habit that the staff and my fellow patients did not always appreciate but which became more necessary to me every day, for I didn't know what else to do with myself. I never took off the hat with the pansies on it. Towards the end of my time in the hospital it was decided that I should work in its tailoring department, where I sewed buttonholes, but even here I did not keep quiet, instead describing every operation as I carried it out. I said, for instance, as I worked looped buttonholes for underwear that I was now working looped buttonholes for underwear, and as I made a bordered or piped buttonhole I said I was now making a bordered or piped buttonhole. After another of the buttonhole workers was driven frantic by my constant talking and tried to thrust her long, thin sewing needle into my breast, it was decided to move me to the darning women, where I still went on talking, and as I pulled the needle through coarse fabric I said I was now pulling the needle through the coarse fabric in little stitches, as far as possible working it over and under a single thread of the fabric at a time. If I was darning a simple tear, I announced that this was a simple tear, and when I was darning multicoloured fabric I would comment that darning multicoloured fabric was a very tricky business. And when I had no remnants of fabric to hand I would say that unfortunately I had no remnants of fabric to hand, so I must watch the pattern very closely and use yarn of the correct colour to replace the missing threads of the weave. After three days one of the darning women threw her darning mushroom at my temples, and I briefly lost consciousness and was moved on to join the mending women. Within a very short time the group of mending women went to Dr Doblhoff, head of the women's section and a university lecturer, who was also the kindly doctor who had given me back my hat with the pansies on my admission, and complained in no uncertain terms of my uninterrupted commentary on what I was doing, whereupon Dr Doblhoff summoned me to see him.

Despite the fact that my constant talking, a psychic disturbance known to professionals as logorrhoea, suggested a deep-seated disturbance of my mental condition which made further hospital treatment seem desirable if not urgently necessary, and might indeed justify my transfer to the incurables ward, said Dr Doblhoff, gently placing the fingertips of his right and left hands together, despite all that, the other patients in the women's section couldn't be expected to be within constant range of the non-stop operation of my vocal apparatus, so on mature reflection he had made up his mind to take the step, which he hoped he could reconcile with his conscience, of discharging me after several months in this asylum, months during which my condition had by no means improved but instead had deteriorated. He had to admit that it hadn't been an easy decision to take, since he was by no means sure that I would be in any state to handle the freedom I was thus regaining sensibly and circumspectly, but in his view the welfare of the majority, as represented by the contingent of mending women who felt severely inconvenienced by my idiosyncrasy, clearly took precedence over that of a single individual, as I might correctly and accurately be termed. It was quite clear in his mind that this view was not unassailable, and indeed in the course of a short and essential consultation with his esteemed friend and colleague the neurologist Dr Sigmund Freud, a man as able as he was ambitious, the latter had expressed lively opposition. Freud considered my discharge from the imperial-and-royal lunatic asylum a mistake which might have serious consequences. Here Dr Doblhoff allowed himself a short pause, which I used to make the sober and diffident remark that as I had been brought up first by

my mother and then by other God-fearing persons in accordance
with the simple and illuminating precepts of the Old and New
Testaments which, to the best of my knowledge, were regarded as
authoritative by a large part of those living in our monarchy, that
is, I had been brought up to revere the exemplary life of Christ
and the saints of the Catholic Church, and accordingly I couldn't
venture to offer any criticism of the professional observations he
had just made, indeed I must admit that I couldn't understand
them at all, yet if he would permit me I would like to point out
that in my view enforced inactivity in his asylum, although it
undoubtedly endeavoured to promote the mental health of all its
patients, and the boredom resulting from that inactivity had been
the reason for my admittedly excessive compulsion to talk. Dr
Doblhoff, who obviously had not expected any comment from me
at all, however restrained, looked at me in surprise, took a
notebook from the breast pocket of his coat, wrote something in it,
and said that such remarks, as simplistic as they were abstruse and
an excellent demonstration of the psychic delusions of the person
offering them, such explanations of highly complex psychic proced-
ures were frequently attempted by compulsives, and were always
of interest to professionals. So saying, he offered me his right hand
and said he wished me well, and after I had folded my bedding
and reported to the matron I could go back to the outside world. I
took his hand hesitantly and said that over the past few months
the imperial-and-royal lunatic asylum had been like a second
home to me, and I hadn't expected to be torn from my new
surroundings so soon, to be honest the outside world he had just
mentioned alarmed me and made me anxious to a very high
degree, couldn't I stay a little longer in this safe refuge, I would try
to dam up my flow of words, I was ready to show my appreciation
of permission to stay in the hospital by doing any kind of work,
even the most menial, and I'd accept a reduction in my rations too
and would willingly submit to physical chastisement, to which I
had become accustomed anyway while I was in the Widow Galli's

household. As he knew, this was the month of February, a most inclement time of year in Vienna, and I would be very grateful to him for permission to stay in the hospital at least for my birthday on the twenty-ninth of February, and not to have to spend it all alone in one of the public parks with the Viennese wind whistling around me. At this request Dr Doblhoff abruptly withdrew his hand and said, with a dismissive gesture, there could be no question of that, what was I thinking of, he was a man who conducted himself with propriety and couldn't hand out privileges, I had no idea how many people were waiting for admission to the imperial-and-royal lunatic asylum, and if all the inmates wanted to extend their stay in the hospital as they pleased, the inevitable result would be chaos; furthermore, so far as he knew, this was not a leap year, so strictly speaking I had no birthday, no, I must go at once, my time was up. With these words he turned away from me and was about to stride off, whereupon, losing my self-control at this brusque answer, I grabbed one of the skirts of his white coat and tried to hold him back, begging him to show leniency and not send me unprotected into the outside world with its unpredictable changes of temperature and the people in it, who for reasons I couldn't explain were often hostile to me, it could be the death of me, a death for which he would have to answer to God and the saints. Dr Doblhoff turned round, pulled at the skirt of his coat and asked how dared I lay hands on a respected doctor who had accompanied his ambitious colleague Sigmund Freud to Paris not long ago, would I kindly let go of him at once, he had made up his mind and wasn't going to change it. When I began to scream, two nurses hurried in, seized me, forced me into one of the shower rooms, undressed me and put me under the ice-cold water of the shower, so I ended my stay in the imperial-and-royal lunatic asylum in the same way as I had begun it.

An hour later, when the matron had given me a much-mended grey-brown cloak left behind by a former patient, with a hood that protected me from the light sleet that was falling, I was walking towards the Inner City with my cardboard case in my hand, and as I walked I maintained the habit to which I had become addicted and described what I was doing. As I went round the corner of Teinfaltstrasse and Herrengasse, observing under my breath that I was now going round the corner of Teinfaltstrasse and Herrengasse, someone suddenly took me by the sleeve and looked inquiringly under my hood. It was Lyuba, who asked me whether I had taken to talking to myself since we met, and when she had embraced me, making the hood slip off my head, she cried in alarm that I looked like a ghost, pale and hollow-cheeked, my eyes were flickering like the eyes of a mentally disturbed person, please would I tell her where I'd been all this time and why I never came back to the editorial offices in the basement, or the bed-woman's hut on the banks of the Danube, the feather-sorter, the conjuror Anton Kratky-Baschik's third girl assistant and she herself had been dreadfully anxious about me, and now she could see with her own eyes that their anxiety had by no means been groundless. I said it was true I had been through various experiences since I saw her, for instance at this moment I was coming away from the imperial-and-royal lunatic asylum in Vienna 9, which she might take as confirmation of her impression of my appearance, whereupon Lyuba, wringing her hands, said, oh really, I couldn't be left to myself for a minute without stumbling from one misfortune into another, thank goodness she had found me, and from now on she would look after me again. As we went along Herrengasse towards the Michaelerplatz it was quite an effort for me not to tell Lyuba we were now going along Herrengasse towards the Michaelerplatz, but instead to listen as she told me the sad end of the story of her carefully planned first edition of the *Maidservants' Clarion.*

Just imagine, she said, just imagine, on the evening before publication an official from the imperial-and-royal censorship authority turned up quite unexpectedly in the editorial office in the basement demanding to see the journal, a request with which she and the feather-sorter, who was there with her, had to comply.

He had gone redder and redder in the face as he perused the journal, had finally slammed it down on the desk and said that in the name of His Majesty the Emperor of Austria and King of Hungary he was confiscating all copies on the spot, in short the entire edition of the journal, which obviously constituted subversive literature intended to incite a whole social class and put radical ideas into its mind by slanderously attacking non-existent evils. He told us, said Lyuba, that we had only our youth and absence of any previous criminal record, not to mention his own leniency, to thank for the fact that it was quite likely no proceedings would be brought against us. Then the official lowered his voice, pinched Lyuba's cheek and the feather-sorter's chin, and said there was no need for women to bring themselves to public notice in so importunate and unfeminine a way, if at all, he himself was a happily married man, just coming up to his silver wedding, to be suitably celebrated on March the seventh in the back room of the Café Sperl in Gumpendorferstrasse, and over many years of marriage he had had plenty of opportunity to observe, in the person of his own wife, how much more effective a gentle and diplomatic approach proves in the pursuit of certain aims. Then the official went up the steps to the door, turned once more at the top of the stairs and asked her, Lyuba, and the feather-sorter to be good enough not to leave the place until further notice, on getting back to his office he would immediately give orders for a small detachment of his assistants to deal with the matter and take the journals away. When Lyuba, who had been struck dumb with alarm, found her tongue again and asked what about the basic right of freedom of the press in this country, what about liberty to distribute opinions, news, information and other ideas, as ratified in Article Thirteen of the Imperial Basic Law of 21 December 1867, the official from the censorship office smiled tolerantly again, wagged his forefinger playfully at them and said they, Lyuba and the feather-sorter, surely didn't doubt his knowledge of the laws introduced by our wise monarch, but he was happy to inform them that in some circumstances that article applied only in part, and in certain cases it could be set aside entirely.

As Lyuba ended her tale of the premature closure of the *Maidservants' Clarion* we were passing the Café Griensteidl in the Michaelerplatz, and she fell silent, stopped outside a window, looked in, pointed to a pale young man of serious appearance wearing an old-fashioned starched high linen collar, who was sitting immersed in a broadsheet newspaper at a table, and said that gentleman, whom she happened to know, was a dramatist, he had told her in confidence that one of his comedies had a good chance of being produced very soon at the nearby Burghtheater. At this moment the young man glanced up from his newspaper and noticed Lyuba, but when she waved to him through the window pane he turned his eyes haughtily away and looked at the waitress, who had just stopped by his table.

When I asked Lyuba whether I could share one of the bed-woman's maize-straw mattresses with her for the next few nights, because I was homeless for the moment, she sighed and said the old woman kept raising her price per night, and since she had been devoting all her time and abilities to planning the *Maidservants' Clarion* before the journal was seized, it was some time since she had been able to find the necessary sum, and she had been obliged to look around for somewhere else to spend the night. She was now sleeping in the tunnels of the underground canal and sewer system, and if I liked I could accompany her, she was in pleasant if not select company there, and I gave her the impression of desperately needing company myself.

So it was that I spent the night covered with my new and voluminous grey-brown hooded cloak on a heap of rags by the side of one of the slow-flowing collecting canals of the Vienna River, in the company of several youngish men who Lyuba introduced to me as totters, unemployed persons combing the sewers and canals daily in search of coins, metal and other usable items. I shook hands with them, except for one who was lying beside Lyuba's resting place wrapped in a blanket, and all I could see of him was his shock of hair, but as it was quite dark in the tunnel of the canal, and the small projecting platform where we lay was illuminated only by the weak light of a faint paraffin lamp, I could make out the men's features only indistinctly. I was greatly surprised next morning when the man lying beside Lyuba threw off his blanket, stood up, stretched, yawned and then bent down to my friend, who had just woken up herself, and kissed her tenderly. For the young man was none other than Milan Havelka, the woodcutter from the Bohemian Forest, who had helped me to run away from the Ursuline convent in Prague, and who I had thought would now be employed in one of the brick kilns to the south of Vienna. Lyuba put her arm lovingly around the neck of the young man, who had stubble on his chin, and then turned to me and said this was Milan who had left his Slav homeland, just like her, and set out for Vienna in search of a better life, they had met about two months earlier in the Merry Vintner Inn, a lucky coincidence if you believed in coincidences, but she personally thought their meeting was more like a stroke of fate, and now she knew why she had made the arduous journey from Maribor and exposed herself to harassment from the inhabitants of Vienna ever since her arrival. Milan Havelka looked at my face, frowned, then recognized me and said this was incredible, it was the boarding-school miss, how did I come to be here in the underground tunnels of Vienna, I didn't seem to have been very successful in my hopeful plans for getting a position in a respectable bourgeois household in this city, as he would allow himself to conclude from my appearance, which was a little less well-groomed than when we had met on the Charles Bridge. Then he indicated his own dirty, ragged garments and said he himself, as I could easily see from the place where he now was and from his clothing, had fared no better, it was true that his brother Karel had kept his word and found him work in a brick kiln in Favoriten but in the first place

285

he, Milan, being descended from a whole tribe of woodcutters, couldn't get used to working in clay, a material alien to him, which was used to make bricks by pouring it into special moulds, and in the second place he had found it hard to stand the heat of the kilns, which could reach nine hundred degrees Celsius or more. In spite of these disadvantages, he had stuck it out for a while in the brick kiln for his brother's sake, using his time to get in touch with other disaffected Bohemian workers, with the aim of importing the Young Czech movement over the borders of Bohemia itself and into the very heart of the Austro-Hungarian monarchy that every honest Czech patriot hated and gradually establishing a network of secret revolutionary cells in the capital, ready to strike and seize power at a given moment. Unfortunately a meeting he had called in the cellar of the Merry Vintner tavern in Vienna 7, a place to which the Slavs so mercilessly oppressed by the absolutist government resorted, had been broken up by the unexpected arrival of three secret policemen, and these corrupt henchmen of the despot, for such Emperor Franz Joseph really was for all he made out he was so close to the people, didn't shrink from arresting all participants in this little gathering. He had subsequently spent several months in Leopoldstadt jail, but they had been obliged to let him go in the end, since there was no proof at all that he had been engaging in any subversive activity. He had avoided deportation back to Bohemia by going underground, for it was on the unfortunate evening when the secret police put such an unexpected stop to his political activities, undertaken with the aim of liberating the Czech people from the Austrian yoke, that he first met Lyuba. She was in the back room of the inn with several like-minded friends, holding a little discussion on the projected founding of a journal for servants which, like the Young Czech movement, aimed to stand up for the independence and self-determination of a group deprived of its rights, and since he had fallen in love at first sight with her, a woman as strong and self-confident as she was maternal and sympathetic, he was naturally anxious to stay near her so that they could continue the fight for social and political justice hand in hand. So saying, he drew Lyuba towards him, and she pressed close to him in an unusually yielding manner, and said that he wasn't discouraged by being obliged to earn his bread just now as one of the poorest of the poor, working as what they called a fat-fisher, one of those scavengers who searched the sewers of Vienna for bones and remains of fat and sold them to soap boilers, one must put up with setbacks in the struggle for freedom, and when the time was ripe they would emerge from the sewer system and continue their interrupted work. Since I was obviously a friend of his new companion in the struggle, he hoped that after the reverses I myself had suffered I would join them and support their endeavours, which must naturally be mine as well.

I was certainly impressed by Milan's remarks, but I said I didn't feel really cut out to take part in ambitious undertakings that aimed to change society, I'd probably do better to look for some new occupation enabling me to serve others directly. Milan replied that he was disappointed, the reasons I gave in my attempt to justify my indifference reminded him of those advanced by his elder brother in answer to the same invitation, his elder brother, like me, preferred to continue providing slave labour for people whose sole intention was to suck the blood out of the likes of us. When Lyuba asked whether I already had something in view, I said that according to the third girl assistant of the conjuror Anton Kratky-Baschik, the conjuror needed a fourth assistant, and I was going to introduce myself to him as soon as possible, to which Lyuba said it was much too late for that, didn't I know that the feather-sorter had applied for the job and got it, and for the last two months she had been letting the conjuror hypnotize her every day, and doing the most amazing things in that condition. This news surprised me slightly, but I pulled myself together at once and said perhaps there were other opportunities for me, I'd heard that the ladies' ensemble in a well-known inn in the Prater needed a zither player, and as I was not unmusical and had some knowledge of playing the piano, which was basically a stringed instrument like the zither, I thought I had a good chance of being taken on. Shaking her head, Lyuba said I'd better do what I must, but this way I would never be free, as for her, she must be off now, she was looking for somewhere new to edit a journal, since the censorship authority had not only confiscated the hand press but had boarded up the door to the basement in Margareten too, and Milan said it was time for him to start fat-fishing, but his offer remained open and I could think it over.

When I had climbed a ladder to the entrance to the tunnels, lifted the manhole cover above and made my way out into the open, I set off for the Café Eisvogel in the Prater. On the way it began snowing slightly, and I pulled the hood well down over my face and began to wonder anxiously how I was going to survive the rest of the Viennese winter until my birthday. When I was outside the café my heart was in my mouth, and however much I told myself that it was because of the long walk, I had to admit secretly that my real reason was fear of meeting the waiter Hans, an emotion conflicting vigorously with my hope of seeing him again. Plucking up all my courage, I entered the café, and an elderly gentleman in a frock coat, holding in his white-gloved hand a tray on which two coffee cups stood, immediately hurried towards me and asked brusquely what I wanted, this was a high-class establishment and I had probably mistaken the door. I said timidly that I wasn't a customer, I'd like to speak to one of the members of the Hornischer ladies' musical ensemble if possible, I had heard from a reliable source that they were looking for a zither player. The head waiter, as he obviously was, seemed to think for a moment, but then he indicated a side door and said the ladies were rehearsing, and I could go in and audition, but he had to point out that they were very well-trained musicians, the lady clarinettist in particular had a high reputation in Viennese musical circles, and he hoped I was clear in my mind about my intentions and didn't overestimate my abilities. After I had thanked the head waiter for his information I went through the side door, through which the faint sound of music could be heard, and entered a hall where the five persons making up the ladies' ensemble, a guitarist, a flautist, a clarinettist, a violinist and a double-bass player, were sitting on a small stage playing a waltz. I stood waiting politely until the piece was over, when the clarinettist, a tall, slim young woman with thin reddish-blonde hair, a pointed chin and colourless eyes jumped down from the stage with her clarinet, came over to me and asked what I wanted. I repeated my request, and when the clarinettist asked what ensembles I had previously worked with, and whether I had ever performed as a soloist, I cleared my throat and said in a subdued voice that strictly speaking I had never performed as a musician before an audience of any size. This confession seemed to arouse some doubt in the clarinettist, for she looked at me suspiciously and said only musicians with concert experience were accepted by the Hornischer ladies' ensemble, although she admitted zither players didn't very often have such experience, and I'd better show her my zither, which she supposed I had brought with me, so that she could see the quality of my instrument for herself. At this request I felt even more awkward and whispered that at the moment I didn't own an instrument, up to now I'd only had the opportunity of practising on a mahogany pianino with a cast-iron frame, but I was willing to buy a zither as soon as my financial situation permitted, and building on what I already knew about music I would quickly acquire skill in playing it. The clarinettist looked at me in astonishment, glanced at her colleagues, who were following our conversation with interest, and then turned her colourless eyes back to me and said she wasn't quite sure that she had understood me correctly, did I mean to say that I couldn't play the zither at all, to which I replied, well, strictly speaking, no, but in the convent where I was educated they agreed that I had musical talent and I was ready to learn, I did understand her reservations but I was asking her to give me a chance to develop my talent and I would do my utmost not to disappoint her. Whispering and giggling reached my ears from the stage, and the clarinettist continued her inquiries, asking who for heaven's sake had advised me to put such an outrageous request to them, the members of the best-known ladies' ensemble in Vienna, and I truthfully replied that a waiter called Hans who worked in this café, whom I had met by pure chance on a little island in the Danube and who had met me again later, also by chance, outside the Rotunda, had told me there was a place vacant for a zither player. At this the clarinettist's naturally rather pale face flushed red, a blue vein stood out on her high white forehead, and she said this could not be true, surely I couldn't be that Bohemian slut who had beguiled her innocent fiancé and was to blame for his being carted off to the lunatic asylum in the Alsergrund, and she advanced threateningly on me. I retreated in alarm and said I didn't know what she was talking about, it was true that the waiter and I had met a few times in the Prater, but I wasn't aware of being to blame for anything, whereupon the clarinettist uttered a screech and made for me, raking my cheeks with her fingernails and screaming that she'd scratch my hypocritical face to pieces, I had ruined her happiness, how could I do such a thing, as if I hadn't known that she and Hans had been going to marry in the Church of Maria Rotunda in March, the menu for the wedding breakfast was already fixed, and now he'd been in the men's section of the lunatic asylum for months, slowly rocking back and forth on his chair and staring straight ahead of him, not respond-ing to anything, all because of me, that Czech floozy he'd fallen for, my name was Rosa, oh, she knew that all right because he kept on talking about me, murmuring that name to himself the whole time. By now the guitarist, the flautist, the violinist and the double-bass player had put down their instruments and come down from the stage to try restraining their indignant colleague and to prevent her from attacking me, and I wrenched myself away in utter confusion, stumbled backwards to the door and then out of the Café Eisvogel, and ran back towards the city centre.

When I had reached the Danube Canal and was rather calmer, and as I crossed the Marienbrücke in the icy wind of February in Vienna that blew the hood from my head, I let the unedifying scene that had just been acted out pass before my mind's eye again, and decided not to give up my plan to learn the zither, in spite of the crushing rejection I had suffered at the hands of the ladies' ensemble. I was upset by the sad news that Hans had lost a good part of his reason over me, and wondered if there would be any point in visiting him, but I feared my presence might overwhelm him completely and plunge him yet deeper into insanity. I was obliged to draw the dismal but obvious conclusion from my experiences of the last few months that none of the saints of Vienna, to whom I had so earnestly applied for protection and favour on my visits to church with the Widow Galli, had been in any position to do their job satisfactorily. The many Madonnas in the churches of the capital had turned out particularly disappointing, most of all the Servant Girl Madonna, and I thought the time had come for me to abandon all of them, if not the Father, Son and Holy Ghost, with a single exception, St John of Nepomuk, who was revered by the immigrant Bohemians in the Church of Maria am Gestade and to whom I would still allow some merit, on the grounds of my origins and the fact that he had brought me and Milan Havelka safe and unharmed down the waters of the upper Vltava, the Schwarzenberg Canal, the Mühl and the Danube and all the way to Klosterneuburg.

Immersed in these blasphemous thoughts, I wandered down the streets of the Inner City and stopped outside Doblinger's, the music shop in Dorotheergasse, since I had seen a piece of sheet music in the window bearing the title 'The Trout', and was reminded of the Schubert song I loved so much. On the spur of the moment I went into the shop and asked the salesman if the sheet music was suitable for zither, at which the young man, whose hair was parted in the middle, raised his left eyebrow, inspected my cloak, slightly dirty after my night in the sewers and the narrow diameter of the entrance to the canal system, and said of course not, the music was intended for piano and voice, as far as he knew there was no zither arrangement of the song, and to be frank he would consider such a thing rather vulgar, he couldn't imagine that if Schubert were still alive he would have approved of it. To make quite sure, however, he would go and look in the zither-music section, and if I waited he would be straight back. With these words the salesman disappeared through a low, dark door, and I let my eyes wander over the sheet music and the musical instruments on display, until they came to rest on a gleaming, brand-new zither.

I no longer remember all the details of what happened then, all I know is that an irresistible longing to possess that instrument came over me, my hands reached out to it, took hold of it, and stowed it away under my voluminous hooded cloak, I turned, left the shop, went a little way along the Dorotheergasse in the direction of the Hofburg, entered the Evangelical church and sat down on a pew, and only there did I realize that once again I had committed the sin of theft, but this time I had not stolen a harmless jar of redcurrant jelly from my employers' kitchen, I had made away with an expensive musical instrument from a highly regarded Viennese music shop in broad daylight. This realization began to horrify me more and more, and despite the fact that half an hour ago I had abjured all and every one of the Madonnas in Vienna I looked desperately around for a statue of the Virgin Mary to whom I could confess my crime and ask for forgiveness, until it struck me that this was, after all, an Evangelical church, which made me feel guiltier than ever, since I couldn't help thinking of my mother and imagining how dreadfully disappointed she would be in me, not only for stealing but for taking refuge with my ill-gotten gains in a heretical place of worship as well. I jumped up from the pew, drawing a rather unharmonious chord from the zither hidden under my cloak, which made the elderly lady in a fur cap and fur collar sitting deep in prayer on the other side of the central aisle a few metres away look up in alarm and glance in my direction, whereupon I made haste to get out of the church and back to the entrance to the sewer system, which I had difficulty in finding, since by now the lid of the manhole was concealed by a layer of snow.

Back in the tunnel, and intending to examine my loot by the light of the paraffin lamp, I sat down on a pile of rags beside Milan Havelka, who was staring gloomily in front of him with his head in his hands, muttering that he'd had enough of his nauseating activity, these sewers stank to high heaven, how could a human being be expected to do such work, the one solution for these intolerable circumstances was political revolt. The sight of the zither, however, aroused his curiosity, he carefully touched the instrument, turned it carefully back and forth in his fingers, stiff and thickened as they were by manual labour, asked where it came from and said appreciatively that I'd relieved the ruling classes of a valuable item, he wouldn't have thought I had it in me, and he asked if I knew anyone who would take the goods off my hands without cheating me, because if not he was ready to introduce me to various very decent fences of his acquaintance. I refused his offer, saying that wasn't the idea, I wanted to keep the zither, learn to play it and then earn my living with it, my mother had always said musicians seldom went hungry. I plucked a couple of strings, and the delicate notes rose echoing in the shaft of the tunnel, so that Milan cupped a hand behind his ear, listened attentively and said it sounded like angelic music, although the sewer system was pure hell and only lost souls and the damned hung around in it. Then a little old man wearing a dark green felt hat, a shabby loden jacket and a pair of stained lederhosen ending below the knee came round the corner of the tunnel on short, crooked legs clad in thick knee-length socks and said what was that he'd heard, what was this he saw, good heavens, a concert zither, a genuine concert zither, and he played a chord with the thumb of his right hand,

293

shook his head and said he had heard a great many zithers in his life, but not one of them had such a heavenly sound. Only then did he look at me more closely, gave me his hard right hand with its black and crooked fingernails and said his name was Hubert, Hubert Egger, and when Milan explained that Hubert was a former Alpine herdsman, not a totter, Hubert added yes, an Alpine herdsman from the blessed country of the Tyrol, more precisely the lower Ötztal, where he had been a cowherd and cheesemaker working on a mountain pasture farm and played the dulcimer in his free time, until one day the mountain farm was torn away by an avalanche, leaving him without a job, so he had decided to leave that blessed countryside by the River Inn and look for work in the capital of the empire. Unfortunately, from his very first day in the imperial capital he had immediately been identifiable as a Tyrolean on the grounds of his west Austrian dialect, which differed in many major points from the colloquial speech of Vienna, and so he had been persecuted with the Viennese xenophobia notorious in all the crown territories, and consequently, despite his efforts, hadn't managed to find any more satisfactory and better-paid activity than scavenging in the sewers of Vienna. He had thought of earning a living by playing the dulcimer, but sad to say his instrument, a large trapezoid zither consisting of a shallow box with two sound holes and decorated with intarsia work in the design of a Tyrolean eagle, had been buried under the snow in the avalanche he mentioned, having been in the Alpine hut at the time of the catastrophe, and he had always lived from hand to mouth in Vienna and could never save enough money to buy a new dulcimer. When Hubert Egger had inspected my concert zither he said if I would let him have the ring he could play the Andreas Hofer song, as a Tyrolean who loved his native land he naturally loved the Andreas Hofer song too, and he'd often played it on the dulcimer in his time. When I asked what ring he meant, I didn't have such a thing, he said a concert zither without a ring to play the strings was like a dulcimer without sticks or little hammers, how come I didn't have that basic knowledge, every zither player knew that! I told him I had only just acquired the instrument but I hadn't been given a ring to go with it, and to be honest I didn't yet know how to play it, but I was hoping I could gradually teach myself the zither, I had been assured more than once in the past I didn't lack musical talent and so I imagined that after a while and with a little practice I could get to the point of accompanying myself in singing simple songs. At this the former Tyrolean Alpine farmer asked what on earth I was thinking of, a concert zither was a highly complex instrument and could very soon be ruined by inexpert treatment, it took years to develop a certain skill on it, but if I liked he'd teach me how to play, it was true that he was best acquainted with the dulcimer typical of the mountain regions, but he thought he could find his way around a concert zither pretty well too, and it would be an honour to make a good musician of an obviously talented girl like me. Having said this the totter stopped, took two slightly curved little wooden hammers from the pocket of his shabby grey loden coat with an air of mystery, and held them triumphantly aloft. These, he explained, were the hammers which that disastrous avalanche had not managed to sweep away, since they had been where they always were at the time in question, to wit in the pocket of his loden coat. While the little hammers wouldn't entirely replace the missing ring they would to some extent serve as a substitute.

So it was that Hubert Egger, born in the Ötztal, taught me the basics of the zither over the next few weeks in my hideout on that little projecting platform in the sewer system of Vienna. Quite soon the Andreas Hofer song and the two Schubert pieces 'The Trout' and 'The Linden Tree' were echoing down the tunnel, causing the totters and fat-fishers, who liked music better than work, to crowd around us and listen. They included Milan Havelka, who said it was a funny thing, for although there were instrument-makers among the inhabitants of the Bohemian Forest, who made a great many items out of wood on account of the wealth of timber in the area, he himself had never been interested in music, nor was he a religious person apart from his family's faith in St John of Nepomuk, but he had to admit that the sweet sound of the zither echoing back from the tunnel walls had an uplifting effect on him, comforted him in his degrading work in the sewers, and gave him strength to hold out and not lose sight of his aim, the founding of a national Czech state. Lyuba sometimes joined us too and said, when I asked her, that all this zither playing was a pure waste of time and simply kept me from more important tasks, but she would admit that some of my pieces did sound very pretty, and it was time I took the zither, climbed out through the entrance to the sewers with it, sat down on the paving stones beside the great entrance to St Stephen's Cathedral and played my little songs as best I could, so that passers-by would throw me a few kreuzers and I wouldn't be a burden on Milan and her any longer, for after all it was they who had paid for my food since I arrived in the canal system, she wouldn't want me to misunderstand, she considered me her friend if not her companion in arms, but as I well knew, she and Milan were short of the necessities of life themselves. I was aware that these reproaches of Lyuba's were justified, but I shrank from playing in the Inner City of Vienna, for I was afraid the sales staff of Doblinger's music shop might pass, recognize the zither as the one that had been on display in their shop, and hand me over to the arm of the law, the Viennese police force, feared by all street musicians and homeless people. When I had confided in Milan Havelka, who said the problem was easily solved and he'd advise me to disfigure the zither by scratching its lacquered surface, thus making the model unrecognizable, I borrowed his penknife and inflicted a number of nicks and cuts on the wooden surface, and after that I smeared the instrument with some of the fat fished out of the sewers by the totters, so that it really did look old and used. I pretended to Hubert Egger, who was horrified by the appearance of the zither next time we practised, that my sleeping place had been invaded by some of the homeless while I was away from it, and they had damaged the instrument out of sheer pleasure in wanton destruction.

A few days later I finally ventured to leave my underground lair and give the people of the city, or rather District One of the city, a taste of my art in the Stephansplatz, an enterprise in which Hubert Egger encouraged me by placing at my disposal not only the little wooden hammers but also a pair of fingerless knitted gloves, the kind worn by street musicians in really cold weather to keep their fingers from freezing and make sure they remained supple. Surprisingly, the Viennese public definitely seemed to approve of my zither playing, an approval expressed not only in occasional compliments from passers-by but in the form of generous amounts of money, which enabled me to show Milan and Lyuba my gratitude and provide for their keep for a while.

In the following period I knew an enrichment and expansion of my life as unexpected as it was pleasing, for my musical activity brought me into contact with other people, most of them from the more remote parts of the empire, like me, who earned their bread in a similar fashion, and all of a sudden I had many friends and acquaintances in Vienna, and could hardly believe that only recently I had been the prisoner of a malevolent witch and religious hypocrite, and had then undergone treatment in the imperial-and-royal lunatic asylum that really did send me out of my mind for a short time. The first musician with whom I struck up an acquaintance was a countryman of mine, a bagpiper from Mühlhausen, who simply came and stood beside me one afternoon and began to accompany my music. He was a great admirer of the famous Bohemian composer Antonin Dvořák, born in his own home town, and took pains to teach me a much simplified arrangement he made for concert zither and bagpipes of the *Slavonic Dances*, which we performed in various parts of Vienna, including the Bohemian Prater, so called because a great many immigrants from Bohemia lived near it, and consequently we had a friendly reception there. Now and then we were joined by two young men from Galicia, one of whom played the hurdy-gurdy and the other the *sopialka*, a kind of shawm, who taught us songs about the deeds of the Cossacks, and if we were in luck we could sometimes join a gypsy band from Temesvar which appeared four times a week at the Casino Zögernitz in Döbling and made a little extra by playing in the streets of Vienna. I also struck up an acquaintanceship with some of the Viennese organ-grinders who went through the city with their barrel organs, either portable or on little carts, turning the handles to set the roller playing the melody in motion and producing the most delightful Viennese songs, some of which I tried to play myself.

Practising my new skills on the zither meant that by the beginning of the Viennese spring I had become well acquainted not only with a number of musicians, most of them as poor as myself, but also with the city of Vienna, its streets and squares, its gardens and inns. The fear I had felt at the idea of having to spend my eighteenth birthday alone and freezing in one of the public parks had been groundless too, for on the twenty-eighth of February (since it was a fact that it wasn't a leap year) Lyuba, Milan and the other totters and fat-fishers had surprised me in my sleeping quarters with a lighted white wax candle, a country sausage and a bottle of Budweiser, whereupon, pleased and grateful, I took out my zither and we all sang the Cabbies' Song to its accompaniment. Thanks to the generosity of the people of Vienna, I could long ago have afforded a maize-straw mattress at the bed-woman's place in Leopoldstadt, and wouldn't even have had to share it with anyone, but by now I had become so fond of my new friends, the homeless of the Viennese underground, that I preferred to go on spending the nights with them beside the collecting channel of the Vienna River, although since the beginning of spring the water level had sometimes been rising alarmingly because of the frequent rainfall, now and then actually reaching our sleeping quarters, and even though the Viennese powers of law and order regularly tried to drive us out of the tunnels of the system. After various trials fate had brought me, a motherless girl, to a large and loving family, and I wanted to show loyalty to it.

But one April day as I was playing the imperial anthem outside the Wedding Fountain in the Hoher Markt with a mute twelve-year-old boy, who also slept in our tunnel and whose only possession was a lustreless, bent old French horn which he never let out of his sight and on which he could play wonderfully well, a fat and well-dressed man with a monocle in his eye, who had been staring pointedly at my zither for quite some time, made his way through our little audience, snatched the instrument from my hand, turned it over, and after briefly examining the wooden base of the zither, held it in front of my face, jabbing his forefinger angrily at a small oval shield stuck to the wood, a feature I had never noticed in my well-planned disfigurement of the instrument's appearance. Months ago, said this distinguished-looking gentleman, months ago a valuable zither, one of those chordophones that may be plucked, struck or bowed and are found in use in different forms all over the world, had been purloined from his shop in Dorotheergasse by a female person wearing a hood drawn over her face, whose features could therefore be made out only indistinctly. When the salesman had noticed this brazen theft he ran out of the shop even though it was snowing slightly, intending to seize the criminal, but the woman seemed to have vanished from the face of the earth. The curved shape of the zither I was playing and its original colour, still recognizable despite the serious damage it had suffered, had reminded him of the stolen instrument, which was why he had acted out of his fundamentally polite and peace-loving character and taken the liberty of examining it. At this point the distinguished-looking gentleman stopped briefly, then raised his voice and shouted, tapping the little shield again, that the label showed this zither was the instrument that had disappeared, he could easily prove his ownership and he would ask the bystanders to help him by acting as the law required, holding the thief and fetching a police officer from the

299

nearby Wipplingerstrasse police station, so that legal proceedings for the punishment of this criminal act could be set in motion. At his words three powerful men, who just now had been swaying back and forth in waltz time to our music, fell on me and twisted my arms behind my back, which made the mute and rather slightly built boy take to his heels along with his French horn, and next moment, hastily summoned by a pretty young woman with a wicker shopping basket who had been humming along to the tune of 'The Linden Tree' only a moment ago with her eyes raptly closed, two uniformed officers appeared, arrested me, and took me off to Vienna Neudorf Women's Prison and House of Correction.

12

While we were breakfasting in the kitchen Aunt Pia opened the paper she took, the *Kurier*, read a little, shook her head and said, oh dear, for the second time in three days a foreign girl had been attacked in Vienna, a young woman from the Dominican Republic who had gone to the Café Diglas in Wollzeile after her German evening class, along with several other students, and around midnight set off for the apartment owned by her fiancé, a Viennese antique dealer, in Vienna 3, and right there in the middle of the embassy quarter, just imagine, in the very middle of the embassy quarter, a stranger with a black stocking mask over his head had pushed her into a not very deep ditch dug by builders and sexually abused her. Once again a right-wing nationalist had admitted the deed, this time in a letter to the editors of the *Kronenzeitung*, *Kurier*, *Standard*, *Presse* and *Ganze Woche*. Aunt Pia put the newspaper down on the table, dunked her bread and butter in her coffee, looked at me and murmured, dreadful, dreadful, on the other hand there was an alarming rise in the number of foreign women like that who were getting engaged to the most eligible bachelors in Vienna, in this instance an antique dealer who lived in the high-class embassy quarter and dealt in Japanese *objets d'art*, and who subsequently married them, thus dashing the hopes of founding families entertained by marriageable Viennese women. The antique dealer himself, as he had stated in an exclusive interview, had intended to marry the sixteen-year-old on Holy Innocents'

Day in the Nine Choirs of Angels Church, there we were again, strictly speaking I myself was one of this set of foreign women limiting the marriage prospects of native Viennese girls, young Herr Horvath's phone calls spoke volumes, he was obviously not to be deterred from what in her view was clearly the behaviour of a suitor by either the anorexia that marked me or my peculiar taste in clothes. And as for the right-wing nationalist, she was not, of course, about to defend his impulsive action, but one had to admit that the percentage of foreigners settling in Vienna was rising to dizzy heights, and that, together with her, Aunt Pia's, deafness, was one reason why she almost never left her apartment, the moment you stepped out into Blutgasse or Domgasse you always had to reckon with being mugged by a Montenegrin, a Slovakian, a Romanian or even a black man and robbed of your savings, and there was no trusting the Bosnian caretaker's grasping husband either, but there, what was she to do, as a helpless old lady she was at his mercy.

I finished my coffee and left the building, and as I passed the horse-drawn cabs outside the cathedral, the driver of one of them, a moustached, red-faced, middle-aged man in black and white check trousers, a black velvet coat and a narrow-brimmed half-height top hat beckoned me over and asked if I lived near here, he'd seen me quite often, you seldom saw such lovely girls in Vienna, and how would I like to meet one of his customers, a rich banker who frequently took his foreign business friends on sight-seeing drives through the city, the banker had a preference for dark-skinned women and as far as he knew didn't mind spending money on that preference. When I had politely declined this offer, I crossed the concourse outside the cathedral and went down Goldschmiedgasse to the Petersplatz, where a lady dressed in deep black, making for the entrance to St Peter's Church, detained me by holding out her right hand, gloved in black lace, and said that if she might permit herself a comment, as a member of the Viennese Association for the Protection of Christian Standards of course she herself firmly believed that all human beings were equal in the sight of God, but she would just mention that not everyone thought so, far from it, and in her view, since it looked as if I had only recently come to this country from warmer climes, I would soon find myself suffering from the prejudices of the average Viennese, who were not very God-fearing people, and she would recommend me not to stay in Austria any longer than was absolutely necessary; having herself gone south by train to Rome not so long ago for a papal audience she could of course understand my desire to travel, but in the end it made more sense to be content with the sphere of life assigned to us by God, rather than crossing the frontiers set by race and nationality in an overweening urge to expand. Well, now she must be going, Father Petrus was waiting for her by the statue of St John of Nepomuk inside the church.

After this insight into the alleged golden heart of the Viennese, the third I'd been granted that morning, I went by way of the Graben and Kärntnerstrasse to the Opera House, took the 95A bus from there to the corner of Margaretenstrasse and Grosse Neugasse, and soon afterwards I was in the Death House. The unsuccessful advances Josef Horvath and I had made to each other during my last singing lesson made me feel distinctly nervous as I anticipated the next one, and I was glad to find Josef, wearing an attractive dark blue linen shirt, letting me in at his door as if nothing had passed between us. I began by spending about half an hour doing my best, on my singing teacher's directions, to perform what he called the tonal change of gear in the back of my head which, said Josef, would make the sound dark, rounded and floating, would dematerialize it, so to speak, and then we set to work on the *Winterreise* again and studied the song 'Numbness', and when Josef sang it to me and I thought I saw an expression of deep sadness on his face at the opening lines, 'I seek the snow in vain / For traces of her foot', I thought of the child he had once been, and on turning my eyes away from him and looking at the portrait of his mother, that long-nosed woman with the low forehead and piercing eyes, I went over to him, sat down on the piano stool beside him, and when his mouth had just formed the words, 'Ah, my poor heart is frozen, / Her image cold within', I closed it with a kiss. This time it was Josef who stood up and led me into the bedroom, which contained a tall bed of dark wood with an ornately carved headboard, a bedside table covered with countless boxes, little bottles and other containers full of medicaments, as well as a huge wardrobe, and had his butterfly cases hanging on the walls, and when he had pushed aside two damp linen sheets hanging from lines, he led me over the threadbare black and brown carpet to the unmade bed with its crumpled pillow, a quilt hanging down over the edge of the bed to the floor, and a not particularly clean sheet with a red hot-water bottle on it. But when we sat down on this bed Josef was overcome by weakness again and sank ineffectually back, clutching his forehead and saying he felt faint, he wondered if this attack was anything to do with our being in his mother's bed where he had slept since her death, and whether the fact that I was sitting on that bed where no one else had ever sat, let alone lain down, except his mother and himself, had caused what he hoped was this temporary draining of blood from his brain. At this I removed Josef's rather plump little hand from his forehead and covered both that forehead and then the rest of the skin on his face with kisses, after which I cautiously turned my attention to his throat and finally to the lower areas of his body in turn, and felt satisfaction and indeed great pleasure as this attempt at resuscitation took effect, filling one part of his body after another with life. In the course of one of the unplanned but passionate movements executed during the next half-hour by the man I had thus raised from the dead, the hot-water bottle slipped to the floor, the boxes of medicaments, tubes of ointment and little bottles of tinctures were swept off the bedside table, and when, during our performance, my eye happened to fall by chance on the face of young Frau Horvath holding her baby son and looking at me from a painting over the headboard, where a picture of the Virgin Mary with the baby Jesus usually hangs in orthodox Catholic Austrian households, I saw her thick black eyebrows draw together in displeasure.

The fact that I had managed, within a relatively short space of time, to resuscitate a man deprived of both physical and intellectual capacity filled me with pride. I didn't by any means feel that my attempts to revive Josef's limp body were a strain, indeed his initial passivity heightened my urge to explore, his surrender lent me unsuspected ardour, the reversal of the usual sexual roles increased my desire, and while I was the enraptured active partner and Josef my willing victim, I felt sorry that it had taken me almost thirty-three years to find such an irresistibly yielding man who so obviously enjoyed my energetic attentions.

A little later, wrapped in the salmon-pink dressing-gown, I was dancing with Josef on the star-patterned parquet of the living-room floor to the tune of *Vienna Blood*, the strains of which had accompanied me as I got off the plane at Vienna-Schwechat Airport, and I can't remember ever being happier in my life. I had my arms around Josef's waist, and he, wearing lightweight pale grey cotton pyjamas, leaned confidently back, his hands clasped behind my neck, abandoning himself to the swirling movement. My feet moved as if of their own accord in the three-four time of the waltz, and as my feet danced, as my left hand held Josef's right hand while my right hand was placed firmly around his waist, I saw his smiling face before me, his flushed cheeks and the little beads of perspiration on his forehead. Never in my life had I led someone else in the dance so confidently, with such pleasure, and I could see from Josef's face that he too was enjoying the harmony of our physical movements as I skilfully steered him past the baby grand he had inherited from his mother, guiding him to one side and back again to avoid colliding with the furniture and lamps she had also left him.

As I went back to my great-aunt's apartment I thought of the day some five months ago when John de Luca had approached me with outstretched arms, crying, 'Anna!' and when, after I had sung him 'The Trout' and 'Swing Low, Sweet Chariot', he had taken my hand, exchanged a few words with the hotel porter, whom he obviously knew and who gave him the key to a room, looking with eyebrows slightly raised at my high-heeled white waitress's shoes as we went towards the lift. In the hotel room on the seventeenth floor John had removed those shoes and the rest of my clothes in a minute flat, and his distinctly dynamic method of operating, his almost too-hasty impetuosity, characteristics which, as I had already noticed, were typical of him, forced me into a total passivity that is not my style at all. How different from Josef!

When John called me late that evening I interrupted him after his first endearment to me and asked him to keep it brief, my singing lessons and my reading were making considerable inroads on my time, whereupon he urged me to book my flight home as soon as possible, November was now over and these four weeks must have been enough to give me a good idea of the city where Freud and his daughter Anna had lived and worked, as well as pushing my voice up to the lyric soprano register, and what was more he was pining for me, how about celebrating our reunion by spending a night in the hotel room on the seventeenth floor where I had given myself to him six months back with an innocence that had both touched and excited him, a positively girlish bashfulness which you almost never found in New York girls, since the majority of them were disappointingly blasé. I told him that during the last month I had become aware of the surprising strength of my links to the city of my maternal forebears, links which must obviously have something to do with a genetically conditioned inclination, or perhaps an unconscious sense of my roots that had been brought to the surface of my conscious mind during my stay, but anyway I wasn't intending to bring my visit to an end as suddenly as he asked, and if he liked he could begin rehearsals with the little Haitian girl whom he thought so suitable for the part of Anna

Freud. After the long pause following this remark, John said quietly that I just couldn't do this to him, the whole project stood or fell with me, did I want the production to come to nothing, what possessed me, suddenly declining to leave what everyone knew was a very dull city full of bad-tempered and depressive inhabitants, a city where there was always a nasty wind blowing, to which I replied he himself had told me some weeks ago that human beings were free agents, and now I wanted to make use of that basic human right, I really couldn't say any more to him at the minute, and anyway I wanted to go back to something I was reading and he'd hear from me in due course. Then I hung up, went back to my room, and began reading the eighth chapter of Rosa's story.

Eight

Vienna Neudorf prison, like all houses of correction for women, was run by an order of nuns, the community of the Sisters of the Good Shepherd, so to my dismay, after escaping the Ursulines of Prague and the Widow Galli with so much difficulty and danger, I was back again in the care of these pious women. On my arrival a description of my person was drawn up, my belongings were taken away from me, my hair was cut short and I was dressed in prison clothing, since the House of Correction was closely linked to the penitentiary. A lame nun called Hermelindis told me about the rules and regulations and the penalties for breaking them. She hardly needed to say, she remarked, that no blasphemous conversation was allowed in this house, devoted as it was to the saving of lost sheep to be restored to the great flock of our Good Shepherd, Lord Jesus Christ, after whom her order was named, it was a house to which the kindly will of God had brought me so that I might acknowledge my sins and begin a new life. Daily attendance at Mass was also compulsory for all inmates, since nothing promoted the transformation and edification of the human soul more than the word of God, in which the offenders had a special course of instruction three times a week, and I was also obliged to take part in this course. Visits were allowed on condition of good conduct but were restricted to a quarter of an hour, since long-term contact with an outside world from which we were shut away in the interests of our own improvement must be avoided. Offences entailing punishment included, in particular, any defiance of our superiors, actions unseemly for a Christian soul of the female gender, and in addition the mortal sin of anger, as well as negligent work and failure to complete the work quota, an offence which partook of another and equally mortal sin, sloth. Anyone transgressing these prohibitions was first cautioned in a personal interview with the Mother Superior, and if the offence were repeated was punished in accordance with the extent of the misdemeanour. She would expressly point out that inmates of this establishment were chained or bound to a stake only in exceptional circumstances, evidence of the high degree of humanity with which wrongdoers were treated here. When Sister Hermelindis had given me a knife, fork and spoon and a tin bowl, she limped ahead of me to the dormitory full of wooden plank beds where I was to sleep in the company of beggars, gypsies, vagabonds, prostitutes, alcoholics and women guilty of lesser offences. She showed me my bed and said the inmates were woken at four-thirty in the morning, after breakfast I was to go to the workroom, where I would be given a task in the wool-treating section; as I might already know, the items made by the inmates of Vienna Neudorf prison were famous everywhere for their quality, the soft, warm nightcaps, stockings, camisoles and indestructible blankets sold like hot cakes in the Tandelmarkt of Vienna. She herself attributed the unusually high morale among the workers to the fact that passages from edifying books were read aloud during working hours.

So it was that next day I sat in the big workroom between Grete, a former kitchenmaid, and a young woman called Frieda who, as Grete whispered to me, had been an unofficial working girl in the Prater and elsewhere and was brought to Vienna Neudorf after a raid carried out by the Viennese police. We were plucking wool, that is to say cleaning it before it was combed and spun. When the nun sitting opposite us at the supervisor's desk brought out a book and asked who would like to read the next chapter of the story of

St John of Nepomuk, which was both a sad tale and wonderful evidence of God's immeasurable grace, I jumped up, startled, and asked to have that privilege, mentioning that St John of Nepomuk was my favourite saint, his sacred influence had left clear traces on the story of my life, so the nun gave me the book and said that although my Bohemian accent was slightly irritating, and new-comers were not usually granted the privilege of reading aloud, she would make an exception on the grounds of my obvious personal attachment to the martyr, and I was to begin reading the legend of that holy man's confidential conversation with King Wenceslas's wife Johanna in the confessional of the Church of St Gall in the New Town of Prague. The pathos and ardour which I tried to inject into my reading impressed both the prison staff and the inmates so much that both groups insisted on my being the reader over the next few weeks and months, a request with which I was happy to comply, since it meant that I was not tempted to resume my behaviour of the lunatic asylum in Vienna 9 and keep commenting aloud on what I was doing, thereby arousing the hostility of the other women.

One day Grete approached me during a walk in the prison yard and asked in a whisper if I was interested in literary works of a delightfully different nature from those that could be borrowed on condition of good conduct from the little library in the House of Correction, works that were smuggled secretly into the place and must be handled very carefully, since we were forbidden to read them. When I said I was quite happy with what the library provided, the only thing I regretted was the absence of cookbooks and works on household management from the shelves, Grete hissed in my ear that she couldn't make me out, how could I feel any enthusiasm for such uninteresting reading matter when I could enjoy exciting novels in serial instalments of eight, twelve or sixteen pages, and when the writers of these novels described difficult situations of human life in amazingly dramatic fashion, making it their business to shine a light into every corner of the depths of the soul and depict adventures, love affairs and crimes in a very powerful way. Before I could object that I preferred reading *The Life of the Devout Maidservant Katharina*, *The Big Book of the Heart of Jesus* or *The Viennese Calendar of the Virgin Mary*, for such works had a good effect on my mental equilibrium, unlike those vivid accounts of human passions that were bound to upset and even distress me, Grete added that right now the serializations of *Demons of the Heart*, *The White Lady of the Vienna Hofburg Palace* and *Innocence Under the Executioner's Axe* were available complete, the fee for borrowing was one kreuzer per number a week, a ridiculously small sum in view of the pleasure these works had so far given everyone who read them and the danger to which she herself and others were exposed in smuggling the novels in. For a start she could recommend the work entitled *Ardent Love and Flames of Fire*, a fascinating family drama set in Vienna of the Biedermeier period, but she ought to mention that numbers thirteen and twenty-seven and the last five instalments were missing, an unfortunate omission on the part of the girl responsible for getting them into the prison. With these words she surreptitiously handed me a set of pages and said she'd let me have a look at the first instalment by the title of *The Black Monk* free, to give me an idea of the high quality of the reading matter she was offering.

A few hours later, having completed my work quota, I was sitting on my wooden plank bed holding the first volume in the *Ardent Love and Flames of Fire* series inserted into the dark red binding of my prayer book, which had a gold cross imprinted on it, so as to avoid arousing the suspicions of the prison staff, and to my surprise I discovered that the former kitchenmaid Grete had by no means been exaggerating when she praised so highly the printed works circulating in Vienna Neudorf Women's Prison and House of Correction. The novel began with such a forceful account of the frightful situation in which the impoverished Count von Falkenau-Gundelrebe, a man of spotless character, found himself as a result of the diabolical machinations of his estate manager

Bodo Kuppelwieser, not to mention the description of the beauty and innocence of his daughter Aurora, who can hardly manage to fend off the advances of the sinister Bodo, that I failed to hear the bell of the prison chapel summoning us to our May devotions to the Virgin, earning myself a reprimand from Sister Benedikta, who said it was certainly creditable to immerse oneself in the prayer book but I mustn't forget that I was part of a community, an unfortunate body of female Christian souls who had stumbled on their winding way through life and were now striving for God's prop and stay, nor must I allow myself to miss the Holy Eucharist and thus deprive myself of the spiritual nourishment of the body and blood of Jesus, so essential to the reinforcement of my faith. And to prevent me from repeating my offence I was to spend the next two weeks on the treadwheel that worked the fulling mill, since the task of plucking wool, obviously only too easy to master, seemed insufficient to teach me discipline.

Work in the fulling mill was exhausting, but had the advantage of proximity to Grete, who had also been sent to work the treadwheel after a stormy argument with Frieda, a quarrel that began when Frieda accused Grete of the theft of a bottle of Blue Portuguese wine given to her as a reward for exceeding her work quota, and in the course of which Grete punched Frieda's left eye so hard that it immediately filled with blood and then closed up and Frieda had to spend three days in the infirmary, something all of us, Grete included, envied her, since the sick were fed on soft-boiled eggs, preserved meat and wine soup, not the watery barley broth given to the healthy. So Grete was able to provide me, unobserved, with further instalments of her sensational novels, which I devoured whenever and wherever I had the chance. The sufferings of young Eudoxia, scourged by the Jesuits of Vienna in the crypt of their church, the unspeakable cruelties of the bloodthirsty Hungarian Countess Bathori and her dwarfish hench-man Ujvari, the protagonists of the cycle entitled *The Iron Maiden* and the fate of the unfortunate bride of the notorious robber

Jaroschinsky so captivated me that a few minutes after I began reading I was no longer aware of my surroundings, and this absence of mind made me quite unable to carry out the tasks allotted to me to the satisfaction of the nuns, who found themselves obliged to punish me with increasing frequency for my negligence.

One day Sister Benedikta told me that a certain Hans Holzer had written to the management of the Prison and House of Correction asking permission to visit me, a request that the Mother Superior had granted, so I was to be in the visiting room of the prison next Thursday at three in the afternoon, to spend a quarter of an hour conversing quietly with my visitor, although naturally any physical contact, even a brief pressure of the hand, was strictly forbidden. This unexpected opportunity made me very excited. So Hans the waiter had at last been discharged from the lunatic asylum in Vienna 9. How had he found out where I was?

During the next few days it was not the adventures of the heroes and heroines of the serial novels that distracted me from my activities; instead the picture of Hans the waiter, already slightly faded, kept coming before my mind's eye. Full of anticipation and full of anxiety too, I counted the hours to Thursday afternoon and finally, in my cleanest smock, with my hair down and not as usual pinned around my head in a simple plait, my knees trembling, I entered the visiting room where Hans Holzer, flanked by Sister Hermelindis and Sister Kordula, both of whom supervised the conversations between visitors and inmates, was sitting at a table and jumped up as I came in, whereupon Sister Kordula's strong hand forced him to sit down again. But no sooner had I sat down opposite him, no sooner had Hans the waiter uttered the words Rosa! and At last! than Sister Hermelindis dragged me to my feet once more, crying that I must be out of my mind, what was I thinking of coming to see a visitor looking like that, the Vienna Neudorf Prison and House of Correction was a decent establishment bent on discipline and order and couldn't afford to have its blameless reputation endangered by inmates appearing with their hair hanging down like gypsies and other worthless vagabonds, I was to plait my hair again at once, go straight to the workroom and fill designated paper bags with powdered dye with due care and attention, naturally I had forfeited permission for my visit, and I could think myself lucky not to have incurred any more severe punishment for my disgraceful behaviour. When Hans Holzer heard this he rose to his feet again and tried to jump across the visitor's table in an attempt to tear me away from the nuns, but after a short hand-to-hand struggle Sister Kordula overpowered him by twisting his hands behind his back with her own iron grasp, and when I lunged forward to help him Sister Hermelindis simply grabbed me by the hair and dragged me after her as she limped swiftly out of the visiting room and down the long corridor to the workroom, so that Hans Holzer's desperate cries soon died away.

After this very upsetting incident I withdrew even more into the world of the serial novels. One evening, when I was sitting on my bed with number thirteen of *The Blackmail Mystery* on my lap, Frieda looked over my shoulder, and before I could hide the novel by closing the dark red cover of my prayer book she said scornfully she'd thought as much, so these were the prayers in which I was always immersed, obviously even I, who had originally given her the impression of being a woman of some intelligence, had fallen for the wiles of Grete, that stupid, greedy kitchen slut, who exploited the wretchedness of the inmates of the prison and supplied them with life at second hand out of pure avarice, capitalizing on our human isolation and constant lack of intellectual stimulation, leading us to believe in a world that didn't exist and that enfeebled us instead of strengthening us for survival in society once we were discharged from the House of Correction. Then she sat down on the bed beside me, put her arm around my shoulders and asked if I wouldn't like to get to know the real, intense world, have genuine experiences, experiences with real live human beings who didn't shrink from exploring their own darker instincts, individuals who did not deny their complex natures, and when I moved slightly away from her and hesitantly said, well, yes, I certainly would, she moved closer again and said if that was really what I wanted then she could only advise me to follow her own trade for a while, there was no better way to acquire a high degree of human maturity within a remarkably short time. When I asked what her trade had been, then, for Grete had said something about her being an unofficial working girl, a term unfamiliar to me since I had not been born in Vienna, she smiled and said it certainly was about time I learned to know life in all its fullness, an unofficial working girl was a woman who sold her body without the permission of the authorities, whereupon I moved a little further away from her again and said practising such a profession struck me at the moment as inappropriate, in fact positively unthinkable, and could hardly be reconciled with the principles taught to me in my childhood. To this Frieda said patiently that she could quite understand why, at my age, I still cherished certain prejudices, she had been just the same in her time. But I would see that as soon as I had become to some extent acquainted with my new social environment, such initial reservations would disappear entirely of their own accord, and I would throw myself enthusiastically into an activity that in many respects was more rewarding than any other she knew. Then she mentioned various places in Vienna, and said when I was discharged I had better go to one of the locations she recommended, preferably in the Prater, where I would find sympathetic and experienced women who would give me a kindly welcome and wouldn't hesitate to introduce me into my new professional circle as soon as I had mentioned her, Frieda's, name.

When I had thanked Frieda for her well-meant advice I was called to the office, where Sister Benedikta gave me a letter addressed to me. It was the first I had received in all my months in prison, and I opened it at once. To my great delight, it was from Hans the waiter, who began by addressing me tenderly as his polka princess from Prague, his Viennese waltz queen, the beautiful dancer of his dreams, whom he was determined to free from the violence of her wardresses and hold in his arms again very soon, twirling to the music of the Schrammel quartet of violins, guitar and accordion. By a strange but fortunate coincidence, he had discovered where I was through a former Alpine farmer from the Tyrol called Hubert Egger, whom he had met in the winding tunnels of the Viennese canal and sewer system where he had been living since his release from the lunatic asylum in Vienna 9, a place to which his desperate love for me had brought him. He kept wondering whether I'd been given the hat with the pansies on it, whether I had believed the claims of the jealous clarinettist from the Café Eisvogel, not a word of them true, and whether I doubted his love. At this point, when I was still only at the beginning of his long letter, I was interrupted by Sister Kordula, who had just come in and who tore the missive from my hand, crying that a convict who was as bad as I was at carding wool, who got all the fibres into a hopeless tangle instead of smoothing them out, had no right to receive letters, and she wondered what work she could give me now, because clumsy as I was I was doing far more harm than good with my two left hands, and the best thing would probably be to throw me out of the prison at once, to which Sister Benedikta said yes, that was undoubtedly the most sensible solution, I spent too much time reading prayers, all that reading had half turned my mind, and she would put this proposal to the prison management at once.

So it was that two days later I was walking back from Vienna Neudorf into the city in my voluminous grey-brown hooded cloak, carrying my cardboard case, with no idea where to find Hans the waiter. Rotten apples and pears with bees buzzing around them lay beneath the trees lining the road, for by now it was autumn, and one clear, sunny day was followed by another. I decided that the first thing to do was visit my last place of residence, underground in the collecting canal of the Vienna River, to look for Hans the waiter, Lyuba, Milan, Hubert and the other totters and fat-fishers, but the little projecting platform in the tunnel which had been our sleeping quarters was now occupied by two unfriendly Polish labourers with a dog, who knew nothing of the whereabouts of my old friends. I walked on along the bank of the canal and finally found a young fat-fisher I knew slightly, born in Eisenstadt, who told me that Lyuba and Milan had been picked up in their hideout by the imperial-and-royal police a few months back, and despite their vigorous resistance they were taken away to Leopoldstadt jail, where they would be kept in secure custody until the beginning of their trial, along with fourteen other Young Czechs, in December for high treason, and in Milan's case if the verdict went against him it could mean sentence of death. As for the Tyrolean mountain farmer, he had gone back to the lower Ötztal last July, saying he'd had enough of Vienna and the Viennese, and now that the snow had finally thawed he intended to go and look for his dulcimer, lost in an avalanche, on the Alpine pastures near the former location of the mountain hut that had been carried away by the snow. As for a waiter called Hans Holzer, he knew no one of that name and trade.

I spent my first night of freedom in the canal and sewer network next to the fat-fisher from Burgenland, who had kindly offered me half his dirty mattress and half the shabby blanket that protected him from the cold, and as I listened to the rats scurrying in the dark and water dripped from the vaulted roof overhead to my forehead I wondered how I was going to earn a living in the immediate future, for I hadn't a kreuzer to my name. It didn't seem worth trying to go into service in some bourgeois Viennese household, after all that had happened to me in such dubious surroundings. I couldn't earn money as a street musician, which I would have liked to do, because I had no instrument. I tossed and turned on the mattress and could not drop off, so that the young man from Eisenstadt briefly woke and said crossly would I for heaven's sake keep still, his work was a great strain and he

317

desperately needed a good night's sleep, and long after midnight I came to the bitter conclusion that, as I saw no other way of re-entering society, I must go off next day to one of the several locations mentioned to me by Frieda and try my luck there as an unofficial working girl. I finally fell asleep towards dawn, with my mother's sad and reproachful face before my eyes.

The first place I tried was the Volksgarten, but as soon as I began mingling with the ladies there, a little too boldly dressed and made up for my liking, as they strolled along the gravel paths, accosted from time to time by elegant gentlemen who offered an arm and walked away with them, I was approached by a slender blonde in bright yellow and a plump brunette in carmine who said indignantly that if I thought I could worm my way in among them unnoticed I was wrong, this was no place for beginners and even a blind man could see I was a beginner, if I wanted to join their ranks I'd have to work my way up slowly, did I think I was some kind of exception, just about all of them here had begun in a small way as perfectly ordinary tarts in the Prater, and anyway clothes like mine – just look at that ugly, voluminous cloak – were quite impossible as working garb, you had to provide attractive packaging for the wares you offered for sale, and surely I must see that my unattractive garments were very bad for business. I protested in some dismay that a series of unfortunate events in my life had forced me, young as I was, to seek a new existence, beginning all over again, so to speak, and a mutual friend of ours called Frieda had advised me to turn to them, saying those good ladies would be sure to help me. At this the lady in carmine cried Frieda, oh yes, that was the Frieda who never showed a trace of solidarity or professional ethics, who brought prices down for selfish reasons of her own, and consequently the others had set the vice squad on her, to the best of her knowledge Frieda had ended up in the House of Correction, I didn't come from Vienna Neudorf too, did I, well, that was the outside of enough, former jailbirds couldn't be tolerated here, I'd better make tracks at once for some byway in the Prater, that was where I belonged together with the common run of tarts, not in one of the finest parks in central Vienna. Before I could apologize and explain that I had acted in good faith, I certainly hadn't meant to be overfamiliar with these good ladies and obviously Frieda had given me a rather misleading account of the situation, I found myself surrounded by a whole troop of the garishly clad women, shouting at me angrily and threatening me with their hatpins and the tips of their parasols, so that I saw nothing for it but to dive for a narrow gap in the increasingly dense crowd and make my escape.

Feeling rather discouraged, and hungry too, I went back to the Prater, recommended by the ladies in the Volksgarten as the place for beginners, but once again I found distrust and hostility rather than the friendly reception Frieda had promised me. To avoid giving further offence by my clothing, I was now carrying my cloak over my arm, and stood in the Hauptallee of the Prater in the boarding-school uniform I wore under it and which was a little too tight for me by now, but after standing under a gas lamp for about five minutes, freezing cold, I was approached by several poorly but prettily dressed young women who asked me suspiciously what I thought I was doing here in my peculiar outfit, their clients were decent hard-working men, they did not suppose I hoped to entice perverts in my schoolgirl dress, really, that was all they needed, and what did I think I was playing at anyway, a newcomer stationing herself in the Hauptallee first off, the places under the lamps were in great demand, surely I knew that beginners started by working in the bushes beside the smaller paths. I apologized politely, explaining that I wasn't Viennese and so I didn't know the customs of the city, and then I wished them good evening, turned into one of the dark little paths to which they had directed me, and stationed myself under an elder bush. Next moment I heard soft footsteps and recoiled in alarm, expecting this to be a customer and my first test, but then I saw that the thin little figure who had approached me and was lighting a cigarette was quite an elderly woman. After the woman had smoked her cigarette and thrown the end away, she gave me a sidelong glance and said in friendly tones that I didn't look to her as if I'd been in the business long, then she came closer to me, looked attentively at my face and said, shaking her head, I must forgive her but the Prater was no place for a young beauty like me, such a pretty, charming girl had opportunities of quite a different nature open to her, I surely wasn't going to be stupid enough to squander my priceless capital on men unworthy of it when I could have a rich, distinguished client for every finger of my hand, youth passed so quickly that you had to use it well, now look at her, Kathi Laimgruber, she'd never been a beauty but she'd been young, oh yes, she'd been young, and now, after twenty years in the trade, she looked like a ruin; no, the fate of a tart in the Prater was not to be wished on anyone, particularly not me, destined as I seemed to be for a more agreeable way of life. If I would take some good advice from an old whore as experienced as she was down-to-earth, I'd buy a standing-room only ticket for one of the Philharmonic concerts held on Sunday afternoons in the beautiful hall of the Musikverein, I'd wear a pretty dress to set off my beauty and look out for a well-situated suitor, she'd be ready to bet I wouldn't have to go home alone. When I said that at the moment various unfortunate circumstances in my life had left me not only penniless but without a roof over my head, for you could hardly call the damp roof of the tunnel in the Viennese canal and sewer system a roof, the woman began rummaging in her fabric bag, pressed some coins into my hand and said it was a pleasure to help a young colleague just embarking on her new life, she herself was poor but not entirely without means, and that sum would be enough to get me admittance to the hall of the Musikverein. With these words, and before I could thank her, my benefactress disappeared into the twilight as inconspicuously as she had emerged from it, and I started back into the city centre.

Next Sunday, wearing my pale lilac dress with its violet lace inserts, full, long sleeves and pleated trimming at the hem, with the hat trimmed with orange and violet pansies on my head and my standing-room only ticket in my pocket, I went to Bösendorferstrasse and the building of the Musikverein, a place known to me from the period of my employment by the Honourable Herr and Frau von Schreyvogl, who had been the lucky possessors of one of the much sought-after subscriptions. The foyer of the building was already crowded with concert-goers dressed in their best, and when I left my hat in the cloakroom, the cloakroom attendant, plucking at the silk flowers, asked if I'd seen Crown Prince Rudolf, he was here today with his wife, Princess Stephanie of Belgium, to hear Brahms's *German Requiem*, they were sitting in the middle of the front row of the circle. When I said I hadn't, the girl added, sighing, that it was a real shame, everyone knew their marriage was pure hell and Stephanie's morbid jealousy drove the heir to the throne, a naturally kind and faithful man, into the arms of other women and was gradually making him turn to drink. The Crown Prince wanted a divorce but the Pope wouldn't grant one, so the marriage went from bad to worse and Rudolf became unhappier and unhappier, a misfortune already clearly reflected in his features. I said I would try to get a glimpse of the Crown Prince from my place in the hall, and then I went up the broad staircase, entered the magnificent hall, stationed myself among the standing-room only concert-goers next to a young man in black, with a beard, thick dark hair and a silver watch hanging from his waistcoat, and looked out for the royal couple, who had indeed taken their seats in the middle of the front row of the circle. The young gentleman beside me noticed my glance and asked whether I knew that the seats of the Crown Prince and his wife were both numbered thirteen, since it was a small oddity of the place that the numbering of the rows, which had even numbers of seats, began with number one on each side. Then he craned his neck in its stiff collar and said the Princess's appearance was a scandal, she was constantly becoming more rigid and formal, getting fatter and uglier every day, no wonder that the heir to the throne sought distraction with prettier and more amenable women in these regrettable circumstances. After he had said this the concert began, and disappointed me slightly, since I would rather have listened to catchy operetta melodies or those Schubert songs that go straight to the heart than a requiem Mass, so I was glad when the interval came, and to my surprise my neighbour invited me to take a glass of wine with him in the buffet. As we drank our Grüner Veltliner he introduced himself to me as Engelbert Korn-häusel and asked, if I would forgive the question, why such an enchanting girl as I was attending a concert unescorted, it struck him as unusual, and perhaps he could offer himself as an escort, such an innocent young creature couldn't be left unprotected against the advances of strangers, and what was my name? When I told him, blushing, the young gentleman cried Rosa, how very suitable, he couldn't think of a more appropriate name for me, and he himself was a man concerned with words, indeed a man who made words his career and used them professionally, for he was a writer, more precisely a dramatist, more precisely still an author of comedies, he wrote seven-act plays in blank verse, always seven-acters because he believed in the power of the mystical number seven, and always in blank verse because he was convinced of the expressive force of unrhymed iambic pentameters, although the number of acts was rather unusual for drama and the verse form also rather unusual for comedies, which explained the fact that so far none of his seventeen dramas had been performed. Would I care to accompany him back to his bachelor apartment over the Café Griensteidl in Schauflergasse after the concert, for he felt a great urge to read me the last three acts of his latest comedy *Dido, or The Broken Lampshade*? I merely nodded, since it seemed to me that the poet, who struck me as curiously familiar in some way, wasn't expecting any verbal comments from me, which was a relief, for my lessons from Fräulein von Roth-Rothenhorst were now long in the past, and I didn't want to endanger this new acquaintanceship by asking what might be the wrong questions.

On our way back to the standing-room only area the Crown Prince in his officer's uniform, his sash and orders, and his wife in a full brocade evening dress with a long train, walked past us arm in arm, and I cast my eyes down in alarm when my gaze happened to encounter the eyes of the heir to the throne.

And so I embarked on my relationship with my first client. Kathi Laimgruber had been quite right in supposing that the hall of the Musikverein would bring me luck. At first I was a little surprised to find that the dramatist treated me very differently from the Honourable Herr von Schreyvogl, and wanted only two things of me: first to lie naked on the moss-green ottoman in his dimly lit drawing room and listen to him as he read aloud what he had recently written, and second to allow him now and then to write his blank verse on my skin with a sharp pen, a request I did not refuse. As soon as Engelbert Kornhäusel learned that I was spending the night in the canal and sewer system of Vienna he said that as good fortune would have it, his was a family which had made a considerable fortune by manufacturing ship's propellers with three or four blades, and he was one of those who profited by it, it would give him great satisfaction to find me accommodation in the Inner City, preferably near his apartment over the Café Griensteidl, a place which he found it essential to frequent, since mingling with like-minded people as he did at the Café Griensteidl filled him with creative energy. When he said this I realized that Engelbert Kornhäusel had been the young man with the newspaper whom Lyuba had pointed out to me as we walked down Herrengasse and past the windows of the Café Griensteidl after I was discharged from the lunatic asylum in Vienna 9, but when I asked him if he knew a newspaper editor called Lyuba Zupan he said he didn't know about her being a newspaper editor, he'd met Lyuba back in the past in the Volksgarten, and she had listened to his work and let him write on her for some time, a revelation that amazed me.

Over the next few months my protector visited me regularly in the spacious room in Metastasiogasse that he had rented, to read to me and write on me. He bought me a high-necked cream satin dress with a bustle and ermine trimming, and a pale pink muslin gown with white tulle appliqué work and a hat to match, made of pelican and swan feathers, he walked arm in arm with me up and down the Nobelcorso between the Kärntnertor and Schwarzenbergplatz, and he took me to the theatre and the Court Opera House; on those occasions it excited him to be the only one who knew I was wearing his verses on my bare skin underneath the satin or the muslin. Every Sunday, wearing my pale lilac dress, I went to morning Mass at the Church of Maria am Gestade, the place of worship favoured by Bohemian immigrants in Vienna, and thanked our patron saint St John of Nepomuk with all my heart for the surprising and happy turn of fate that had brought me a room of my own and a bed all to myself for the first time in my life, for no longer having to spend the night on the hard iron beds of dormitories in boarding schools, hospitals, lunatic asylums and prisons, or sleep in entrance halls, walk-in wardrobes, bathtubs and projecting platforms in the tunnels of sewer systems, and for not having to share my bed with anyone else, not my mother, or Olga, or the feather-sorter or the fat-fisher from Eisenstadt. My one anxiety was how to clean the marks of Engelbert Kornhäusel's pen off my body, since he sometimes insisted on my not washing his writings off for days or even weeks on end, and after some time it became difficult to remove the ink without leaving pale traces of his verse behind. When thorough cleansing by simply treating my skin with a cut lemon and pumice soap was not successful I used turpentine or soap spirit, and when these methods, too, failed me I tried a three per cent solution of hydrogen peroxide, which would get rid of the most obstinate stains.

Until these last few months here in my dismal cell number fifty-five in the Provincial Court in Alserstrasse I have never in my life had so little to do as during my relationship with the young but unsuccessful poet, a relationship conducted on the verbal level as a monologue on his part, and I found it very pleasant. Engelbert Kornhäusel spent most of his time in the company of other men of letters at the round table in the reading room of the Café Griensteidl, and he got into the habit of pacing up and down when he visited my room in Metastasiogasse and recapitulating the content and course of the discussions held by this group, going over them out loud and almost word for word. His peace of mind depended entirely on the artistic esteem accorded to him and his seven-act plays by the group, and unfortunately that esteem kept sinking in the course of our relationship, as a result of which his mood switched more and more between irritation and depression. At first I bore his mood swings patiently, since it didn't seem to me advisable to endanger the improved position in life I enjoyed thanks to the writer's generosity by voicing the slightest complaint, but finally his increasing aggressiveness led to a crisis and the consequent rupture of our common interests. The stern and in his view unjustified criticism of his radically new idea of verse drama on the part of his literary friends, particularly by Hermann Bahr, who had recently returned from the cosmopolitan city of Paris and thus enjoyed a key position, and the young and gifted former grammar-school pupil Hugo von Hofmannsthal, known as Loris, was beginning to undermine his creative power and eventually led to a severe case of writer's block, which was a relief to me at first, since it spared me that tedious scrubbing of my skin. Subsequently, however, Engelbert Kornhäusel took to a habit which had a very upsetting effect on me, and indeed endangered my health. His subconscious inner resistance to the writing of comedies in blank verse continued, but he began working off his resentment at the lack of appreciation shown by his literary colleagues in the form of passionately felt pamphlets, scratching his handwriting into my skin with a violence and fury that was in unpleasant contrast to the tender care with which he had once inscribed his iambic pentameters, so that I sometimes involuntarily groaned when his pen was particularly sharp and violent, and that disturbed him, since he did not appreciate any kind of vocal utterances on my part. In this way our relationship perceptibly deteriorated and my protector, who deserved that description less and less and was increasingly becoming my tormentor, pursued his literary activity even more furiously and scratched his words ever deeper into my skin, leading to increasing blood loss and finally septicaemia accompanied by a high temperature, shivering fits, a rapid pulse and fast breathing, which kept me in bed for weeks and rendered me useless as writing material, and that again reinforced his frustration. One day he came to the room in Metastasiogasse where I was lying in bed, in a state of great agitation and crying out that this was terrible, the Café Griensteidl, a place that for all his arguments with his colleagues was so eminently necessary to his literary inspiration, had fallen victim to the redevelopment projects of the imperial-and-royal court buildings department, which would stop at nothing, and the café was to be closed down. He couldn't imagine life without the place, he couldn't envisage moving to the Café Central in Herrengasse where the group was to meet in future, he was ruined, and saw nothing for it but to seek release in suicide, a project that forced him to put his affairs in order, and among them to give notice that he was stopping the rent for my room at the end of the month. With these words he rushed out of the door again, and I couldn't prevent him, for I was still very weak from the blood poisoning.

So there I lay in my room in Metastasiogasse, sick and abandoned by my protector, unable to climb down the steep stairs to the portal of the Church of Maria am Gestade and kneel on the cold stone floor beneath its Gothic vault, praying to my patron saint to save me in this desperate situation, and I wondered anxiously what I was to do, for there were only nine days left until the end of the month.

One evening a day or two later someone knocked on the door of my room at about eight o'clock, and thinking it might be the caretaker bringing me a cup of tea to drink in bed, to cleanse the blood, I called out an invitation to come in. I was greatly surprised when it was not Frau Doležal who entered the room, but a moustached, red-faced, middle-aged man in black and white check trousers, a black velvet coat and a narrow-brimmed half-height top hat, with a riding crop in his right hand, whom I recognized as Crown Prince Rudolf's personal cab driver Josef Bratfisch, the man whose wonderful whistling had once moved me to tears in the Merry Vintner tavern on the Brillantengrund. When I sat up in bed in surprise, the visitor asked me to forgive his unannounced visit and to have no fear, he had nothing untoward in mind, far from it, he had been sent to me on a secret mission, and as soon as I had given him a chance to deliver his message he'd wager I would be delighted at his patron's request. After I had drawn the coverlet up to my neck and invited the newcomer to sit down with a faint gesture of my left hand, the stocky coachman lowered himself on to one of the two bentwood chairs, making it creak, wiped his forehead with a white-spotted blue handkerchief, and said it gave him pleasure to inform me that his Serene employer, none other than the Crown Prince himself, had expressed a lively interest in my person, in fact felt an attraction to it that in his, Josef Bratfisch's, modest opinion bordered on passionate infatuation. As the Austrian people knew, and it would certainly be no secret to me either, for years our future monarch had been bound before God and man to a non-Austrian wife whose character was in such blatant contrast to his own sociable and kindly nature that for a long time now the couple had appeared together only on official occasions. When I mentioned at this point that it had indeed come to my ears recently, in a Viennese concert hall, that the Crown Prince had been obliged to endure unprecedented torments in his marriage for years, Herr Bratfisch nodded several times and said, yes, yes, he could see I was in the picture, and consequently he was sure I'd look kindly on his master's wish to meet me as soon as possible. When I asked on what occasion the eye of the heir to the throne had fallen on my humble person, since as far as I was aware it could only have been in the concert hall I had just mentioned, the Crown Prince's coachman said, oh no, by no means, Crown Prince Rudolf had been observing me for a long time, he had seen me not only in the hall of the Musikverein but also at a performance of the *Magic Flute* at the imperial-and-royal Court Opera House, wearing an enchanting cream dress, and a performance of Grillparzer's play *The Waves of Love and the Sea* at the Burgtheater in an equally captivating pale pink dress with matching feathered headdress, on a young gentleman's arm, and his inborn love of all that was beautiful had been so inflamed by my regular features, perfect figure, graceful movements and in short all the enchantment radiated by my person that he had confessed to him, Josef Bratfisch, who could be described as not only his personal cabby but also his close confidant, which filled him with pride, that he hadn't been able to sleep for weeks. I said I felt greatly honoured by the undeserved notice of Rudolf von Hapsburg, indeed most distinguished by it, but as he could easily see an attack of septicaemia, from which I was now luckily getting better, made it impossible for me to go out just yet, to which Josef Bratfisch made haste to say no one wanted to anticipate my full recovery and he would merely allow himself, with my kind permission, to pay me a short daily visit and inquire after my esteemed state of health.

Sure enough, Josef Bratfisch knocked on the door of my room every evening after that, always around eight, sat down on the bentwood chair, talked to me and brought me little presents from the Crown Prince, intended to please me and hasten my recovery: flowers, champagne, confectionery, vol-au-vents and other delicious and easily digestible dishes. The attention paid to me by so distinguished a man improved both my physical and my mental condition very quickly, and four days later I felt able to agree to meet the Prince in one of the famous *chambres séparées* of the Hotel Sacher, to which Herr Bratfisch drove me with his team. I decided to wear the pale lilac dress and the hat trimmed with pansies on this occasion, although they were both a little shabby by now, since the heir to the throne had already seen my other two dresses, and the translucent pallor of my skin, which was partly a result of the blood poisoning, was set off to good advantage by the lilac of the dress. In the hotel foyer a resolute-looking lady smoking a cigar received me. She introduced herself as Frau Sacher, and making very kind remarks took me up to the first floor, where the Crown Prince was already waiting for me. His natural and unaffected behaviour immediately soothed the agitation which had overcome me during the drive in the horse-drawn carriage, and his inconspicuous clothing, which as he later told me deliberately laid no outward emphasis on his position through the wearing of orders, sashes, epaulettes or swords, so as not to make me feel insecure, inexperienced young creature that I was, also contributed to the relative informality of the following exchanges between us.

When I let the sad but improbable events of my life pass before my mind's eye now, shortly before my execution, as those condemned to death commonly feel impelled to do, it seems as if the months following that first encounter with Rudolf in Frau Sacher's *chambre séparée* made up to me for all the other trials and tribulations of my unsatisfactory female existence. It is true that Rudolf could hardly be described as a good lover in the strict sense of the term, it is true that despite repeated attempts he never really once succeeded in doing what the Honourable Herr von Schreyvogl had done so effortlessly, but the designated heir to the throne showed me more tenderness and understanding, particularly at the beginning of our relationship, than I had ever before encountered from any man in my life. Unlike the dramatist Engelbert Kornhäusel, moreover, he was anxious that as a child of the people, to whom he was bound by a firm link of mutual esteem and with whose simple representatives he cultivated close contact, I should give my opinion on a wide range of the subjects

329

weighing on his mind, from the lamentable overweight of his wife Stephanie and the underweight of his mother Elisabeth, which was in curious contrast but equally deplorable, to what in his opinion was his father's entirely misguided policy on the nationality issue, and even to the question of whether suicide in youth can be justified from the viewpoint of the suicide himself, and how certain it is that the time of a man's death may be read in the lines of his hand. After only our third meeting Rudolf said it was time I left that poky little room in Metastasiogasse, a place that did not match my generous heart and also reminded him disconcertingly of his eccentric predecessor, and he was sure I would allow him to provide me with a little villa in Oberdöbling, for our relationship, new as it was, gave him more happiness than he would have thought possible and formed a healthy corrective, one daily becoming more important to him, to his tendency to melancholy, an inheritance from his mother, who came from a Bavarian family unfortunately very prone to mental disturbances.

So it was that a little later I was living in a ten-roomed villa near Döbling Cemetery with an old Moravian married couple, as frail as they were discreet, who looked after the house and garden, something that filled me with amazement when I remembered how recently I had been obliged to figure among the wretched inmates of the Vienna Neudorf Women's Prison and House of Correction. Rudolf insisted on my leaving the villa only in his company, a wish with which I willingly complied at first, since in my boundless adoration of the Crown Prince I devoted my whole existence exclusively to receiving him, giving him pleasure, and once he had left preparing for my next encounter with him. He paid me frequent visits, usually in the company of his personal cabby, who took us on long drives, when the weather was fine, to the nearby vineyards where we drank new wine in the company of all kinds of people from all classes of society, danced, sang melancholy songs or had Josef Bratfisch whistle them to us.

One warm July evening we were in high good humour, sitting

on weathered wooden benches under a walnut tree in the Heuriger tavern known as the Last Drop in Heiligenstadt, drinking dry white wine and eating bread and pork dripping in the company of Bratfisch and his amiable wife, when a so-called rack wagon, one of those unsprung farmer's carts in which you could drive cheaply from the city centre to the nearby villages, stopped outside the inn. Idly, we watched the passengers getting down from it, and I could hardly believe my eyes when I saw that the couple who got out last, a tall, thin woman with thin red-blonde hair, a pointed chin and colourless eyes, and a young man with dark blond curls, were the jealous clarinettist from the Café Eisvogel in the Prater and Hans the waiter, whom I had sought in vain all over Vienna. When I saw how Hans Holzer gave the clarinettist his hand to help her down from the cart, and how she took it, jumped down, put her arms round his neck and kissed him, I once again, after a long interval of time, felt that sharp pain as if a thin needle were piercing my heart. At that moment Hans Holzer looked in our direction, and he slowly removed the clarinettist's arms from his neck and walked past us into the inn, his eyes lowered. Shaken by this unexpected encounter with the waiter, I drank several glasses of the dry wine and then, swaying slightly, went into the tavern myself to order another jug. As I passed the table where Hans and the clarinettist were sitting, the latter suddenly recognized me, rose to her feet and came round the table, not fully sober herself, crying out that she didn't believe it, here was that Bohemian floozy again, the one who haunted her fiancé's mind to this day and was the reason why he still hadn't kept his promise of marriage, the little tramp for whose sake he had gone all that way on foot to Vienna Neudorf Women's Prison when she was a convict there, oh yes, convicted of theft, as well she knew, her fiancé, a decent man, hadn't shrunk from visiting a convicted thief in prison, there was something very wrong about all this, I'd bewitched him, that's what I'd done, bewitched him, everyone knew Bohemian women were witches, every last one of them, Bohemian women knew all kinds of magic arts, but she wasn't afraid of me, she'd show me what came of getting across a member of one of the best ladies' musical ensembles in Vienna. With these words she picked up her clarinet, which was lying on the wooden bench, and went for me with it, whereupon Hans Holzer, who hadn't yet said a word, jumped up and came out from behind the table, slightly drunk too, wrenched the clarinettist's instrument away from her after a tough struggle, stood in front of me, breathing heavily, and said he was surprised by the path I'd taken since our first meeting on the little island in the Danube, when the innocent magic of my girlish nature had immediately cast a spell on him. Both then and in our later meetings in the Prater I had given him the impression of being a modest and reserved female, yet one who at the same time was capable of very deep feelings, a person determined to earn her living by honest labour, an impression which no doubt had deceived him, since he now found me here consorting with the powerful, indeed openly courting their favour, in the company of those who put on a show of being friends and protectors of the people but were really anxious only to take advantage of the powerlessness and good nature of their subjects and enrich themselves by exploiting them as a labour force. If I thought he didn't know about my escapades since I had been released from the House of Correction then I was much mistaken, I couldn't pull the wool over his eyes any more, and he, who had unfortunately lost his reason for a brief time because of his enduring sentiments for me, was here and now finally breaking with a woman who had thrown in her lot with a corrupt and rotten political system and was taking advantage of it as shamelessly as, conversely, the rulers took advantage of the likes of us, I was an imperial-and-royal cocotte, a Hapsburg whore, he was ashamed of me. While Hans Holzer hurled these insults at me, the clarinettist tried desperately but in vain to get him to hold his tongue, for the other guests at the inn had noticed us, and Bratfisch the Prince's personal cabby was standing in the doorway listening with interest. It was true that Rudolf had not concealed his liberal inclinations from me, but the things Hans Holzer was saying were so abusive not only of me but of the ruling house that I acted quickly to avert danger from the man who had succeeded in touching my heart, went back out of doors to join the Crown Prince, and said the new wine had given me a headache and I'd like to go back to Oberdöbling, a wish with which Rudolf immediately complied.

It was a long time before I could get this unexpected reunion with the waiter Hans out of my mind, and it cast a slight shadow over my previously unclouded happiness with the heir to the throne, a happiness that I soon felt he too seemed to find less intense than at the beginning of our connection, for his relationship with his father, never good, was perceptibly deteriorating and weighed upon our own, and he would often vent his anger with the monarch in my presence with a violence that alarmed me. The Emperor's political ideas were hopelessly outdated, he said, as he progressed further into old age he kept making irreparable mistakes in statesmanship, he was already so senile that he, Rudolf, could not imagine that his father had the slightest idea of the content of the hundreds of documents to which he put his signature daily, in addition his bigotry was barely tolerable, for instance he, Rudolf, thought it tasteless for his father to wash the feet of twelve unappetizing old men every year on Maundy Thursday. Then there were the eternal and deadly dull family dinners which he, Rudolf, was obliged to attend, he couldn't stand the stress of those family dinners any longer, that hypocritical atmosphere among blood relatives pretending to love each other but really hating and despising one another with every fibre of their hearts, he couldn't understand why his father insisted on these family dinners. And he was getting meaner and meaner, turning into a typical old skinflint, you had to haggle with him over every kreuzer, sometimes he wished the old man would finally choke to death on his bronchial catarrh. If the Crown Prince's increasingly frequent outbursts of hostility towards Emperor Franz Joseph caused me considerable concern, I was even more distressed by his attacks of melancholy, when he would drink vast quantities of champagne laced with cognac and keep talking about suicide, saying the gods were right to see that those whom they loved died early, all existence was vain and empty, and his wife, that thorn in his flesh, would soon be standing by his open grave, unable to torment him any more. When he entered the drawing room of the villa in Oberdöbling one afternoon with a skull in his hand, and on my recoiling in horror asked if I loved him deeply enough to die with him, for he had long been tired of life, I said I didn't know how a human being could even toy with the idea of laying hands on himself, my mother, who as he knew had been a simple cook, had drummed it into me in my early youth that life was a gift of God and must in no circumstances be thrown away on pain of forfeiting eternal bliss, did he want to burn for ever in hell, the place destined for suicides, at which Rudolf uttered a short and bitter laugh and said he wondered what he had done to deserve being constantly surrounded by females who, with the exception of his mother the Empress, a highly intelligent woman even if given to moodiness, got on his nerves with their sentimental twaddle, their stupid nattering, and lacked both the courage and the deeper metaphysical understanding to accompany a man of his complex nature, resembling Faust on the one hand and Hamlet on the other, into the house of death. But I'd soon see, if I myself wasn't prepared to make the little sacrifice which to him seemed so natural, some other woman would not deny him this loving service, and would willingly keep him company in death along with this specially dissected skull which the Jewish anatomist Emil Zuckerkandl had kindly let him have.

Nor was it the painful idea that I had finally lost Hans Holzer, together with Rudolf's violent mood swings, that impaired my enjoyment of life, which only recently could have been described as effervescent: the hostility of my rivals disturbed my original harmonious relationship with the Crown Prince. Rudolf had never concealed from me that I was not the only woman to enjoy his favours, and at the very beginning of our relationship had explained that a man of his rank and temperament could not possibly concentrate his desires permanently on one woman alone, he hoped I would understand that because of his position he was constantly led into temptation, a temptation to which, he confessed, he succumbed in so far as his powers allowed. In spite of my youth he thought me sensible enough to make no objections of any kind if he turned his attentions to other young women of Vienna, tender, pliable creatures like me, for after all the future ruler of a gigantic empire must sometimes mingle with his future subjects to win their love and confidence. To this request I had replied that he need have no fears on that count, my mother, a gentle and God-fearing woman, had always urged me to share all I had joyfully, just as our Lord Jesus Christ did, for strange as it might seem, she had said, if you gave, it was given unto you again. However, I had not expected that not all the Crown Prince's women would be of the same mind as me, a mistake which only a little later turned out to have serious and indeed life-threatening consequences.

One Sunday afternoon I was standing in front of the big mirror in the ten-roomed villa in Oberdöbling, trying on a light summer straw hat trimmed with rose petals and apple blossom which the Crown Prince had brought back for me from a short stay at the spa in Abbazia, when I suddenly heard a loud and angry voice. Turning round, to my surprise I found myself facing a tall, full-breasted lady in a dark taffeta dress, who was wearing a huge black hat adorned with a stuffed sparrowhawk and carrying a bright blue perfume bottle in her black-gloved right hand, while with her other hand she easily fended off the frail Moravian married couple who were trying to prevent her from entering the room. So she had tracked me down at last, cried the lady, so this was our fine Crown Prince's latest conquest, still hardly more than a child, just like him, perverted lecher that he was, a man whom even the most severe impairment of his potency brought on by excessive alcohol consumption, from the dismal consequences of which she, Liesl Pernerstorfer, had had to suffer for years in her capacity as the oldest and therefore highest-ranking of Rudolf's mistresses, could not induce to abstain from those dreary affairs that led him into the most repulsive nooks and nauseating crannies of the Austro-Hungarian monarchy. She had no intention of being ousted by a flat-chested child like me, as Rudolf had suggested when he remarked to her that the older must make way for the younger, that was the law of Nature, no, she had no intention of having her hard-earned allowance cut or even discontinued just because I was temporarily in his favour, temporarily, she repeated, for like most of his conquests I wouldn't enjoy that favour for long, I was nothing but a passing fancy, a nine days' wonder in the Crown Prince's bed, she hoped I was clear about that, nothing but a nine days' wonder. Then the stately lady fell silent for a while, looked me up and down, and finally said that seeing me like this, so pale and thin, she felt positively sorry for me and had quite changed her mind about her original plan of throwing the vitriol in her perfume bottle in my face and thus once and for all preventing my occupying any long-term position in the hierarchy of the Crown Prince's mistresses. If she knew Rudolf, and she had certainly known him since the year 1878 when she initiated the timid youth into the mysteries of physical love, he would very soon tire of me of his own accord, so every drop of her vitriol would have been wasted, and then it would be she and not I who lived in this villa, it was only a matter of weeks. So saying, the imposing lady turned on the heel of her gleaming black buttoned boots and, followed by the helpless Moravian couple, left first the drawing room, then the house, and finally the property itself.

After this experience I developed the habit of behaving with caution on the short walks in the immediate vicinity of the ten-roomed villa that Rudolf would now permit me, looking behind me now and then in case anyone was following me. One afternoon, when I was sitting on a bench under a weeping willow in Döbling cemetery, worrying about the increasing frequency with which Rudolf spoke of suicide, a fat, elegantly dressed lady with a small round hat and a black veil hiding her face emerged from behind Count von Lodron's tombstone and pointed a gun at me. Speechless with shock and unable to move, I stayed where I was. The weapon she was holding, said the lady by way of preamble, in a foreign accent with which I was not familiar, was a semi-automatic Browning pistol, more precisely the pistol with which she was going to put an end to my existence in the next few minutes. She was not prepared to tolerate the offensive way in which her husband, that violent drunk, flaunted his mistresses a moment longer, not only had she been obliged to accept his scandalous relationships over the years with Kuranda, Pernerstorfer, the Vetseras both mother and daughter, and worst of all that snake in the grass Caspar, not only, quite apart from them, did she have to put up with the countless short, sometimes very short affairs in which the Crown Prince engaged during his drunken expeditions through the suburbs of Vienna night after night, now he had the impudence to add yet another to the quota of his regular mistresses, namely me, a Bohemian servant girl, as she had learned, a vagabond convicted of theft, this was the end, this really was too much. When she remembered the trust and confidence with which she had followed her fiancé to a foreign land, leaving Brussels at the age of fifteen, imagine that, only fifteen, when she remembered how earnestly she had tried to become a good Austrian, she felt deep sympathy for the child she had been at that time. Today she couldn't understand her naive readiness to be impressed by the reception accorded her by the Viennese, the full extent of whose stupidity and spite she had understood only much later, inexperienced as she was – when she thought of the *Myrtle Waltz* specially composed for her by Johann Strauss, the magical firework display at Schönbrunn with the initials R and S sparkling in the dark night sky, the procession in the Prater with sixty-two court carriages, performances by military bands and the Vienna Male Voice Choir, the gymnastics and fencing displays, the gala dinner in the Redoutensaal of the Hofburg, over a hundred covers in gold plate and sixty-four covers in silver, and above all the wedding ceremony performed in the Church of St Augustine by Cardinal Prince Schwarzenberg in the presence of twenty-four bishops and archbishops, when she thought of all this the tears came to her eyes. Her life had been nothing but a series of mistakes, nothing but constant disillusionment, the Austrians, particularly the Viennese and even more particularly the court of Vienna had wrecked all her hopes, she should have stayed in Belgium in the care of her beloved father King Leopold and her mother good Queen Marie Henriette. With these words Crown Princess Stephanie, for it was she, lifted her little veil and passed the back of her right hand, in which she was holding the Browning semi-automatic, over her pale and swollen face, the sparse yellow hair over her forehead, and the small eyes set deep in her flesh, which did indeed have tears in them. If I only knew the sufferings she had endured and probably still had to endure, she said tearfully – oh, no one could have any idea of the full extent of the ruinous effects of her unhappy marriage to the Crown Prince, a man entirely delivered up to his dubious activities and increasingly showing himself to be given to mentally sick fantasies, a man whom she had at first adored, an emotion she was sure I could understand as a woman in general and as her husband's lover in particular. Obviously overcome by pain at the thought of her husband's infidelity, the Crown Princess swayed to and fro, put the hand holding the pistol to her temple, and then sat down beside me on the green-painted wooden bench erected by the imperial-and-royal cemetery management. Overcome by a sudden sense of feminine solidarity, I put my arm around the poor woman's shoulders, whereupon, sobbing out loud, she buried her head in my breast, and the Browning semi-automatic slipped from her hand into my lap. I picked it up cautiously and stowed it away in my brightly embroidered fabric bag from Gödöllö in Hungary, a present from Rudolf. When I had given Stephanie time for a good cry I asked how she had come to Döbling Cemetery, and when she said she had taken a one-horse carriage which was waiting for her a little way off, I rose, helped her solicitously to her feet, and led her out of the cemetery to her carriage.

After this, Rudolf's visits to Oberdöbling became less frequent, which did hurt me, but I became really anxious only when Frau Bratfisch turned up in the ten-roomed villa one cold morning at the end of January 1889 and told me that her husband, without intending to look, had found four farewell letters on the Crown Prince's desk, clearly in his own hand, addressed to his daughter Valerie, his wife, Baron Hirsch and Mizzi Caspar, and again by pure chance had found in a drawer of the desk thirty thousand gulden to be given to Caspar and a Browning semi-automatic, discoveries which reinforced her and her husband's long-held suspicions that their master was tired of life, and gave grounds for the very worst of fears. For heaven's sake, she urged, I mustn't withdraw from the poor world-weary man the beneficial and soothing influence I had always had on him, I must do everything in my power to persuade him to remain in this world, vale of woe as it admittedly sometimes was for all of us.

When Frau Bratfisch had left I made haste to my dressing room, pulled out the bottom drawer of the rosewood chest of drawers adorned with early seventeenth-century Persian miniatures where I had stowed away the colourfully embroidered fabric bag from Gödöllö containing the pistol after my encounter with the Crown Princess, and found my suspicions confirmed. The bag was empty. I sent the old Moravian couple off at once with an urgent message to the hunting lodge at Mayerling, where I knew Rudolf was at this moment, but no sooner had they set off than Josef Bratfisch arrived in great haste in his cab and told me that in the early

339

hours of the morning the future monarch and his mistress Baroness Vetsera had been found shot dead in Rudolf's bedroom in Mayerling, both corpses lying on the bed along with a skull and a Browning semi-automatic pistol.

13

That morning I was woken by a deep, long-drawn-out musical note, and as I woke I realized that the sound had come to me from a dream and was made by Magnolia, striking a huge gong with the head of a felt-covered mallet.

Magnolia. While I was abandoning myself to her touch the day before, my eyes closed, the faces of the Tutor and my mother had come before me, singing in duet, 'Now the ice cracks and disperses, / Now the soft snow melts away', and then their faces, mouths open and eyes turned to heaven, their throats clad in blue sailor collars edged with white, retreated into the background and faded, their voices died away and were drowned out by the sound of a drum beat, soft at first but gradually becoming louder, by the rhythm of the drumsticks, initially slow and then speeding up as they beat on the taut membrane, and I saw the narrow white sole of Magnolia's foot, which in fact was sliding up my calf, coming down again and again on the pedal of a big drum, I saw her hands which were really caressing my hips beating a regular rhythm on the skin of a drum tautly stretched to breaking point, her fingers outstretched, and the rhythm of the drumming rang in my ears, spread from them like a wave right through my body, ending with a mighty blow on the tanned calfskin head of the copper kettle-drum which has six to eight screws to adjust it and is the most important percussion instrument in the orchestra.

I had slept wonderfully well and felt better than ever before in my life, a circumstance which, once I had got up, induced me to collect the boxes, cans, little bags and flasks of medicaments lying scattered on the bedroom carpet with a view to throwing them straight in the anthracite-grey rubbish bins in the yard of the Death House. On the way down I met Fräulein Haslinger, who stared at me in alarm and asked what had come over me, I mustn't go down these stone steps barefoot with my dressing-gown half undone on a cold day in early Advent, whereupon I pressed the plastic bag of medicaments into her hand without a word, turned and ran upstairs again two steps at a time, causing the former pastoral assistant to call after me, saying I obviously had a temperature already, no wonder, there were bound to be unfortunate consequences if I neglected my health like that, and she'd bring me a bottle of cough syrup at once.

When I had eaten a hearty breakfast and put on the new black roll-neck sweater I'd bought in Rauhensteingasse from Alexander, Gentleman's Outfitters, the one Magnolia had admired recently as we were strolling through the city when she saw it in Alexander's window — so I went back and bought it next day, having succeeded in selling the portrait of Schubert by Kriehuber in the flea market to an American tourist, who instantly believed every word I told him about its unique value as a work of art — I went back to the bedroom and took the butterfly cases off the wall one by one, for when I had told Magnolia about my financial problems she suggested that I could try finding a buyer for the dead butterflies, you never knew, collectors sometimes paid high prices for such items. As I left the room with the cases, I tried to avoid meeting my mother's gaze in the painting above the bed, for she had always told me not to part with my butterfly collection in any circumstances, saying the collection would always remind me of its donor, namely herself, my mother, and of my happy childhood, but as I went out I was incautious enough to turn back for a moment and cast my mother an apologetic glance. The expression on her face as she watched what I was doing betrayed fury out of all proportion to the extent of my crime, and I told her with some annoyance that she was overreacting, the Austrian laws of inheritance say that a sole heir, in this case me, can do as he likes with his legacy. I then hesitated for a moment and added that I wasn't putting up with any more interference from her in other areas of my life either, she'd been able to see for herself yesterday afternoon that I was a grown man now, and I intended to stop visiting her grave quite so often too. Then I put down the butterfly cases, took the picture off its hook and placed it on the floor, facing the wall.

Although I had been banned from the Dorotheum, I decided to visit the auction house one more time, and I left my apartment. No sooner was I out in Kettenbrückengasse than the lady from the tobacconist's came out of her shop and asked what had become of my pure wool scarf, we were past the first Sunday in Advent now and not many people could afford to go out and about in Vienna without a scarf after the first Sunday in Advent, and when I told her my scarf was hanging on a hook in my wardrobe in the Death House, she said, shaking her head, she was beginning to wonder whether that African beauty I'd been seen with for quite some time was really looking after me as well as the people of this quarter claimed. Just before I reached the underground station the pharmacist met me on the way to her pharmacy, and cried, oh, poor Herr Horvath without his scarf, what a misfortune, and then she put a hand to her neck and handed me her own woolly scarf with a black and red flower pattern and a broad grass-green border, saying I could make do with this for the time being, she'd nearly reached the pharmacy anyway. I refused her kind offer and went on, and when I reached the steps leading down to the underground I saw her out of the corner of my eye, still standing in the street with the scarf in her hand, staring at me with her mouth open. The old lady from Kettenbrückengasse was already waiting on the platform with her little spaniel, which had its eyes bandaged, and she was just launching into an account of her pet's unsuccessful cataract operation when she interrupted herself in the middle of

her second sentence, stared at my throat and said for goodness'
sake, where was my scarf, I wasn't wearing my scarf, but just then
the train came in and I boarded it without exchanging a word with
the old lady.

When I reached the auction house I found the Various Antiquities
department and showed my four butterfly cases to an expert. The
expert said the Dorotheum didn't need any butterfly collections,
there was no market for them, but when I asked him to find a
specialist butterfly expert, he said he'd see what he could do and
went off. About five minutes later he came back with a tall, thin
man with greying brown hair and pale, blurred features, who
leaned over my cases with a magnifying glass, examined butterfly
after butterfly intently with the corners of his mouth turned down,
and kept slowly moving his head back and forth. I was in the act of
putting the three cases he had already examined under my arm,
feeling discouraged, when the expert, who was just bending over
the fourth, uttered a small shriek and said, a Pink Rose, this was
incredible, *Pachliopta kotzebuea*, a native of the Philippines, an
extremely rare species, being so timid, and consequently hardly
ever found in butterfly collections, also frequently confused with
the Common Rose, of similar appearance, which settles on the flora
of south-east Asia in huge flocks just after the rainy season. In any
case, this discovery must be reported immediately to Professor
Priem, head of the Lepidoptera Department at the Natural History
Museum, of course such a find must be made available for public
viewing as soon as possible, and he rather thought the Natural
History Museum would be making me an offer to buy in the very
near future.

After receiving this information, which gave grounds for great
hopes, I left the auction house and called Magnolia at once from a
telephone kiosk on the Graben to tell her she'd given me good
advice, it looked as if my Pink Rose butterfly was going to rid me
of my financial worries at a stroke, and when she had briefly
interrupted me, saying Pink Rose, how strange, I added that I'd

also seen her in a dream and as far as I could tell, since I had no
appropriate criteria for comparison, I loved her. Magnolia said in
her smiling voice that she knew, she knew, and it made her very
happy, but she was going to hang up now, she'd just begun reading
the ninth chapter of the blue notebook, and Rosa was in a state
which gave cause for concern.

Nine

The shattering news of the Crown Prince's death cast me into
the depths of despair and brought into my life, which had run
such a surprisingly fortunate course since my meeting with the
Prater prostitute Kathi Laimgruber, a change that was far from
being for the better and indeed led straight to my ruin. Not only
was I, a motherless girl, robbed of the most powerful patron and
protector I had ever known, I also felt I was to blame for his
suicide and the death of Baroness Vetsera, since my inexplicable
negligence had given him the chance to get hold of the weapon
that had been used, and I wondered if Stephanie was suffering
similar pangs of conscience. In my grief I shut myself up in the
ironing room and couldn't be induced to take any nourishment
even by the patent persuasions of the Moravian husband and
wife, communicating with me through the closed door. Only
when the old lady urged me to leave at once because there were
two police officers at the wrought-iron gate, obviously wanting
to clear up the still unexplained matter of the fingerprints on
the pistol, and she didn't know how long her husband would be
able to hold them off, did I emerge from my painful musings,
pack the bare necessities in my cardboard case and put on my
old grey-brown hooded cloak, and when the Moravian woman
had made the sign of the cross over me with rapid fingers,
shedding tears, I left the property, which was surrounded by a
wall, through a small door at the back of the house and crossed

Türkenschanzpark in the direction of Gersthoferstrasse and so on into the city centre, intending to seek refuge in the canal and sewer system of Vienna once again.

When I came to the little projecting platform in the tunnel, the fat-fisher from Eisenstadt was just reading the two Polish labourers and their dog a report from the *Wiener Zeitung* of the mysterious circumstances surrounding the tragic death of Crown Prince Rudolf and Baroness Mary Vetsera, circumstances connected among other things with the still very obscure part played by a young woman whom the Crown Prince had frequently visited in Oberdöbling over the last few months and of whom the police had not yet given any further details. All that was known for certain was that the projectile from the Browning semi-automatic pistol, a weapon easily acquired since it was advertised for sale in the newspapers, had passed through the left temple of the heir to the throne, made its way right through his brain, and finally emerged from the Crown Prince's head two centimetres above his right ear. Only when I took off my cloak to sit down with them did the fat-fisher notice me. He came towards me, looking pleased, greeted me and then asked in surprise what I was doing here, I didn't look as if I was one of the inhabitants of the Viennese underground any more, and I looked down at the pale yellow satin dress embroidered with little white roses which Rudolf had brought me back from Paris and said, sadly, that appearances, as so often, were deceptive, and this dress was all I had left of my recent vain attempts to earn an honest living.

So it was that I shared the mattress and blanket of the young man from Burgenland again that night, and when he heard me weeping in the dark he didn't complain that I was disturbing his sleep, but took me and my pale yellow satin dress astonishingly gently in his muscular arms.

Next day, 4 February 1898, I set off in my slightly crumpled yellow dress and my mended grey-brown cloak, with its hood drawn well down over my face because it was snowing, and besides, I wanted to be sure no one recognized me as the Crown Prince's former companion, and made my way to the chapel in the Hofburg where Rudolf's corpse was lying in state on view to the population of Vienna for a day before his funeral, the hundred and thirteenth Hapsburg to be laid to rest in the crypt of the Capuchin church where I had so often prayed to the life-sized statue of the Madonna of Lourdes. I stood waiting in the queue for several hours, freezing cold, before I could enter the black-draped chapel, approach the tall catafalque surrounded by candles, and look for the last time at the face of the man for whom I had felt such deep affection. As I gazed at Rudolf's waxen face and saw the mortal wound inflicted by the Browning semi-automatic, as I heard the angelic voices of the choirboys singing up in the gallery, I was overcome by such grief that I tried to fling myself on the coffin, wailing aloud, but the other people in the queue prevented me, seizing hold of me and taking me back out into the Josefsplatz. Suddenly I remembered the little blue perfume bottle that Liesl Pernerstorfer had brought with her when she visited the ten-roomed villa in Oberdöbling, and I dragged myself through the snow to the nearest grocery store and asked for some diluted vitriol, an item in common use as a cleaning fluid. Then I went slowly with the bottle towards the Church of Maria am Gestade, to withdraw my confidence from the last of the saints whom I had expected to provide me with comfort and aid, namely St John of Nepomuk, since he hadn't proved himself worthy of that confidence either. I opened the tall door and entered the empty church, and when I had gone straight to the statue of the patron saint of Bohemia and formally withdrawn my allegiance from him, I sank to his feet on the stone floor, leaned back against his plinth and put the bottle of vitriol to my lips.

At that moment a figure emerged from the shadows below the organ gallery and a man with thick black hair and a black moustache, wearing a brown peaked cap and a brown cravat, came towards me and took the bottle from my hand. I did not resist. He supposed I was another decent Bohemian whom the Viennese had brought to the brink of despair with their boundless malice and spite, he said, fortunately he happened by chance to be in the church frequented for choice by his countrymen to offer up a small prayer for his brother, accused of high treason against the Austro-Hungarian monarchy, who was now in Leopoldstadt jail and who, with his woman companion, had been waiting months for his trial to begin. I pricked up my ears at this information and said could the prisoner by any chance be Milan Havelka, a supporter of the Young Czech movement born in the Bohemian Forest, to which the stranger replied, yes, indeed, that was the very man, his unfortunate younger brother who had inherited their paternal grandfather's seditious disposition and had always given him, as an elder brother who felt responsible for him, a great deal of anxiety. At these words I rose to my feet, supporting myself on the plinth of the statue, and cried that this was amazing, I knew his brother and his brother's comrade in arms Lyuba very well, Milan had told me about him, his brother Karel, and how he had found him, Milan, work in a brick kiln on the Laaerberg when he first arrived in Vienna. To this Karel Havelka, for thanks to yet another of those positively incredible coincidences that occurred in my life in astonishing numbers it was indeed he, said in surprise, yes, that was right, but both his brother and he had soon been sacked from the brick kiln because Milan couldn't keep his inflammatory nature under control and had begun inciting the workers to take revolutionary action. After that, because of his love for horses and in the absence of other career opportunities he, Karel, had taken work as a waterer or cab-horse groom, one of those who gave the cabbies' horses food and water, groomed them, and by way of thanks for their devoted attention to the animals had to put up with bad treatment by the cabbies themselves, members of a profession erroneously thought to be close to the people but really very haughty. As Karel Havelka was telling me this I studied his face and recognized him as the man who had once stood in the Stephansplatz among Lyuba's horsy friends, whose likeness to his brother Milan I had noticed, and I was amazed at the mysterious manner in which our Creator keeps separating people and then reuniting them. For his part, Karel looked attentively at me and then asked whether anyone had ever told me that although I was blonde and fair-skinned I bore a certain resemblance to the Empress Elisabeth, he had a very special feeling for the Empress Elisabeth although he didn't intend to go into it more closely at the moment, but anyway he was glad to have met me, wouldn't I take a cup of hot tea with him in the Café Drechsler where the cabbies went, this cold February weather was a great trial particularly to the poorer people of Vienna such as himself and as he supposed me too, both of us being immigrant Bohemians. I hesitated for a moment, then thanked him for his invitation but said that for various reasons I was in no frame of mind just now to visit a place of entertainment such as a coffee house, particularly one frequented by coachmen. With this I turned to leave the church, but Karel Havelka barred my way and said our encounter seemed to him a significant one, I mustn't deny him any hope of seeing me again, to which I replied he need have no fear, if God wanted us to meet again then we would. Before I opened the door my rescuer added that he didn't know why I had wanted to poison myself, but in his opinion there could be no good grounds for such a thing, and he trusted that after our encounter, which he saw as a sign and an omen, I would never consider taking so rash a step again. So saying he put his hand lightly on my left shoulder, and I looked up at him, smiled for the first time in days, removed his hand gently with my own, opened the church door and went down the stone steps.

With the optimism and confidence so characteristic of me, unfounded as they strictly speaking were, I thought that the grief and rage I felt at Rudolf's death would wear off, and my *joie de vivre* would get the better of my anxieties again, but after a while I had to admit to myself that I wasn't going to be able to recover so soon from this blow of fate, the worst that I had known apart from my mother's death. I felt a strange sense of apathy and lethargy which made it impossible for me to pursue any profitable activity, and so I went on living with the outcasts of society in the canal and sewer system of the city of Vienna, sharing with them what little money I had brought with me from the villa in Oberdöbling, which consequently soon ran out. My grief and weariness soon affected my appearance, and I need not have gone on pulling the hood of my grey-brown cloak over my head to disguise myself, since few would have suspected that the pale, emaciated woman with tangled hair, a bewildered expression on her face and wearing slovenly clothing was Crown Prince Rudolf's mistress, recently so elegant and the picture of health. As for the circumstances of the Crown Prince's death, the official version at first was that Rudolf had suffered a heart attack, and a little later that the couple had died in a suicide pact, but it was rumoured that Crown Princess Stephanie, whom the Austrian people could easily believe capable of an act of violence, what with the stormy scenes and embarrassing quarrels between herself and her husband that had occurred in public with increasing frequency over the last few years, had already been interviewed by the police several times, and had more to do with the tragedy than the authorities would admit, but her high rank protected her. As for the mysterious young woman whom the dead man had honoured with his frequent visits during the last months of his life, said the newspapers, she had disappeared without trace.

Unable to shake off my pain and the immoderate grief against which I had no defence, I fell into the habit of spending a great deal of time with the two Polish labourers and their dog, as well as the fat-fisher from Eisenstadt, and resorted more and more often to the strong potato schnapps which the Poles had sent to them every month from Lublin, and the more mildly flavoured cherry brandy that the man from Eisenstadt sometimes got from his home in the Burgenland, since the alcohol relieved my sufferings and comforted me, at least in the short term, for the loss I had endured through the workings of blind fate. At the risk of giving offence to the more innocent and sensitive of those who may perhaps read this account, I must admit that in my need for affection, and through the abatement of a sense of feminine modesty brought about by the consumption of intoxicating liquors, I allowed myself to have physical as well as friendly intercourse with these outcasts from human society. Once I had crossed the moral barriers set up by the religious and secular authorities of my time, abandoning the decorous behaviour instilled into me as binding upon my sex, I continued down the dubious path on which I had begun when, following the advice of the unofficial working girl Frieda, I approached the garishly dressed ladies in the Volksgarten, a path that hastened my decline and led me straight into the depths of human vice. Disillusioned by the blows of fate and disappointed by the despicable behaviour of most of my fellow men, I determined to turn my back on the so-called powers of good and deliberately ally myself to those of evil, and I wandered the city dressed in rags and with matted hair, bawling out 'The Trout' and 'The Linden Tree' and drinking, offering my body for the price of a sparse meal, a glass of schnapps, a poor bed for the night, and after that I would give myself more and more often for nothing to the abandoned and despised, ruined and damned of Vienna, men without work or shelter, without feelings or conscience, petty thieves, soldiers, unskilled and day labourers, the homeless, poor creatures who were worked to the bone, exploited, their feelings deadened, in whom I began to see myself as if in a mirror, and who humiliated and degraded me so that they would not be alone in their degradation and humiliation.

As a result of this way of life I finally became ill, and when I could hardly keep on my feet any longer I dragged myself with the last of my strength to the far bank of the Danube, making my way for the second time to Black Sophie in her strange little cottage. She examined me on the plank bed in the little room with the dried plants and iron stove, while the black cat with the white triangular patch on its forehead licked my face, and diagnosed general physical debility as a result of excessive alcohol consumption, lack of sleep and insufficient nourishment, as well as a syphilitic infection in its early stages. Naturally this information terrified me, but when Black Sophie saw my fear she said there was no cause for concern, as the disease was not far advanced the prospects of a cure were excellent, a recipe for a medicine from her mother's book consisting of pig dung burned to ashes and several hairs from an intact virgin would cause the symptoms to die down gradually and prevent the first stage from being followed by a second, let alone a third. An even swifter cure could undoubtedly be achieved if I had sexual intercourse with an executioner, admittedly something that could not easily be done, for one reason because the Viennese Provincial Court's present imperial-and-royal executioner Selinger was no longer particularly fit to perform such a service on account of his age, although she had heard that his assistant Josef Lang, a man in the prime of life, showed himself very amenable to such requests, which were in fact put to members of his profession with astonishing frequency. To strengthen me and build me up in general she recommended me to carry wood shavings from a tree that had been struck by lightning about my person, and said she'd be happy to sell me such shavings for a ridiculously small sum. The speed with which Black Sophie had made her diagnosis and the certainty with which she had prescribed her various remedies impressed me so much that I confided in her, telling her how shamefully I had been used by both Providence and those closest to me, and I asked whether there was any way in which I could avenge myself if not on Providence at least on ill-disposed human beings. When Black Sophie had looked at me thoughtfully and in silence, she said that of course one could harm others, indeed even cause their death, by performing certain magical rites; for the benefit of interested persons she had copied out some of the simpler of these rituals from the book she had inherited from her mother, who came from the Karst, and she was willing to let me have a copy of them at cost price. If the magic didn't have the desired result within a week she would return me the entire sum, though she couldn't remember that a customer had ever required her to do such a thing, since the magic spells, for such they were, were extremely efficacious.

Sure enough, my state of health did improve within a few weeks, which confirmed my confidence in Black Sophie's arts and made me decide to follow her advice and seek out the imperial-and-royal executioner Selinger's assistant to complete my cure. I went first to the porter of the Provincial Court in Alserstrasse, who told me not without suspicion and some reluctance that Josef Lang and his wife Franziska ran a coffee house in Simmering Haupstrasse, and if I really wanted to, I could find him there. To ensure that I didn't seem so repellent to the executioner's assistant that he would turn down my request flat, I washed myself and my clothes in the water of the Danube, on the banks of which, after previously spending some time in the company of Bohemian brickworkers and sleeping at night beside the kiln where the bricks were fired, I had found shelter in a dilapidated little boathouse made of unplaned old planks perfunctorily nailed together. I combed my matted hair in front of a fragment of mirror glass I had found in the hut, and then I went off to the suburbs, where I did indeed find Josef Lang behind the counter of his coffee house and fell into conversation with him. Among other things, this affable and loquacious man told me that although he was not from a family of executioners, but had first trained to be a carpenter, then worked as a stoker, and now, as I saw, kept a coffee house, his chances of rising from the position of Karl Selinger's second assistant to being his successor were not bad at all. He must say he felt a certain attraction to the idea of this admittedly rather unusual profession, and could easily imagine himself exercising the responsible post of executioner until he reached retirement age. When we had talked about one thing and another for a while, I said in a jocular tone that I believed executioners had always been credited with mysterious abilities, among them extraordinary sexual powers, and I wondered if that also applied to their assistants, to which Josef Lang, flattered, said it was true that the members of the profession held considerable charms for the ladies, women of very different social classes quite often approached him personally or in writing, asking for a rendezvous, which he sometimes granted. And he also received letters from persons asking him for a piece of the rope that had strangled some wretched creature, or at least a few fibres from it, since such an item was popularly believed to bring luck. When I asked whether it was true that executioners and their assistants were able to cause a person to feel passionate love, to cure jealousy, to help barren women conceive and even conjure up spirits, as some said, my interlocutor smiled enigmatically and said that popular belief exaggerated, but he certainly thought he could provide remedies for certain ills, for instance he had already freed several people from nightmares that had afflicted those poor souls regularly, and he was in a position to perform certain practices that cured sexual diseases, against which the members of his guild were immune. Here I made haste to say that this was my own position exactly, I had a slight case of the French disease, and could he cure me of it, for a proper fee, of course, to which the executioner's assistant said, well, he could try, and he'd take the liberty of visiting me in the near future.

So it was that one evening soon afterwards the executioner's second assistant Josef Lang, the very man who, by virtue of yet another of those incredible coincidences that have so often determined the course of my life, will be placing the noose round my neck in a few days' time, came to the boathouse on the banks of the Danube where I had taken shelter and immediately cured me of first-age syphilis by a single performance of the sexual act. This fact revived my spirits, and so did the prospect of paying back those who had treated me unjustly, tormented me, injured me purposely or out of stupidity, and had persecuted and done me harm with their wickedness and malice. I therefore withdrew into the dimly lit boathouse and concentrated on Black Sophie's magic spells just as the Widow Galli had once concentrated on hers. First I wished that a bottle of cleaning spirit placed on the window sill in the sun while the wife of Regional Postal Manager Lindner, who had exploited my labour so thoughtlessly and shamelessly and who was so vain, was cleaning her whalebone corset, would explode in the heat, the splinters of glass would disfigure her pretty face, and that disfigurement would lead to the Regional Postal Manager's leaving his wife, whose extravagance had long been an anxiety to him anyway, obliging her to earn her living as a parlourmaid and be as unfairly treated by others as she had treated me. Then I closed my eyes, thought of the Honourable Herr and Frau von Schreyvogl breakfasting lavishly in their bedroom, and murmured quite a long spell which was meant to bring about the bankruptcy of the Schreyvogl and Sons silk factory in Vienna 7, so that the couple in whose household I had often had to go hungry would be reduced to destitution and have the greatest difficulty in getting their daily bread for themselves and the twins. And when I had wished galloping consumption on Helene and Marie, the daughters of Deputy Spa Director Gerstner, as well as their mother, and for their father, who was my father too, not that that had prevented him from slipping into bed beside me in the attic bedroom, a case of syphilis proceeding unchecked to the third stage with all its unpleasant symptoms, including large inflamed tumours and the consequent painful collapse of his entire nervous system, when I had summoned up all my powers of concentration and memorized a complicated magic spell intended to cause the convents of the Ursuline nuns in Prague and the Sisters of the Good Shepherd in Vienna Neudorf to be struck by lightning and burned to the ground, I hurled what I thought was the most powerful spell of all at Wieden and the Widow Galli, who had mistreated me so mercilessly, a spell designed to strike her dead with a loose stone falling from the masonry of the Church of St Joseph where she had played the organ, when she was on her way to early Mass there.

Since Black Sophie's advice had helped me more than once already I was sure that the magic spells from her mother's book wouldn't fail me, and the terrible revenge I was taking on my enemies would strike them within a week at the latest. In my mind's eye I pictured the horribly disfigured countenance of the Regional Postal Manager's wife, the Honourable Herr and Frau von Schreyvogl worn to mere skeletons and their twins utterly debilitated for lack of food, the Widow Galli's smashed skull, and the charred bodies of the pious nuns discovered by the firemen of Prague and Vienna Neudorf respectively, and these ideas filled me with satisfaction such as I had never felt in my life before, rekindled my will to live, which had been almost extinguished for quite some time, and infused new energy into me, so that I began paying more attention to my appearance again, took better care of my body and cleaned and mended my clothes, with the result that I no longer spent almost all my time hiding away in the boathouse but resumed my walks through the suburbs and the Inner City, stealing or begging food.

One afternoon, when I was sitting on a bench in the Stadtpark not far from my former place of employment on the Ring, while the spring sun shone on my face, Frau Navratil, caretaker of the building at 18 Stubenring, passed me pushing a pram, and I seized my opportunity to greet her and ask how the Honourable von Schreyvogls were. When Frau Navratil had looked suspiciously at me and finally recognized me, she said in unfriendly tones that unlike me, for I didn't look as if I had done very well for myself in the meantime, which didn't surprise her, the Slav race being notable for its indolence and stupidity, as Ritter von Schönerer correctly stated, unlike me the extremely amiable von Schreyvogls were constantly and industriously endeavouring to improve their position in life, endeavours that were bearing fruit, for the silk factory had seen an unprecedented boom in business and developed into a flourishing company, and furthermore the union of the couple, who were as much in love as on the day of their wedding, was now blessed with four children, if I liked I could take a look at Roswitha Albine, the youngest member of the family, a really dear little creature if a little too plump, which came of good living, the Honourable Herr von Schreyvogl and his wife, not to mention the twins and Sixtus Isidor, born in October of the year before last, were slightly overweight too, although incidentally it suited them all. So saying, Frau Navratil turned away from me and pushed the pram on. I sat there on the bench for quite a long time, stunned to discover that one of Black Sophie's guaranteed spells didn't work, and indeed it was evident that the opposite of what I wanted had happened. Finally I rose and went off, deeply disturbed, towards the Judenplatz, to ask after the health of the wife of the Regional Postal Manager from the market woman who supplied her with country produce from the Waldviertel. I was greatly disappointed when, in answer to my question, the blonde farmer's wife clapped her hands and cried, oh, the Regional Postal Manager's wife, didn't I know that she had finally left her mean old husband, who did nothing but sit about in inns and coffee houses, and entered into a new relationship with an officer of the Eighty-fourth Household Regiment, ten years her junior, very good-looking and from a family rolling in money, whom she had met at the Emperor's ball through her son, elegant young Lieutenant Georg? Only yesterday she'd been to this stall in the company of the dashing soldier to buy two nice fat geese, you could see how happy she was, beaming all over her face and looking ten years younger herself. I quickly took my leave of the farmer's wife, feeling cast down, went down Kurrentgasse, Steindlgasse and Milchgasse to the Petersplatz, and had just decided not to ask after the whereabouts of the Widow Galli when that lady herself, dressed in deep black as usual, emerged from the Baroque portal of St Peter's Church with its magnificent façade in the company of Father Peregrin and stopped outside the church to talk to him, and overcome by sudden curiosity I hid around the side of its projecting structure to overhear their conversation. Dismayed, I heard Father Peregrin congratulate the widow on her unanimous election as honorary president of the Viennese Catholic Association for the Protection of Christian Standards, her excellent state of health allowed the association every prospect of profiting by her devout and wise leadership for a long time to come, and as he had told her, its members were uncommonly proud of her invitation from the Holy Father to a private audience, to which Cardinal Grober and two of his ministrants would accompany her, a private audience, just imagine, such an honour was very seldom granted to a woman.

After these disappointing and sobering discoveries, I decided to take the arduous walk to the other bank of the Danube for the third time, past the Dechantlacke and between two blind arms of the Danube, and make my way to Black Sophie's cottage to call her to account. When I complained that as far as I'd been able to check, not a single one of her magic spells had taken the slightest effect, so I was expecting her to refund my money in full, the witch replied indignantly that anyone could say that, how was she to know I was telling the truth, I'd have to produce conclusive evidence of the legitimacy of my complaints, no evidence, no money, that stood to reason. When I objected, asking how I could prove that the Regional Postal Manager's wife had not been disfigured by the exploding bottle of white spirit, the Widow Galli had not been struck dead by a falling stone, and the Honourable von Schreyvogls were not going hungry, Black Sophie said impatiently that was my business, and now I must forgive her, I had interrupted her in the middle of assembling a complicated and sensational recipe, a mixture of pulverized quail brains, filings from bells, fourteen dried juniper berries gathered on the day of the Assumption of the Virgin Mary and various other ingredients, which would enable her either to cure or to cause epilepsy. At this I raised my voice and said her methods were dishonest, not to say criminal, and I wouldn't hesitate to spread abroad this opinion of her in and around Vienna, whereupon the black cat with the triangular white patch on its forehead hissed at me, and the thin woman in her loose black garment rose to her full height, pointed to the door with her outstretched right arm and told me to get out of her sight at once if I didn't want her to use the powers she possessed against me, it would be easy for her, Black Sophie, who was known and feared beyond the borders of the Austro-Hungarian monarchy, had regular intercourse with the mightiest of magicians, the most clairvoyant of witches and the most reliable of enchanters, to do me a great deal of harm and inflict some extremely unpleasant diseases on me by witchcraft, so if I valued my life I had better get out that minute. I turned on my heel, fled from the cottage, and decided that after these discouraging and disagreeable experiences of the Black Art I would abjure it while there was still time, and I consigned the double sheet of squared paper with Black Sophie's handwritten magic spells on it to the waters of the Danube flowing past my boathouse.

One warm, cloudless spring day soon afterwards I was standing near the pleasure house in the Hauptallee of the Prater, which was lined by many onlookers enjoying the sight of all the flower-decked carriages in the annual Korso or flower parade held there, when a man standing behind me in the dense crowd poked a finger into my back and said would I kindly get out of his way, where would we be if everyone behaved like me and simply pushed her way to the front, what was the point of his taking up his position in the Hauptallee of the Prater an hour before the flower parade began so as to have a good view if thoughtless people disregarded the most elementary rules of civility without the slightest scruple? I turned and told the middle-aged man with the grey top hat and round-framed glasses that as far as I could see I was a head shorter than he was, and since he had mentioned civility I would allow myself to point out that a gentleman usually let a lady go first, whereupon the man looked at me sharply and said what did I mean a lady, unless he was much mistaken I was that depressive with the strong tendency to self-chastisement whom they had been obliged to remove forcibly from the hospital where he worked because the other women patients complained of her constant talking. I looked at this unfriendly gentleman in my own turn and recognized him as Dr Doblhoff, the university lecturer who worked at the lunatic asylum in Vienna 9. He immediately went on and said, yes of course, now he remembered, I'd seized him by the skirt of his doctor's coat, an awkward scene, and how was I now, he hoped I hadn't been tempted to commit suicide again since my stay in the asylum. I replied that to be honest, I had to admit that in consequence of the truly insuperable obstacles constantly thrown in my way by a malevolent fate, I had not only toyed with the idea of suicide again, I had even tried to put it into practice, although unsuccessfully, and when Dr Doblhoff asked where I was living I told him truthfully I had found accommodation in one of the empty buildings along the Danube and was living, so to speak, from hand to mouth. The lecturer seemed to be thinking this over, and then he said hesitantly that since I had kept reciting recipes from cookbooks during my attacks of logorrhoea he supposed, and admittedly he might be jumping to conclusions, that I would be able to prepare those dishes, most of them of Bohemian provenance if he remembered rightly, to which I replied that my mother, who had been cook to the family of the Deputy Spa Director in Marienbad for a long time before her early death, had indeed taught me cookery skills, although unfortunately I had never had a chance to put them into practice yet. Here Dr Doblhoff took my arm and steered himself and me carefully and swiftly through the people waiting to watch the parade and towards the garden of the Second Coffee House, where he gently made me sit down on a chair at one of the round tables and asked what I would say to becoming his housekeeper for a while and running his household, which consisted of only one person, namely himself, because he had no children and his wife's sickness with the so-called Viennese disease, also known as consumption or tuberculosis, had kept her in sanatoriums almost constantly for the last few years, an offer which I accepted there and then.

So it was that a few days later I was making Braised Goose Bohemian Style for the first time in my life in the kitchen of the comfortable apartment where the lecturer in nervous diseases lived at 16 Berggasse, Vienna 9, and I had to keep looking at the fattest of Dobromila Rettigova's four cookbooks, which was lying open beside me, since I lacked experience in the art of cookery. I was all the more pleased to find that the lecturer, who after the early death of his parents had been brought up by his maternal grandmother, a native of Königgrätz, and who loved Bohemian cooking, enjoyed the goose I had bought from the nearby Jewish butcher Sigmund Kornmehl, which I had braised in half a litre of white wine and seasoned with bay leaves and tarragon. After I had made all his favourite dishes in turn – clear soup with slices of white bread dipped in egg and fried, oxtail, fried calves' brains and Prague fillet, as well as various delicious Bohemian desserts such as cream-cheese dumplings, plum dumplings, yeast pastries with sweet fillings, rolled pancakes stuffed with sweet cottage cheese, and yeast dumplings filled with plum jam – dishes which fortunately all and without exception earned his unreserved approval, Dr Doblhoff took me aside and said he liked my cooking very much, the consumption of the meals I obviously conjured up with such ease on his table delighted him, since he was a hard-working man constitutionally inclined to enjoy the pleasures of life but with no time to indulge them, and he hoped I would remain with him as cook and housekeeper for a long time to come. He must tell me that he not only had his medical duties treating the insane at the lunatic asylum in Vienna 9, he also aspired to an academic career, so that his free time, of which he didn't have much in any case, was entirely devoted to the writing of a thesis qualifying him as a full university lecturer, and once completed and published, this thesis would cause a great sensation in and beyond Vienna, since in it he was trying to get on the trail of phenomena – indeed, he was already on their trail – which would advance and in fact revolutionize the exact science of the functioning of the human mind, still in its infancy, in a most extraordinary manner. Because of the resentment of his Viennese colleagues, who were as mediocre as they were ambitious and did all they could to put obstacles in the path of any scientist more talented than themselves, envying him the slightest success and seeking to harm him wherever possible, because of his undoubtedly well-founded fears that some of these colleagues might make use of information incautiously entrusted to them for their own ends, thus depriving him of the fruits of his scientific endeavours, he was keeping the results of his investigations to date strictly secret, the one man with whom he sometimes exchanged opinions was Sigmund Freud the lecturer in neuropathology, whom he admired, a very trustworthy scientist of high moral integrity from whom he had nothing whatever to fear in that respect. Ever since they had attended the new Salpêtrière hospital for nervous illnesses in Paris together, working there for several months under the internationally famous Professor Jean Marie Charcot, their friendship had become closer, and the boundless admiration he entertained for Dr Freud, together with his increasing need to be near that highly talented man, was the reason why he had given up the apartment he inherited from his parents in Hietzing and moved here to Berggasse, where Freud himself had recently come to live with his wife Martha and their children Mathilde, Martin and Oliver. With these words Dr Doblhoff drew me over to one of the tall windows of his living room, pushed the thin net curtain aside, put one arm lightly around my shoulders and with the other pointed to the comfortable building opposite, with the butcher Kornmehl's shop which I patronized on its ground floor. That was the building where Freud lived, he said, and from this window he could watch the comings and goings of his colleague and his colleague's family; indeed, he could often cast a glance into Freud's lighted living room in the evening, which gave him great satisfaction. Then he smiled and added that he was aware that his veneration of the neuropathologist, whom he regarded as a father figure although their difference in age was only slight, went beyond the usual bounds of esteem, not only was he developing gestures and mannerisms characteristic of the other man but even similar symptoms of illness, for instance he had recently suffered from stomach pains such as those that had afflicted Freud for years, and had also been distressed by nasal catarrh, from which again the man he admired suffered. To these revelations by my new employer I said that I had received a very good education for the child of a simple cook, but Fräulein von Roth-Rothenhorst, my governess in Marienbad, had never mentioned anything about any science of the human mind, nor had the nuns in the Ursuline boarding school in Prague where I had spent quite a long time, so he must forgive my ignorance and explain in more detail what his researches were about, to which the doctor said he would try to give me an explanation, although a greatly simplified one, and told me that from observation of his own dreams and those of his patients he was increasingly coming to the conclusion that even as children people suppressed disagreeable feelings to a greater or lesser degree, but that these disagreeable feelings still made themselves felt unconsciously and had an indirectly disruptive effect on the conduct of the person concerned. By means of a process which he called free association and which played a key role in dreams, it was possible to uncover the suppressed material and thus limit or entirely eliminate the unpleasant consequences to which they had given rise in that person's life. I made haste to say I thought I understood what he was talking about, after all my mother, who died prematurely, had ascribed great importance to her dreams and tried to interpret them with the help of the *Dream Book of the Pharaohs*, a work unfortunately no longer in my possession, but here Dr Doblhoff interrupted me a little impatiently and said he supposed I wasn't comparing his strictly

scientific study of dreams with the simple, arbitrary interpretations that had been attempted time and again in superstitious ages,
and to this day were still offered to gullible customers by gypsy
women at fairs and other calculating and greedy persons, ultimately it was this very ignorance which in many people, and
undoubtedly in my own case, caused constitutional neurotic
compulsions to emerge from their state of latency and encouraged
mental breakdown. I replied he must forgive me, I didn't understand these complicated arguments, but I did think my dreams had
sometimes given me very useful instructions on what to do in
difficult situations, whereupon Dr Doblhoff cried, oh, what a pity,
sometimes he came close to despairing of the ignorance of the
lower social classes, particularly their female members, and the
impossibility of teaching them anything, I could spare him my
positively criminally naive opinions and go and dust the antique
pieces which he had recently taken a great interest in collecting,
once again following the example of Dr Freud. So saying he went
into the smoking room to light a cigar, another of his colleague's
habits that he had adopted, and I picked up the feather duster and
passed its soft feathers carefully over the little statues, stones,
potsherds and plaster busts standing on Dr Doblhoff's desk and in
a glass case. On this occasion I also removed the dust from the
glass protecting a photograph on the desk showing a woman with
a thin face, sad eyes, a knot of dark hair and a chain round her
neck worn over a lace blouse and carrying an oval locket, which as
I concluded from the inscription in spiky, narrow handwriting and
dark blue ink to the bottom right-hand corner of the photograph
and saying 'Forever True, Your Aphrodite', must be Dr Doblhoff's
absent wife. He had told me that after several visits to the
Semmering area, the Riviera and Davos, which unfortunately could
do very little to improve her poor health, she was now at the spa of
Merano in the South Tyrol and pinned all her hopes on its
beneficent climate, hopes of which he naturally did not wish to
deprive his wife, but which in no way seemed justified by the latest

disturbing findings of the lung specialists, whose diagnosis was so alarming that he had recently felt moved to have his wife's name provisionally added in memorial lettering to the epitaph on the family vault in the form of a round classical temple in Hietzing Cemetery, underneath those of his grandparents and parents as well as his aunt. Her unusual first name, Aphrodite, had been chosen by her father, a former professor of classical philology at the University of Vienna. He hoped I wouldn't misunderstand him: ten years ago, when he married his wife, who was a few years his senior, in the church of the convent of the Salesian Order of nuns, it had been a love match, but you had to face the incontrovertible medical facts, and they did not suggest that she would recover from consumption, for that widespread illness which was the cause of almost half the deaths in Vienna had attacked Aphrodite out of the blue and developed in a very short time to tuberculosis of the apices of the lungs, so that large parts of her lungs had already collapsed. As Dr Doblhoff had also confessed to me, he tried to forget his grief over the progressive deterioration in his wife's health through his work as an assistant doctor at the Alsergrund lunatic asylum and during his very interesting conversations with Freud, and in addition through his participation as a cellist in a string quartet consisting entirely of doctors from the aforesaid lunatic asylum, who devoted themselves to the chamber music of Schubert in particular and met every Wednesday evening at the home of one of the musicians; and now, even more recently, I too had brightened his largely joyless existence with my skills as a cook and my general loving care for him. He was also pleased by the turn for the better taken by my mental health since I came into his household, frail as it had been for so long, the calm and regular daily round of a housekeeper's activities obviously had a good effect on my psychological constitution. Then he added that all the same he couldn't help noticing that I seldom left the apartment, I seemed to be a rather retiring person, like himself, what did I think of taking a walk with him next Sunday in the grounds of

Schönbrunn Castle, in particular visiting the newly built palm house, the biggest glasshouse on the continent of Europe, where rarities of the plant world from all over the earth were displayed in three large pavilions. I said that I was glad he had mentioned my state of mind, it was true that I felt very happy in his household and his presence, and I had for some time been meaning to thank him expressly for taking me in, an orphan almost ruined by my dealings with my inconsiderate fellow humans, and I was happy to accept his invitation to a walk on Sunday.

A few days later we were sitting in the sun on a stone bench in one of the alleys of Schönbrunn Castle park, which are laid out in a star shape, and while we watched a man standing at a great height on a wooden scaffold on wheels, clipping one of the hedges rising to some ten metres, Dr Doblhoff talked about his scientific research into dreams, of the way in which there is less repression in sleep, but something called dream censorship still comes into play, distorting the dreams that were constructed as neurotic symptoms, and told me how, through intensification, displacement and dramatization, dreamwork transfers latent ideas into the manifest content of the dream. I felt moved to complement these remarks by mentioning that I remembered dreaming last night that his wife had entered the little maid's room where I was sleeping, wearing a pretty travelling costume of dark grey worsted and carrying two cases, and said she was just off by the post coach to Trieste and would then take the Southern Railway to Vienna, a journey to which she looked forward with excitement but slight concern, for a hundred and seventy thousand navvies had worked for decades building this line, on which engines known as adhesion locomotives climbed incredible rises and passed through fifteen tunnels and over sixteen viaducts, and I said that my late mother would probably have interpreted this dream as the return of a person believed dead. Once again Dr Doblhoff interrupted me, sounding slightly annoyed, and said that although by chance his wife did happen to own a dark grey worsted costume I might spare him such tedious interpretations, the fact was that the lung specialist treating her in Merano, a European authority of the first rank, had telephoned two days before and told him that the idea of performing pneumothoracic therapy on Aphrodite, that is to say, blowing air into the area of the pleura, thus compressing the lungs, eliminating them from the breathing process and healing them, could not be put into practice, since the costal pleura itself was already affected, and moreover she was getting steadily weaker, coughing blood more and more frequently, and to be honest he, the lung specialist, could scarcely envisage any partial restoration of his patient's health, let alone a complete cure, on the contrary he, her husband Dr Doblhoff, must prepare himself to become a widower within six months or possibly earlier. When I exclaimed in horror that this was terrible, Dr Doblhoff put an arm gently round my shoulders, looked sadly in the direction of the Fountain of Neptune and said, yes, of course it was terrible, life in general was terrible, and so was the fact that he, being as he had told me constitutionally very much disposed to enjoy the pleasures of life, had been obliged to forgo the joys of married life for years and sleep in a half-empty matrimonial bed, I couldn't imagine how cold it sometimes was in his half of the bed, or rather how cold it used to be, for since I had been making that half of the bed every morning, straightening the sheet, plumping up the pillow and smoothing the coverlet, when he lay down at night in his half of the bed made so carefully, even lovingly by my hand, he felt as if the sheet were not so clammy any more, the pillow not so cool and the coverlet not so freezing. At this compliment I felt the blood rise to my cheeks, and to hide my embarrassment I turned away and took from the round wicker basket beside me the half of a cold pork knuckle I had cooked the previous evening, blanching it in boiling water for five minutes, then taking it out to score the rind across in both directions at intervals of a centimetre, rubbing salt, pepper and four cloves of garlic into the rind and then sprinkling it with plenty of caraway, after which I put it rind down in a covered pan in the oven with a little water and cooked it at medium heat, finally taking off the lid and letting it roast to a crisp in the heat from above. I now cut bite-sized portions for two in silence, laid them on slices of black bread and handed one portion to my employer, who bit into the rosy meat, sighed slightly and said he hadn't eaten a pork knuckle like that since his maternal grandmother died, and he thanked the happy chance that had led him first to meet me in the lunatic asylum in Vienna 9 and later to come upon me again at the flower parade in the Prater. Half an hour later we were walking among and beneath the tropical plants in the palm house, and quite soon the humid temperature had so dazed and wearied me that without putting up any resistance to speak of I allowed Dr Doblhoff to draw me behind a banana plant, cover my face and throat with kisses, and slip his practised cellist's hand under the violet lace insert of my pale lilac dress.

The next few months in the apartment at 16 Berggasse in the Alsergrund passed in an atmosphere of peaceful routine that I would never have thought possible after the eventful life I had led until quite recently. Every morning Dr Doblhoff went off to the lunatic asylum, and I tidied the bedclothes on both sides of the marital bed, which he had insisted on my sharing with him after that incident behind the banana plant in the palm house, a wish with which I complied hesitantly at first but soon not without enthusiasm, since what we did underneath the big framed painting showing Dr Doblhoff and his wife at their wedding, and under the batiste and damask bedclothes, did much to restore me to a state of harmonious equilibrium and cheerful relaxation after my life had been thrown so badly off course since the death of Crown Prince Rudolf, and my own well-being increased in proportion to what, if I could believe the gloomy reports delivered by Dr Doblhoff – and I did believe them – was the decline in Aphrodite Doblhoff's state of health. Both in the kitchen and the bedroom I went to a great deal of trouble to provide active assistance in alleviating the sad fate of a man whose mortally sick wife was undergoing one open-air rest cure after another on the terrace of a Merano sanatorium in a mild climate and dust-free air, although they hardly gave any grounds to hope for a positive result, and Dr Doblhoff repeatedly assured me that he appreciated these endeavours of mine very much indeed, as he did my assiduous care for the maintenance of his home, furnished on the model of Dr Freud's own spacious apartment at 19 Berggasse. Like my former protector Engelbert Kornhäusel, my employer hated female chatter, so I got into the habit of never interrupting his conversation on subjects limited to the state of his wife's health, his own work in the lunatic asylum and on his thesis on dreams, and his fertile scientific exchange of ideas with Dr Freud, at most accompanying them by a few sounds of confirmation, encouragement or regret. When the other three members of the string quartet, one of them, as Dr Doblhoff told me, a specialist in hypnosis at the lunatic asylum and the other two specialists in electrotherapy, met once a month in the sitting room of his apartment, I was expected to enter the room in silence when the sound of the instruments died away and then, without a word, give the first and second violinists, the viola player and finally their host trays on which I had arranged little triangles of black bread spread with egg, fish, liver sausage and Liptauer cheese in pretty patterns. I also, after being twice reprimanded, gave up bothering the hard-working doctor, who was so unhappy in his private life, with accounts of my dreams and any small attempts I might make to interpret them, keeping it to myself that Frau Doblhoff appeared to me in the bedroom almost every night in an ever-changing wardrobe, announcing her imminent return from the South Tyrol.

After three months of harmonious life with Dr Doblhoff at 16 Berggasse my period failed to appear and I began suffering from dizziness, loss of appetite and nausea, complaints which reminded me alarmingly of my service in the Honourable von Schreyvogls' household and which did not remain a secret from Dr Doblhoff,

who patted my cheek affectionately and said he was sure I
wouldn't mind if the viola player, a conscientious and ambitious
medical man who before training in hypnosis, out of a pure desire
for scientific knowledge, had been a gynaecologist, were to
examine me after their next string quartet rehearsal; as for
himself, Dr Doblhoff, he could think of nothing better than to be
given a child, that symbol of eternal growth, by the charming
young creature that I was. I thought of the almost nightly
appearance of Aphrodite Doblhoff in the bedroom and asked
quietly how such a gift was to be reconciled with the existence of
his wife, however endangered her health, a remark that Doblhoff
waved away, saying smilingly that the expert in Merano had told
him by telegraph that at present his wife was shaken by fits of
shivering more or less the whole time, and was suffering from the
last or at least the penultimate stage of consumption, in a word she
was practically on her deathbed, so I mustn't have the least anxiety
on that score, even love matches were sometimes brought to a
premature end by the incalculable workings of fate. When I asked
why his marriage had been childless, he took a key from a drawer
of the Biedermeier sideboard in the drawing room, and without a
word, but gesturing to me to follow him, took it into the room he
called a dressing room, where he opened a walnut trousseau chest
adorned with rustic carving and showed me the clothes inside it,
telling me that here were the six little nightgowns, six little jackets
and six umbilical bandages, six towelling nappies and six muslin
nappies, three shawls, six bibs and facecloths, two swaddling
bands and feeding bottle, two medium-sized hand towels and
three little pillows with their pillowslips which had been bought
back in the past when Aphrodite was expecting, although alas, not
for long, since the tuberculosis which had already infected her, as
it more easily and frequently does infect tall, slender people like
herself, so-called asthenic physical types, than other people, had
made her too weak to carry the child to full term. I put my hands
over my face and cried, oh, that was terrible, whereupon my

employer put his own hands gently on my shoulders and said again of course it was terrible, life in general was terrible, a fact he frequently lamented in his conversations with his colleague Freud, who incidentally, to his, Dr Doblhoff's, slight surprise seemed to be transferring the main interest of his own research from the study of hysteria to the field of dreams, his own, Dr Doblhoff's, subject.

The viola player who was a gynaecologist and a specialist in hypnosis diagnosed pregnancy a few days later, and during the next few months Dr Doblhoff was more tender and considerate of me than ever before, helping me to smooth the bedclothes and dust his collection of antiques, and taking me gently in his arms when I woke from my sleep with a start, for the nightly visitation of Frau Doblhoff, who had recently taken to appearing in nothing but a long white nightdress, was assuming increasingly alarming features, and she would come very close to my side of the bed, leaning over me and coughing so that a spray of little drops of blood fell on me and the white batiste coverlet, and gasping that it was one thing for me to take over the side of the bed that was hers by right, after all, whatever her husband claimed, theirs had never been a love match, but she wouldn't have my brat wearing the baby clothes she had once placed in the trousseau chest for her own child, no, she would prevent that by infecting me and the fruit of my womb with unpleasant bacteria in short order, oh yes, she would by no means shrink from so doing. The father of my unborn child, as a man who had been trained in medical practice before he turned to studying the human mind and was consequently familiar with physical processes, also explained the changes that take place during pregnancy, since my mother, Fräulein von Roth-Rothenhorst and the nuns of the Ursuline convent boarding school in Prague had all imparted a good deal of useful information but had left me totally in the dark about such facts as these, merely telling me that pregnancy is an extraordinarily impressive part of a woman's life and the subsequent experience of motherhood overwhelming. Apart from the slightly alarming dreams in which I saw visions of Aphrodite Doblhoff's pale, emaciated figure at my bedside, nothing disturbed my peace of mind; after my loss of appetite, dizzy feelings and nausea passed off, as they soon did, I felt extremely well physically, and when Dr Doblhoff laid his head on my belly in the bed, told me the precise number of days yet to elapse before the birth of the child and said the time would pass like lightning, I must just wait and see, his son would be following in his footsteps in no time and continuing the scientific work he, Dr Doblhoff, had so confidently begun, he would undoubtedly show a sense of family feeling, which didn't necessarily seem to be the case with Dr Freud's sons, to their father's occasional regret, in fact Freud's temper wasn't very good at present, since the Viennese Medical Association, to whose members Freud had given his important lecture as long ago as 1886, had been delaying the granting of his application for a full professorship for seven years now, not that that surprised him, Dr Doblhoff, nothing else was to be expected of the medical men of Vienna, of course they were as ignorant as they were perfidious and scarcely a talented man was safe from their plots and intrigues, he hoped his son would be endowed by nature not only with his own remarkable scientific talents but with enough presence of mind and knowledge of human nature to assert himself, actively assisted by his father, against that corrupt clique, that cold-blooded cabal – when Dr Doblhoff laid his ear on my belly like that I felt something that is commonly called happiness. When I then stroked his slightly greying, wavy dark hair and said cautiously, we'd see, we'd see, we couldn't absolutely count on our child's not being, for instance, a girl, or, for instance, having qualities quite different from those he hoped for, he removed my hand from his hair, raised his head, looked at me sternly through his round glasses and told me not to be annoying, his picture of the future had always proved accurate, he saw everything as clear as crystal and in detailed outline before him, including our wedding in the Nine Choirs of Angels Church, which would take place relatively soon after poor Aphrodite was laid to rest in the family vault in Hietzing Cemetery and in any case before the child's birth. He could also see the first summer holiday we would take with our son in the Semmering area and his first day at school, and when I quietly objected that perhaps it was not right, if not positively wicked, to anticipate fate like this, he asked what did I mean, anticipate, after all I was the one who always pestered him with dubious and inexpert interpretations of my dreams, and I might consider myself lucky to be as honestly and exclusively loved by a man as I was by him.

So the days passed by, I continued to enjoy good health, my girth increased and my mobility decreased, and finally the birth of the child, which was to be attended by the viola-playing gynae-cologist, whose hypnotic powers Dr Doblhoff expected to cause a certain amelioration of my labour pains, was only a few weeks away. One day, when we had brought up from the cellar the cherrywood cradle that had been in the Doblhoff family's posses-sion for generations and were just carrying it over the threshold, a telegraph boy handed a telegram to my employer on the landing between the upper ground floor and the mezzanine floor, and as soon as he had glanced at it he suddenly put the back end of the cherrywood cradle down on the grey and red chequered terrazzo floor of the landing. Expecting the telegram to contain the sad if not unexpected news of Aphrodite's death, I said consolingly that the laws of existence were as unfathomable as they were inexor-able, one person was born and another died, my late mother had always believed that you had to accept such natural vicissitudes of fate with equanimity, to which Dr Doblhoff whispered that this was impossible, the specialist in Merano had sent a telegram to say that Frau Doblhoff's condition, as if miraculously, had taken a turn very much for the better when they began giving her a new drug scarcely more than a few months ago and he, the specialist, didn't think it was too much to assume that she, Frau Doblhoff, would be

able to travel to Vienna on the Southern Railway at the beginning
of next week, accompanied by a trustworthy person; at any rate
he, the expert, thanked God for such a cure and was sure that he
too, Dr Doblhoff, whom he, the expert, would very soon inform of
the precise time of his wife's arrival, would also thank God in due
form. Since the invalid had already announced her return to me
several times before this, I was less shattered by the news than
might have been expected, so I picked up the front end of the
cherrywood cradle again and asked my employer to take the other
end, continue on our way into the apartment with me in spite of
this unforeseen event, and put the cradle in the corner of the
former dressing room which we were intending to make into a
nursery, a request with which Dr Doblhoff complied with total
apathy. Then he withdrew into the smoking room for several
hours, and finally, around five in the afternoon, opened its door
and summoned me in.

In view of the complete change in the circumstances, he said,
automatically passing his right hand over the pair of doves made
of pure white Augarten porcelain shown billing and cooing as they
stood on a little table, a wedding present from his parents-in-law,
as he had told me long ago in response to my query, in view of this
new and unexpected state of affairs we must contemplate measures that were inevitably to some extent other than our original
intentions. Since he knew Aphrodite as well as a man can know a
woman with whom he made a love match years ago, and on the
grounds of this knowledge concluded that she would reclaim her
half of the matrimonial bed as soon as she arrived back at 16
Berggasse, he must suggest that I left that half of the bed, which I
was now unlawfully occupying, and go back to the maid's room,
which was the right place for me after all. As for the imminent
birth of his son, this, because of the equally imminent return of
Aphrodite, now presented more problems than expected, problems
for which, however, he had already found a solution which he
hoped would suit all parties involved, including his son. I must see

that my delivery could not now be performed, as originally planned, by the viola-playing specialist in hypnosis with his obstetric and gynaecological training while I occupied half of the matrimonial bed, which would inevitably entail some awkwardness in view of the new situation, and he was sure I would agree to move to a place entailing less awkwardness than the matrimonial bedroom and bring the boy into the world in the spacious, peaceful and germ-free padded cell in the lunatic asylum in Vienna 9, attended by his aforesaid colleague. I was horrified by the idea of my child's first seeing the light in the cramped, cold, windowless little room where I had once been locked up, and the sudden shock made me go straight into labour. Overcome by pain of a kind I had never known before, I sank down on the upholstered bamboo seat by the window, clutched my belly and said I didn't feel well, could the baby possibly be arriving earlier than expected, to which Dr Doblhoff, who always had the number of days and weeks until my delivery in his head, said that out of the forty weeks, that is two hundred and eighty days, thirty-seven weeks, that is two hundred and fifty-nine days, had now passed, and of course babies were sometimes born prematurely, but he assumed that a person with a talent for the exact sciences, like his son, would not deviate more than two days either side of the due date, the twenty-ninth of May, so I wasn't to worry, perhaps the Bohemian-style crayfish poached in beer that we ate for lunch hadn't agreed with me; delicious as they had been, you never knew with crayfish. When the pains, which I was too inexperienced to recognize for what they were at the time, grew stronger and I groaned aloud, Dr Doblhoff said river crayfish poisoning wasn't something to be taken lightly, it would probably be best to call in his general practitioner Dr Leodolter from Strudlhofgasse at once.

On his arrival, the doctor looked at the colourless liquid which by now, to my dismay, had run down my legs and emerged from under the hem of my dress to form a little puddle on the parquet floor, he said, ah, there we were, the waters had already broken, and he went straight to the Schottenring and came back with a hired cab. As I went down the steps, supported by Dr Doblhoff and the doctor, my pains increased, and in the cab the worst of them came on, pains which I now know, as I didn't at the time, to have been the contractions of the second stage of labour, when you bear down to hasten the birth process. Because of a moment's incaution on the part of the cabby, who was urging the horses to go faster, we collided with the corner of a building in taking a bend, causing the left forewheel to suffer a broken spoke which made it necessary for the vehicle to stop for quite some time, and as a result my daughter Aphrodite, to my relief, was born not in the padded cell of the lunatic asylum in the Alsergrund but in a stationary cab on the corner of Sensengasse and Lazarettgasse.

14

I put down the blue notebook. Aphrodite was far from being a usual girl's name in Vienna, and not only Dr Doblhoff's wife and Rosa's newborn daughter but my own grandmother had been called Aphrodite. I rose, went to the kitchen where Aunt Pia was sitting at the table skinning a calf's brain, and said in a loud voice that while looking for bedclothes I had opened the chest in Wilma's room by mistake and so had come upon an old blue notebook which I admitted, and I apologized at the same time, I had opened out of sheer curiosity, and to be honest I hadn't just opened it, I had read almost all of it. When Aunt Pia stopped skinning the calf's brain and looked at me in outrage, I boldly went on and said I was sure she would know the identity of the woman called Rosa Havelka, née Tichy, who told her own story in it so movingly, I'd wondered whether she might be a distant relation, a member of the Bohemian branch of our family, to which Aunt Pia said first she was greatly surprised to find me turning her household upside down without her express permission, and second, as for the blue notebook it had been in the chest for decades, I couldn't expect an old lady of eighty to know all the details of the origin of every item in her apartment, she only remembered vaguely that the notebook had come into the family's hands through the agency of a nun. I immediately asked whether by any chance this nun was a member of the community of the Good Shepherd, to which Aunt Pia replied impatiently that she didn't know about that, perhaps I'd stop bothering an old woman just waiting for death to release her and instead of pestering her with unnecessary questions I should call my mother, my mother was very well informed about the family, and perhaps I would also allow her to get on with this calf's brain, she was going to fry it with eggs, a dish which she supposed, delicious as it was, I would probably refuse to touch, like almost everything she cooked.

I did as Aunt Pia told me, called my mother, and told her that Rosa Havelka, whose autobiography I had found in the chest in Wilma's room, had had a daughter called Aphrodite, and as this was an unusual name I wondered if there was any connection between this person and my grandmother, who bore the same name, to which my mother said, slightly annoyed, what chest was I talking about, she didn't know any such chest, anyway Aphrodite was a perfectly usual girl's name, newborn baby girls were often called Aphrodite not only in the United States but also in and around Austria, the two continents, so far apart in space, shared the inheritance of the Greeks, Aphrodite meant beauty, charm, youth, everything parents could wish for their children, and now I must forgive her, but she had to get back to drawing up the questionnaire about the sensual appeal to American voters of the lady who was Secretary of State, she'd been working on it for days.

Next Sunday Josef, who had by now received Professor Priem's generous offer to buy the Pink Rose butterfly and accepted it on the spot, invited me to a performance of Schubert's Mass in E Major in the Golden Hall of the Musikverein, and when I went to the ladies' room before the beginning of the concert, the attendant, carefully wiping the lavatory seat for me, asked if I'd seen the Federal President, an usherette had told her the Federal President was in the audience with his second wife, all the people of Austria, herself included, were glad to see him achieve this late-come happiness, everyone knew that his first marriage had been a severe trial from beginning to end and for the last few years had existed only on paper, anyway she very much hoped that the Federal

President's wife would visit the ladies' room, since such a visit was the only way she, the ladies' room attendant, could get to see prominent ladies who attended the concert, I was better off in that respect. Then Josef and I found our seats in the front row of the stalls, and gave ourselves up to the music of Schubert played by the orchestra of the Vienna Philharmonic and sung by the choir of the Vienna Musikverein, and glancing sideways at my singing teacher it struck me that he looked very like the composer and I wondered why I hadn't noticed it before. In the interval a former member of the Vienna Boys' Choir whom he knew, now a bassoonist in the Baden spa orchestra, approached us in the buffet holding a mock-salmon roll, looked me up and down thoroughly as he bit into it, and began talking to Josef about the average salaries of members of Austrian spa orchestras. He then pointed with what remained of his roll to an elegant couple standing not far away from us and whispered that there was the Federal President, the Federal President and his second wife, and when I looked that way the Federal President's eyes briefly met mine and I looked discreetly down.

For about a week, to be precise ever since the morning after the afternoon when I shared Josef's mother's bed with him for the first but not the last time, I had not been feeling quite myself. Much to Aunt Pia's anxiety I ate even less than before, I sometimes had a dizzy spell as I walked around the city, and I usually felt nausea before getting up, complaints that became slightly worse every day and when my period failed to appear sent me off to the St Mary Magdalene Pharmacy to buy a pregnancy test, causing the pharmacist there to give me a conspiratorial smile and say poor Herr Horvath had been so cheerful recently, he no longer dragged himself around with his shoulders stooped and hardly came into the pharmacy at all, which she naturally deplored as owner of the business, but welcomed as his adviser in matters of health and lifestyle over many years; between ourselves, what poor Herr Horvath needed was a little family, a little family would make a different person of poor Herr Horvath in no time at all.

The test was positive, and I wondered anxiously how Josef would react to the revelation that in all probability my very first attempt to resuscitate him had left me in an interesting condition: anxiously because it was to be expected that like all the other men I'd ever known before him he'd say what, a child, was I out of my mind, there could be no question of a child, he hoped I realized he was saying so not in his own interests but first and foremost in mine, I was an artist and my fulfilment as a woman had to come second, or rather what was commonly taken to be fulfilment as a woman but on closer inspection only very rarely was, as an artist I had to serve my public, my public had a prior claim on me, where would we be if women artists pursued such ends, which fundamentally were purely selfish, and above all where would art be? But if I felt unable to refrain from my deeply self-interested wish for a child, he was sorry, but I'd have to look around for someone else to father it, he was sure I'd have no difficulty in finding some irresponsible individual, someone who thought more of his so-called personal happiness than anything else, an egotist not prepared to make the smallest sacrifice to art. That was what they'd all said, including John, who had walked back and forth on the dove-grey fitted carpet of the seventeenth-floor hotel bedroom in midtown Manhattan where we met every Wednesday afternoon after our first encounter, waving his hands in the air to lend his words more force, and who had then stopped in front of the window with a view of the Chrysler Building, briefly examined the skyline, then turned and added that the three children God had given him, for naturally children were gifts of God, had deliberately been conceived with a woman who was not at all artistic, you could only have children with a woman who was not at all artistic if you didn't want to risk disaster, even the smallest spark of artistic talent made a woman totally unsuitable for motherhood, only fools thought a woman's artistic talent could be combined with motherhood.

All this was going through my head as I walked through the stalls of the Naschmarkt on my way to Kettenbrückengasse, and the closer I came to the Death House the more despondent I felt. How could I burden a man who might not be quite as frail now as at the beginning of our acquaintanceship but was still weak, was still a child himself, with the information that I was expecting another? As I went upstairs to the second floor I met the pastoral assistant on the landing between the first and second floors, with a copy of *Die Presse* open in her hand, and when she saw me she began reading me a piece from it reporting that the neo-Nazi in the stocking mask had struck for the third time in the Augarten near the flak tower at around two in the morning, when he had robbed a girl from Isfahan, in her third semester studying computer science here, first of her clothing and then, as the doctor in casualties and emergency later clearly established, of her virginity, leaving a detailed account of what he had done next morning on the answerphone in the Iranian Embassy and demanding among other things the sacking of all Iranian taxi drivers in Vienna from their jobs. These cases seemed to be taking an unexpected turn, since the statements of the antique dealer who had been questioned on his girlfriend's rape at first purely as a matter of routine had become perceptibly more contradictory, and the Viennese police were beginning to wonder whether this internationally known specialist on netsuke, small Japanese objets d'art used to fasten kimonos, aged fifty-seven and three times divorced, might not have more to do with the three cases than anyone supposed at first, particularly as a brief search of his apartment in the embassy quarter, six rooms and a conservatory, had brought to light a collection of miniature warships from the period of the Third Reich, thus establishing the connection with Nazi ideology. The antique dealer obstinately persisted in claiming that the warships had been given to him by his parents at family parties here in Vienna in his third and fourth years of life, a claim which did not particularly impress the shrewd members of the

Vienna Police Department of Anti-Austrian Intrigue. Fräulein Haslinger looked up from *Die Presse* and said, terrible, terrible, if I asked her, such incidents ultimately rose from nothing but the fundamental lack of faith everywhere these days, and in addition of course a Vietnamese or Iranian girl couldn't count on God's protection with as much certainty as Christian Catholics, and when I objected that the young woman from the Dominican Republic might well be a Catholic, Fräulein Haslinger said possibly, but in her opinion the true faith decreased in proportion to its geographical distance from the Vatican. As I walked on she called after me that I seemed rather nervous, would I like to colour in a copy of the outline of the famous south rose window in the cathedral of Notre Dame in Paris, a window thirteen metres in diameter, she could let me have a copy and the coloured crayons too if I needed them, and I'd find that my peace of mind was restored in no time at all.

Josef, who as I saw when he opened the door had lost a little more weight, which again suited him, welcomed me in cheerfully and said, just imagine, over the last couple of days three young people had phoned saying they were thinking of taking lessons from him, the events of the last few weeks had shown him that I clearly brought him luck, a remark which I seized upon as the occasion to say that I wasn't so sure of that, because I was equally clearly pregnant, whereupon he looked at me, beaming, took me in his arms and said I had no idea how happy my news made him and by a strange coincidence, since as he had said he was sure that the consistent run of good luck he'd enjoyed for over a month now was connected with my entry into his life, he had been just about to ask me to marry him at Christmas in the Nine Choirs of Angels Church, the apartment was big enough for both of us to follow our own professions without getting in each other's way too much, he would give singing lessons in the living room and I could study my parts in the utility room, and as for the daughter we were expecting in midsummer next year, the little room facing north would be a positively ideal nursery for a future concert pianist. Some time in the next few weeks we'd go down to the cellar for the pearwood cradle in which he himself lay as a baby, bring it up here and dust it off, and he would tell the receptionist the good news straight away, so that she could get to work knitting and crocheting the baby clothes we'd need after Elisabeth's birth, he'd help out with that too, he hoped I wouldn't mind if we called the baby Elisabeth after his mother who had looked so like Sisi, and in memory of the beautiful Empress herself. When I said he had no idea how relieved I was by his reaction, so far my experiences with men had been rather negative, and not one of them was seriously prepared to take the role of a father in the usual sense of the word, Josef said that never having known his own father, the only child of the unmarried daughter of a famous composer, he was determined to spare Elisabeth the same fate.

That afternoon we worked together on the proper vocal expression of Schubert's song 'Courage!' and we had never performed a song so well together, nor had our voices been so harmoniously combined as at the end of the lesson, when we sang together: 'Cheerful in the world we go / in the wind and weather! / If there is no god on earth / We'll be gods together.' In the evening Josef insisted on escorting me back into the city centre, saying that in my condition I needed his support, you could slip only too easily on the streets of Vienna, wet with rain as they were at the moment, and the florist had pointed out that it got dark very early at this time of year and she'd advise him not to let his African beauty go out alone at night, an extreme right-winger in a black stocking mask was striking fear and trembling into the hearts of foreign girls living in the city, the numbers of whom were undeniably growing the whole time.

As we crossed the Stephansplatz we saw a young blonde girl musician sitting cross-legged on a piece of cardboard outside the cathedral and playing a dulcimer, and Josef threw her a five-schilling piece, which she caught skilfully in her left hand, clad like her right hand in a brightly coloured fingerless knitted glove, briefly interrupting the accompaniment of the music she was playing, and he said it was a long time since he'd heard the signature tune of *The Third Man*.

Around ten in the evening I called John at his production offices on the corner of Fifth Avenue and Fifty-first Street and told him he'd have to do the show without me, unforeseen circumstances meant that I neither could nor would leave Vienna at present. I heard him taking a deep breath to begin on an answer and then I hung up, went to Wilma's room and sat down on the bed with the blue notebook, and when Aunt Pia knocked at the door saying excitedly that the gentleman with the lovely deep voice wanted to speak to me at once, it must be something important, from his tone he seemed to be absolutely beside himself, I put the notebook down again, opened the door for a moment, went past the surprised eyes of Aunt Pia to the telephone, put the receiver back on, took it off again and placed it carefully on the lace doily protecting the vulnerable surface of the little round Art Deco table where the phone stood. Then I went back to Wilma's room and read on.

Ten

On Dr Leodolter's advice and at my employer's expense, I spent the two weeks after my delivery in a small private hospital near the Türkenschanzpark between Oberdöbling and Gersthof, where I soon recovered from the stress of the birth. Dr Doblhoff, disappointed and annoyed that I had borne him not a son but a daughter, who being female offered hardly any prospect of the continuation of his researches, visited me twice. The first time he brought me the present of a yellow rose, and having placed it in a vase he moved the iron chair in the hospital room close to my bed, sat on it, and told me that his dear wife had arrived by the Southern Railway a few days ago, she had made a wonderful recovery in the fresh mountain air of the South Tyrol, she was looking very well and had been cured of tuberculosis of the apices of her lungs, which really was a miracle, and now that she was back on her side of the bed, to which she had returned as was only natural on the very first evening, he had to say that a love match once made was a love match for ever, and even though his wife didn't cook nearly as well as I did he was happy to have her back in his household. Considering that they had rediscovered each other, and he was sure I would be glad of that too, he didn't expect I'd have any objection to his suggestion of calling the child Aphrodite, a small and admittedly rather sentimental token of esteem on his part to the person with whom he had shared his life for many years, even if, understandably enough, that person never

387

knew anything about the existence of her little namesake. So I would see it was all for the best, I need feel no anxiety on his behalf, said Dr Doblhoff, rising to his feet, the only thing that had given him some slight cause for concern these last few days was hearing from some medical students that his esteemed colleague Dr Freud was discussing dreamwork with increasing frequency in his lectures at the General Hospital, using terms obviously developed not by him, Freud, but by himself, Dr Doblhoff, terms which had come up in the very interesting private conversations the two of them had enjoyed so long and in such a friendly fashion. He couldn't think Freud, that very serious-minded neurologist, was doing it with any dishonest intention, Freud was above any low suspicion, yet he did feel some slight surprise at these borrowings, probably due to mere coincidence. And now he must be off, he and Aphrodite were going to attend a gala performance at the Court Opera that evening.

A few days later Dr Doblhoff paid me his second and last visit. Having added a white carnation to the yellow rose in the vase, he sat down on the iron chair again and said it was time to discuss my and Aphrodite's future, and he suggested that I return to the labour market as soon as possible, I'd spent enough time in this wickedly expensive private hospital and his financial means were not inexhaustible. Fortunately he had connections upon which he had been able to call, connections with court circles which would allow me to work in the Hofburg Palace as a silver cleaner and table-setter, an honourable profession, in fact a positive rise in the social scale for a female of humble background who had already to number a sojourn in the lunatic asylum in Vienna 9 among the episodes of her eventful career, and that was not a particularly good recommendation in a search for work. As for little Aphrodite, he had made arrangements for her to be accommodated in a clean, well-run babies' home in Taborstrasse in Vienna 2, he hoped I would agree to these dispositions. Then he shook my hand, thanked me for the delicious meals I had made him as his housekeeper, and expressed his very good wishes for my future.

So it was that when Aphrodite had been handed over to the care of the Discalced Carmelite nuns who ran the babies' home, I started work only a week later as silver cleaner and table-setter in the Tableware Chamber, as it was called, of the Hofburg Palace in Vienna. When I passed through the gate in Michaelerplatz into the Burghof, the imperial sentries were just changing guard in their gold-braided uniforms and their waving plumes, and I thought optimistically that for all the adversity I kept encountering, fate must mean well by me after all, having brought me straight to the centre of a huge empire and now allowing me to earn my bread in one of the most magnificent royal palaces to be found anywhere in the world. I went off to the court kitchens, which you entered from the palace courtyard known as the Schweizerhof, reaching them by way of a flight of stairs leading down to twelve low-ceilinged, vaulted hall-like rooms with broad pillars, where I introduced myself and was initiated into my new job by the head silver cleaner, a plump, blonde lady who said she hoped I was aware of the responsibility that went with the position of fourth silver cleaner upon which I was now entering, it would be my task to clean the place settings of gold and silver for the court table as well as the state vessels, that is the epergnes for fruit and sweetmeats made of gilded bronze with cut-glass inserts, and to lay that table. She hardly needed to emphasize that very special care must be taken over the cleaning and maintenance of the Great Milan Service, as it was known, of gilded silver, used exclusively at dinners in honour of heads of state or on other very special occasions. But now she must go and see at once to the family dinner, which as always took place at seven in the evening, the flower arrangements from the court nursery garden at Schönbrunn hadn't arrived yet, and the first silver cleaner would explain everything else. So saying the head silver cleaner took me into a kitchen furnished with copper pots and pans, basins of water for live fish, and large iceboxes, where three silver cleaners were sitting at a table pouring boiling water over silver candelabra to remove remnants of wax, then rubbing them down well with a cloth, and finally buffing them to a sheen with the finest silver-cleaning powder. The first silver cleaner handed me a small candelabrum and said I could sit down with them and start work, and while I sat there at the table polishing the candelabrum she explained that the silver and gold place settings were placed in soapsuds made from good white soap without any other ingredients, then boiled for a few minutes and finally rubbed dry with fine sawdust, and after that these items would be perfectly clean and shining. The cutlery and plates could be protected from tarnish by wiping them over with collodion diluted with ethyl alcohol, and to remove spots left by egg on the spoons you heated them in a boracic solution or rubbed them with soot. Then the third silver cleaner, a young girl with a small, triangular face, chestnut curls and lively hazel eyes who was busy cleaning a golden plate with burned and pulverized ammonium carbonate, dug me gently in the ribs with her elbow and said, giggling, that when Empress Sisi was staying in the Hofburg, which she did less and less frequently these days since she was so often away on her travels, they sometimes had the opportunity of laying the table in her apartments in the Amalientrakt area of the palace; Empress Sisi, who had always been rather odd, had been getting more peculiar every day since her fiftieth birthday, she was constantly exercising to keep her slim figure and ate almost nothing but a soup made of beef, chicken, venison and partridge, she also often drank ox blood, or more precisely the juices from six kilos of beef, and regularly consumed five to six raw egg whites, which she, the third silver cleaner, thought revolting. Here the first silver cleaner snapped at the third and said it wasn't our place to mock Their Majesties, Herr Wetschl the household steward had expressly forbidden it, and anyway Empress Elisabeth was one of the most beautiful women in Europe, she hadn't put on an ounce since she arrived as a very young bride, and she still weighed no more than fifty kilos, a large man's hand could span her waist and her hips measured an astonishing sixty-five centimetres, so she, the third silver cleaner, had better watch her wagging tongue. At this the third silver cleaner put down the golden plate, shook her curly head and said the first silver cleaner must be joking, the days when Empress Sisi had been a beauty were long gone, after all she was approaching sixty, and it was easy to see why she wouldn't have her picture taken any more and covered her face with a black veil, everyone knew she had a nasty rash on it, a remark that made the second silver cleaner, who was just dipping a silver knife with rusty marks on it into a solution of vinegar, say that was a lie, the Empress Elisabeth's complexion was as flawless as ever, and who should know better than she did, since before she became second silver cleaner she had spent quite a long time as assistant to Fanny Angerer, the Empress's favourite hairdresser and like herself a native of Spittelberg where her father was a barber, and she consequently had seen the Empress at close quarters and had even had the privilege, with several other hairdresser's assistants, of washing her wonderful dark hair, using vast quantities of raw egg yolks and about twenty bottles of French brandy, and had some-times held up the Empress's long, thick, silky braided tresses when the weight of her extraordinary crowning glory gave her a headache. It was true that the Empress had become a little eccentric, but you had to remember that her marriage to the Emperor had never been what you might call happy, and that her only son had died by his own hand, and she, the second silver cleaner, felt bound to defend that lonely, ageing woman, who had no influence at court and suffered from sciatica and severe nervous disturbances, against the thoughtless comments of igno-rant know-alls like her, the third silver cleaner, and she hoped that I, the new girl who was going to share a room with them – Maria, Wilhelmine and herself, Johanna – in the servants' quarters of Hofburg would show a little more respect for the Hapsburg family. I refrained from letting the three girls know that I had been only too well acquainted with the Empress's son while he was alive, and agreed to their suggestion of going to the Prater next Sunday to watch a big cab race.

On that first evening in the Hofburg I lay beside my new colleagues in my narrow bed in the servants' quarters as they talked to each other, whispering and giggling in the dark, and I thanked God I was so well off in my new post. The work was not strenuous, I was in pleasant company, there was plenty of food and compared to what had been set before me during my previous career in service it tasted excellent, and my job left me enough time to visit my daughter at weekends in the babies' home, where she was undoubtedly being very well cared for and suckled by an experienced wet nurse. My regret that the return of a woman believed as good as dead had put so sudden an end to the domestic bliss with Dr Doblhoff which had seemed within reach was more than compensated for by the joy I felt at the existence of little Aphrodite, and anyway Dr Doblhoff hadn't turned me out into the street like the Honourable von Schreyvogls, but had found me work and provided for the upkeep of our child, behaviour towards a female servant which must be accounted extremely generous.

Next Sunday, after laying the long table in the Redoutensaal, Maria, Johanna, Wilhelmine and I, dressed in our best, went off arm in arm to the Prater, where all Vienna had gathered on the Krieau trotting course to watch the cab race. Since on our wages we couldn't afford tickets to go in, we positioned ourselves by the fence around the racetrack, from where we could see the racing, and I could hardly believe my eyes when, on the box of a magnificent black cab at the front of the field, I saw none other than Karel Havelka, wearing the black velvet coat and waistcoat, check trousers, spotted white cravat and half-height top hat that were the cabby's characteristic costume, urging on his two horses with a long whip. Unfortunately he soon fell behind, and reached the finishing line second from last, whereupon he got down from his cab with his head bowed, moved away from the other participants and towards the ornamental fence, and leaned against it not far from where we were. He looked so disappointed that I couldn't help approaching him, putting my hand through the fence and laying it comfortingly on his right shoulder, whereupon he turned and said, smiling, why, if it wasn't the girl from the Church of Maria am Gestade who was so tired of life, he wasn't at all surprised to see me here, he'd known for certain that he would meet me again and I looked very nice in my pretty pink dress, much better than back then in winter, I didn't seem to have been doing too badly since then. I said that at the moment I couldn't complain, and he appeared to have been doing well too, for since he had taken part in the famous cab race in the Prater I concluded that he was no longer obliged to work for the cabbies as a groom but had become independent, to which he said, oh, it was his dream to be an independent cab driver and a dream that would probably never come true, but he was glad enough to have become a cabby in public employment, even if they were little better off than the grooms, since the authorities came down hard on the slightest infringements of the Regulations for Cabs and One-Horse Carriages, on one occasion he had failed to pick up a fare and had been put under arrest for three days, and on another occasion, when he had declined to take a fare on what he thought were good grounds, he had been given ten blows with a stick, well, the poor working folk of Austria-Hungary had to put up with outrageous injustice of that kind and he was coming to understand his younger brother. I asked Karel Havelka if Milan and Lyuba were still in Leopoldstadt jail accused of high treason, and he said yes, they were, the trial had been postponed, but there was a prospect of the Emperor's pardoning some of the accused on his birthday next August, or at least reducing their sentences. Since he loved his younger brother, despite Milan's seditious nature, he was hoping for the best. When I was about to leave after talking for some time to my fellow countryman, he detained me by taking hold of the full muslin sleeve over my left arm and said this time I didn't get away from him as easily as on our first meeting, and how about going bathing with him next Saturday in the Holzer River swimming pool on the left bank of the Danube below Kronprinz-Rudolf-Brücke, he was sure I too felt it was unusually hot for the time of year, he insisted on my coming, we'd meet at two on the afternoon by the left-hand pier of the bridge on the city side. I looked up at Karel, smiled at him, removed his hand gently with my own, and returned to Maria, Johanna and Wilhelmine, who had been following our conversation with the greatest interest, showered me with questions about the dark-haired cabby on our way back to the Hofburg, and said I mustn't hesitate for a moment to accept his invitation, such an invitation was an amazing stroke of luck for me, an unmarried mother, what a good-looking man, and a cabby too!

Next Sunday, when I had visited Aphrodite in the babies' home in Taborstrasse and reassured myself that she lacked for nothing with the Discalced Carmelites, and since the first, second and third silver cleaners hadn't stopped urging me to do so all week, I set off for the Danube to meet Karel Havelka by the third pier of Kronprinz-Rudolf-Brücke. After paying for our admittance at the cash desk of the Holzer open-air swimming pool, where we were given bathing suits and towels, and after we had put on the bathing things in the changing rooms, we lay down near the water in the early summer grass, and I must admit that I thought my fellow countryman very attractive with his thick black moustache and in a bathing suit of horizontal yellow and black stripes, and he impressed me a great deal when he jumped into the river, parting the waves with powerful strokes, because I have never learned to swim myself, in fact my mother, who couldn't swim either, forbade me to learn, saying that a person born on the twenty-ninth of February, and a Saturday at that, was in great danger of drowning. While Karel swam in the Danube, I looked around among the other bathers on the grass, and to my surprise saw Engelbert Kornhäusel, who I thought had taken his own life in his grief over his literary friends' criticism of his work and the closure of the Café Griensteidl. The dramatist, wearing an elegant dark-blue bathing suit, was sitting behind a female on a towel and writing on her back with a pen, and on closer inspection I saw that in so far as one could see from this distance, that definitely plump back belonged to none other than the von Schreyvogls' former parlour-maid, who had been so suddenly sacked by her mistress but whose shin, nonetheless, was privileged to be stroked affectionately by her former master a little later. Suddenly Engelbert Kornhäusel paused in his literary activity and looked up, and for a second our glances met before he lowered his eyes to that beautiful if plump back again and went on writing. At the same moment Karel, whom I had failed to notice emerging from the water in my surprise and pleasure at finding that my former protector had not committed suicide after all, startled me by placing his wet hands on my shoulder blades.

On the warm, moonlit early summer evening following that hot early summer afternoon at the Holzer open-air swimming pool, I wandered with Karel Havelka along the bank of the Danube, which was gently lapped by the gleaming waters, and when Karel stopped, raised my chin with his forefinger, turned my face up to the full moon and said he hadn't been mistaken, there really was a similarity between me and our Empress, and when he then brought his face closer to my own moonlit features and first the tips of his moustache, then the rest of the moustache and finally his mouth touched my lips, I did not resist, and was glad that Maria, Johanna and Wilhelmine had pestered me so long, saying that as an unmarried mother I mustn't let this unique opportunity pass me by without seizing it.

Next morning the sun woke me, shining in through one of the two attic windows in Karel's room on the bed where we lay, and I turned my head to one side and examined Karel's profile, his straight forehead, powerful nose and strong chin, and instead of that piercing sensation of a thin needle thrust into my heart that I always felt at the sight of Hans Holzer, my throat constricted and my bowels ached. Then the man who didn't know he had spent the night with an unmarried mother, let alone a thief, prostitute and former inmate of the lunatic asylum on the Alsergrund, opened his eyes with their thick, black lashes, smiled at me, stroked his moustache and my hair and said he had slept wonderfully well, and all because of me, who had given myself to him with an innocence that not only touched but excited him, a girlish timidity that you almost never found in Vienna, the Viennese women he had met so far were mostly prostitutes, hardened thieves who had stolen the money from his pocket, hysterical females fit for the lunatic asylum, or careworn unmarried mothers whose brats yelling in the next room would very soon drain a man of all desire, yes, now he stopped to think of it, the unmarried mothers were the worst of the lot, always talking about their children, always tiresomely insisting on knowing they were provided for, he personally had no time for children, children bored him. I was quick to say I could see what he meant, I wasn't fond of children either, not in the least, to which Karel replied that he was glad we were of one mind there, and it opened up the possibility of our continuing and deepening our acquaintanceship, which had begun under rather unhappy circumstances but was undoubtedly the will of Providence, and since yesterday evening, or more precisely last night, had developed so pleasingly; he was of an age when a man seriously thought of settling down, and he confessed that my delicate reserve and my likeness to the Empress Elisabeth fascinated him, had I never tried wearing my hair like hers, it would suit me very well. When I objected that I was fair, not dark-haired like the Empress, and anyway my hair was much shorter and less luxuriant than hers, and I would never succeed in achieving anything like her magnificent crown of hair, Karel said that made no difference, it was just a matter of emphasizing the similarity of our features a little, couldn't I try for his sake, here and now in his room, in front of the admittedly rather small and dull mirror over his chest of drawers. So I got up, stood in front of the mirror and braided my hair into several plaits which I wound round my head, and then turned to Karel, who had been watching from the bed and now moved his head slowly back and forth and said it was incredible, incredible, with my hair worn like that I was the image of the Empress, I must know he had adored the Empress Sisi for years, or to be precise since he was four years old. When I asked how that had come about, he said that as a young woman Sisi and her imperial husband had visited Bohemia, and his, Karel's, father, a woodcutter from the forests of southern Bohemia and also an ardent admirer of the Empress's beauty and charm, had made the difficult journey in his horse-drawn cart from the Bohemian Forest to Prague to see her. He, Karel, then aged four, ran after the cart as it drove away from his parental home, crying, and his father finally took pity on him, lifted him up on the box and took him to Prague, where they had mingled with the crowd waiting for the arrival of the imperial couple, standing by the side of the street near the City Hall in the Old Town. Although, as he said, he couldn't have been more than four at the time, he had never forgotten the moment when Sisi and Franz Joseph drove past them in a golden coach drawn by eight snow-white horses. The Empress's supernatural beauty as she smiled and waved to her Bohemian subjects had impressed him deeply as he, a poor, barefoot woodcutter's child who naturally had never been out of the Bohemian Forest before, stood there open-mouthed, staring at that lovely face, that magnificent chestnut hair with the sparkling diamond stars in it, the mauve dress and the little jacket trimmed with Siberian silver fox fur, and he didn't know what had come over him. Since then he had never stopped thinking of the Empress, his first love, taking a close interest in everything to do with her, and the fact that she had grown older hadn't made the slightest difference to this passion, for passion it was. I slipped back into bed with Karel, laid my head with its crown of hair on his shoulder, and said that since a happy stroke of fate had led me to the Hofburg, where I had recently taken the post of fourth silver cleaner and table-setter, I knew from a reliable source, namely the second silver cleaner, that despite her rank, beauty and wealth the Empress wasn't happy, whereupon Karel started up and cried, what, I worked in the Hofburg, that was amazing, what a privilege, I must know he had dreamed for decades of being taken into the service of the imperial couple, preferably as a coachman in the imperial-and-royal stables, he'd told me how besotted he was with horses, a passion he shared with Sisi who, as he understood from the newspapers, was an excellent horsewoman and rode boldly out on horseback in a black velvet habit, with a top hat and tall laced boots with spurs, three pairs of gloves worn one on top of the other, and her fan stuck in her saddle. He had to admit that he had tried several times to climb over the wall of the extensive park round the Hermes Villa and catch a glimpse of Empress Sisi galloping along on her Hungarian thoroughbred in the untouched woodland landscape among the deer and wild boar, but the wall was so high that he had never yet succeeded. It was one of his finest daydreams to be taking jump after jump beside her at a full gallop on an English racecourse, although of course he was aware that such dreams could never be fulfilled, for he knew that it was the sturdy, red-haired and rather deaf Scotsman Bay Middleton who had the privilege of riding at the Empress's side, a man of whom he felt bitterly jealous, just as for years he had been green with envy of Gyula Andrassy who, according to the gazettes, had succeeded in winning a permanent place in Sisi's heart on his first meeting with her, an occasion on which the Hungarian count had worn a coat embroidered with jewels, with a tiger skin flung over his shoulder. Then Karel gave me an inquiring glance and asked if I could understand such a passion, a passion with no realistic basis at all, an affection that had already lasted decades and so far had prevented his forming any significant connection with another woman, to which I replied I couldn't entirely put myself in his place, but I could to some extent see how he felt, for I had loved my mother, who sad to say died much too young, I had loved her very dearly, an emotion that could probably be compared with his feelings. At this Karel embraced me and cried happily that I was the first woman to understand his complex personality, even in the Church of Maria am Gestade he had known that our meeting was an extraordinarily fateful one, and when it came to the point he was a man of decision, so he was asking me here and now, in his bachelor bed in Vienna 8, whether I would marry him some time in the next few weeks, preferably on the Feast of the Assumption, in that same church.

Kind young reader with these lines before your eyes, try as a woman to understand the reasons that moved me, an unmarried mother and all alone in the world, first to consider the honourable offer of a fellow countryman whom I had found decidedly attractive in his black and yellow striped bathing suit, and by no means repulsive either during our first night together in his attic bedroom in a small and dilapidated building in Josefstadt, although I did not exactly love him in the usual sense of the word, and finally to accept him. I was tired of making my way through life always alone, I wanted to spend the rest of my days with a husband to whom I was married in the sight of God and man, I wanted to care for him and be protected by him, and not least to share my bed with him for ever, a bed from which the men I had known so far had always stolen away very soon. And dear young reader, please also try to understand something that is very hard to grasp, the fact that I couldn't summon up the courage to tell Karel Havelka about my daughter Aphrodite, then in the care of the Discalced Carmelite nuns, that I denied my own flesh and blood, for I knew that such a revelation would instantly make him withdraw his generous offer.

So it was that on the Feast of the Assumption I walked past the statue of St John of Nepomuk to the altar of the Church of Maria am Gestade beside Karel and followed by my bridesmaids Maria, Johanna and Wilhelmine, who carried the train of my wedding dress, a strikingly good copy of the dress Sisi had worn when, not yet seventeen years old, she married the young Emperor on 24 August 1854 in the Church of St Augustine, illuminated on the occasion by fifteen thousand candles and draped with red velvet, my future husband having unhesitatingly paid the larger part of his savings to have that copy made. My three colleagues were quite beside themselves with excitement when I told them about my wedding plans and exclaimed what a good match, they didn't know of another unmarried mother in or around Vienna who had succeeded in making anything like such a good match, and when I told them that Karel intended to spend the rest of his savings on a little honeymoon in Ischl they clapped their hands and cried, Ischl in the beautiful Salzkammergut, how enviable, as for them, they'd never been further than Pötzleinsdorf. Sure enough, directly after the wedding breakfast at the Merry Vintner on the Brillanten-grund, where the guests, besides several waterers and cab-horse grooms, included a number of my old acquaintances from the sewer system of Vienna, among them the fat-fisher from Burgen-land, although to our regret neither Milan nor Lyuba could come because they were still in prison, directly after the wedding breakfast we took the post coach to Ischl, where we spent a few days in a small inn and went for walks in the area, visiting among other places the imperial villa, which Karel was absolutely bent on seeing since it was where Sisi and Emperor Franz Joseph had met, a fact already known to me from my lessons with Fräulein von Roth-Rothenhorst. Imagine, said Karel as we stood in front of the magnificent building, putting his arm round my shoulders, ima-gine Sisi arriving from the Starnberger See dressed in mourning, in a high-necked black dress because one of her aunts had died, with her hair in plaits, overshadowed by her more beautiful and well-educated older sister, who had been picked as the Emperor's bride, but the lithe and lissom 23-year-old young Emperor in his smart general's uniform didn't hesitate for a moment, and had fallen in love at first sight with the child Sisi still was at the time, something that he, Karel, could understand only too well. And in our little room at the inn in the evening, when I took down the crown of hair I now wore daily at my husband's request and undid my plaits, Karel came up behind me, took me in his arms, the muscles of which he exercised twice a week at an athletics club in Meidling in the company of other cabbies and factory workers, butchers' and salters' journeymen, and asked me to go to the wigmaker Schnabl in Papagenogasse when we got back and buy at his, Karel's, expense a wig of long, thick chestnut hair, in a word hair like the Empress's in her youth. At this request I objected that I was really perfectly happy with the fair hair I had inherited from my mother, God rest her soul, even if it was straight and not very luxuriant, and besides it was midsummer, I would be sure to feel unbearably hot under a wig, and what would Maria, Johanna and Wilhelmine say if I turned up in the Hofburg wearing a hairstyle reserved for our Empress, whereupon Karel parted my hair at the back of the neck, kissed the parting lovingly and said he didn't entirely understand me, a young wife must read her husband's every wish in his eyes and couldn't refuse him such a small request, one that I would certainly not regret complying with if I could be persuaded to keep the wig on at night in the matrimonial bed as well. To this I said we'd see, and anyway I could go and see what the wigmaker Schnabl had in stock.

Two days after our return from Ischl the great popular festival in the Prater held annually in late August in honour of the Emperor's birthday took place, and Karel and I mingled with the crowd and walked in high good humour along the Hauptallee of the Prater. When we came to the Third Coffee House, a shabbily dressed, emaciated couple hurried towards us, greeting us with effusive affection, and we were just about to turn away from these strangers in painful embarrassment when the bearded, hollow-cheeked man asked if he had changed so much that his own brother didn't recognize him, whereupon Karel first looked hard at the man's face, then fell on his neck and cried was this possible, why had no one told him that the Emperor really had given an amnesty? In answer Milan Havelka, putting his arm round Lyuba – for it was they – said that we had no idea what they'd suffered in prison under investigation, in the prisons of the Austro-Hungarian monarchy those accused of high treason were treated worse than robbers and murderers, they had been free since yesterday and for the time being had moved into the tunnels of the canal and sewer system, but with the aid of a Flemish anarchist they had met in prison were about to set out for Rotterdam to take ship to America and try their fortune brewing beer in the Midwest of the United States, Czech beer was in great demand there, and perhaps they could import the Young Czech movement to the States and continue the project on which they had begun, the necessary destruction of the Austro-Hungarian monarchy. In any case, they couldn't stay a week longer in a country where the slightest liberal endeavour was suppressed with disproportionate brutality, they had recently heard that a few years ago the forty-six-metre statue of a woman known as the Statue of Liberty, erected in Paris and given to the Americans by the French as a gift, had been set up at the entrance to New York harbour on a plinth forty-seven metres high, a profoundly symbolic gesture that filled them, Lyuba and Milan, with the utmost confidence. But now we must drink to our unexpected reunion in the nearby inn The Whale, a place well worth seeing because its main entrance was through the lower jaw of a sperm whale caught in the Bering Sea, the beer was excellent, and we must explain to them, Milan and Lyuba, what strange and fortunate stroke of fate had brought us, Karel and Rosa, together.

After we had exchanged news at length over Hungarian goulash and Brünn beer of what had happened to us since we last met, Lyuba and I took our bags and went to the ladies' room together, and while we were waiting in line for our turn I told the best friend I had ever had, apart from Olga, that I had a daughter called Aphrodite now in a babies' home in Taborstrasse, of whom Karel, who hated children, must not know if I were not to jeopardize my marriage to him, a situation that made me particularly anxious because the child's father had recently threatened to stop his monthly payments to the Discalced Carmelites, since his invalid wife was confined to her sickbed by another attack of tuberculosis and nothing would help her but an expensive stay in a sanatorium in Davos. Lyuba thought for a little while, and then said she had found the solution to the problem: suppose Milan and she took little Aphrodite first to Rotterdam and then to the Midwest of the States with them, I must know how few chances were open to a servant's child and a female child at that in this country of ours where property was so unjustly distributed, but the new world they were about to enter would offer Aphrodite, which if I asked her was a very peculiar first name, entirely different circumstances in which she could live a happy and carefree life, and now that Lyuba came to think of it, as a mother I positively owed Aphrodite this opportunity.

Devout reader, with your feminine feelings you will have opened your eyes wide with horror on deciphering the above lines, wondering how anyone could put such a suggestion to a mother, but pray calm yourself, try not to judge too hastily, and remember that every mother has her beloved child's future at heart, a future very likely to be a sad one in Austria-Hungary, a future that would have obliged my daughter to tread the same thorny path that her mother had trodden before her. Believe me, the decision to let my child go cost me the greatest effort, believe me when I say that the pain I felt when I hugged and kissed Aphrodite for the last time two days later before entrusting her to Lyuba can be compared in intensity only with my grief when I sat by my mother's deathbed and she closed her eyes for ever, and believe me too when I tell you that I had nothing but my child's good in mind in parting from her. And when, in the near future, I must lay my shorn head in the noose of the former executioner's assistant Josef Lang, now the imperial-and-royal executioner, my last thought will be for my child who, as I have heard from Lyuba, is attending school in a city called Minneapolis in a state called Minnesota, and in her free time helps my friends, now married, to brew a bottom-fermented, strongly hop-flavoured and very light-coloured beer with an eleven per cent wort content.

15

The horse race in the Krieau, which I was watching from the second row of the grandstand through the opera glasses inlaid with mother-of-pearl that I had inherited from my mother, was in full swing. Magnolia, wearing a blood-red skirt and with her little plaits flying under her black riding hat, was in the lead with two other women jockeys, and as she made for the next jump I rose and cheered her on as loud as I could. Magnolia, I shouted, take the fence, and she spurred her chestnut thoroughbred on and flew over the fence, the hat falling off her head, and galloped on. Then the Empress Elisabeth made her way forward on her tall English mount, and although she was riding side-saddle in a long, black velvet dress, she caught up metre by metre, and kept hitting her horse with her crop until she was riding beside Magnolia, neck and neck, and her red-haired Scottish riding master, who was sitting beside me in the stand, jumped up too and shouted, Lizzy, you can do it! As if in a film close-up I saw the Empress's face looming large before me, and then it was my mother's face, distorted and ugly, and I cried, come on, Magnolia! and the sound of the crop grew louder and louder and I woke up. I could still hear a sound, and realized that someone was throwing pebbles at one of the bedroom windows. I stumbled out of my mother's bed and opened the window, and saw Magnolia standing there with a blue book in her hand, looking up at me and saying, Josef, let me in.

A little later I was sitting at the kitchen table drinking pepper-mint tea with Magnolia and telling her she ought not to have come to Kettenbrückengasse on foot at midnight from the building on the corner of Blutgasse and Domgasse, she knew they hadn't caught that extreme right-winger with the stocking mask yet, but she simply interrupted me and said this was important, she'd found out that Rosa was her great-grandmother. When I asked what gave her this peculiar idea she replied it was all perfectly clear, Rosa and Dr Doblhoff's child born in the stationary cab on the corner of Sensengasse and Lazarettgasse was called Aphrodite, and her grandmother had been called Aphrodite too, they were one and the same person. Here I objected that Aphrodite was certainly an unusual girl's name, but the coincidence of the name on its own didn't prove her theory, and anyway I had no idea what she was talking about, she must remember that I knew almost nothing of Rosa's autobiography. Here Magnolia leaned over the kitchen table and said in an urgent tone that didn't I understand, Lyuba and Milan had taken little Aphrodite to the Midwest, more precisely to the state of Minnesota and even more precisely to the city of Minneapolis, and when I asked who on earth Milan and Lyuba were she said she'd explain more about that later, but it was a fact that her grandmother had been at school in Minneapolis. When I said in some confusion that she was quite right, I really didn't understand a word of this, she explained impatiently that in Rosa's story Aphrodite's foster parents had set up as brewers in Minneapolis, and the surname of her, Magnolia's, grandmother Aphrodite had been Havelka, just like Rosa's, for the simple reason that Milan, who was foster father to Rosa's daughter, her grand-mother, had been Rosa's husband's younger brother. At this I clutched my forehead and said I was sorry, this story was abso-lutely beyond my powers of comprehension, you couldn't expect someone woken suddenly from the first phase of deep sleep to get the hang of these complicated relationships on the spot, where-upon Magnolia leaned back in the kitchen chair, began to laugh and said I was right, but anyway she was going to call her mother straight away, from here if I didn't mind, because only now did she understand why her mother had been reluctant to talk about it, it was extremely awkward to acknowledge that your own grand-mother had been executed for murdering her husband. I stood up, went over to Magnolia in my salmon-pink dressing-gown, raised her from the kitchen chair and said great-grandmothers, grand-mothers, mothers, my head was going round and round, why not put off the telephone call for a little while and spend the rest of the night with me in my mother's bed, she mustn't forget I had new pupils to whom I must devote my attention, so I needed my rest, teaching singing was a strenuous business and what was more, once we'd spent the considerable but not inexhaustible sum I had earned from the sale of the Pink Rose butterfly, it would be the basis of our family income. Magnolia smiled and said she'd go along with that suggestion, on condition that before she went to sleep she could read the rest of the tenth and last chapter of Rosa's story, having interrupted herself so suddenly in the middle of it.

Some time after Lyuba and Milan had left, I moved out of the servants' quarters of the Hofburg and into Karel's attic room in Josefstadt, a home too cramped for a married couple, and soon afterwards my husband said we could hardly move without bumping into each other in this poky attic room, a young married couple had a right to decent accommodation, and something must be done about our housing situation at once. Then he added that he had told me about his dream of working as a coachman in the imperial-and-royal stables some day, couldn't I ask around among the Hofburg staff, perhaps there'd be some prospect of his realizing that dream, and I thought about it for a while and then said I couldn't imagine the silver cleaners and table-setters, the cooks, assistant cooks and kitchenmaids, the butler's staff, the lackeys who waited at table and the sauce chefs being very helpful to me in this way, but I did have another idea, I could turn to the person whom I had to thank for my present situation, who might perhaps be willing to put in a word for my husband too. Karel replied that he appreciated my support, although it was quite natural, of course, for a newly married wife to stand by her husband, and it would be in my own interests too to help him fulfil the dream he had cherished so long of being somewhere near his Empress, I'd soon see an instant improvement in his temper, which had been rather gloomy because of his unsatisfactory situation in life. When my husband admitted so frankly to his need to be close to his first great love I felt a twinge of jealousy for the first time in my life, but I immediately suppressed that feeling and said I would get in touch with the person I had mentioned as soon as possible. Before Karel set off for the cab rank on the Graben he asked, in passing, whether I had been to see the wigmaker Schnabl in Papagenogasse yet.

A few days later, when I entered the court kitchens wearing a flowing wig of genuine red-brown human hair, the head silver cleaner flung her hands up to her white cap in bewilderment and asked what all this was, I couldn't go about in the Hofburg in a wig that made the Empress's unique way of dressing her hair look ridiculous, particularly since this was one of those rare, brief periods when, having returned unexpectedly from Corfu, she was back here in her apartments in the Amalientrakt expecting her table to be laid by the table-setters, which included me, the head silver cleaner didn't mind how I went about in Vienna, although she wondered what my husband, who in the opinion of the first, second and third silver cleaners was as delightful as he was experienced, would think of such headgear, but anyway my hair had to look neat and tidy at work, and I'd better take that monstrosity off my head immediately. So I meekly put my false hair down beside the hand-operated spit on which four hundred fowls could be roasted all at once in an hour, and with Maria, Johanna and Wilhelmine I went off to the Amalientrakt to lay the silver for the Empress's breakfast in an understandable state of great excitement, for I had seen her only once, and then she was deeply veiled and driving in a black coach in the Prater.

When we opened the door to her apartments a female voice said the table was to be laid in the drawing room as soon as possible, and we entered that room hesitantly and on tiptoe. The sight of the Empress, no longer young but slim as a reed and in my eyes wonderfully beautiful, who was wearing a coal-black silk dress with a long train and trimmed with pitch-black ostrich feathers, had her long hair undone and was swinging from an exercising ring fitted in the doorway between the drawing room and her boudoir, and before whom we curtseyed deeply, has made an indelible impression on my memory. We made haste to lay the table and left the Empress's apartments, curtseying again.

In the evening I told Karel about this momentous encounter, and he urged me to describe every detail of the Empress's appearance and the furnishings of her rooms, and finally said, sighing, I had no idea how he envied me my experience, only an appointment as imperial-and-royal court coachman, and the prospect of occasionally getting a glimpse of the woman he adored that such an appointment would entail, would liberate him from the torments of his yearning for her presence and thus make our life together into a satisfactory marriage, indeed our marriage was already developing in a very promising way through my agreeing to wear the chestnut wig in various situations. Once again I suppressed my budding jealousy, and one day soon afterwards I visited Dr Doblhoff in his consulting room in the lunatic asylum in Vienna 9 to ask him to use his influence in court circles on my husband's behalf, and also to tell him that he could stop the payments for our daughter, since she was no longer with the Discalced Carmelites but had left recently for another continent. On hearing of my marriage Dr Doblhoff said he hoped I hadn't made up my mind to that step overhastily, and he was also sorry for it because now that his wife was back in a sanatorium he had been going to suggest that I return to keep house for him until further notice, although he must say that my decision about little Aphrodite was a considerable relief to him both emotionally and financially. Then he said he would get in touch with Count Paar, the Emperor's general adjutant and an intimate friend of his parents-in-law, and perhaps the Count could do something for my husband. I said I greatly appreciated his helpfulness, for I knew what a busy man he was and I thought he looked rather tired, to which he replied bitterly that that was because of the perceptible deterioration of his relationship with Dr Freud, whose character, unfortunately, was not as honourable as he had always supposed, for to his great disappointment and indeed indignation the neuropathologist had told him that he was planning to publish a pioneering work on the interpretation of dreams based on the discussions between the two of them, and had shown him part of the manuscript, on reading which he had immediately realized that Freud had stolen the results of his own research, the fruits of years of intensive reflection, a manner of conduct not untypical of persons of Semitic origin, and that the father figure he had idolized was in fact no better than a mean, common thief. However, added Dr Doblhoff, that was life, life spared you nothing, you always had to expect setbacks, he would continue his path of exploration of the dark interior of the human mind and was probably about to turn to a new and extremely interesting field, the study of obsessive-compulsive neuroses. I then said that since he was talking of the human mind, I would like to ask him, just by the way, about certain kinds of behaviour on my husband's part: he dwelt in what might almost be called a morbid manner on a past love, which naturally made me jealous, for instance he wanted me to do my hair in the same way as this person, and wear similar clothes, he was drawn to places linked with her, and in a word I was a little uneasy. Dr Doblhoff said I needn't worry, what I was describing seemed to be a harmless case of obsession deriving from an early sexual inhibition and the fixation that went with it, a mild disturbance that in his opinion wouldn't have a very harmful effect on our marriage; he thought that given suitable understanding on my part the symptoms would soon die down of their own accord, and in any case he would advise me to comply with my husband's wishes as far as I could. And now he must ask me to get off his couch, since it was booked for the next hour by his patient Emma O., who suffered from compulsive brooding.

Dr Doblhoff did indeed put in a good word for my husband, and only a few weeks later Karel began his new job as imperial-and-royal court coachman in the imperial-and-royal stables, so the dream of his life had come true. At the same time we moved into a roomy apartment above the stables, which went with Karel's new appointment, and these two changes led to a considerable improvement in his temper, which in its turn had a good effect on my own state of mind, and as a result my status as a married woman satisfied me more and more every day. On the advice of the *Housewives' Golden Treasury*, which I took out of my old cardboard case for the first time in a long while, I decorated our new home and took pains to follow the guidelines for married women and housewives laid down by the author of the book, according to whom the wife managed the home with pleasure, love and zeal, welcomed her husband lovingly after his day's work and lavished affectionate attentions on him, a course of conduct that guaranteed her greatest happiness and was in itself her finest reward. After work in the Tableware Chamber I hurried home and went to great pains to prepare everything so that Karel, whose hours of duty ended a little later than mine, would have no cause for any complaint on his own return. And if he did take exception to something, I thought of my mother, who had always said that nothing was more satisfying than to be of service to one's neighbour. I also did all I could to approach Karel's ideal and that of my mother and the *Housewives' Golden Treasury*, and to become a truly feminine creature who ensured her own happiness and the happiness of others by radiating feminine kindness, mildness and helpfulness, gentle understanding and sympathy, always giving with open hands and from a full heart, never obstinately maintaining her own point of view but showing herself yielding and conciliatory in any argument. If my powers ever failed me briefly in pursuit of this ideal, I called to mind a story my mother had told me in the attic bedroom in Marienbad about a woman she admired called Griselda, an uncommonly patient and obedient person. When my husband approached me one day asking me if I couldn't do him the small favour of blackening my teeth a little, he remembered that when, at the age of four, he had first seen the Empress Sisi on her visit to Prague her teeth had been rather black, a feature that made her even more attractive to him, if I saw what he meant, then my study of the *Housewives' Golden Treasury* and my memories of my beloved mother's principles made it not too difficult for me to comply with this wish, even if I found it rather odd at first. Nor did it cost me anything to listen attentively when Karel told me in detail about the carriages and state coaches, the caparisons and harnesses for hacks and carriage horses in the imperial-and-royal stables which he had to look after in his work, particularly the so-called imperial coach in which Princess Elisabeth of Bavaria, the future Empress, rode on her way to her wedding in the Church of St Augustine, as well as the black neo-Baroque court funeral coach. Towards the end of his accounts he would always say quietly that his heart's desire was to drive Empress Sisi just once in her life in the official state coach, a vehicle representing the late culmination of Viennese coach-building, a wish that, as he well knew, could hardly be realized, because for one thing the Empress was almost never in Vienna, and for another she would be driven by no one but her personal coachman, so consequently his, Karel's, secret ambition was to be successor to that coachman, an endeavour in which he had no doubt he would be supported in due course by my connections with Dr Doblhoff and Dr Doblhoff's connections with Count Paar. He was also sorry that his place of employment was not in the immediate vicinity of the Hofburg, Schönbrunn or the

Hermes Villa, those places where the Empress stayed when she was in Vienna, and that as a result nothing had yet come of his hopes of seeing her.

So weeks, months, and even several years passed by, and I became accustomed to the calm routine of married life, its regularity broken only by certain and to me rather unwelcome diversions caused by the state of mild obsession into which Karel's persistent infatuation with the Empress Elisabeth now and then cast him, and I sometimes thought with amazement of my turbulent past, which seemed to me like someone else's life. Following Dr Doblhoff's advice, I tried to show understanding for my husband's occasionally rather peculiar wishes, agreeing, for instance, to have a copy of the dress the Empress had worn on her visit to Bohemia, which Karel had drawn from memory on a piece of paper, made by the Slovakian dressmaker in the alterations shop on the corner of Wollzeile and Postgasse, as well as good copies of other clothes worn by Sisi, and he tried to help the dressmaker by showing her photographs cut from the newspaper in which the Empress was wearing these clothes, even though these fancies of his caused us temporary financial difficulties and earned me the envy of Maria, Johanna, Wilhelmine and the head silver cleaner, who said I was vain and accused me of trying to raise myself above my station. It was only when Karel asked me to try to get my weight down to the fifty kilos that Elisabeth had weighed all her life that I felt some reluctance, and his request that I would expose myself to draughts now and then when I had the chance, to induce the fits of coughing so characteristic of the Empress, caused our first matrimonial quarrel. When I accused him of thoughtlessness and heartlessness Karel said I was the heartless one, if I loved him as much as I said I wouldn't hesitate to risk contracting slight pulmonary disease, like the Empress, and employ suitable means of achieving the anaemia that had lent Elisabeth her inimitable elegant pallor, I'd soon see that such signs of illness would increase his desire for me inordinately, and would therefore be for my own good. So I dried my tears and tried to comply with his wishes as best I could, an endeavour that first led to my fainting several times because of insufficient food and excessively tight lacing of my corset, and later resulted in a severe attack of pneumonia with a high temperature as a result of my frequently standing by a window left open to admit the winter cold, an illness that prevented me from doing my work as a silver cleaner and table-setter for three weeks, something not at all well received by the head silver cleaner.

Soon after my recovery I decided to visit Dr Doblhoff again and confide to him my concern over my husband's increasingly strange behaviour, but Dr Doblhoff once again reassured me and said such conduct was nothing unusual among obsessive-compulsive neurotics, it was the reaction to a suppressed desire of a sexual nature in early childhood and represented compensation for it, nothing more. Before I left I told Dr Doblhoff another of the dreams I'd recently had, in which I desperately tried to prevent my husband from stabbing Empress Elisabeth through the heart with a file, but Dr Doblhoff immediately became impatient and said the short period of our shared past on which we could look back gave me no right to waste his time with nonsensical tales, his patients needed him urgently, he was also in the course of starting proceedings against that Jewish traitor and deceiver Freud, for the man whom he, Dr Doblhoff, had with unpardonable naivety thought so honest was well on the way to claiming authorship of the findings laboriously acquired by himself, Dr Doblhoff, in the field of obsessive-compulsive neurosis, something that must at all costs be prevented, and to cap it all Aphrodite was at death's door in Davos, which led him to ask once more whether I wouldn't be willing to take over the running of his household at 16 Berggasse again.

When I had declined this request of Dr Doblhoff's, I left the lunatic asylum and went back to the matrimonial home, where I found my husband standing in front of the long mirror in our living room in one of the dresses copied from Sisi's wardrobe, the delicate rose-pink silk gown with its wide crinoline which she had worn on her arrival in Vienna as the Emperor's fiancée. When I asked what he was doing, he said calmly perhaps I'd be good enough to go into the bedroom and fetch the chestnut-brown wig of genuine hair made by the wigmaker Schnabl in Papagenogasse, put it on him and tell him how it suited him, whereupon I ran weeping into the boxroom and locked myself in. About a quarter of an hour later my husband's insistent knocking made me open the door, and when I saw him standing there still in the dress, with a red-brown wig on his head, I burst into tears again and cried that I wasn't sharing a bed with him for a single night longer, from now on I would sleep on the divan in the boxroom, whereupon Karel took me so tenderly in his muscular arms developed at the athletics club and at present covered with pink silk that I was unable to put my threat into practice but let him carry me, sobbing quietly, through the bedroom doorway and to our matrimonial bed.

Next day I told Karel I couldn't go on living with a man who was in the grip of a passion for another woman so strong that he actually tried to turn himself into the beloved, but Karel begged me not to leave him, saying he was sure his passion, admittedly uncontrollable so far, would die down if he finally had an opportunity to see Empress Sisi a second time, to see her as she was now, a woman of almost sixty long past her youthful bloom, the sight would sober him, would release him from his unhealthy desires and enable him to turn to me at last. As a table-setter, he said, I had access to the Empress's apartments, and if I valued the continuance of our marriage, as he supposed I did, I could smuggle him into them. I thought for a while and then said I'd see what I could do, and he must get himself a black mask to wear over his eyes, just in case, and when my husband looked questioningly at me I said I would tell him what it was for when the time came.

A few weeks later Empress Elisabeth and her lady companion came back from a short visit to French-speaking Switzerland, and I set about putting my plan into action. When the head silver cleaner told us table-setters to lay the table next day for the fortifying broth the Empress intended to take at noon, I said casually that it wasn't worth the four of us traipsing off to the Amalientrakt just to lay a single soup plate and a single gilded spoon, my colleagues were very busy preparing for the court ball, and if she, the head silver cleaner, had no objection I would set the Empress's table myself, to the best of my knowledge there were supplies of place settings in the Empress's private kitchen in her apartments. The head silver cleaner agreed to my suggestion, so I was able to tell my husband that evening that the moment when he would see the Empress at close quarters was very near, he was to be ready with the black mask intended to prevent his being recognized during his secret visit, an announcement that cast him into a state of high excitement.

Next day we entered first the Burghof and then the Amalien-trakt together, arousing no suspicion, and when we reached Elisabeth's private kitchen I asked Karel to keep quiet and wait for me. I went into the kitchen, where Theresia Teufel, Sisi's cook, was busy preparing the fortifying imperial broth from beef, chicken, venison and partridge, I took a gilded soup spoon and a deep plate from the china cupboard, left the room and climbed with my husband up the stairs to the Empress's apartments. When I knocked I heard the Empress's voice telling me to bring the plate into the bathroom where she, the Empress, was taking a bath in warm olive oil, for as she expected I knew, olive oil keeps the skin smooth, whereupon I cautiously pushed down the door handle and opened the door, indicating to Karel that he was to put on the black mask and follow me, and went on into the Empress's bathroom, the door of which was half open. I curtseyed, and carrying the soup plate and the gilded spoon I went over to the Empress Sisi lying there in the big copper tub, giving Karel an opportunity to see his first love through the half-open door, but when I turned to leave the bathroom my husband suddenly rushed

416

through the doorway and was about to jump into the tub with her and embrace her, whereupon the Empress began to scream, a reaction that made Karel abandon his project and take to his heels, and since the many imperial-and-royal guards stationed at strategic points in the Hofburg were so slow to answer Elisabeth's cries for help, he succeeded in escaping.

As a consequence of this incident, as surprising as it was disagreeable, I was summoned to account for myself to the head steward, who said sternly that it was irresponsibly negligent not to have closed the door to the Empress's apartments after entering them, thus giving the opportunity of entrance to the masked man who must have been acting from the worst of motives and unfortunately had not yet been found, he had probably been lurking outside the door waiting for such a moment, and I was dismissed without notice.

When I returned to the matrimonial home over the imperial-and-royal stables after my sudden sacking from my job in the imperial-and-royal court kitchens, I found Karel pacing up and down in a state of great agitation on the parquet living-room floor, wringing his hands. He immediately began heaping reproaches on me, asking how I could have involved him in a venture which had done the very opposite of what was intended, namely to cure him of his passion for the Empress, but instead had made it flare up again with extraordinary ardour, on seeing her lying in the copper tub like a beautiful mermaid with her loose hair wet he had lost his head, Sisi wasn't at all old and faded, as he had expected, but even more desirable because of her greater maturity, and now what was he to do, his ill-starred affections would drive him to distraction, and as his wife it was my duty to stand by him. At these words I thought apprehensively of the dream I had had the night before, in which Karel, holding a knife, had followed a woman with long chestnut hair going up a narrow spiral staircase, but I tried to hide my anxiety and calm my husband to the best of my ability. We soon went to bed, and when I woke briefly that

417

night, the other half of our matrimonial bed was empty, but since Karel would sometimes get up several times in the night, go to the kitchen and drink a glass of water I thought no more of it, but turned over and went back to sleep.

Two days later I read in the *Reichspost* that around midnight, in the Hauptallee of the Prater, where prostitutes waited for clients, an unknown man had tried to rape three of them in turn, but luckily he had not succeeded in any of the three cases, since the women had defended themselves vigorously and driven off their attacker, a stocky, broad-shouldered, middle-aged man whose features could not be made out in the darkness. A striking feature of the case was that all three women had been tall and slim, with long, thick, red-brown hair, which suggested that the perpetrator had special preferences, and women of this type were advised to be cautious if they went out at night, since experience suggested that the man might strike again. When I read these lines I remembered that when I briefly woke up on the night in question Karel had not been in the matrimonial bed, and the information about the women's red-brown hair made me uneasy, but then I dismissed the faint suspicion that had risen within me, and indeed reproved myself for allowing such an outlandish idea into my head. My husband might have some peculiar habits, but he was not a violent man. That evening Karel skimmed through the paper, shook his head and said a woman couldn't feel her life was safe in this city, I must be careful not to go out in the evening except in his company, obviously there was a monster roaming near the Prater.

When I was leaving home next morning to go to the fish market by the Danube Canal and buy carp, the wife of Archduchess Valerie's personal coachman, who also lived over the imperial-and-royal stables, asked me if I'd heard that a seventeen-year-old washerwoman had been overpowered and abused by a man outside the Ulrichskirche on her long journey home from choir practice with the Dornbach Folk Chorus, just imagine, outside a church, and she was found there in a bad way a few hours later; the description the poor child had given of the perpetrator coincided in almost every respect with the one the Prater prostitutes gave of their attacker, it seemed that there was a successor to the Beast of Ottakring who had prowled Vienna six years ago. The strange thing was that when the girl came back to her senses her teeth had been blackened, a circumstance that no one had yet been able to explain, but at any rate it wasn't safe to venture out of doors after seven in the evening, Vienna wasn't what it had been ten years ago, that was what came of the influx of ethnic groups of inferior race from the outlying regions of the Empire, particularly Jews from the east, Ritter von Schönerer was quite right, but now she had to be on her way, fresh rolls from the Baumgartner bakery always sold out fast in the morning. So saying, Frau Bartok hurried away, and I stood there for some time in the hall of the building to recover from the shock I had been given by mention of the victim's blackened teeth. On my way to the fish market the suspicion I had so easily been able to quell two days ago arose in me again, and this time I couldn't shake it off so easily. As soon as I had bought two Danube carp, not too fat, from my usual fishmonger I decided to go and see Dr Doblhoff at once, unannounced, and I was lucky enough to meet him as soon as I entered the lunatic asylum, in one of the pale lime-green corridors of the building. When he had asked me with a touch of annoyance what problem brought me to him today, he hoped it wasn't too urgent because he was on his way to see his lawyer in Blumenstockgasse, there was no end in sight yet to the proceedings against that wretched caftan-wearing Jew Freud, which were costing him a mint of money, I asked him straight out if he thought it possible for someone to turn to crime because of what he called an obsession, to which my former employer and doctor replied that it was entirely out of the question, a neurosis was not a psychosis, he had already assured me several times that my husband's behaviour must be considered the mere vicarious satisfaction of a suppressed conflict between the two tendencies of libido and resistance, and perhaps I would now stop pestering him about this tiresome matter, and when I added that I was beginning to fear my husband was leaving our bed by night to go out and rape women, Dr Doblhoff stared at me and said he very much hoped that the monstrous and absurd accusation I had just made was not the symptom of a new outbreak of the derangement which had once made it necessary for me to be confined in the lunatic asylum, and I had better go home and lie down for a few hours.

On my way home to the imperial-and-royal stables, I decided to stay awake if I could next night to make sure that Karel spent it entirely in the matrimonial bed, and by dint of drinking several cups of fresh coffee around six in the evening I succeeded in doing so. I held my breath when my husband rose without a sound at midnight, slipped into his clothes, flung the tiger skin lying beside the bed over his shoulder, and left the bedroom. When I heard the front door quietly closing I too got up, put on my old grey-brown hooded cloak, fastened the black mask over my face, and followed Karel at some distance through the dark, empty streets of the city of Vienna, along Siebensterngasse and down Stiftgasse and Lindengasse to Mondscheingasse, where to my surprise he hid behind the trunk of a plane tree a few metres from the Merry Vintner tavern and bent his gaze on the front door of the inn, whereupon I in my turn hid in the entrance of a building and kept watch on my husband. Before long a female figure came out of the front door of the inn and, walking fast, passed first Karel and then me without noticing either of us, whereas at close quarters I recognized her as the waitress Slavka, a pretty young woman born in Ljubljana who has a wealth of chestnut hair. As soon as Slavka had disappeared round the next corner, Karel followed close on her heels, and when he too had turned into the side street I followed him myself at a distance of about fifty metres. The echoing sound of Slavka's heels was all that broke the silence of the night; the waitress was walking fast towards the suburbs, and as she crossed a little park, my husband quickened his pace, caught up with her, flung himself on her, held her mouth shut and wrestled her to the ground, at which I ran to the pair of them, flung myself on the tiger skin over Karel's back and bit him as hard as I could on the back of the neck, so that he screamed with pain, let go of the waitress, shook me off and disappeared among the lime trees. Thereupon, and without a word, I helped the young woman, who was sobbing quietly, to get to her feet, then turned and without answering her when she asked who I was, or letting her detain me, returned to the Inner City and our matrimonial home and got back into bed. Soon afterwards Karel cautiously opened the bedroom door, took off the tiger skin and spread it on the floor beside the bed again, undressed and also lay down to sleep.

Next day was a beautiful, clear autumn day, to be precise it was 10 September 1898, and I decided to make use of the sunny weather to clean the windows of our apartment. I was just standing on a first-floor window sill, wiping over the panes with a rag and a solution of diluvial chalk, an infallible method of making glass spotless and shining, when Frau Bartok, weeping aloud, came to the open window of the apartment next door and called, in tears, oh, what a tragedy, had I heard already, the Empress Elisabeth was dead, treacherously assassinated, an Italian anarchist had thrust a file into her heart on the banks of Lake Geneva, oh, the poor Emperor, what a good thing he had Frau Schratt or he would probably never survive the news, such trials as the poor man had to bear, the House of Hapsburg was under an unlucky star, what a misfortune, if you asked her she'd never trusted those Italians, deceitful creatures, the lot of them. While I was still struck by amazement at finding my dream of the file as an assassination weapon had come true, if in a slightly different form, my husband came out of the stables, let himself drop heavily on the living-room sofa, and buried his face in his hands. It was incredible, he then sighed, only two hours ago he had received word of his appointment as coachman to the Empress, her previous personal coachman having suffered a sudden stroke, one of the dreams of his life had been fulfilled, but too late, for only an hour ago he had learned that Empress Elisabeth was no longer among the living, he would never drive her in her state coach, the only drive on which he would take her would be her journey in the imperial funeral coach to the Capuchin crypt, where she was to be buried beside her son.

I went over to Karel, a broken man sitting there on the living-room sofa, stroked his head comfortingly, and couldn't believe that this was the same man who had followed a young woman right through Vienna last night with a tiger skin over his shoulder and had tried to rape her. Frieda the unofficial working girl must have been thinking of such contradictory characters as his when she talked to me in Vienna Neudorf Prison and House of Correction and spoke of the shadow side of human beings and the complex nature of certain individuals, these were the experiences she had recommended to me, this was the real, intense life she had suggested I lead. I looked at Karel's scalp, where the hair was thinning, thought of my good mother and what she would have said of my present existence, and then I sank down on the sofa beside my husband, laid my head on his shoulder and began to weep.

That evening I read in the late edition of the *Reichspost* that the sexual offender terrorizing Vienna, who had obviously taken recently to wrapping himself in a tiger skin, a gesture eloquently indicative of his nature as a ravening beast, had struck again, attacking the waitress Slavka C., aged twenty-three, in a lonely park on the outskirts of the city last night, and the fact that the attempted rape had not succeeded was due to a mysterious figure who had hurried to the young woman's aid, whereupon the man had fled. The account went on to quote Slavka's statement, in which she described first her attacker and then her rescuer, who had worn a voluminous hooded cloak and a black mask and had fallen on the man fearlessly, and without whose intervention she might well not be alive now. She asked her guardian angel to come forward and accept the reward of a waitress's monthly wages that she was offering in gratitude for the assistance rendered.

Next night I went to pains not to go to sleep again, but unfortunately did not succeed, and when I woke up in the morning my husband was stretching in bed beside me and said he had had a very good night's sleep, he felt considerably better, and was in a position to accompany the dead Empress on her last journey to the Capuchin crypt without collapsing on the coachman's box in grief for his loss. I glanced surreptitiously at Karel, and suddenly I remembered the golem of whom Olga used to speak so often in the old days in the Ursuline convent in Prague, and I felt afraid of this man who shared my bed and board but whose soul was still a mystery to me. When Karel had gone to the stables I unfolded the *Reichspost* with trembling fingers and read to my horror that the monster in the tiger skin had claimed another victim, Wilhelmine H., employed as a silver cleaner in the Hofburg, who was on her way home from a performance at an inn in Floridsdorf where the popular Vienna salon yodelling artist Luise Montag had been appearing, a performance that went on until the early hours of the morning, when the pervert pulled her into some bushes, abused her and forced her to have intercourse. According to the victim's statement, the criminal had groaned the name Elisabeth several times during the rape, a clue that the authorities intended to follow up zealously.

The certainty that my pleasant, cheerful former colleague had been attacked and abused by my husband made me very angry, and I decided to abandon the marital loyalty I had maintained so long, go to Wipplingerstrasse police station and tell the police what I knew. But I had hardly begun making my statement to the officer on duty, a sullen young man with straggling hair receding from his forehead and a long scar on the left cheek, when he interrupted me and said, sounding bored, that so far as this case was concerned the police were taking no more statements, it was about to be solved, and when I cried that I knew the rapist, it was my husband and he must be arrested immediately to prevent him from ravaging the female population of Vienna any longer, the young man looked me up and down stolidly and told me not to talk nonsense, adding that although he was not authorized to tell me anything about the state of the case he would do me the kindness of informing me that a former inmate of the lunatic asylum in Vienna 9, a maniac who was a danger to the public and had already several times threatened the lady who shared his life, a well-known musician, with her own clarinet, was under strong suspicion of the rape, so I had better keep my deranged suppositions to myself, we chronically underemployed Viennese housewives had nothing better to do than bother the Viennese police, permanently labouring under a heavy workload as they were, with our fancies. At the mention of the supposed rapist my heart missed a couple of beats, for there could hardly be any doubt that this was Hans Holzer, whom I had last seen in the Last Drop Inn in Heiligenstadt, and who was now in danger of being unjustly suspected of dreadful crimes, and I took the sleeve of the officer's uniform and begged him desperately to listen to me, because I was telling the truth, the monster with the tiger skin was none other than my husband Karel Havelka, whereupon the officer, raising his voice, said this had to stop, would I please immediately let go of him, a police officer whose job it was to maintain public order, or he would have to take extreme measures, arrest me in the name of the law and lock me in the sobering-up cell of Wipplingerstrasse police station until I had calmed down.

Dear reader, put yourself in my position, the position of a woman whose life had been heading inexorably, as if guided by fatal forces, towards the hopeless situation in which she finally found herself, a union sanctioned by church and state with a husband whom she did not love in the usual sense of the word, who had turned out quite early to be a prey to dubious impulses and was later revealed as a violent criminal, far away from the only man, with the exception of Crown Prince Rudolf who had met his death prematurely, for whom she had ever felt really deep affection, and whom she could not protect from suspicions as outrageous as they were unfounded, and then, dear reader, pity me.

The night after my visit to Wipplingerstrasse police station I did not have to make any effort to stay awake, but tossed and turned, full of anxiety and uneasiness, beside my husband, who appeared to be sleeping peacefully, and waited for the beginning of the day on which Elisabeth, Empress of Austria and Queen of Hungary, was to be laid to rest. Towards midnight my eyes closed, and half asleep I saw Karel before me, sitting at the barred window of a prison cell writing, Karel with the executioner's assistant Josef Lang placing a cape round his neck and grinning, and I woke from my drowsy state with a start and saw that the other side of the bed was empty and the tiger skin had gone. At the same time I heard footsteps in the street below the open windows of our apartment, and I jumped up, threw on my hooded cloak, took a carving knife with an oak handle from the drawer of the kitchen dresser, hid it in the folds of my cloak and hurried out of the apartment and out of the building, just in time to see Karel disappearing round the corner of Hofstallstrasse and Babenbergerstrasse. Once again I followed him through the deserted Inner City of Vienna, walking at a safe distance behind him over the Opernring, down Albrecht-gasse and Tegethoffstrasse, and past the Capuchin church to Kärntnerstrasse and the Stephansplatz, where my husband con-cealed himself in the entrance of a building at the opening of Jasomirgottgasse opposite the huge doors of the cathedral, where he seemed to be waiting for something. I stopped at the corner of Stock-im-Eisen-Platz and stepped behind a board fence marking off a building site at the end of the Graben, a position from which I could see Karel in the light of the gas lamps through the gaps in the fence, although he could not see me. Soon afterwards the cathedral bells rang, a signal that midnight Mass was over, and the congregation came out of the building, first in a throng and then one by one, and dispersed over the concourse outside. One of the last to leave the cathedral was a tall, slender, willowy girl with a beautiful dark crown of hair and a large black shawl around her shoulders. She turned to look at the nave again as she came out, bowed her head, crossed herself and then went along the right-hand side of the cathedral to the back of the building. At this Karel emerged from the darkness of the entrance of the building in Jasomirgottgasse and went the same way as the girl, whereupon I too ventured out from behind the fence and followed my husband. Next moment the late churchgoer turned into a building which has a public thoroughfare running through it from the Stephansplatz leading directly into Domgasse, and Karel quickened his pace and finally caught up with the girl as she stopped outside a building on the corner of Blutgasse and Domgasse and prepared to open the tall doors. From a few metres away I saw her turn a large wrought-iron key in the lock, without noticing her pursuer, and then she went into the building, followed by Karel. The door slowly began to close, and before it was finally shut I too slipped through the opening and saw Karel holding the girl with one hand, placing the other over her mouth, and pushing her along the corridor and through one of the low iron doors opening off it. I slipped through the door behind him, groped my way in the musty darkness down a spiral staircase that obviously led to the cellar of the building, and heard suppressed cries for help, which I followed. Beside the wooden partitions of the sections of the cellar and in the light of the full moon falling in through a small window, I saw the tiger skin over my husband's back as he forced the girl up against the wall of the cellar, and at the sight I was overcome by blind fury with the man in whom I had been so deceived, and by an irresistible desire to protect this young member of my own sex, and I drew the carving knife from the folds of my cloak and thrust it up to the hilt into the tiger skin and the human flesh beneath. Karel let out a scream, slowly sank down beside the girl, who stood there frozen with terror and wide-eyed in the moonlight beside the cellar window, without entirely letting go of her, and finally lay there motionless and curled up on the cold trodden-earth floor of the old vaulted cellar.

So it was not Karel Havelka, the man to whom I was bound by the holy sacrament of marriage, who drove the late Empress Sisi that same day in the Hapsburgs' black funeral coach, in which her son Rudolf who departed this life in such unfortunate circumstances had already taken his last journey, through the mourning crowds of Viennese to the Capuchin crypt, as he would have wished, but Tibor Bartok, the Archduchess Valerie's Hungarian-born personal coachman and our neighbour above the imperial-and-royal stables.

I remember the next few days only vaguely as a series of examinations, interviews and interrogations, at the end of which I found myself back in Vienna Neudorf Women's Prison and House of Correction, but this time not as a prisoner who had committed the relatively petty crime of stealing a concert zither, but as the murderess of my husband. It was some time before I understood what the lawyer assigned to give me legal aid who visited me in my cell was obliged to tell me: in my case he could not plead self-defence, since it was not I whom my husband had been about to rape but the eighteen-year-old umbrella seamstress Juliane Kalb; and furthermore the fact that I had surreptitiously approached my victim from behind and our marital relationship were both regarded as aggravating circumstances, and in view of the present state of the law I must expect to be condemned to death by the rope. Moreover, the umbrella seamstress whom Karel Havelka was following on the night in question and who lived on the corner of Blutgasse and Domgasse, and was in good health, had said that in her opinion there was no need to kill the man, a view that he, the lawyer, shared, after all Havelka had no criminal record and had never offended in any way except for minor infringements of the Regulations for Cabs and One-horse Carriages of 1854. When, in a failing voice, I protested that I

427

myself had witnessed my late husband's attempted rape of the waitress Slavka Cencic, the lawyer shook his head gently and said no one would believe me, particularly because, as I probably didn't yet know because of the rapid pace at which events had been moving, Hans Holzer, unemployed, had decided after a long stay in police custody, and after some initial denials, to confess to all the previously unsolved cases of the rape or attempted rape of Viennese women over the last few weeks, a confession that he did not think would help the unfortunate man much, since he was a former inmate of the imperial-and-royal lunatic asylum in Vienna 9, and the expert psychological opinion provided by a lecturer in nervous diseases who worked at that institution was very incriminating.

At these shattering revelations, I at first refused all food and sank into deep despair, for I could not believe that in a constitutionally governed western state, which according to Fräulein von Roth-Rothenhorst is what the Austro-Hungarian monarchy was, an entirely innocent person could be accused of a terrible crime, and a woman who had indeed murdered her husband, but only to protect another woman from the most dreadful physical violence, could be condemned to death. This initial despair was followed by a period of hope, which again gave way to hopelessness, and so confidence and pessimism alternated until, as the months passed by, I regained my composure and resigned myself to the inevitable. I am now waiting calmly for my execution, and as for the advice of the Sisters of the Good Shepherd, who urge me to repent of my crime, take stock of the state of my soul before I die and reconcile myself to the fate assigned to me by God, I reject it firmly and with equanimity. My earthly existence is over, and all my hopes are that I will soon be reunited with my dear mother and with Olga. I am not afraid of my third and last meeting with the former executioner's assistant, now the imperial-and-royal executioner Josef Lang, who was kind enough to cure me of first-stage syphilis, for as he once convincingly assured me in his coffee house in Simmering, my death from cerebral paralysis or a heart attack will occur within only forty-two to sixty-five seconds, and any slight twitches that may follow that period of time will be mere reflexes. My corpse will then, according to the custom, be taken down after an hour, and the scaffold will be dismantled within three hours. As for the place in the Central Cemetery where the Entreprise des Pompes Funèbres firm of undertakers will bury the yellow-painted coffin bound with twine and containing my mortal remains on the night after my execution, it is a matter of perfect indifference to me.

16

When I returned from the Death House in the morning to the apartment on the corner of Blutgasse and Domgasse to phone my mother, the sun was shining and the cupola of the temple, made of countless gilded leaves, was gleaming as I passed it. I thought of my great-grandmother, who had walked the same streets in this city a hundred years ago, and I suddenly felt very close to her, a woman so different from me, but one whose boundless patience and willingness to sacrifice herself, incomprehensible as I found them, had been her greatest asset, just as Josef's weakness was also his strength.

Aunt Pia, who was standing by the stove cleaning a pig's head, turned as I came in and said she had been worried sick, what possessed me to spend the night out, thank goodness the identity of the right-winger who had raped those three young foreigners was almost one hundred per cent certain now, she had just read that the antique dealer from the embassy quarter was under grave suspicion, who'd have thought it, a man who would attack his own girlfriend wearing a black stocking mask, human nature was very contradictory. And as for young Herr Horvath with whom, as his constant phone calls showed her, I was obviously consorting very frequently and at whose place she supposed I had spent last night, it was her opinion that a girl of good family ought to think about her reputation a little more. If I wanted to win the heart of one of the most eligible bachelors in Vienna, incidentally an amazingly good catch for a coloured girl, which after all I was, then I should show a little more reserve. I decided to take no notice of these reproaches from Aunt Pia for the moment, went over to the little Art Deco table in the hall with the telephone on it and called my mother, who replied in a voice drowsy with sleep, which reminded me that it would be four in the morning in New York City, and I apologized, but at the same time I made use of my advantage in taking her by surprise and told her straight out that she was the granddaughter of a criminal executed by the imperial-and-royal executioner Josef Lang in April 1900, something that, thus caught unawares, she made no attempt to deny, and indeed she admitted it. When I asked why she had never told me about this member of the family, she said she didn't have the courage to confess that her immediate ancestors included a woman of such dubious reputation. On my asking her to explain the family relationships in the Bohemian line in rather more detail, my mother sounded impatient and said of course she loved me as a mother should love her child, but even maternal love has its limits, and it verged on the outrageous to wake a political scientist intensively working on a comprehensive opinion survey in the early hours of the morning just to cast light on the family tree, a family tree which apart from that one point was no different from anyone else's with respect to the moral integrity of its members. If I insisted on an explanation of these irrelevancies I had better ask Aunt Pia, Aunt Pia had always known all about the family. So saying, my mother put the receiver down and I went back to the kitchen, where Aunt Pia was just putting the pig's head in a pan of boiling water, and asked her to elucidate, to which she said I made excessive demands on a weak, deaf old lady, but since I obviously wasn't to be diverted from my probing questions she would try to explain it all to me. Here she sat down at the kitchen table, and when I had sat down opposite her she said that, as she had already indicated, early in the 1950s a nun aged around seventy had appeared in the building, approached the then caretaker, a Croatian woman from Agram whose work

432

was rather slipshod in a manner typical of southern Slavs, and asked where she, Aunt Pia, lived. This nun, one Beata Maria Postl, a member of the community of the Sisters of the Good Shepherd, had given her the blue notebook saying that it contained the sad, tragic autobiography of Rosa Havelka, the murderess of her husband, who had handed it to her in a rather different form, on pale green lined paper, in the condemned cell of the Provincial Court prison in Alserstrasse, where she, Sister Beata Maria, was supposed to be giving the unfortunate woman spiritual consolation during the last hours before her execution by the rope, a consolation that the sinner, unrepentant to her last breath, had incidentally refused to accept, though she had pressed those pages into her hands, saying she could do what she liked with them. Soon afterwards Rosa Havelka, accompanied by the priest and the prison governor and flanked by four guards, had been led by the two executioner's assistants to the gallows yard, where the imperial-and-royal executioner of the time, Josef Lang, was already waiting for her. When she, Aunt Pia, had asked at this point what business of hers the autobiography of an obviously pitiable woman but one entirely unknown to her could be, the nun asked her to be patient for a moment and she would soon explain the connection. After the execution of the murderess, she had kept the piles of loose sheets of paper in a cupboard in her cell for decades and had quite forgotten them until one day, in clearing out her cell, she had come upon them again and decided to copy out the autobiography which had been carelessly scribbled down, making a few altera-tions, to provide a warning to young girls who had gone astray and whose reintegration into society had been her concern all her life. So saying she, the nun, gave her, Aunt Pia, the fat blue notebook and said this was the work, she wanted her, Aunt Pia, to take it and do as she liked with it, for with very few exceptions the girls, most of them as incorrigible as Rosa Havelka herself, had shown no interest in it. When she, Aunt Pia, had asked again what made the nun think of presenting her of all people with this work, the nun replied that her researches conducted at various parish and registry offices in Vienna, Lower Austria, Bohemia and Moravia had revealed the information that Rosa Havelka, whose maiden name was Tichy, like hers, Pia von Hötzendorf's, was a blood relative of hers, although a distant one, and since she, Frau von Hötzendorf, was also the only member of Rosa's family still alive and living in Vienna that she, the nun, had been able to trace, there was no one to whom she could give the document but her, Frau von Hötzendorf. Rather impatiently Aunt Pia said it was true that her maiden name was Tichy, Tichy was a very common Czech surname, in and around Vienna you could find countless Tichys, but she still didn't understand how her life, which had so far run along well-regulated lines, could be linked with that of a woman who had murdered her husband, to which the nun had replied that she supposed she was right in conjecturing that Aunt Pia's grandfather Wenzel Tichy had come to Vienna around the middle of the nineteenth century from the neighbourhood of Pilsen, a town in western Bohemia known for its breweries, and in Vienna had worked first as a plasterer and then in stucco, a question to which she, Aunt Pia, replied in the affirmative. And when the nun went on to say she supposed it was also correct that this Wenzel Tichy, Aunt Pia's grandfather, was born the second of nine children of a Bohemian smallholder in a village near Pilsen she, Aunt Pia, replied that it was perfectly possible but she didn't know for sure, she had never taken any particular interest in the Bohemian branch of the family and had hardly known her grandfather, to which Sister Beata Maria said that her investigations had clearly shown that her, Frau von Hötzendorf's, grandfather Wenzel Tichy and Libussa Tichy, Rosa's mother, were brother and sister, so that her, Frau von Hötzendorf's, father Zdenek and Rosa were cousins, even if they had never met, which no doubt answered the question she, Frau von Hötzendorf, had put at the beginning of their conversation. Then she again offered her the notebook which Aunt Pia had earlier refused, but which she now took without further objections, went to the door and said she hoped that the blessing of God might be with Aunt Pia in all she did and ensure that her future fate continued to be happier than that of her unfortunate blood relation.

After telling me this, Aunt Pia collapsed on the kitchen chair and said in a faint voice, now I could see what my inquiries, more like interrogations if I asked her, had done, she was utterly exhausted, only eating the pig's head could reanimate her, although even that wasn't certain, but in any case it was to be hoped that my morbid curiosity was now satisfied with the discovery that I had a murderess in the family, a revelation that had not given her, Aunt Pia, any satisfaction to speak of in the past, and of which she had never, for good reasons, told the Major, a man of very good family and distantly related on the paternal side to Field Marshal Radetzky. When her head with its thin white hair dropped forward, I hurried around the table in alarm, raised it and gave the old lady a glass of water to drink, whereupon she revived slightly.

So it was true. Rosa Havelka, née Tichy, was my great-grandmother, a relation of whom, unlike my mother and Aunt Pia, I was not ashamed, but for whom I felt sympathy.

The doorbell rang. I opened the front door, and there before me stood John in a white suit, looking pale and tired for lack of sleep, hair untidy and leaning with one hand propped on the door frame. When he had embraced me, rather hastily, as I thought, he said that after I had refused to talk to him on the phone he had immediately caught a night flight to Vienna to come and take me back to New York City, I must go and pack my bag and we'd drive straight to the airport, in reply to which I politely asked him to come in and led him towards the living room past the kitchen, and when he looked through the half-open kitchen door and saw Aunt Pia, slowly recovering, he asked, horrified, whether that spooky person was my relation, how could I live in such sinister surroundings, if he'd known the conditions in which I was obliged to exist here he'd have reserved me a room at the König von Ungarn Hotel at once, why for heaven's sake hadn't I said a word about it, it looked as if he'd arrived just in the nick of time, Vienna was no place for me, he'd guessed as much from the start, and he was sure I'd be pleased to hear that until the premiere he was entrusting my further voice training to an outstanding if wickedly expensive singing teacher to whom Callas herself had turned in her day when she was at her wits' end. By now we were in Aunt Pia's living room with its population of dolls, and John started with surprise again and said this was horrifying, you were watched the whole time by countless glass eyes in here, how on earth had I been able to bear it, dear little nut-brown doll that I was, where was my bag, the next plane took off in an hour and a half.

At this point I decided it was time to interrupt John's torrent of words by saying I had no intention of returning to New York City, I was expecting a baby by my singing teacher and was going to marry him at Christmas in the Nine Choirs of Angels Church in central Vienna. At this John removed a Norah Wellings rag doll and a very beautiful Japanese porcelain doll in a sea-green silk kimono from the seat of an armchair made by the firm of Thonet and upholstered in burgundy velvet, and sat down on it. What did I mean, he asked after a pause, what did I mean a baby, I was an artist, an actress, a singer, a dancer, he'd offered me the chance of a lifetime, such a chance had to be seized, what was I thinking of, I mustn't let such a chance go just because I suddenly found myself in the family way, a state of affairs which, incidentally, could be quickly and easily remedied once we were back, and furthermore I knew he was crazy about me, he had been looking for me and me alone in the person of the little Haitian girl whose skin was a shade paler than mine and with whom he had been up in the elevator to the seventeenth floor of the hotel in midtown Manhattan now and then out of melancholy, pure gloom because of my absence. Then he brought the palm of his hand down on the round table in the living room and said, right, time to go now, to which I replied that if he liked I'd be happy to accompany him to the nearby airport terminal outside the Hilton Hotel, we could take the short cut through the Stadtpark, and he looked at me for a long time and then laid his head on the tablecloth of white cotton-linen embroidered with stem stitch and began weeping, thus showing me unmistakably, if without words, that he had taken it in at last. Slowly I went around the round table to him, drew him to his feet and left the apartment with him, passing the kitchen, where Aunt Pia was just cutting a piece off the now tender left ear of the pig's head with an old silver table knife, and then led him, the tears still running constantly down his cheeks, out of the building, along Domgasse and Schulerstrasse, and then over the Parkring and through the Stadtpark to the Vienna Central terminal. Here I sat him down beside a thin lady in the bus, which was ready to leave, and he let me do so apathetically, although he had stopped shedding tears. I pressed a kiss on his forehead, and as I was turning to leave, the thin lady, to my surprise, addressed me in friendly tones and said, what a coincidence, we'd sat next to each other over a month ago on the flight from New York to Vienna, the gentleman in the white suit obviously wasn't feeling very well, and if it was all right with me she'd keep an eye on him. I looked at the lady's face and recognized the thin brunette who had told me about the six famous tapestries in a Paris museum, and when I asked her, out of civility, where she was going this time, she said Paris, of course, her mother had begun copying the second of the Lady with the Unicorn tapestries, a superhuman task for someone of seventy-four, and had asked her to take a close look at the colours of the background and describe them when she got back. Then she asked me where the gentleman in the white suit was going, and when I said New York, she repeated, smiling, New York, undoubtedly New York was very impressive, but personally she preferred Paris.

SARA GEORGE

The Journal of
Mrs Pepys
Portrait of a Marriage

The highly acclaimed, bestselling fictional journal of the wife of our most celebrated diarist.

'An altogether enchanting novel . . . sheds a brilliant beam into the dark interior of this 17th-century household and with compassion elegantly scripts a couple's most intimate moments' *Scotland on Sunday*

'Sara George has succeeded admirably in finding a voice – and a sweet, innocent but intelligent and warm voice it is – for one of the many women half-hidden from history by their dominant menfolk' Margaret Foster

'Pepys's wife finds her voice . . . all the more powerful for being partial' *Daily Telegraph*

'Anyone who thinks that Bridget Jones epitomises an existence turbulent with trials and tribulations should take a look at Elizabeth Pepys's journal . . . The minutiae of daily life against the huge events of fire and plague echo Pepys but in a far more accessible form; Elizabeth is an attractive creation and this piece of "faction" makes a spirited tale' *Independent on Sunday*

0 7472 5761 2

review

LILIAN FASCHINGER

Magdalena the Sinner

'Meet Magdalena Leitner, codename "the Sinner". She is a killer seven times over, clad in a second-skin, black leather motorcycle suit. She is Austrian – but not the yodelling type. Rather, she's bent on a singular, sinister mission: to force her confession upon the village priest she has kidnapped at gunpoint . . .

'As she tears through the European Union in search of love, liberty and in pursuit of happiness, Magdalena charges at the windmills of bourgeois mores, Church hypocrisy, nationalist instincts, and our selfish failure to listen to or care for others . . . Unfettered by moral scruples or social constraints, our leather-clad heroine acts out every woman's most subversive wish – and every man's – as she roars through conventions on her Puch . . .

'In the end, we, like the priest, are wholly in Magdalena's spell, and want this magical morality tale to go on and on and on' Cristina Odone, *Literary Review*

'Faschinger rings the changes with wit and ingenuity . . . Magdalena is a spellbinding raconteur' Margaret Walters, *The Sunday Times*

0 7472 5459 1

review

Now you can buy any of these other **Review** titles from your bookshop or *direct from the publisher.*

FREE P&P AND UK DELIVERY
(Overseas and Ireland £3.50 per book)

Hens Dancing	Raffaella Barker	£6.99
The Catastrophist	Ronan Bennett	£6.99
Horseman, Pass By	David Crackanthorpe	£6.99
Two Kinds of Wonderful	Isla Dewar	£6.99
Earth and Heaven	Sue Gee	£6.99
Sitting Among the Eskimos	Maggie Graham	£6.99
Tales of Passion, Tales of Woe	Sandra Gulland	£6.99
The Dancers Dancing	Éilís Ní Dhuibhne	£6.99
After You'd Gone	Maggie O'Farrell	£6.99
The Silver River	Ben Richards	£6.99
A History of Insects	Yvonne Roberts	£6.99
Girl in Hyacinth Blue	Susan Vreeland	£6.99
The Long Afternoon	Giles Waterfield	£6.99

TO ORDER SIMPLY CALL THIS NUMBER

01235 400 414

or e-mail <u>orders@bookpoint.co.uk</u>

Prices and availability subject to change without notice.